KU-034-590

Praise For Bestselling Author Stephen Leather's Spider
Shepherd Series:

'As tough as British thrillers get' *Irish Independent* on *Hard
Landing*

'One of the strongest and most outstanding books of his career
to date. Another real scorcher ... so gripping I just could not
put it down' *www.eurocrime.co.uk* on *Rough Justice*

'The sheer impetus of his story-telling is damned hard to resist'
Daily Express on *Cold Kill*

'*Rough Justice* is a top drawer thriller with blood-soaked action,
terrifyingly real villains, spine-tingling menace and a pulsating plot
with serious ethical issues at its heart. Another class act from Mr
Leather' *Lancashire Evening Post*

'This is an aggressively topical novel but a genuinely thrilling one,
too' *Daily Telegraph* on *Cold Kill*

'A brilliant read that stands out of the morass of so-so military
thrillers around nowadays' *News of the World* on *Hot Blood*

'A tightly-plotted, heart-racing read' *Daily Mail* on *Hard Landing*

'Authentic stuff' *Observer* on *Hot Blood*

'High-adrenaline plotting' *Sunday Express* on *Soft Target*

'In brisk newsman's style he explores complex contemporary
issues while keeping the action fast and bloody' *Economist* on
Dead Men

About the author

Stephen Leather was a journalist for more than ten years on newspapers such as *The Times*, the *Daily Mail* and the *South China Morning Post* in Hong Kong. He began writing full time in 1992. His bestsellers have been translated into more than ten languages. He has also written for television shows such as *London's Burning*, *The Knock* and the BBC's *Murder in Mind* series. You can find out more from his website, www.stephenleather.com.

STEPHEN LEATHER

FAIR GAME

HODDER

First published in Great Britain in 2011 by Hodder & Stoughton
An Hachette UK company

First published in paperback in 2011

1

Copyright © Stephen Leather 2011

The right of Stephen Leather to be identified as the Author
of the Work has been asserted by him in accordance with the
Copyright, Designs and Patents Act 1988.

A CIP catalogue record for this title is available from the British Library

B format paperback ISBN 978 0 340 92498 3
A format paperback ISBN 978 1 444 71617 7

Typeset in Bembo by Palimpsest Book Production Limited,
Falkirk, Stirlingshire

Printed and bound by Clays Ltd, St Ives plc

Hodder & Stoughton policy is to use papers that are natural, renewable
and recyclable products and made from wood grown in sustainable forests.
The logging and manufacturing processes are expected to conform
to the environmental regulations of the country of origin.

Hodder & Stoughton Ltd
338 Euston Road
London NW1 3BH

www.hodder.co.uk

For Juliet

It was a big bomb, a mixture of fertiliser, diesel oil and aluminium powder with industrial detonators and a mobile phone trigger. It had been three days in the making and now took up most of the back of the white Transit van. The explosives had been packed into aluminium beer kegs, each with double detonators. They had been stacked into the van, two dozen in all. Hundreds of six-inch nails had been duct-taped around the kegs to add to the lethal shrapnel. The wires from the detonators led to a central trigger unit which was connected to a Nokia mobile phone. It was a big bomb and a deadly one, designed to destroy its target and kill or maim anyone inside.

The bomb had been carefully constructed by a fifty-year-old man who had driven up from Limerick. The bombmaker had been making explosive devices for the best part of three decades and had been taught by experts. He had been involved in the London Docklands bombing in February 1996 that had put an end to a seventeen-month ceasefire, and had helped build the bomb that had devastated Manchester city centre just four months later. When the IRA had lain down its arms in 2005, he had joined the Continuity IRA but within a year had switched to the Real

IRA, whose Republican views were more in line with his own.

Once he had finished putting the bomb together he had driven back to Limerick, and if all went to plan he would be sitting in front of the television with his wife and three daughters when it exploded.

The man who was going to drive the van to its target was a sixty-year-old farmer from Warrenpoint, on the northern shore of Carlingford Lough. Willie Ryan was a committed Republican, like his father and his grandfather before him. He had left the Provisionals long before the peace process had begun because he was dissatisfied with the way things were going, and he had immediately joined the Real IRA.

The van had been stolen from Galway and driven across the border to Ryan's farm. The plates hadn't been changed. There was no need – the next meeting between the Garda Síochána and the Police Service of Northern Ireland to discuss stolen vehicles wasn't scheduled for another two weeks.

Before he had driven back to Limerick, the bombmaker had explained to the four men in the cell how to detonate the bomb. It wasn't rocket science. The phone had to remain switched off until the van was in place. Then, and only then, was the phone to be switched on. All it took was a call to the number and the moment that the call went through to voicemail the detonators would explode.

'Are you all right, then, Willie?' asked Seamus Maguire, the leader of the cell, and at twenty-six the youngest. He was dark haired and fair skinned, wearing a Trinity College sweatshirt and cargo pants.

Ryan nodded as he pulled on a pair of black leather driving gloves. 'I'm fine,' he said.

Maguire put a hand on the older man's shoulder. 'I'm not going to teach my grandmother to suck eggs, but stay below the speed limit. If anyone stops you, stay calm and we'll take care of it.' He nodded at the other two men, Gerry O'Leary and Ray Power. They were hard men in their thirties, and they were both checking their weapons, brand-new Glocks. 'Gerry and Ray will be behind you all the way. You're not going to be stopped but if you are you sit tight and let them handle it. No playing the hero, OK?'

Ryan smiled without warmth. 'Like I said, I'm fine.' He finished putting on the gloves and cracked his knuckles. 'Fine and dandy.'

Maguire checked his watch. It was time. 'Right, guys, let's do it,' he said. It would take thirty minutes to drive to Old Park police station in North Belfast, by which time it would be getting dark. The plan was for Ryan to get into the car with O'Leary and Power and drive away while Maguire stayed behind to detonate the bomb.

'Rock and roll!' said Power, punching the air.

They all jerked as they heard a vehicle drive up outside. 'Are you expecting anyone, Willie?' Maguire asked.

Ryan shook his head. 'Could be a friend of the wife's.'

'Gerry, have a look-see,' said Maguire.

O'Leary reached inside his jacket pocket and pulled out a gun. He walked on tiptoe to the barn door.

Maguire gestured at Power and he also pulled a gun out from under his jacket.

O'Leary eased the door open and slipped out. Power and Maguire crept over to the door. Time crawled by but they heard nothing. No shouts, no gunshots, no footsteps. Just the cawing of crows in the distance and the sound of a tractor in a far-off field.

'Gerry, are you OK there?' shouted Maguire.

There was no answer. Ryan came up behind Maguire. 'If it was the cops, they'd have blown the doors off by now,' muttered Power.

'Gerry?' shouted Maguire. 'You OK?'

O'Leary appeared at the door, scowling.

'What's happening?' asked Maguire. 'What is it?'

'Father bloody Christmas,' said a voice, and the door was kicked in by a man in a ski mask and a knee-length black leather coat holding a sawn-off shotgun. A second masked man burst into the barn, holding a Glock. The man with the shotgun kept the twin barrels pointing squarely at Power's chest. A third masked man wearing a brown leather bomber jacket pushed O'Leary into the barn and then pointed his handgun at Maguire.

'Drop your gun, sunshine. However this plays out you'll be dead if you don't,' said Leather Coat.

Power looked over at Maguire, screwed up his face as if he was in pain, and threw his gun down to the floor. The masked man with the Glock walked over, picked it up and stuffed it into his belt in the small of his back.

Leather Coat reached into a pocket and pulled out a cloth bundle. He tossed it to the ground in front of Maguire. 'There's four hoods there, put them on and then stand with your hands behind you.'

'Who are you?' asked Maguire.

'I'm the guy who's telling you what to do, and if you don't do exactly as I say I'll shoot you in the legs and then put the hood on you myself. Now do as you're fucking well told.'

Maguire bent down and picked up the hoods. He handed them to Ryan, Power and O'Leary and one by one they hesitantly pulled them down over their heads and then stood with their hands behind their backs.

The two men with Leather Coat walked behind the hooded men and used plastic tags to bind their wrists.

'Now listen to me and listen good,' said Leather Coat. 'We're going to walk you outside and put you in the back of a van. If you try to run I'll shoot you in the leg and put you in the van. If you shout or even say anything I'll shoot you in the leg and put you in the van. So however this pans out, you're all going in the van. And if I do have to shoot you, we won't be swinging by Casualty.'

The four hooded men were herded outside and one by one pushed into the van. They lay on their backs as the rear doors slammed and the van drove off. An hour later they reached their destination and the rear doors were opened.

'Right, out,' shouted Leather Coat. The two men in ski masks bundled the four hooded men out and pulled off their hoods. They were standing in an empty metal-sided factory unit, the oil-stained concrete floor suggesting that it had once been home to heavy machinery.

Leather Coat held up a small stainless-steel box the size of a packet of cigarettes. There were three aerials of varying lengths sticking out of the top and a small red light glowed on the side.

'Anyone know what this is?' Leather Coat asked.

'It's a mobile phone jammer,' said Maguire.

'Well done you,' said Leather Coat. 'You're not just a pretty face. Just so you know, this has been on for the last thirty minutes and so it's been blocking all mobile phone transmissions. If any of you are hoping that you're being tracked through the GPS in your phones, you can think again.'

'No one's tracking us and anyway our phones have been off all day,' said Maguire. 'They have to be off while we're around the bomb.'

'The cops have phones that transmit sound and position even when they're powered off,' said Leather Coat.

'What are you talking about?' asked Maguire. 'Who are you?'

'I'm the man asking the questions here, that's who I am.'

'A name would be nice.'

'Yeah, well, a night in bed with Angelina Jolie would be nice, but that ain't gonna happen. You're Maguire, right? The so-called brains of this outfit?'

Maguire nodded. 'What the hell's going on? Who are you? Are you cops?'

The man chuckled. 'You think we're fucking cops? If we were fucking cops we'd be in here with Hecklers and bullet-proof vests and a helicopter overhead.' He gestured with his gun. 'Down on your knees. All of you.'

The men did as they were told.

The two men in ski masks went through the pockets of the men and placed their wallets and mobile phones on the ground in front of them.

Leather Coat placed his phone jammer on the ground, and then straightened up.

'Here's the thing,' he said. 'One of you is a fucking traitor. One of you is a rat. The bloody SAS have got the police station staked out and I'm pretty sure that as we speak the cops are on the way to Willie's farm to liberate the bomb.'

He grinned. 'At which point they're in for a hell of a surprise because we've swapped the mobile phone trigger for a timer.' He looked at his watch, a chunky Casio. 'So in about twelve minutes they'll all be blown to pieces.'

'What's this about?' said Maguire. 'We were on a mission.'

'Your mission was blown,' said Leather Coat. 'And one of you four blew it.'

Maguire shook his head. 'That's not possible,' he said.

Leather Coat pulled a Samsung mobile phone from his back pocket and held it up. 'We took this from a Special Branch officer in Belfast this morning. He was receiving text messages about a large Anfo bomb being prepared by a Real IRA cell.'

'But no one knows what we are doing,' said Maguire. 'Just the four of us and the Operations Director. The OD is the only member of the Army Council who has details of the operation.'

'I'm here on the OD's authority,' said Leather Coat. 'He wants the rat dealt with.'

'I know these men, I've known them for years.'

'Yeah? Well, maybe you don't know them well enough.'

'We're not rats,' said Ryan. 'And fuck you for saying we are. I was just about to drive a one-ton bomb into Belfast, so I don't need anyone telling me that I'm a rat.'

'We'll soon find out,' said Leather Coat. He bent down and switched off the jammer. He waved his gun at his two companions. 'Switch on their phones,' he said. 'Be quick about it.'

The two men checked the mobile phones, then moved to stand behind Leather Coat.

'Don't worry, the phones won't be on long enough for

the cops to get a trace,' said Leather Coat, taking a phone
from his pocket. He looked at the screen. 'Just have to wait
until we get a signal.' He nodded. 'There we are, four bars.
Good old Orange.' He looked over at the four men. 'Anyone
want to confess, before I call the number that we got from
the Special Branch cop?' The four men said nothing. Leather
Coat grinned. 'Let's go for it, then,' he said. He pressed the
green button and watched as the pre-programmed number
flashed across the screen.

There was a silence lasting several seconds and then the
phone in front of O'Leary burst into life. The James Bond
theme echoed around the warehouse.

'There you go,' said Leather Coat. 'How easy was that?'

'O'Leary, you bastard!' screamed Maguire.

'He's working for the cops?' shouted Ryan. 'How the hell
did that happen?'

Leather Coat walked over to the ringing phone and
stamped on it. It shattered into a dozen pieces. Then he
walked behind O'Leary and kicked him in the middle of
the back. O'Leary fell forward with a grunt and lay face
down, gasping for breath. 'If it was up to me we'd have a
long chat with you, you rat bastard, but the OD wants you
dead,' said Leather Coat.

Two shots rang out in quick succession and Leather Coat
staggered back as blood spurted from two chest wounds.
His gun fell to the ground and he stared at the man who'd
shot him, his forehead creased into a surprised frown.

It was the man in the bomber jacket who'd fired the shots.
The man standing next to him started to scream as he
swung his Glock around but the shooter fired again, two
shots that caught him high in the chest, just above the heart.

The man fell back, his mouth working soundlessly, and he slammed into the ground.

The shooter slid his gun back into its holster and stood looking down at O'Leary. 'See what you've done?' he shouted. 'See what your stupidity has gone and done?' He walked over to the second man that he'd shot and pulled out a set of keys from his pocket.

O'Leary twisted around, trying to look up at the shooter. 'Who are you?' he asked.

'I'm the man who just saved your life.'

'Are you a cop?'

'Are you?'

O'Leary nodded. 'Special Branch. Long-term penetration. I've been undercover for more than two years.'

'Yeah, and in all that time did no one tell you about sending text messages to your handler?'

'That's the way he wanted it.'

'Then he's an idiot. You make calls and you use payphones or throwaway mobiles. You don't send texts because text messages can come back to bite you in the arse.'

'OK, I get it,' said O'Leary. 'Now will you untie me?'

The shooter bent down and picked up Ryan's mobile phone. 'Help's on the way.'

'You can't leave me here like this,' said O'Leary.

'It's your bed, you lie in it,' said the shooter.

'Who the hell are you?'

The man walked away without answering. He ripped off his ski mask as he left the warehouse and tossed it to the side. He tapped out a number on the mobile he'd taken from Ryan, putting it to his ear as it rang out.

'Yeah, it's me. Spider,' he said. 'It's all gone tits up. You need to get a team to this location now. You can track the GPS.'

'What went wrong?' asked Charlotte Button, Spider Shepherd's MI5 handler.

'Special Branch had an undercover guy on the team. He's here. They were going to kill him. Why the hell does the right hand not know what the left's doing?'

'I'll find out,' said Button. 'Are you OK?'

'No, I'm not OK,' said Shepherd. 'I've just killed two men. And you'd better tell the cops on the way to the farm that the van's on a timer, set to go off in about six minutes.'

'I'm on it,' said Button. 'We've got your location, we're on our way.'

'I won't be here,' said Shepherd. He tossed the phone away and jogged over to the van.

There were seven men and a woman sitting at two tables at the back of the café, all Somali by birth but all with British citizenship. The café was in a run-down area of Ealing in West London and it was owned by one of the men, Simeon Khalid, whose hands were clasped together around a tall glass of iced water. He was a short, stocky man with skin the colour and texture of old leather, his fingernails were bitten to the quick, and he looked a good ten years older than his true age of twenty-four. Simeon Khalid was the name that he used on official papers, but even that was not his true name. The British demanded a family name and a first name so that was what he had given them, but in Somalia men and women were not named that way. Somalis did not have surnames. They identified themselves with a given name followed by the father's given name and the grandfather's. They effectively had three first names, but the British didn't understand that so when they insisted on a family name he had given them Khalid, the name of his father. They had accepted that and Simeon Khalid was the name on his driving licence and his tax file, and it was the name on the British passport that he was eventually given. Simeon Khalid had nothing but contempt for the British but he was happy to take advantage of their stupidity.

There were four Somalis sitting at the second table, two teenagers in cheap suits and ill-fitting shirts, and an older couple, worried parents. The woman was holding back tears, occasionally dabbing at her eyes with a lace handkerchief. Her husband was a big man but stooped with age, and he sat with his arms folded and stared straight ahead, a battered trilby on the table in front of him. The two teenagers were the accused, and they were the reason that the *gar* had assembled.

A Somali man in his twenties was standing at the door to the café, looking out. 'He is coming, Wiil Waal,' he hissed.

Crazy Boy nodded. At the *gar* he was referred to as Simeon Khalid but among his friends and within the Somali community he was Wiil Waal, Crazy Boy. The *gar* was where the Somali community resolved conflicts and where justice was handed out. Two of the men sitting opposite Crazy Boy were in their seventies, elders of the Somali community, men whose wisdom was revered and whose judgement was accepted by all. In between them sat a man in his fifties, bald and overweight and wearing a crumpled linen jacket, his lips blackened from chewing khat leaves. He was the aggrieved party and he wanted justice from the *gar*.

The man who ran the café was in his sixties, and had

been one of the first refugees to leave Somalia after the civil war began in 1991. He had worked hard, but a gambling habit meant that he had little to show for a lifetime of toil and he now worked for Crazy Boy. Crazy Boy nodded at him and the man began busying himself at the tea urn. A middle-aged man in a raincoat pushed open the café door. His name was Sadiiq and he nodded at Crazy Boy. Crazy Boy nodded back. Sadiiq had also sought refuge in England at the start of the civil war and had been one of the first Somalis to move into Ealing. He sat on the local council and was often sought out by journalists to comment on news stories involving the Somali community. Sadiiq held the door open so that his companion, an old man in a heavy wool coat, could enter. He was in his seventies with a full head of curly hair that had gone grey many years earlier and his knuckles were swollen with arthritis. '*Ma nabad baa?*' he said as he took the empty seat next to Crazy Boy. The question wasn't addressed to anyone in particular, it was the standard Somali greeting. 'Is it peace?'

The men at the table nodded and mumbled, '*Waa nabad.*' It is peace.

Sadiiq pulled up a chair and squeezed in between two of the elders, muttering an apology.

'I am sorry for my lateness,' said the old man in Somali. 'My wife is ill and I had to change her dressing.' The man's name was Mohamed Dhamac Taban, and all the men at the table knew that his wife was dying from cancer. No one knew for sure how old Taban was, not even the man himself. His birth had never been registered in Somalia and he had made up a date when he'd arrived in England in 1985.

'The *gar* is not in session until you are at the table,' said

Crazy Boy. 'We all hope and believe that God will smile at your wife and help her in your time of need.'

Taban nodded without smiling, accepting the kind words but knowing in his heart that there was nothing that could be done to help his wife.

The waiter appeared with a tray of glasses containing milky black tea flavoured with ginger, cinnamon and green cardamom pods. He carefully placed a glass in front of each of the men and a bowl of sugar cubes on each table.

Crazy Boy waited patiently for Taban to sip his tea. As the oldest member of the Somali community, Taban was the head of the *gar* and was entitled to deference and respect but Crazy Boy knew that the old man wouldn't live much longer than his ailing wife. Once he had joined his Maker, it would be Crazy Boy who ran the *gar* and who administered justice within the Somali community. Crazy Boy gestured at the teenagers at the adjacent table as Taban put down his glass and smacked his lips. 'We are here today to pass judgement on two boys who attacked and injured another. That boy, Nadif, is now in hospital. He was stabbed in the stomach and his throat was slashed.'

'He will live?' asked Taban.

'Yes, he will live, but he will be scarred for life,' said Crazy Boy.

Taban looked at the man sitting between the two elders opposite him. 'You are Nadif's father?'

The man nodded.

'I trust God will care for your child and hasten his recovery,' said Taban.

'Thank you.'

'Your wife is not here?'

'My wife passed away, five years ago.'

'I am sorry for your loss, may God watch over her soul,' said Taban. He looked over at the next table. 'Those are the boys who hurt him?' he asked Crazy Boy.

Crazy Boy nodded as he stared at the two teenagers. One of them, the younger, was listening to an MP3 player, his head bobbing back and forth in time to the music. The other was toying with a bottle of sauce. Taban tapped his knuckles on the table to get their attention. 'Take out the earphones,' he said, pointing at the teenager with the MP3 player. 'Show some respect.' The teenager did as he was told and stared sullenly at the tabletop.

The father of the boys continued to stare straight ahead but the mother smiled at Taban. 'We are so sorry for what happened,' she said. 'My boys are good boys, they have never been in trouble before.'

That was a lie, Crazy Boy knew. The two teenagers were well known in the area as bullies and thieves. But he held his tongue.

'They have apologised to the boy?' asked Taban.

'Not yet,' said the mother. 'But they will. They will go to the hospital and tell Nadif that they are sorry for what they did. They will beg his forgiveness.'

Taban sipped his tea.

'We need to agree on compensation,' said Nadif's father. 'We need to agree an amount. His injuries are bad, he will not be able to work for many months.'

'Does he have a job?' asked Taban, placing his glass of tea back on the table.

'He is a mechanic.'

'And what does a mechanic earn?'

The father shook his head. 'I do not know. He gave me money every week but I do not know how much he earned.'

'Five hundred pounds a week,' said Crazy Boy. 'More, perhaps. That's what a mechanic would earn. More with overtime.'

'Does four thousand pounds sound reasonable?' asked Taban.

Nadif's father looked across at Crazy Boy. 'That is a pittance,' he said. 'My son almost died. They attacked him like dogs. For what? For his wallet and his mobile phone?'

'Is that true?' Taban asked the mother of the two boys.

She opened her mouth to speak but her husband held up his hand to silence her. 'The boy spoke ill of my daughter, their sister,' the man said. 'He called her a whore, he said that he had seen her with a white boy.'

'That is a lie!' snapped Nadif's father. 'My son did nothing. He said nothing. They attacked him and now he lies in hospital.'

'Did they steal his wallet and phone?' Taban asked the father of the boys.

'Both have been returned,' said the man. 'But that is not why they were fighting with Nadif. Nadif abused their sister and that is why they struck him.'

'They slashed him with knives,' said Nadif's father. 'He said nothing about their sister. That is a lie.'

'They have admitted their guilt and compensation will be paid,' said Taban slowly, choosing his words with care.

'This isn't right,' said Nadif's father. 'If I had gone to the police they would be in prison now. But they sit over there as if they didn't have a care in the world. Do they look sorry for what they did to my boy? Do they look as if they care?' He glared at the teenagers. One of them sneered back at the man but his mother slapped his shoulder and he looked down at the table.

Taban leaned forward and took the father's hand in his. 'Everyone here feels your pain,' he said. 'That is why we have the *gar*, to make things right. That is how we do things. We do not go to the police, we do not use the infidel's courts. We sort things out within our community. That is the way it has always been and it is the way it always will be. We do not allow the infidel to pass judgement on us. We resolve our own conflicts.'

The father nodded. 'I understand,' he said.

Taban let go of the man's hand and sat back. 'How much do you think would be reasonable by way of compensation?' he asked Crazy Boy.

'Four thousand pounds is not enough, not considering the injuries,' Crazy Boy said to the men at the table.

'How much, then?' said the father of the boys. 'They have admitted their guilt, they have expressed remorse, what was taken has been returned. We want to put this behind us and move on.' He toyed with his trilby.

Taban looked at Sadiiq. 'What do you think, Sadiiq?' he asked.

Sadiiq nodded thoughtfully. 'The injuries are severe and the attack was unjustified,' he said. 'Eight thousand pounds is what should be paid. And when Nadif is well enough to receive visitors, the two boys must go and ask his forgiveness.' He looked at Nadif's father. 'That forgiveness will be granted.'

The father nodded.

Taban looked at the parents of the teenagers. 'So eight

thousand pounds from your family, to be paid by the end of the week.'

'Thank you,' said the father.

His wife nodded quickly. 'Thank you so much,' she said. 'May God bless you.'

Taban looked across at Nadif's father. 'An apology will be made, and compensation will be paid. The matter will then be closed.'

Nadif's father nodded slowly.

'Then our business here is concluded,' said Taban. 'Let us all go in peace.'

The parents hurried out of the café with their teenagers, avoiding eye contact with Nadif's father.

Crazy Boy stood up. Nadif's father looked up at him expectantly and Crazy Boy patted him on the shoulder. 'I am sorry about what happened to your son,' he said. 'Tell him I'll see him tomorrow.'

The man nodded and muttered his thanks.

'Is there anything you need?' asked Crazy Boy.

The man shook his head, but Crazy Boy pulled a wad of fifty-pound notes from his pocket and peeled off half a dozen. He stuffed them into the man's hand, then patted him on the back.

Two Knives already had the café door open for Crazy Boy. He had remained at the door throughout the *gar*. He was one of Crazy Boy's foot soldiers, his most loyal. His true name was Gutaala, which meant 'Leader', but Two Knives was no leader of men, he was a follower. It was Crazy Boy who had given him his nickname when they were teenagers in Somalia. He hurried down the street after Crazy Boy.

'I don't understand, a fine is nothing,' said Two Knives.

'Why didn't you really punish them? They put Nadif in hospital and they know he works for you.'

'Because true punishment has no place in the *gar*,' said Crazy Boy. 'And the money isn't a fine, it's compensation.' He put his arm around Two Knives. 'You think the old men there would agree to true punishment, to an eye for an eye?' He shook his head. 'They believe that the shame that is brought to a family is punishment enough. That and money ends it in their eyes.' He gripped the back of his friend's neck and squeezed tightly. 'But not in mine, brother,' he said. 'You will wait for the family to pay the money, and then you will do what has to be done.'

'I don't understand,' said Two Knives. 'The *gar* decided that the family pays compensation and that is the matter closed.'

'That they did,' said Crazy Boy. 'But what the *gar* decides and what I decide are two different things. You wait until the blood money has been paid and then you and your brothers pick them up and show them what happens to anyone who crosses us. I want them to lose their hands and their feet and their pricks and their heads and I want the pieces fed to dogs. Do you understand?'

Two Knives grinned and nodded. 'That's more like it,' he said.

'Make sure that no one sees you pick them up, make sure that no one can connect what happens to them to me. But I want them to die screaming and I want to see a video of their last moments.'

'It will be a pleasure,' said Two Knives.

Ahead of them was a large Mercedes. The driver already had the door open for Crazy Boy and another of his bodyguards was standing by the front passenger door. Crazy Boy slapped Two Knives on the back and climbed into the car.

Charlotte Button was sitting at a corner table in a West Belfast pub, wearing a cheap coat and with a half pint of Guinness in front of her. There was a copy of the *Belfast Telegraph* on the table with a pair of wool gloves and by her feet a Tesco carrier bag filled with provisions.

Shepherd bought a Jameson's whiskey with ice and sat down opposite her. 'I wouldn't have thought you'd shop at Tesco,' he said. 'I would have you as more of a Waitrose customer.'

'It's cover,' she said. She gestured at her coat. 'I'm trying to blend. You don't think I'd wear this for any other reason, do you?'

Shepherd smiled. The coat and the bag of shopping might have been in character but she was too pretty and too well groomed to blend and she was wearing a slim gold watch on her wrist that belied any attempt to pass herself off as a Belfast housewife.

He sipped his whiskey. 'I have to leave today,' he said.

She slid a sheet of paper across the table. 'You're booked on half a dozen flights out of Belfast this evening,' she said. 'Or you can drive and take the ferry.'

'The car stays here,' said Shepherd. 'And there's a good chance they'll be watching the airport and the ferry terminal. I'll take the train to Dublin and fly from there.'

'I'll make the reservations,' she said. 'I'll text you the booking references.'

Shepherd shook his head. 'I've tossed the phone and the Sim card,' he said. 'I'll buy my own ticket.'

'You're angry,' she said, and it was a statement and not a question.

'Damn right I'm angry,' he said. 'My life is on the line, here, Charlie. Everyone in that warehouse saw me shoot those guys.'

'I know. I'm sorry.'

'This isn't about apologies, it's about the mother of all cock-ups. The whole point of me going undercover is that I go in and out with no one knowing what's happened. I gather intel, but someone else clears up the shit.'

'Spider, you're not telling me anything that I don't already know.'

'I think it needs spelling out, Charlie. I shot two members of the Real IRA. They know what I look like.'

'But they don't know who you are.'

'That's not the point,' snapped Shepherd. 'The point is that they know what I did and if I ever cross paths with them again . . .' He threw up his hands in disgust. 'Bloody amateurs.'

'We can make sure that you never work in the Province again.'

'And what if they come looking for me, Charlie? What are you going to do? Put me in the witness protection programme? I spent more than three months in Ireland, I must have been caught a thousand times on CCTV. If they have access to any of the cameras then they'll have my picture.'

'Your legend was watertight. If they do go looking for you they'll be looking in the wrong place. They think you're an American, remember?'

'They're not stupid, Charlie. They'll know that the Americans wouldn't put one of their own people undercover in Northern Ireland.'

'But they won't know who you are or where to look for you.'

'We shouldn't even be in this position,' said Shepherd. 'I was blown, Charlie. My cover was blown to smithereens mid-operation. That's never happened before.' He sighed and shook his head contemptuously. 'How the hell could something like that happen, Charlie? How could MI5 and Special Branch be on the same case and not know?'

'Because we were coming at it from different directions,' said Button. 'Special Branch had an operative undercover in the cell, you were getting close to the Operations Director. They knew what the target was, but for whatever reason didn't share that intel.'

'And if the Real IRA hadn't got that Special Branch inspector's phone, the operation could have gone ahead and a lot of people could have died. What was going through their minds, Charlie? Don't they know we're on the same side?'

'I'm assuming that if the undercover agent hadn't been blown they'd have ambushed the bomb along the way. The SAS were ready and waiting.'

'Again, if the Sass were there, why weren't we told?'

'We've no direct link with the SAS, Spider. That would go through the Cabinet Office in London.'

'So no one had the big picture, is that what you're saying? If that's the case, it's no wonder that things go wrong.'

'It's complicated,' said Button.

Shepherd smiled thinly. 'Yeah, that's what I say to Liam whenever he asks me a difficult question. Complicated or not, what happened yesterday was a major fuck-up, if you'll pardon my French.'

'I can understand how angry you are.'

'Can you, Charlie? When was the last time you shot two people? I shot them because it was the only option I had, but if it had been handled differently we could have taken them alive.'

Button nodded but didn't say anything.

'Answer me this, Charlie. MI5 and the Northern Irish cops are both after the dissidents, right? So why don't they share intel? Why don't they talk to each other?'

'It's a question of trust, or the lack of it,' said Button. 'It goes back to the 1998 Omagh bombing. MI5 had pretty good intel that there was a major bomb planned for Omagh or Londonderry but didn't inform the RUC and twenty-nine people died. And even before then there was the alleged involvement in shoot-to-kill cases.'

'Alleged?' said Shepherd. 'Didn't Sir John Stevens say in his report that they'd helped the UDA in fifteen murders and been involved in fourteen attempted killings and sixty-two murder conspiracies?'

'You and your trick memory,' said Button. 'Anyway, we're talking about water under the bridge. Their murderers are all back on the streets, so it's no use now bitching about what MI5 might or might not have done back in the day. But trust is a two-way street, Spider. And MI5 have plenty of reasons not to trust the PSNI. Back in 2002 the Provos broke into PSNI headquarters at Castlereagh and stole a stack of files. The Chilcott review looked at the break-in and recommended that MI5's role in Northern Ireland be expanded. The PSNI weren't happy, of course, especially when word went around that MI5 itself was behind the break-in.'

'Any truth in that rumour?'

Button chuckled. 'You don't really expect me to answer that,' she said.

'Dark forces,' said Shepherd.

'Dark forces or not, the lack of trust means that communication isn't what it should be. The PSNI has a tendency to hang on to the assets it has because it thinks it gives them an edge over Five. Five regards the PSNI as inherently unreliable so intel sharing isn't high up its list of priorities.'

'And because of that, two men died. At my hands.'

'You saved their agent's life, Spider. And I can tell you, he had a wife and two kids.'

'Yeah? Well, one of the guys I shot had five kids, Charlie. And his widow's going to be bringing them up alone.'

'They knew what they were doing, Spider. Nobody forced them to join an execution squad.'

'I know that,' said Shepherd. 'But all it would have taken was for someone at the PSNI to let Five know that they had a man in a bombing cell and to have worked with us. And how the hell was the operation blown in the first place? How did they get the Special Branch officer's phone?'

Button smiled wryly. 'You won't like this,' she said. 'It was in his coat in a pub and it got stolen. By the time he realised it was missing it was too late.'

Shepherd shook his head in disgust. 'Bloody amateurs,' he said.

'The guy you saved, he wants to meet you,' said Button. 'He wants to thank you.'

Shepherd grimaced. 'Not interested,' he said. 'I'm due some time off, right? Six months undercover with hardly a break.'

'Take as long as you want. And you should talk with Caroline Stockmann.'

'I don't need a shrink, Charlie. I won't be losing any sleep over what I did.' He looked at his watch. 'I've got to go. Can your guys clean up the flat?'

'Of course,' she said. 'I'll have your things sent on to Hereford.'

'There's nothing there I need,' he said. 'It was all part of the legend, there's nothing personal. Burn the lot. What about you? Are you going to London?'

'There's a debriefing at Loughside tomorrow. I'll be in London later this week.'

Shepherd stood up. 'I'll see you when I see you,' he said.

She looked up at him, the concern obvious in her eyes. 'Are you OK?'

Shepherd shrugged. 'I've been better,' he said.

Shepherd got back home in Hereford at four o'clock in the morning. The house was in darkness and he made himself a cup of coffee and two slices of toast. He had just bitten into the second slice when Katra appeared at the kitchen door. She was wearing her favourite pink flannel pyjamas and had tied back her dark brown hair into a ponytail. She blinked the sleep from her eyes as she smiled.

'Dan! I didn't know you were coming back today,' she said. Katra had worked for Shepherd for more than three years but still had a noticeable East European accent that betrayed her Slovenian origins, though there was also a trace of Australian from the hours that she spent watching Antipodean soap operas.

'Neither did I,' he said.

'Are you OK? You look tired.'

'It's been a long day,' he said. 'How's Liam?'

'He's fine,' she said, sitting down at the kitchen table. 'He said he'd had trouble getting hold of you on the phone.'

He nodded. She was right. It had been more than three days since he'd spoken to his son. 'I've been really busy,' he said.

Katra gestured at the fridge. 'Do you want me to cook you something? I could make you an omelette or scrambled eggs.'

'Toast is fine,' he said. 'Then I'm straight to bed. He's been doing his homework?'

'Eventually,' she said. 'I have to nag him.'

'I'll talk to him,' said Shepherd. 'But no problems?'

Katra shook her head. 'Everything's fine.'

'No girlfriend yet?'

Katra laughed. 'If there is he hasn't told me.' She got up, went over to the sink and poured herself a glass of water. 'Are you back for a while?'

'Fingers crossed,' he said.

'Liam's playing football on Saturday.'

Shepherd raised his coffee mug. 'I'll be there,' he said. 'Now you go back to bed.'

Katra nodded and went upstairs. Shepherd finished his toast and coffee, put his plate and mug in the sink and headed up to Liam's bedroom. His son was fast asleep, curled up with his back to the door. He tiptoed over and bent down over the sleeping boy. He watched him for almost a minute, fighting the urge to ruffle his hair because he didn't want to wake him.

He went along to his own bedroom and set his alarm clock for seven. It meant that he'd only have just over two hours' sleep but he wanted to be up with Liam.

He went to sleep the moment his head touched the pillow, and it seemed no time at all before his alarm was buzzing. He pulled on the same shirt and jeans that he'd worn before he went to bed and padded down to the kitchen. Katra was in the kitchen scrambling eggs and preparing to stir in the cheese that Liam loved.

'You hardly slept,' she said, popping bread into the toaster.

'I wanted to see Liam before he goes to school. Is he up yet?'

'I checked, he's showering.'

'I'll take him to school,' said Shepherd.

She looked over her shoulder. 'Are you sure? You must be tired.'

'I'm fine,' he said, switching on the kettle. 'How was he while I was away?'

Katra carried on stirring the eggs. 'He's a good boy, you know that.'

'No problems at school?'

She shook her head. 'He's doing really well. They had a maths test two days ago and he got ninety-four per cent.'

'Wow,' said Shepherd.

'And he's doing really well at football.'

'I'll watch him on Saturday.'

'He'd like that. You know he misses you.'

Shepherd sighed. 'I know.'

She smiled. 'At least you're home for a while now,' she said. 'Do you want some eggs?'

'My eggs?' asked Liam, appearing at the door. He was

wearing his school uniform but his tie was loose around his neck.

'Hi,' said Shepherd. He went over and hugged him and kissed the top of his head.

Liam squirmed out of his grasp. 'Dad, I'm not a kid,' he said. He sat down at the kitchen table, gulped down orange juice and bit into a slice of toast.

'When did you get back?' he asked.

'Early this morning,' said Shepherd. 'And don't talk with your mouth full.'

Shepherd ate his toast and drank his coffee as Liam bolted down his breakfast, then he went back upstairs for shoes and socks.

By the time he got back to the hall Liam was at the front door with his backpack on. 'Tie,' said Shepherd.

Liam tied it half-heartedly.

'Properly,' said Shepherd.

'It's the style,' said Liam. 'Everyone wears them like this.'

Shepherd picked up the keyless remote for the BMW X3 and opened the door. 'After you, your lordship,' he said, and did a mock bow.

Liam shook his head sadly and walked out. Shepherd followed him. 'So how long are you staying for?' asked Liam as he climbed into the car.

'A few days at least,' Shepherd said. 'Maybe a week or so. I'll definitely be at the game on Saturday. Katra says you're playing a blinder these days. Seat belt.'

Liam fastened his belt as Shepherd started the car. 'Can I ask you something, Dad?'

'Sure. Anything. You know that. Just so long as it's not going to cost me anything.'

Liam pulled a face. 'That might be a problem, then.'

'I'm joking, Liam,' said Shepherd. 'What's up?'

Liam took a deep breath as if he was steeling himself to break bad news. 'Can I go to boarding school?'

It was the last thing that Shepherd had expected to hear and his jaw dropped. 'Can you what?'

'Boarding school. Can I go to boarding school?'

'You've been watching those Harry Potter movies again, haven't you? You know they're not real?' He drove slowly away from the house.

'I'm not six, Dad.'

'Yeah, I know that, but boarding school isn't all midnight feasts and learning to do magic tricks.'

'How do you know what it's like? You never went to boarding school.'

That was true, and it made Shepherd pause. All he knew about boarding schools came from what he'd read and seen on television; he had no first-hand experience at all. 'I know it means being away from home for months at a time,' he said. 'It means being at school twenty-four hours a day.'

'So?'

'So I'd miss you not being here. You're fourteen and soon you'll be leaving home for good. I'd like to spend time while you're still around.'

'I'm thirteen, Dad. Fourteen is months away.'

'But you'll be going to university when you're eighteen. That's only four years.'

Liam sighed and folded his arms. Shepherd didn't have to be an expert in reading body language to know that his son was upset about something.

'What's wrong, Liam?'

The boy sighed again. 'OK, look, it's not as if you're here much, is it?'

'I've been away a lot, I know. I'm sorry. I'll try to be at home more if that'll help.'

'You always say that, Dad. You always say you'll spend more time at home but you never do. And you've just been in Ireland for almost six months.'

'I was back most weekends.'

Liam shook his head. 'No, you weren't. Maybe once a month you came back.'

Shepherd took his right hand off the steering wheel and ran it through his hair as he realised that his son was right. The Northern Ireland operation had been as dangerous as they came and every time he had left the Province he'd been putting himself at risk. 'It was a tough job, Liam.'

'They're all tough jobs, Dad. And they all need you to be away.'

'So what do you want? You want me to stop doing what I do and get a job in an office?'

Liam's eyes narrowed. 'Would you do that?'

Shepherd felt his stomach churn as he realised that he was having the same conversation he'd once had with his wife, a conversation that had resulted in him leaving the SAS.

'It's my career,' he said.

'It's your life,' said Liam, which was exactly what his mother had once said to Shepherd, and he smiled despite himself.

'Sometimes I have to be away, there's nothing I can do about that,' said Shepherd. 'I try to be here as often as I can and I phone every day when I'm away.'

Liam shook his head. 'No you don't,' he said. 'Sometimes you don't phone for two or three days. You're always sorry when you do eventually call and you always bring me a present when you come back, but . . .' He tailed off and didn't finish the sentence.

'I'm sorry,' said Shepherd.

'You don't have to keep apologising, Dad, I'm not a kid. I understand about your job and I know what it means to you. This isn't about you. It's about me.'

'So how does boarding school help?'

'I don't know. I just thought . . .' He shrugged and looked away. 'I just thought it might make things better, that's all. Better for everybody, you know.'

'Is there a problem at school here?'

Liam shook his head. 'No, it's OK.'

'You're not being bullied or anything?'

'Of course not,' said Liam disdainfully.

'So what's the problem?'

'It's not a problem,' said Liam. He sighed again. 'I'm just fed up being here on my own.'

'You've got Katra.'

'Katra's great but she's not my family and she's a girl.'

'You've got your grandparents.'

'And I'd still have them if I was at boarding school. Dad, it's no biggie.'

'It is a biggie,' said Shepherd. 'It's about you leaving home.'

'It's boarding school, Dad. That's not leaving home. I'd be back at holidays and half-terms and you can visit at weekends. I don't see what the big deal is.'

'There's the cost, for a start.'

Liam scowled. 'So it's about money? I thought with all the overtime you work that money wouldn't be a problem.'

'Of course it's not about money.'

'So why talk about the cost?'

Shepherd fought the urge to smile. He hadn't realised how forceful and devious his son had become. It seemed like only yesterday that he'd been changing his nappies and wiping away his tears, and now he was arguing his case as confidently as any adult. 'OK,' he said quietly. 'Let me think about it. But answer me one thing. What's put this in your head? Something must have sparked it off.'

Liam shrugged carelessly. 'Well, a friend of mine left school here to go to boarding school and he says it's great.'

'Where is his school? The new one?'

'In the Lake District. He says there are no girls there, which is great, and they get to play sports every day and they've got an amazing swimming pool. They do lots of day trips to the lakes and he's learning to sail. It sounds great, Dad.'

Shepherd smiled. 'It does, doesn't it? I might see if I can book myself in for a few months.'

'It's for kids, Dad.'

'I was joking,' Shepherd said. 'Are you serious about this? It's not just a whim?'

'I want to do it, Dad. Really.'

'OK,' said Shepherd. 'I tell you what, you get me the details of their website and I'll take a look.'

Liam's face brightened. 'And then I can go?'

Shepherd wagged a finger at him. 'Then we'll talk about it.'

'But you're not saying no?'

'I'm saying I'll look at the website and we'll talk about it.' They were a hundred yards from the school entrance and he slowed the SUV. 'Do you want me to drop you here?'

'Why, can't you take me to the gates?'

'I thought teenagers didn't want to be seen with their parents.'

'Dad, this is a BMW X3. Do you think I don't want to be seen in a cool car like this?'

Charlotte Button didn't call Shepherd for a week. He'd been working full-time on the Northern Ireland job for almost six months so he was due plenty of time off, and she was also well aware how mentally exhausting it was to work undercover. Shepherd spent his days lounging around the house and simply enjoying the fact that he was Dan Shepherd and not Matt Tanner, Real IRA enforcer, and that he didn't have to be constantly thinking about what he was going to say next. He ran for at least an hour a day, usually across nearby fields, wearing his old army boots and carrying a rucksack filled with bricks wrapped in newspaper, and he worked on the garden, mowing the lawn, cutting the hedges and weeding the flowerbeds, and finally got around to repairing a leak in the roof of the garage.

He made a point of taking Liam to school every day, and picking him up every afternoon. He stood on the touchline and cheered with the rest of the parents as Liam's team lost 3–1 on Saturday and he took him shopping for new clothes and school shoes and ended up buying a pair of football boots that cost more than any footwear that Shepherd had ever owned.

He kicked a football around with Liam in the garden,

and had Sunday lunch with Liam's grandparents at their home, and helped him with his homework. He enjoyed being a father again and not having to deal with the stress of constantly having to pretend to be someone else, but he was still happy to hear Button's voice because that meant that she had a job for him.

'Everything OK?' she asked.

'All good,' said Shepherd.

'And Liam's OK?'

'He's thinking about boarding school. I'd like to pick your brains sometime. Your daughter is a boarder, right?'

'And loves it,' said Button. 'How about you pop down to London in a day or two.'

'For a chat about boarding schools or because you've got something for me to do?'

Button laughed. 'Cabin fever already? I thought you wanted time off.'

'I do. Of course I do.'

'I know you, Spider. You need to work or you start howling at the moon.'

'Is that a yes, then?'

'There's an assignment that needs your particular skills and I'd like to run it by you. But it's not pressing. Whenever you're ready to get back in the saddle is just fine. You've racked up a stack of overtime and days in lieu over the past year.'

'That's the way it goes,' said Shepherd. 'I can hardly tell the bad guys I've got to clock off, can I?'

'I've had a word with the powers-that-be and they're happy to pay you for the extra days off, if you want. It'll be a nice windfall. Or you can take the days.'

'It's a nice change not to have to be worrying about overtime and whether or not I'll be paid for working on my off days.'

'That's the War against Terror for you,' said Button. 'The police are getting their budgets slashed but MI5's money is still flowing.'

'Funny that, because you're a thousand times more likely to be mugged or killed by a hit-and-run driver than blown up by a terrorist.'

'What newspaper are you getting your information from?' she asked.

'Depends on who I am,' said Shepherd. 'Matt Tanner read the *Belfast Telegraph* and the *Irish Republican News*. Me, I still read the *Daily Mail*. But I like the *Sunday Times* at the weekend.'

'That explains it,' she said. 'Anyway, funding worries aside, can you come to London day after tomorrow? I'll get an office fixed up near Paddington.'

'No problem,' said Shepherd.

'And at some point you're going to have to have a chat with Caroline Stockmann.'

'Because of what happened over the water? I already told you I don't need to see a shrink. I'm sleeping just fine, no guilt, no flashbacks, no remorse. If I had to do it again I wouldn't hesitate. No post-traumatic anything.'

'I'm glad to hear that, but you're overdue your six-monthly psychiatric evaluation,' she said. 'I'll get her to give you a call.'

'I'll count the minutes,' said Shepherd.

'I wouldn't,' said Button. 'That's the sort of behaviour that might get you red-flagged on a psychiatric evaluation.'

*   *   *

Shepherd caught the last train of the morning to London. The office that Button had arranged for their meeting was above a Chinese restaurant in Queensway, a ten-minute walk from Paddington Station. On the way he stopped off at a Starbucks and bought himself an Americano and a breakfast tea for her.

He deliberately walked past the door at the side of the restaurant and then stopped suddenly to look in the window of a shop selling tacky souvenirs and check that he wasn't being tailed. When he was satisfied that no one was following him he doubled back and pressed the button for the second-floor office. The locking mechanism buzzed and he pushed it open.

There was a pile of mail on the other side of the door and a rack on the wall where there had once been a fire extinguisher. The stair carpet on the lower flight of stairs was torn in places but there was no carpet at all on the upper section, just bare boards that were cracked and chipped and which squeaked with every step that he took.

Button opened the door for him and smiled when she saw that he was holding two Starbucks cups. He held one out to her. 'English breakfast tea,' he said.

'You're such a sweetie,' she said. She nodded for him to sit down and closed the door. It was a nondescript office with a large teak desk that was bare, except for her briefcase and a Newton's Cradle with chrome balls, and a matching empty bookcase. There were white plastic blinds over the window and a cheap plastic sofa facing a square coffee table on a threadbare carpet.

'Salubrious,' he said, looking around.

'It was the best safe house I could find at short notice,'

she said. She was wearing a blue blazer over a white and blue checked dress and her chestnut hair was an inch or so shorter than when he'd last seen her in Belfast. 'MI5 does have a particularly nice office in the British Museum but I thought you'd be happier being closer to Paddington.'

Shepherd took off his coat and sat down on the sofa. Button picked up her briefcase, pulled over a wooden chair and sat down opposite him. She clicked the double locks of her case, opened it and took out an A4 manila envelope.

'How much do you know about pirates?' she said, opening the envelope.

'Yo-ho-ho and a bottle of rum?'

'Not so much Long John Silver, more Somalis in the Gulf of Aden.'

'Holding ships for ransom and making a mint, from the sound of it.' He frowned. 'But East Africa is a bit out of MI5's manor, isn't it?'

'Turns out it's a bit closer to home,' she said, pushing a couple of surveillance photographs across the table. One was a close-up of a short, stocky man in a hoodie, his head down as he spoke into a mobile phone; the other was of the same man but wearing a Chelsea shirt and climbing into the back of a large Mercedes. 'This is Wiil Waal, or "Crazy Boy". His real name, in as much as Somalis have real names, is Simeon Khalid.' She put down a close-up of the man's face. 'He's twenty-four but looks older.'

Button slid out another photograph and pointed at a mugshot of a black man in his forties, his face pockmarked with old acne scars, his nose squashed flat against his face. 'This is his elder brother, Abshir. He was taken by security forces in northern Somalia in 2010 and is behind bars awaiting trial. He was one of the founders of the new wave of Somali pirates, a particularly nasty piece of work, and an Islamic fundamentalist. He's worth in excess of twenty million dollars but the US have got most of it. The Treasury Department targeted him a while back and have been freezing his assets wherever they can find them. The family business was taken over by one of Crazy Boy's uncles.'

She put two more photographs on the table, surveillance pictures of a group of half a dozen hard-faced men in a skiff, AK-47s slung over their shoulders. She tapped the face of one of the men, in his late forties with two gold front teeth and a thick scar across his chin. 'This is the uncle. He runs things out in Somalia but since Abshir was taken into custody Crazy Boy has been pulling the strings from here. The uncle's name is Blue.'

'Blue?'

Button shrugged. 'Somalis are big on nicknames. His has something to do with his skin colour being so black that he's gone beyond black and blue. I think you've got to be Somali to get it. Anyway, so far as we know, he doesn't do anything without checking with Crazy Boy first. We think Crazy Boy plans the operations, funds them, then repatriates the profits and washes them through his businesses here.' She gestured at the surveillance photographs of Crazy Boy. 'He came to the UK about four years ago. And you'll like this, he lives in Ealing. Not far from your old house.'

'Small world,' said Shepherd. 'Why Ealing?'

'There's a very large Somali population there now, and in Southall. It probably has something to do with the proximity to Heathrow.'

'The airport?'

'More specifically, the khat leaves that Somalis like to chew. It has to be eaten fresh and there are supplies coming in every day to Heathrow. Ealing is close to the airport so the Somalis there are guaranteed the freshest leaves. The fresher they are the better the buzz, apparently.'

'And this khat isn't illegal?'

Button shook her head. 'Not yet,' she said. 'It is in some countries but not in the UK. The principal ingredient is an amphetamine-like stimulant and the World Health Organisation has classified it as a drug of abuse. You'll see Somalis chewing it as naturally as smoking a cigarette.'

'I don't remember seeing that many Somalis when I lived in Ealing.'

'There's been a huge increase in the last few years, but even so they tend to keep to themselves. The women are at home most of the time and the men go to their own social clubs. They don't mix much. The number of Somalis in the area has probably trebled since you moved to Hereford.' She tapped the photograph. 'Crazy Boy has the brains of the family, it seems. He bought himself passage across Europe and into the UK, slipped through in the back of a truck from Calais with half a dozen genuine asylum seekers.'

'And got asylum, presumably.'

'He was on track,' said Button. 'He had false papers and a top immigration lawyer.'

'But Five must have known who he was, right?'

'Not then,' said Button. 'He came in under the radar. We knew that he'd left Somalia but no one knew where he'd gone. And to be honest, even if we had known there wouldn't have been much we could have done. We didn't have his

DNA or fingerprints so all he had to do was to stick to his story and he'd get asylum.'

'The world's gone crazy, Charlie. You're telling me a Somali pirate can just waltz into the UK and end up with a British passport?'

'It's not as simple as waltzing, but most of Somalia is a war zone so any Somali who can get into the UK is pretty much assured of asylum status.'

Shepherd sat back. 'Like I said, the world's gone crazy. And why the UK? Presumably they all pass through Europe, why don't they claim asylum there?' He held up his hand. 'Don't tell me, it's because we're a soft touch and because once they hit British soil they can claim a free house and full benefits.'

'Actually Crazy Boy did apply for and received benefits while his application was processed, even though we believe he had access to overseas funds of the order of ten million dollars. He obviously couldn't touch that because it would have blown his application.'

Shepherd shook his head in disgust.

'If it makes you feel any better, he dropped his asylum application two years ago.'

Shepherd frowned. 'But he's still in the UK? How come?'

Button tapped another photograph, this one of Crazy Boy with an overweight black woman with dreadlocks holding a baby that had been wrapped in a multicoloured cloth. 'He married this woman. Haweeya Bergman. A German national. She fled Somalia in 2002 and married a German who had British citizenship too. She got a British passport and a German one, divorced him and moved to the UK. When Crazy Boy married her he got British citizenship and German citizenship. The baby she's holding is Crazy Boy's. A son. The son was born in Britain so getting Crazy Boy out of the country is now nigh-on impossible.'

'The woman, how old is she?'

'Thirty-nine.'

'And Crazy Boy is twenty-four, you said.'

'That's right. Your point is?'

'Well, forgive me if this is sexist and ageist, but she's a fair bit older than him and with a face like a bulldog chewing a wasp, so I don't see how anyone can think it's a love job.'

Button feigned dismay. 'Spider, the courts have to take people at their word. If they say they want to be together until death do them part, then who are we to pour scorn on their choices?' She grinned. 'It's as clear as day that he married her for the passport, and had the child because that gives him extra security. But the simple fact is that he's now in the UK to stay. He's brought in several million pounds, he's purchased a large house in Ealing and he's set up two restaurants in the area, along with a Somali shop and a café. He's also active in the *gar* system.'

'*Gar?*'

'Somali criminal courts, where judgement is handed down by the community elders. Crazy Boy is unusually young to be running a *gar* but after several elders died or ended up in intensive care, he was invited on board. In his area of Ealing he effectively functions as judge and jury, holding sway over several thousand Somalis.'

'So if he's a legitimate businessman and happily married father, what's Five's interest?' asked Shepherd.

'I didn't say anything about him being legitimate,' said Button. 'His businesses are almost certainly money-laundering fronts and he's continuing to run the family's piracy operations out in Somalia. He sends money out to fund the pirates and brings back the profits. He runs a gang that also deals in drugs, mainly marijuana, but we think he also imports coke and heroin through Somalis in Amsterdam. But our interest is because there are terrorism considerations. Serious considerations.'

She took another surveillance photograph out of the envelope, this one of a tall black man wearing desert fatigues and cradling an AK-47, his face half masked by a black and white checked scarf. There were half a dozen other men similarly attired standing around him.

'This is Ahmed Abdi Godane, the leader of Somalia's al-Shebab movement and an al-Qaeda stooge. He's based in northern Mogadishu and he's a nasty piece of work. He's effectively created an African Taliban and he's been issuing fatwas against everything from televised football to pop music. He moved into the major league during the World Cup when he organised two massive suicide bombings in Kampala. He's directly responsible for seventy-six Ugandans dying for no reason other than the fact there are Ugandan peacekeeping troops in Somalia. All our experts reckon that he's gearing himself up for a major attack on the West.'

'And the UK connection?'

Button tapped the photograph again. 'We have evidence of telephone traffic between Godane and Crazy Boy's uncle just days before the attacks in Kampala.'

'They could have just been talking about the match,' said Shepherd.

Button flashed him a tight smile. 'We don't know what they were talking about, but the mere fact that they are in contact sends up a lot of red flags. We're looking now for financial movements between the pirates and al-Shebab and if we find them, then we've opened up one hell of a can of worms.'

Shepherd nodded slowly. 'I get it,' he said. 'If Godane blows up a US embassy in Africa and the Americans find out that the UK has given citizenship to the man who paid for it . . .' He grimaced. 'It's going to screw up the special relationship, isn't it?'

'There is no special relationship, not any more,' said Button. 'That's the problem. If Crazy Boy is funding al-Shebab terrorism, then yes, we're going to look bloody stupid if we've given him a passport. The last thing we want is for the Americans to be pushing for extradition while Crazy Boy gets defended by a pack of human rights lawyers.'

'Led by our own Cherie Blair, no doubt.' Shepherd laughed. He held up his hands as Button glared at him. 'OK, I shouldn't be flippant, but it's hard not to be cynical, isn't it? How the hell do we allow this to happen? How do we get to the stage where a Somali pirate with al-Qaeda connections is able to live in the UK? Why don't we just sling him out?'

Button tapped the photograph of the woman and child. 'His family,' she said. 'And human rights legislation.'

'But he lied to get into the country. He said he was an asylum seeker when he wasn't. Then he switches horses midstream and marries a Somali woman with German nationality and gets her pregnant despite the fact that she's ugly as sin and twice his weight.'

'It's the law,' said Button.

'But at any point Five could have told the UK Border Agency or the Home Office who he is and had him sent home.'

'Five doesn't work like that, Spider,' said Button. 'We don't reveal our files to immigration tribunals.'

'I think a quiet word in the right ear might have helped, don't you?'

'And then a lawyer starts demanding to know where information about his client came from? That would be a can of worms that we wouldn't want opening.'

'We still have D notices, don't we?'

'Not for criminals, we don't. For terrorism and national security, yes. But not for criminals like Crazy Boy.' She smiled sympathetically. 'I understand exactly what you're saying, Spider. And I'm in total agreement. But we have to follow the law. If we start bending or breaking laws simply because we don't agree with them, where do we end up?'

'Anarchy,' said Shepherd. 'That's what I'm expected to say, right? And no one in their right mind wants anarchy? But really, Charlie, I don't see that anyone would choose to be in the situation we're in with scum like Crazy Boy. They break the rules when they feel like it and cry foul when we trespass on what they see as their human rights.'

'Please don't tell me that life isn't fair, Spider, you know how I hate it when you do that.' She sipped her tea. 'So, do you want to hear what the job is?'

'I'm all ears,' said Shepherd. 'I'm assuming that you want me to go undercover, is that it? With a peg leg and a parrot on my shoulder?'

'Leaving aside the fact that you're the wrong colour, the pirates don't trust outsiders,' said Button. 'But Crazy Boy doesn't operate like the other pirate groups. Most of them tend to prowl around and seize whatever ship they come across, but we believe that Crazy Boy has started targeting specific ships, based on who owns them and what they're carrying. We're pretty sure that he's getting inside information from at least one London-based company. That's where we want to use you.'

'Why me, Charlie? Sitting at a computer all day isn't what I do best.'

'It's undercover, Spider, and no one does undercover better than you. And no one's better than you at spotting who's wrong.'

'You flatterer, you.'

'I know it's not the same as infiltrating a gang of armed robbers or drug dealers, but in the grand scheme of things it's just as important. Maybe more so. Crazy Boy's pirates have taken six ships that we know about in the past two years. And the last four were all carrying containers for the same freight forwarders based in London. It could be a coincidence, but we think there's something going on. The freighters were all similar vessels on similar routes, all coming from China via the Suez Canal and so passing through the Gulf of Aden close to Somalia. It's possible that Crazy Boy is getting information from someone at the company. Most of the pirates used to operate by just prowling around and attacking any ship they found, but in the past few years they've started taking a more intelligence-led approach. We know they've been placing people in ports who then radio ahead when they spot a likely ship leaving, and we know of at least one hijacking where they had their own man on board as a seaman.'

'So you want me to do a Father Christmas and find out who's been naughty and who's been nice?'

'Exactly,' said Button. 'Their head office is in Hammersmith so they're not too far from Ealing. Thirty-seven employees, of whom only twenty have access to ship and cargo movements. We've looked at assets and checked bank accounts of everyone at the company and we can't find anyone who's suddenly come into money or who has any obvious connection with Crazy Boy, but four ships in a row is just too many to be a coincidence.'

'Not if they have cargo on hundreds of ships.'

Button shook her head. 'They use most of the world's shipping companies, depending on where they're shipping to and from, so they are spread pretty wide. But the only pirates who've taken a ship carrying their cargo have been working for Crazy Boy. Our intelligence guys have run the probabilities and they're sure that there's some connection between Crazy Boy and the freight company.'

'I'm not sure that it's going to work, sending me undercover in a company. I've never worked at a desk, you know that. I was with the Paras then the SAS then the cops and then SOCA and I never so much as opened a drawer or used a photocopier.'

Button laughed. 'We'll put together a legend that doesn't make your lack of typing skills an issue,' she said. She took out a pale green thumb drive and gave it to him. 'There's a rundown on the company and the likely suspects,' she said. 'I understand your reservations, but you're a chameleon, that's your skill. You can blend into any situation, you get people to like you and to accept you. That'll work as well with a group of office workers as it does with a gang of bank robbers or a terrorist cell. It's the only way, Spider. If we send in the cops to start questioning people up front then they'll know that we're on to them and shut down.'

Shepherd put the thumb drive in his pocket. 'When?'

'We've got to put together a legend and fix you up with a flat. Three or four days. Unless you want more time off.'

'Next week will be fine,' he said and sipped his coffee. 'So what's the ultimate aim? To put Crazy Boy behind bars? Or deport him?'

'If we can get him on conspiracy, we'll move for sure. A lot depends on how he's getting the intel from the company, if he's doing it for himself or through an intermediary. We're watching his money, too. It's possible we'll get him on money laundering. Deportation is doubtful in view of his British citizenship.'

'And how much of this is a backside-covering operation in case the Americans come to you with a terrorism angle?'

She raised her eyebrows. 'I'm not that devious, Spider.'

'Maybe not, but your bosses almost certainly are.'

'I've been tasked with investigating Crazy Boy because British ships are at risk and there appears to be a British company involved. I mentioned the al-Shebab link just so you'd be aware of the potential political implications. If we can make a case against Crazy Boy he'll be charged, that's for sure. We won't be dragging our heels, I can promise you that.'

'And if it does kick off in Africa while he's in prison, it stops being a UK problem.'

'That's fair,' said Button. 'Plus if we have him in prison on criminal charges and the US apply for extradition, it'll be a lot easier to hand him over. It's one thing for the human rights brigade to shout about the rights of a poor refugee, but they're less likely to get hot under the collar about a Somali pirate with terrorist links.'

Shepherd finished his coffee and looked at his watch. 'You don't mind me heading back to Hereford?'

'Absolutely not,' she said. 'I just wanted a face-to-face chat and to give you the thumb drive. I've got a meeting at Thames House all this afternoon.' She grinned. 'They're big on meetings, unfortunately.'

'How's Zoe, by the way?' asked Shepherd.

'Sixteen going on twenty-five,' she said. 'Liam's serious about boarding school, is he?'

'Seems to be. He's mentioned it a few times.'

'Zoe's at Culford School,' said Button. 'They've been brilliant. Especially after Graham died. It always made sense for her to be a boarder because Graham and I were working all the hours God sends. We had a string of au pairs but they never really worked out.'

'That's why I think it might be good for him. I've been away a lot over the past year or two and it doesn't seem to be getting any better.'

'He's not just using it as a threat? Trying to get your attention?'

Shepherd shrugged. 'He puts up a good case. I'm away a lot and there's no sign of that changing. If he was in the right school, he might do really well. And they're usually big on sports, which he's keen on.'

'Well, Zoe loves it,' said Button. Her eyes narrowed. 'You've still got Katra, right?'

'Sure, and she's great. But I'm away all the time and he's an only child.'

'That was the thing that swung it for Zoe,' said Button. 'It's different if they've got siblings but when they're on their own they really are better off with children their own age.

Gives them social skills and they get their own network of friends. Zoe goes skiing with one of her pals and her parents and last year she spent two weeks in Hong Kong with one of the boarders whose family runs a hotel chain in Asia. And whichever way you look at it, they do so much better academically. There's no chasing them to do homework, very little in the way of discipline problems and you can be reasonably sure that some inner-city wannabe gangster isn't going to mug them for their mobile phone or lunch money.'

'Are there any downsides?'

Button nodded slowly. 'Oh yes,' she said. 'You lose them that much quicker.'

'In what way?'

Button sighed. 'They grow up so fast anyway but when they're away at school it seems to happen quicker. They become more independent, they learn to sort out their own problems, stand on their own two feet.'

'That's good, right?'

Button winced. 'Of course it's good, but there are times when you wish it didn't happen so fast. They only have one childhood and the bits you miss you never get back.'

'But on balance it's a good thing?'

'I think so, yes. If you want I can get you a brochure for Culford. Or they have a website you can look at.'

'Yeah, the website's fine, but I'm hoping to find something closer to Hereford.' He stood up and as always when saying goodbye he was confused about what to do. A handshake seemed too formal, but she was his boss so a hug or a kiss on the cheek seemed too personal. He grinned and gave her a small wave.

She smiled back with an amused glint in her eye and he

knew that she sensed his confusion. She mimicked his wave. 'You take care, and polish up your secretarial skills, just in case.'

The Mercedes pulled up in front of a terraced house in Southall. 'Wait outside, I won't be more than ten minutes,' Crazy Boy told his driver. The driver nodded. Crazy Boy jerked his chin at Two Knives. 'Get the case out of the boot.' Two Knives was a cousin, a fierce fighter when he had been a pirate, the man that Crazy Boy had used to carry out hostage executions when shipping companies had been slow in paying ransoms. Crazy Boy had given him the nickname because when he boarded a ship he always had two large curved knives, one on either hip. He had joined Crazy Boy in London a year earlier after paying ten thousand pounds to a group of Chinese traffickers. The Chinese were the best traffickers in the world. No one was better at moving people, arms or drugs. He had applied for asylum and his lawyer had assured him that he would have British citizenship within three years.

The driver pressed the switch to open the boot as Crazy Boy and Two Knives climbed out of the car. Crazy Boy sneered as he looked up and down the road. The houses were small and uncared for, the brickwork stained and crumbling, the paint peeling from the doors and window frames, the windows unwashed. The pavements were covered with litter and there were cubes of broken glass in the gutters, relics of smashed car windows. Three Indian women waddled by in brightly coloured saris, each pushing a stroller, gossiping away in Hindi. One of them glared at Crazy Boy and said something to her companions and they all laughed.

Crazy Boy knew that the Indians of Southall hated the Somalis. There had been dozens of cases of Somali teenagers being assaulted by groups of Asians and Somali shopkeepers were always having their windows smashed. He glared at the women and shook his fist at them. 'Never seen a black man with a big car?' he shouted in English. 'Think we all live in the jungle, do you?'

The women averted their eyes as they hurried away.

'Back to your foul-smelling hovels, you Indian cows!' he screamed.

The women began to run, their pushchairs bouncing along the uneven pavement.

Crazy Boy mimed firing a gun at them. 'Bastard Indians,' he said. 'They hate us, you know that? They came here to do Whitey's work and then they bring in their cousins with arranged marriages and look down their noses at us. We fought to get into this country. We killed. They crawled in on their bellies and they think they're superior to us?'

'Bitches,' agreed Two Knives, pulling a suitcase out of the boot. He looked around and then slammed the boot shut. The case was heavy and he had to use both hands to carry it to the front door.

Crazy Boy pressed the doorbell and heard a faint buzzing sound from the back of the house. A few seconds later he heard shuffling feet and a woman in full burka opened the door. She scrutinised them through the slit in her headdress and then opened the door wide to allow them in.

Crazy Boy went first, heading straight down the hallway to the kitchen at the back of the house. Two Knives followed him with the suitcase as the woman shut the door and disappeared into the front room.

The man sitting at the kitchen table was in his sixties with a straggly beard that was streaked with grey and white. He was wearing a Fair Isle sweater over a long grey Jubba jacket and baggy grey trousers. In his right hand he held a *misbaha*, a string of Islamic prayer beads. There were ninety-nine beads on the string, corresponding to the ninety-nine names of Allah. He tended to use them as worry beads rather than as a means of religious devotion. The man's name was Muhammad al-Faiz but everyone who did business with him called him the Arab. He had been in England for nine years and already had eleven children with his three wives in the country. The wives lived in separate houses paid for by housing benefit, and all were claiming invalidity payments as the Arab knew a Bangladeshi doctor who was happy to sign them off as epileptics for five hundred pounds a time.

The Arab stood up, hugged Crazy Boy and kissed him on the cheek. 'You are well, brother?' he asked.

'Always,' said Crazy Boy. He waved at Two Knives, who swung the suitcase on to the kitchen table and unzipped it. Inside were dozens of brick-size bundles of fifty-pound notes. 'One and a half million, to be transferred to my uncle in Mogadishu,' said Crazy Boy. 'He will want paying in US dollars, the same as last time.'

The Arab nodded his head. 'That is not a problem. The conversion will be done on the day that the money is transferred. The current exchange rate is 1.44, I believe.'

He opened a cabinet above the sink and took out an electronic banknote counter. He unplugged a kettle and plugged in the counter. 'Can I offer you a drink while I do the count? Mint tea, perhaps?'

'After all this time you do not trust me?' Crazy Boy laughed.

The Arab smiled as he took one of the bundles out of the case and slotted it into the top of the counter. 'My friend, I trust nobody,' he said. 'That is why I have lived so long.' He pushed a button on the front of the counter and the notes began to whirr as a red LED counted them off. 'Would you care for tea, my friends, because this will take some time?'

'Tea would be good,' said Crazy Boy, sitting down at the table.

The Arab continued to count the money, breaking off only to make and serve glasses of hot sweet tea garnished with fresh mint leaves. Crazy Boy sat and sipped his drink and waited. He wasn't offended at the Arab's insistence on checking every note. Business was business. He was equally thorough when he was paying money out.

When the Arab had finished he opened a door to a room which had once been used as a larder but which now contained only a safe almost as tall as he was. There was an electronic keypad on the door and the Arab tapped out a six-digit number and pulled open the door with a grunt. He put Crazy Boy's money on to a shelf in the middle, closed the door and joined him at the table. He picked up his glass of tea and toasted Crazy Boy before drinking. 'So business is good?' asked the Arab.

'The ships still sail, the ransoms are paid, all is well with the world.'

'I hear that the infidels are doing more to protect their ships.'

Crazy Boy shrugged. 'They try, but there are too many ships and the sea is too large. But you are right, the pickings are not as easy as they once were. Still, he who does not seize opportunity today will be unable to seize tomorrow's opportunity.'

The Arab smiled. 'You Somalis have a proverb or saying for every occasion,' he said.

'It is the way we pass down our wisdom from generation to generation,' said Crazy Boy. 'One of our proverbs is that Somalis never utter a false proverb.'

The Arab chuckled. He poured more tea into Crazy Boy's glass. 'Simeon, one of my countrymen would like to meet you. There is a matter he wishes to discuss with you.'

Crazy Boy frowned. 'And what would that matter be?'

The Arab scratched his beard and smiled apologetically. 'I am afraid I am a mere middleman in this. He knows that I do business with you and thought that it might make you more comfortable if the approach was made through someone you know.'

'You spoke to him about me?' said Crazy Boy, his voice hardening.

'He approached me, that's all.'

'He came here?'

The Arab shook his head as he fingered the beads of the *misbaha*. 'It was at the mosque. Please don't worry about this, he is a good man, a good Muslim, and he wanted to make the approach through me rather than to approach you direct because he did not want to cause you any offence.'

'You told him that I send money to Somalia?' Crazy Boy's eyes flashed angrily. 'This is not acceptable. I do business with you because I don't want the world and his dog to know what I am doing. That is what I pay you for, privacy.'

The Arab waved his hands as if warding off an attack. 'Please, no, do not misunderstand me. Of course I did not say anything about what passes between us. I would not stay in business for long if my tongue was as loose as that.' He put a hand on Crazy Boy's arm. 'Brother, all that happened is that he spoke to me after prayers, and asked that I get you to contact him. It was a sign of respect that he did that. I know him and I know you. He merely asked that I pass on a request for a meeting. Our business was not discussed. Nor would I ever talk to anybody about what takes place here.'

Crazy Boy nodded. 'OK. I'm sorry. Of course I trust you, how could we do this business without trust?'

'Simeon, we Arabs also have many proverbs, one of which is this: "A foolish man may be known by six things: anger without cause, speech without profit, change without progress, enquiry without object, putting trust in a stranger and mistaking foes for friends." I hope that by now you consider me a friend. I more than anyone understand that one should not put one's trust in a stranger, but this man is not a stranger to me. I would trust him with my life. He is a good man and a good Muslim.'

'But what does he want with me?'

'To talk, Simeon. Just to talk.' The Arab took a sip of his tea. 'His name is Mamoud al-Zahrani. He is staying at the Hilton Hotel in Edgware Road.'

'So I am summoned, is that it?'

The Arab smiled and shook his head. 'Of course not, that's not what I meant. He has a suite there and it's a convenient place to meet, that's all.'

'Who is he, what does he do?'

'Like me, he is also a middleman, but his connections are more political than mine.'

'The Saudi royal family, you mean? He speaks for the sheikhs?'

'He speaks with the sheikhs, but that is not what I meant by political.' The Arab lowered his voice. 'All I am asking is that you speak with him, Simeon. Hear what he has to say.'

Crazy Boy nodded. 'I'll think about it,' he said.

Shepherd was sitting in front of the television half-watching a chat show in which a woman pregnant for the fourth time was about to undergo a lie detector test to see if she had been unfaithful to her current boyfriend. The host of the show, with a reptilian smile and a Savile Row suit, was egging the audience on as they shouted abuse at the woman, an overweight bleached blonde in a pink leisure suit and silver ankle boots. Shepherd could tell from the woman's body language that she wasn't lying, she wasn't being unfaithful and the baby was her boyfriend's. He wondered why anyone would expose themselves to such hatred and ridicule on a show that was presumably seen by millions. The boyfriend was no catch, either, and had the clothes, posture and haircut of a man who'd spent a few years in prison and who would probably be back behind bars before too long. They seemed a well-suited couple, but Shepherd felt sorry for the woman's kids.

On-screen the woman pushed herself up out of her chair and began screaming insults at someone in the audience, spittle flying from her mouth as she ranted and raved, her belly wobbling like a bowl of jelly. Two security men moved in to stop her diving into the audience, most of whom were now standing up and baying abuse at her. It was the first time in years that he had watched daytime television and Shepherd realised that he hadn't missed much.

He picked up his remote and clicked through to Sky News. He was sitting on the sofa with his computer on his lap. He'd plugged in the thumb drive that Button had given him and was reading the briefing notes about the freight-forwarding company in Hammersmith and the personnel who were suspected of helping Crazy Boy choose his targets off the coast of Somalia. He wasn't looking forward to going undercover in an office where the only danger he faced was the risk of a paper cut. As an undercover cop and later as a SOCA operative he'd taken on some of the biggest villains in the country, and in Northern Ireland he'd gone under-cover to get close to terrorists, and while he understood the need to bring down a pirate warlord like Crazy Boy, he didn't think that Button was making the best use of his talents. Still, on the plus side he'd be able to get home at weekends and there'd be no problems phoning Liam each evening.

He heard the phone ring and Katra answered it almost immediately. She came into the sitting room, holding the phone. 'Caroline Stockmann,' she said.

Shepherd muted the sound on the television. 'My favourite psychologist,' he said. 'What can I do for you?'

'I think you know,' said Stockmann. 'Charlie thought it might be a good idea if we got together, plus you're overdue your biannual.'

'The biannual psychological review was in my police contract and my SOCA contract but I don't remember seeing it when I signed on with MI5.'

'And your memory is good, isn't it?' said Stockmann.

'Virtually photographic,' agreed Shepherd. 'Eidetic, they call it.'

'The thing is, Charlie would very much like us to sit down for a while. And as you know, what Charlie wants, Charlie does tend to get. But whatever it may or may not have said in your contract, you do have to have a biannual.'

'I'm in Hereford, Caroline.'

'And isn't that a coincidence.' She laughed.

Shepherd didn't say anything for several seconds. 'Please don't say you're stalking me, Caroline.'

'It's more of a Muhammad coming to the mountain situation,' she said.

'It's not the first time you've said that,' said Shepherd. 'It's either that or you claim to be doing some work for the Regiment.'

'What can I say? It's as if you can read my mind.'

Shepherd sighed. 'Where would you like to meet?'

'How about the same place we met last time I was in your neck of the woods. Not a booth, because I know how much you hate sitting in booths, not being able to push them out of the way and all.'

'When?'

'Anytime this afternoon. You give me a time.'

'Two o'clock.'

'Two o'clock it is.'

Shepherd put down the phone. 'Who was that?' asked Liam.

'My stalker.'

'Your stalker?' Liam gasped. 'Are you serious?'

'Joke,' said Shepherd. 'It's someone from work.'

'You said you were on holiday.'

'I am, she just wants a chat. An hour or two at most.'

'Is it your boss?'

Shepherd shook his head. 'No, that's Charlotte Button. This lady is someone else; she has to do a report on me to say that I'm doing my job OK.'

'Like a school report?'

Shepherd nodded. 'Yes, that's pretty much what it is.'

'I hope you pass.'

Shepherd laughed. 'You and me both.'

Shepherd got to the pub early but Stockmann had beaten him to it and had installed herself at a circular table close to the booths that overlooked the car park. 'The early bird,' she said, raising a half-full pint of bitter in salute.

'Excellent tradecraft.' Shepherd laughed. 'Always get to the meeting first and sit with your back to the wall.' They shook hands and then Shepherd went over to the bar and bought a lager shandy, heavy on the lemonade. 'So what time did you get here?' he asked as he sat down opposite her.

'I was already in town when I phoned,' she said.

'You were taking a risk, weren't you? What if I wasn't around?'

'Well, first of all I knew you were, and second of all they do a good pint here and serve a ploughman's lunch that's one of the best I've ever tasted, so it wouldn't be the worst thing in the world to be here on my own for a couple of hours.' She gestured at the remains of a ploughman's on the table.

'So I'm guessing you didn't come all the way over to Hereford just for me?'

The psychologist nodded. 'I'm here for a few days,' she said. 'I actually am doing quite a bit for the Regiment.'

'Checking that they're fit for purpose?'

'To be honest, most of what I'm doing involves former members of the Regiment. Guys who've left and are finding it difficult on the outside. You've got to look pretty long and hard to find a group of people more prone to suicide than former SAS troopers.' She sipped her beer.

'That's the truth,' said Shepherd. 'Going from a full-on life of combat to Civvy Street can be a shock to the system. It was hard enough for me to move into policing. It must be a hell of a lot worse to go to a desk job or working on a building site.'

'Or just sitting watching TV all day, or in the pub. Not everyone who leaves the Regiment gets another job. You hear about the guys who go back to Afghanistan or Iraq and make a fortune freelancing and everyone knows about the ones who become best-selling authors, but a lot of guys end up on the scrap heap. That's pretty hard to accept when you're only in your thirties.'

'So what do you do, ring them up and ask them out to the pub for a chat, same as you do with me?'

Stockmann chuckled. 'You're a whole different ballgame, Dan,' she said. 'All I'm doing with you is checking to see that you're on an even keel. Some of the guys I'm dealing with now, they're shipwrecks and raising the *Titanic* doesn't come close.' She took another sip of her beer and put down her glass. 'The thing is, they're not the sort of men who are going to admit that they've got a problem, never mind ask for help. But if we can get them back to the Regiment for a reunion or some other excuse, it gives us a chance to put out some feelers and offer them support where they need it, be it financial or psychological.'

Shepherd laughed. 'You're a devious sod, aren't you?' he said. 'You get them up here on false pretences, that's what you're saying.'

'We tell a few porkies, yes,' said Stockmann. 'But for all the right reasons.' She nodded at his glass. 'No Jameson's today?'

'I'm hanging out with Liam later,' he said.

'Sorry, I didn't mean to take you away from your family.'

'A couple of hours won't matter much, and it'll give him time to catch up with video games.' He sat back in his chair. 'So I'm guessing that this has more to do with what happened in Northern Ireland than it does with a biannual review that may or may not exist.'

'It exists, Dan,' said Stockmann. 'That wasn't a porky. But yes, Charlie wants me to raise what happened with you.'

'What happened? I shot two men, Caroline. Shot them and killed them. And please don't ask me how I feel about that.'

'Why? Because feelings don't come into it?'

'Because it's the standard psychiatrist's question, isn't it?' He held up his hand. 'And before you correct me, I know that you're a psychologist.'

'Do you know the difference between a psychologist and a psychiatrist?' She answered the question for him. 'About fifty pounds an hour.'

'And who gets the better pay?'

Stockmann smiled. 'The psychiatrist, of course. They're the real doctors. We psychologists, we're the ones with the doctorates who can't prescribe drugs.'

'I'm sure that Charlie pays you well.'

She shrugged. 'Frankly, Dan, I don't do this for the money.'

'So why do you do it? Public service?'

She smiled thinly. 'Something like that,' she said. 'I do value what you and your colleagues do, and in my own small way I like to think that I'm helping.' She swirled her beer around her glass. 'So, have there been any repercussions? After what happened in Northern Ireland.'

'Job-wise?'

'You know what I mean, Dan.'

'Am I sleeping? Yes, like a baby. Am I eating? Like a horse. Do I waste even one second regretting what I did? No.'

'I'm not sure that's true, Dan,' she said quietly. 'I mean, I'm sure you're sleeping and that you haven't lost your appetite, but I know you well enough to know that you don't take a life without it affecting you in some way.'

Shepherd shrugged. 'OK, if anything it pisses me off.'

'It makes you angry?'

'Being put into the situation is what I'm annoyed at. The guys I killed were stone-cold killers and they'd have killed me if I hadn't killed them, but it could have been handled differently.' He drank some of his shandy, not because he wanted to drink but to give himself time to gather his thoughts. Caroline Stockmann had a very easy way about her, but at the end of the day she was there to compile a report on his ability to do his job and she had a mind like a steel trap. 'How much did Charlie tell you?'

'Pretty much everything,' she said.

'Including the fact that the whole operation was a cock-up?'

'That's not the word she used,' said Stockmann. 'But I gather that was the drift.'

'I went into a situation where there was another under-cover operative that I wasn't aware of. The men I were with were going to execute him.'

'You saved his life.'

'I saved one and I took two, which any way you look at it means I'm one down on the deal.'

'It's not the first time you've taken a life in the line of duty, though, is it?'

Shepherd looked at her steadily. 'It's not what I did, that's not what I'm angry about. It's the way that it happened. Yes, I've taken lives before, but it's always been because there was no other choice. In Northern Ireland, I was in a situation that could have been avoided if people had been behaving professionally.'

'And who do you blame for that?'

'What, you want me to blame Charlie, is that it?'

'Do you think she was at fault?'

Shepherd frowned as he considered the question. Eventually he shook his head. 'I think she probably did everything she could, it was the Northern Irish cops that screwed up. They ran their operation without letting Five know. Five is responsible for all anti-terrorism operations in the Province so the cops must have deliberately not shared their intel. And by doing that they put their agent at risk.'

'Do you think that's what has made you so angry? You can empathise with the agent?'

'Probably, yes. That could have been me. I could have been the one facing an execution squad and I might not have been so lucky.'

'It wasn't luck that saved him, Dan. It was you.'

'Did Charlie tell you that one of the Special Branch cops left his phone in a pub and that's how they found out there was an undercover agent?' He scowled. 'Bloody idiots,' he said. 'Lions led by donkeys, isn't that what they said about the infantry during the First World War? That's what it feels like, Caroline. Like I'm being run by idiots who couldn't find their own arses using both hands.'

'Are we talking about Charlie now?'

Shepherd shook his head. 'Charlie's sound,' he said. 'I trust her completely. But that doesn't mean to say that I trust her bosses.'

'Is that what's happening, you're losing confidence in the people you work for?'

Shepherd sighed. 'It's a worry, but it doesn't prevent me from doing my job,' he said. 'Now it'd be a different matter if I was working for the PSNI and they dropped me in it the way they dropped their guy in it.'

Stockmann smiled. 'You know that they were going to be called the Northern Ireland Police Service until they realised that people would be grabbed by the Nips?'

'Are you serious?'

'It was well down the legislation route before it was pointed out how ridiculous it would sound.' She took another sip of her beer, watching Shepherd carefully over the top of her glass.

'I'm not bitching about the job,' said Shepherd. 'The job's fine and I'm perfectly capable of doing it.'

'I understand that, but you're clearly unhappy.'

'You kill two people, Caroline, and tell me that you're happy about it.'

'Is there anything you could have done differently?'

'Me? No, nothing. They were going to shoot the cop and I only had seconds to react. And once I'd shot the first guy, the second guy was getting ready to shoot me. It was me or him.'

'It was combat?'

Shepherd nodded. 'Exactly.'

'And is that why there's no guilt? Because it was kill or be killed?'

'Guilt isn't the right word,' said Shepherd. 'I'm very conscious of why I did what I did and I would have preferred not to have done it, but if I hadn't shot the first guy then the cop would have died and if I hadn't shot the second guy he would have killed me.'

'So it's the fact that you reacted instinctively that takes away the guilt?'

Shepherd smiled. 'You sound like you're planning to do a paper on the subject.'

Stockmann's eyes sparkled with amusement. 'Funnily enough, I was thinking of doing something on post-traumatic stress disorder. But my question was more about finding out what makes you tick.'

'The training removes the guilt, pretty much,' said Shepherd. 'The Regiment trains you over and over until you react instinctively.'

'But that just makes you carry out the task effectively,' said Stockmann. 'It's like training conscripts to use a bayonet. Teach them well enough and on the battlefield they'll do it instinctively but the training doesn't help them cope with the guilt they feel years later.'

'Different sort of training, different sort of combat,' said

Shepherd. 'Wars with conscripts pit ordinary men against ordinary men. That's why they could climb out of the trenches on Christmas Day and play football. Professional soldiers are a different thing altogether.'

'What if it wasn't combat?' said Stockmann quietly, as if she feared being overheard.

'You're talking hypothetically?'

'Of course.'

'Then I think outside of a combat situation, the taking of human life is probably harder to deal with. I don't think I could ever be a sniper, for instance.'

'Because?'

'Because a sniper is killing when his own life isn't on the line. A sniper lies in wait and then shoots when his victim isn't expecting it.'

'You were shot by a sniper, in Afghanistan, weren't you?'

Shepherd rubbed his shoulder. 'It was more of an ambush than a sniping,' he said. 'The guy had a regular assault weapon rather than a sniper's rifle but yeah, we weren't in a firefight and he only took the one shot and then vanished.' He grinned ruefully. 'Though I doubt that he is losing any sleep over what he did, me being an infidel and all.'

'I guess that's the answer to my question, isn't it?' said Stockmann. 'If you feel morally justified in killing, there shouldn't be any guilt.'

Shepherd nodded slowly. 'I guess so.'

'So have you killed outside a combat situation?'

Shepherd didn't reply. He took a long, slow drink of shandy.

'Is that a question you'd rather not answer?' asked Stockmann.

'Is this you asking, or Charlie?'

The psychologist frowned. 'What do you mean?'

'Did she ask you to ask me that question?'

'It doesn't work like that, Dan. This isn't an interrogation. It's an assessment.'

Shepherd took a deep breath, forcing himself to relax. Stockmann wasn't the enemy, but the question had caught him off guard.

'So why would you ask me a question like that?'

'Because of the nature of your career. You were a soldier, you were in the SAS, you moved to the police, then the Serious Organised Crime Agency, and now you're with MI5. I was wondering if during the course of those different jobs you'd ever been asked to take a life in a situation where combat wasn't involved.'

'Because?'

'Because I'd be interested to know how you reacted. Whether guilt kicked in afterwards.'

Shepherd nodded slowly. He didn't like lying to the psychologist, but she had given him no choice. Yes, he had been in situations where there had been no combat, where he'd helped to cold-bloodedly take the lives of men who were no immediate threat. And no, there had been no guilt afterwards. But he couldn't tell Caroline Stockmann. He shrugged carelessly. 'It's never happened,' he said.

'That's a relief,' she said. 'From your point of view, I mean. It's not something I'd want to put to the test.'

'What about you, Caroline? Do you think you could take a life?'

She laughed carelessly. 'Me? Good gracious, of course not,' she said. 'How on earth could I? I don't have the strength, mental or physical. I'm one of life's victims.'

'That you're not,' said Shepherd. 'But say you were at home and a rapist broke in and you had a knife.'

'That's a lot of ifs.'

'It's only two,' said Shepherd. 'Rapist. Knife. Do you stab him to save your life?'

'I suppose so, yes.'

'And suppose someone was about to kill your husband or wife. Would you kill them?'

'Yes,' she said, more confidently this time.

'See, you do have what it takes,' said Shepherd.

'If pushed, anyone can kill, is that what you're saying?'

Shepherd nodded. 'And if you were defending your child, I don't think there would be any guilt. Do you?'

'I suppose not.'

'Now let's take it a step further. Suppose someone murdered your child. And you knew without a shadow of a doubt who'd done it. Would you kill them if you could?'

'That's too hypothetical, Dan.'

'How can anything be too hypothetical? It's a simple question.'

'But not one that I can answer in the abstract. We can't take the law into our own hands.'

'You think the criminal justice system is working, do you?'

'You're very good at that, aren't you?' she said.

'Good at what?'

'At deflecting questions by changing the subject. You do it so subtly that one's hardly aware of you doing it.'

Shepherd chuckled. 'It's a necessary skill when you're undercover,' he said. He put up his hands. 'Sorry, go ahead. Ask away.'

She raised her glass. 'Thank you so much,' she said, before

taking a sip. She put down her glass. 'Let's talk about your career path,' she said. 'I know that joining the police from the SAS was a big step. Because of your late wife.'

'She wanted a quiet life, she was fed up with me risking everything for Queen and country. I don't think she realised it was going to be out of the frying pan into the fire.' He smiled at the memory of his wife, Sue, who'd died in a senseless car accident when Liam was just seven years old.

'But when you moved from the police to SOCA, it had more to do with Charlie than anything?'

Shepherd shook his head. 'I hadn't met her before I joined SOCA,' he said. 'I was with a police undercover unit that got absorbed by SOCA, and she was in charge.'

'Why did you leave the police?'

'I wasn't given a choice,' said Shepherd. 'SOCA took over the undercover unit and I was told I could start working with them or start pounding a beat in a uniform. SOCA was threatening to cherry-pick all the big cases so there wouldn't have been much to do as a regular cop. I have to say that it didn't work out that way, though.'

'Why's that?'

'SOCA has been a bit of a failure,' said Shepherd. 'Too many pencil-pushers and too many box-tickers, too many chiefs and not enough Indians. Can you name any major SOCA successes over the past couple of years?'

Stockmann nodded. 'I'd be struggling,' she said.

'Don't get me wrong, some of the work was challenging but at the end of the day all the investigations were cost-led. If it looked as if a target was going to be too expensive, we'd let it slide. The powers-that-be only wanted us to chase the cases that they knew we'd win, which basically meant that we never went near the top villains.'

'That must have been frustrating,' said Stockmann.

'I put up three drug barons based in Amsterdam who between them are responsible for half the cannabis and probably ten per cent of the cocaine that reaches the north of England, but I was told that there weren't the resources to go after them. So that was that. If we don't go for them and the Dutch aren't bothered, they effectively have a free pass. And the thing is, they know it. So what's the point of having a law enforcement organisation if it doesn't uphold the law?'

'I assume that's rhetorical,' said Stockmann. 'But I understand what you're saying. Is that why you were happy to move to MI5 with Charlie?'

'It was one of the reasons. Better the devil you know . . .'

'And how are you finding the Secret Service?'

'It's not that secret, these days,' said Shepherd. 'It's like every man and his dog knows what we do.'

'And the work's challenging?'

'Espionage, terrorism, major crime.' Shepherd nodded. 'Plenty of variety, plus they're not as budget conscious as SOCA was.'

'Well, I suppose 9/11 and 7/7 were a big help financially,' said Stockmann. 'The government put billions into security and they weren't overly concerned about where it went.' She swirled her beer around her glass. 'And how did you feel being in Ireland?'

'It's not my favourite place,' he said. 'The SAS aren't best popular, despite the peace process and all. Plenty of people still bearing grudges.'

'Was it tough?'

Shepherd shook his head. 'Not really. My legend was that I was an IRA sympathiser, brought up in the States and with five years in the Marines. That way it didn't matter if my accent was all over the place. I was introduced through an undercover agent in New York and got close to the Real IRA's Operations Director. We were gathering evidence against him and the rest of the Army Council.'

Stockmann shuddered. 'I don't know how you can do that, get close to men who would kill you without hesitation if they knew who you were.'

'The trick is to stop them ever finding out,' said Shepherd. He sipped his shandy.

'And how are things at home?' Stockmann asked.

'Ticking along nicely,' said Shepherd, 'though the absent father thing isn't working out as well as I'd hoped. I'm spending a lot of time away from home.'

'Your son still misses his mother?'

'Of course. We both do. But I don't think either of us is grieving any more.' He smiled. 'Liam's just asked me about boarding school.'

'That J. K. Rowling has a lot to answer for,' said Stockmann.

'I think he realises it's not all magic spells and teachers with beards, but it caught me by surprise.'

'How old is he now?'

'Fourteen next birthday.'

'He's growing up.'

'That he is. I'm just not sure that he's ready for boarding school.'

'It might make things easier, job-wise. With your absences.'

'True. But I like the fact that he's there whenever I get back.'

Stockmann nodded thoughtfully. 'Which is great for you, but you have to look at it from your boy's point of view. He's forever waiting for you to come in through the front door, or for the phone to ring.'

'Not much of a life, is that what you mean?'

'I'm not saying that, but at least if he was boarding he wouldn't be expecting you every evening, would he?'

'I suppose not,' said Shepherd.

Stockmann finished her beer. 'Well, I think that's us done,' she said.

'You don't want another one?'

'I'm working all afternoon,' said the psychologist. 'I'll need a clear head.'

'And what's the prognosis?' asked Shepherd. 'Am I fit for purpose?'

Stockmann laughed. 'Of course you are, Dan. But you knew that before you even sat down.'

'That's good to hear.'

'It always amazes me what little effect your profession seems to have on you.'

'Water off a duck's back,' said Shepherd. He grinned as he stood up and extended his hand. 'See you in six months.'

Seamus Maguire looked up as he heard the rattle of a key in the lock of his cell door. The officer who opened the door was a new face, in his late forties with thinning hair and a beer gut that protruded over his belt. 'Your solicitor's here,' he said, pushing the door wide. 'Hop to it.'

Maguire got off his bunk. He was wearing a prison-issue

tracksuit. They'd taken his sweatshirt and cargo pants off him when he was arrested, along with his shoes. Now he was wearing an old pair of trainers that were a size too big. Maguire hadn't complained; he didn't want to give them the satisfaction. He could take anything they threw at him, they were the enemy and he was at war. 'I didn't ask for a solicitor,' he said.

'Ask or don't ask, I don't give a flying fuck,' growled the officer. 'I'm told to take you along for a meeting with your solicitor and that's what I'm doing. Now get the fuck out of this cell or you can whistle for your tea tonight.'

The prison officer led the way along the landing and down a flight of metal stairs. He unlocked the gate leading off the cell block and stepped back to allow Maguire to go through, then relocked it. He took Maguire along a corridor to the visitors' hall. There was a private room just before the double doors that led to the main hall and the officer jerked a thumb at it. 'Your brief's in there,' he said. 'I'll be waiting here, come out when you're done.'

Maguire let himself into the room. There was a single table, bolted to the floor, and four grey plastic chairs on spindly metal legs. There was a middle-aged man in a brown suit sitting at the table, a battered briefcase by his feet. Standing in the corner of the room was a woman in a dark business suit, her red hair tied back in a ponytail. Maguire sneered at the man. 'I don't need a solicitor,' he said. 'I don't recognise the Police Service of Northern Ireland and I won't be recognising the British court that tries to judge me.'

The man shrugged and took out an iPod. He pushed white earphones into his ears and settled back in his chair. He folded his arms and closed his eyes.

'What the fuck?' said Maguire.

'Don't bother about him, Seamus, he's just my ticket in here,' said the woman. She gestured at the chair. 'Sit yourself down, now.'

'What?' said Maguire, totally confused. 'Who the fuck are you?'

'I'm the woman who's been sent to find out how and why you managed to fuck up so badly. So do as I said and sit the fuck down.'

Maguire stared at her. She was in her late twenties, and while her accent was Irish she wasn't from Belfast. The border maybe. Or even from the Republic.

'Are you with the Ra?'

She pointed at the chair. 'Best let me ask the questions, Seamus. We'll get along much better that way.'

Maguire sat down and cupped his hands together. 'I didn't tell them anything,' he said. 'I haven't said one word since they arrested me. And I won't be recognising the court, or their justice system. I'm insisting that I be treated as a political prisoner.'

'Very noble of you, Seamus.' She sat down opposite him. 'Now what the fuck happened?' she asked.

'It wasn't my fault,' said Maguire.

'At this stage it's not about blame, it's about finding out what happened,' she said. 'The Army Council needs to know what went down because the cops aren't saying anything.'

'How much do you know?'

The woman pointed at his face. 'Don't fuck with me, Seamus. Your balls are on the line and I'm holding the knife. If I don't go back to the Council with a true account of what happened, you'll be dead before you even get to trial.'

'Do you know about O'Leary?'

The woman frowned. 'What about O'Leary?'

Maguire ran his hands through his unkempt hair. 'It all turned to shit,' he said. 'O'Leary was working for the cops. Undercover, double agent, I don't know what the fuck he is but he's got a Special Branch handler. The bomb was never going to get anywhere near the police station, the SAS had it staked out.'

'We knew that one of you was a traitor, but we didn't know it was O'Leary,' said the woman.

'Who did you think it was?' he asked, and before she opened her mouth to reply he saw the answer in her eyes. 'Me?' he said. 'You thought it was me?'

'You were the youngest, Seamus,' said the woman. 'You had less of a track record.'

'You bastards,' hissed Maguire.

'What happened?' asked the woman. 'Shots were fired, we know that much, but we don't know who got shot. Who was shooting, Seamus? Was it the cops?'

Maguire frowned. 'Is that what you think? The cops?'

'We don't know what to think because there's been a news blackout,' said the woman. 'That's why I'm here. So if not the cops, what the hell happened?'

Maguire sat back in his chair and folded his arms. 'We were ready to go. The bomb was armed, Willie knew exactly what he had to do. Then three men in ski masks burst in. Nasty bastards.'

'One of them had a long leather coat?'

Maguire nodded. 'He was the one giving orders.'

'That was Declan Connolly. He was the Council's man. He was there to nail the traitor.'

'Yeah, well, he did that. He put the four of us into a van

and drove us somewhere, then pulled some stunt with a phone. O'Leary's phone rang and he said that O'Leary was a rat. So the guy, Connolly, puts a gun to O'Leary's head and says he's going to shoot him and then the shit hits the fan. One of the other guys shoots Connolly in the chest, twice, then he turns and shoots the other guy. Fast, professional, he doesn't say anything.'

'What did he look like, the shooter?'

'He was wearing a ski mask. Bit under six feet, jeans, trainers, bomber jacket. Glock.'

'Were the jeans black? Or blue?'

'Black.'

'And the jacket? Brown leather? Elasticated waist? Bit worn?'

Maguire nodded. 'That's him.'

'Did he say anything?'

Maguire shook his head.

'Did you get a feeling that this guy was a cop too, like O'Leary?'

'He wasn't with O'Leary. He just high-tailed it out of there like he was the bloody Lone Ranger or something. He took Ryan's phone and left. The cops turned up twenty minutes later. They took us all away.'

'Including O'Leary?'

'Yeah, but I haven't seen him since. I haven't seen Ray or Willie either, though.'

'Ray and Willie are being held in different prisons. O'Leary's vanished. The shooter, did he say anything before he left?'

'Yeah, he was pissed off big time because of what had happened. He asked O'Leary if he was a cop and he said he was. O'Leary said that he'd been undercover for two years. Can you believe that? Gerry fucking O'Leary was a rat for two bloody years.'

'What else did the shooter say?'

'Something about being an idiot for using his phone. Not sending text messages. My ears were still ringing from the shots so I couldn't make out everything he said. But he was as angry as hell. O'Leary asked him to untie him but he wouldn't.'

'Anything else?'

Maguire shook his head. 'That's all I can remember,' he said. He leaned forward. 'What happens now?' he asked.

'We try to minimise the damage that O'Leary's done,' she said. 'They've already arrested McGrory in Limerick and there'll be more arrests to come. Then we'll go after the shooter.'

'I meant me,' said Maguire. 'What happens to me?'

The woman smiled coldly. 'You, Seamus? You're well fucked.' She nodded at the solicitor, whose head was bobbing back and forth in time to whatever music he was listening to on his iPod. 'You're doing the right thing not bothering with a lawyer. You can plead guilty or not guilty, but whatever you do it's going to be life. You know that, right?'

Maguire nodded glumly.

'The word from the Council is that they want you to refuse to recognise the court and insist on political prisoner status,' she said. 'Go on to a dirty protest if need be.'

'That's what I've been doing since they banged me up,' said Maguire. 'I keep telling them I want off the wing. But they're just ignoring me.'

'Stick at it,' she said.

'What about Ray and Willie?'

'I'll be going in to see them.'

'Do you think they'll put us together?'

'Maybe after the trial,' said the woman. 'Not before. They don't want you exchanging information. But look on the bright side. The fight has only just started. At some point down the line there'll be a settlement and you'll be released to a hero's welcome. All you've got to do is hang on in there. *Tiocfaidh ár lá*,' she said. Our day will come.

Maguire nodded. '*Tiocfaidh ár lá*,' he echoed.

'What do you think?' asked Button, looking around the sitting room. They were on the tenth floor of an apartment block in Praed Street, part of the Paddington Basin development. The building was just a short walk from Paddington Station, and the flat had two bedrooms and a good-sized bathroom and had been fitted out with modern Italian furniture and a big-screen LED on one wall.

Shepherd nodded. 'It's good,' he said. There was a framed photograph on a table of a man and woman in their sixties. 'My parents?'

'Eric and Elsie,' said Button, handing him a manila envelope. 'Details are all in here. You're Oliver Blackburn and you work for a consultancy firm in the Midlands but you've been based in London for the past two years. If anyone checks the lease of this place they'll find that you've been here for eighteen months.' She gave him a box of newly printed business cards and a BlackBerry. 'The numbers on the card go through to this mobile and to an office in Birmingham, an MI5 front that we use for a lot of legends.' She grinned. 'We're better at this than SOCA ever was.' She sat down on a leather and chrome chair and crossed her legs. 'Basically the company in Hammersmith has been told that a consultant is being sent in to look at ways of increasing efficiency. That way you can wander around and ask all the questions you want. You'll be given a desk but it's then up to you to go where you want and pretty much do as you want.'

'And who there's going to know who I really am?'

'No one,' said Button. 'Even the managing director thinks you're the real thing. We've arranged it through the main holding company's chief executive, and other than him no one knows who you are.'

'Consultant covers a multitude of sins, doesn't it?'

'Exactly. You can arrange interviews with all our suspects and ask them anything you want.'

Shepherd sat down on a black leather sofa as a shaven-headed man in a tight-fitting Armani T-shirt and faded jeans came out of the main bedroom carrying a clipboard. He was Damien Plant and he was one of MI5's dressers, who supplied the props to back up any legend. 'There's half a dozen suits in the wardrobe,' he said. 'I've given you a dozen shirts, handmade by a firm in Birmingham, but I've left the shoes up to you. All in all it's much nicer gear than you had in Belfast.' He handed the clipboard to Shepherd. 'Just sign at the bottom.'

Shepherd scrawled his signature and gave the clipboard back to him.

'You can keep the clothes once the operation's done,' said Plant.

'They can go to charity,' said Shepherd. 'I'm not a great fan of suits. Do I get a car?'

'No need,' said Button. 'You can get to Hammersmith from Paddington easily enough.'

'Well, my work here is done,' said Plant. He shook hands with Shepherd, kissed Button effeminately on both cheeks, and left.

'You'll be glad to hear that Caroline Stockmann gave you a clean bill of health,' Button said to Shepherd as the front door closed.

'She's a good judge of character,' said Shepherd, opening the manila envelope. He slid the contents on to the coffee table. There was a year-old driving licence with his photograph and the address of the flat, and a three-year-old passport, both in the name of Oliver Blackburn.

'The licence and passport are the genuine thing so you can use them anywhere,' said Button. There was an American Express credit card showing that he had been a card member since 1998 and a Nationwide debit card. He grinned at Button but she was already wagging her finger at him. 'Emergencies only,' she said. 'But if paying a bill with one of them adds to the legend, all well and good. Just remember that everything goes through the accounts department and they use a very fine-tooth comb.'

'I presume I'm there until I find out who's helping Crazy Boy?'

'As long as it takes,' she said. 'But I wouldn't think it'll take you too long. We're not talking about a career criminal here, when all's said and done. And at least no one's likely to shoot you.'

'That'll be a nice change,' said Shepherd.

Manhunt was Crazy Boy's favourite game. He could slaughter and maim and torture with impunity, and the graphics were as close to real as you could imagine. The one thing he didn't like was that his actions were controlled by the mysterious Director, who kept issuing orders. In the real world, Crazy Boy was the giver of orders, not a taker, and if Manhunt was real the first thing he would do would be to put a bullet between the Director's eyes. In the first level he had to kill the Hoods, a gang of blacks and Hispanics, and the graphics were so good that some of the guys he got to kill reminded him of men he knew back in Puntland. Then he went after a white supremacist gang called the Skinz and that was the part he liked best, marauding through a city killing whites. He wondered what it would be like to do it for real, to pick up an AK-47 and walk down Oxford Street, shooting at random. There were other gangs he had to kill, the Wardogs and the Innocentz and the Smileys, but it wasn't as much fun killing them as it was with the Skinz.

He let rip with a shotgun and blew the head off a gangster with a shaved head then shot him in the chest for good measure as he sank to his knees. 'Yes!' he shouted as he moved to the right and shot two thugs, one in the groin and one in the face.

'Behind you!' shouted Two Knives. 'They come at you from behind!'

'I know that, I know that,' said Crazy Boy, reloading as he turned. He let rip at the three hoods who'd been coming up behind him. Blood sprayed across the street and the men fell back and smacked into the tarmac. 'Die, you scumbags!' he screamed.

He was sitting on a huge overstuffed sofa that had come with the house when he'd bought it. In fact all the furniture had come with the house, a five-bedroom mansion in one of the most expensive areas in Ealing, standing in two acres of immaculate gardens. The house had belonged to an Indian businessman who had left the country at short notice with an Inland Revenue investigation team hard on his heels. The house and contents had been put up for auction six months after the businessman had arrived in New Delhi and Crazy Boy had bought it through an offshore company, one of more than a dozen that he controlled. When he had moved in he hadn't needed to bring anything other than his Xbox and collection of video games.

The Indian's taste had been towards the ostentatious and the walls of the sitting room were decorated with ornate gilt mirrors and framed photographs of old sailing ships, which Crazy Boy had taken as a good sign, considering his chosen profession. His feet were resting on a huge piece of thick glass that lay on four large marble balls, which the estate agent said had been carved by an artisan outside Milan. Above were three large chandeliers that hadn't been cleaned since Crazy Boy had moved in and were already covered with dust and cobwebs. At one side of the room, next to the French windows that led out to a paved terrace that ran the full length of the house, was a sideboard that would have looked at home in Versailles, not that Crazy Boy had ever heard of Louis XIV or his palace. On one end of the sideboard was a four-foot-tall glass sculpture of dolphins frolicking in white-tipped blue waves, and on the other was a porcelain figurine of a fairy-tale coach being pulled by four white horses. In the middle was a porcelain mermaid sitting in a mother-of-pearl-lined shell.

A biker waving a heavy chain came rushing out of an alley and Crazy Boy shot him in the chest and quickly reloaded. A black Humvee came roaring down the road and Crazy Boy let loose with the shotgun. The first shot took out the windscreen, the second blew the nearside front tyre and the third turned the head of the driver into a bloody mist. The BMW spun off the road and crashed into a shop window.

There were three cheap Nokia mobiles next to the Xbox and the one in the middle rang. 'Get that, yeah,' said Crazy Boy.

Two Knives picked up the ringing phone and looked at the screen. 'It's your wife.'

'Your wife?' said the young blonde girl sprawled on the sofa across from Crazy Boy. 'I didn't know you were married.' She was a hooker that he'd ordered from a West London escort agency, eighteen years old and only recently arrived from Latvia. There was another one, a brunette with pneumatic breasts, upstairs in Crazy Boy's bed.

Crazy Boy pointed a finger at her as he carried on playing. 'Shut the fuck up, bitch,' he said. 'Find out what she wants,' he told Two Knives.

The blonde pouted and rolled over, hugging a cushion. Crazy Boy had paid four thousand pounds to have the girls for a full twenty-four hours but he was already bored with them even though there were still a few hours to go.

He carried on playing his game while Two Knives answered the phone and spoke to his wife. The woman was his wife in name only. He had married her for the passport that came as part of the package and the only reason he'd made her pregnant was so that no one could ever argue that it was a marriage of convenience and because being the father of a European citizen gave him additional rights.

He switched his shotgun for a handgun and fired six shots into the chest of a streetwalker.

Sitting on two winged armchairs by the window overlooking the garden were two Somalis, Levi's and Sunny, big men who had worked for Crazy Boy since he'd arrived in England. They were both distant cousins with relatives working for Crazy Boy back in Somalia and both had been granted asylum in the United Kingdom after paying ten thousand dollars each to a Chinese people-smuggler in Mogadishu.

On a table between them was a huge Waterford crystal bowl full of fresh leafy khat twigs. As they watched Crazy Boy play his video game, they kept reaching into the bowl, stripping off leaves and chewing on them. They had eaten khat from the age of ten, and neither could remember a day when they hadn't enjoyed the buzz that came from the plant's cathinone psychoactive drug. Khat grew naturally in the mountains of Kenya, Yemen and Ethiopia, and every day tonnes were exported across Africa wrapped in banana leaves to keep them fresh, and more was flown around the world to satisfy the cravings of expatriate Africans. More than three-quarters of exported khat was sent to the United Kingdom for the two hundred and fifty thousand Somalis who now called England their home. It could be bought in London, fresh off a plane, for £3 a bundle. Freshness was important, for within forty-eight hours of being picked the cathinone started to decay and lose its potency. Crazy Boy had fresh khat delivered to his house every day.

There was a gilt desk with legs fashioned in the shape of an eagle's wings in one corner and on the wall behind it was a bank of flatscreen monitors that gave more than a

dozen views of the exterior of the house and garden. Two
Knives had supervised the installation of the twenty-thousand-
pound CCTV system and he'd done a good job – there
wasn't a single blind spot anywhere. Two Knives had also
arranged for all the windows of the house to be replaced
with bullet-proof glass and for the fitting of a high-tech
burglar alarm system. Crazy Boy wasn't convinced that he
needed the latter as there was an arsenal of weapons in the
house and there were always at least three of his bodyguards
in residence, but Two Knives had convinced him of the
necessity.

The rest of the house was as luxurious as the sitting
room. In Crazy Boy's bedroom there was a bed that was
ten feet square with silk sheets that were so smooth that it
was like sleeping on ice, and opulent furniture, most of
which still had Harrods price stickers attached. There was
a marble-lined bathroom leading off the bedroom, with a
Jacuzzi big enough for three people, which Crazy Boy often
put to good use. It was the first place he'd taken the two
hookers when they'd arrived on his doorstep the previous
evening.

Two Knives put the mobile phone back on the coffee
table. 'She wants money,' he said.

'Bitch always wants money,' said Crazy Boy.

'And she wants to know when you're going round to see
your boy.'

'That boy's so ugly I think they threw the kid out by
mistake and kept the shit that came out afterwards,' said
Crazy Boy, shooting a black mugger in the groin three times
and then blowing a big chunk of his skull away. 'What she
want the money for anyways?'

'She says she has to pay the car insurance and she got a fine for speeding and she wants the boy to go to baby school.'

'I give that bitch ten grand a month and she goes through it like it was water,' said Crazy Boy. He sighed as he switched back to the shotgun and blew out the windows of a passing car. 'How much she want?'

'Five grand,' said Two Knives.

'Take it round tonight, yeah,' said Crazy Boy. 'But tell the bitch she have to make do with what she get every month. Bitch so ugly she not worth half what I give her.'

Crazy Boy's wife lived in a three-bedroom semi-detached five miles from the mansion. He'd bought it through an offshore company and every month he gave her ten thousand pounds in cash for living expenses. According to Two Knives she'd developed a drug problem above and beyond the khat leaves that she used to chew – he'd seen drugs in the house. Crazy Boy knew that the woman wouldn't be stupid enough to get involved with another man so the drugs could only have been hers. He had no problem with that just so long as she didn't get into trouble with the police, but at some point she was going to have to be slapped and brought into line. There was no call for her ringing him up and asking for money and trying to use their kid as leverage.

'Someone's at the gate,' said Sunny, pointing at the CCTV monitors.

Crazy Boy paused the game and looked over at the bank of monitors. There was a black Bentley parked in front of the gates, its grille only inches from the bars. 'We know anyone with a Bentley?' he asked Two Knives, who'd gone over for a closer look at the screen.

'Bentley's for old men,' said Two Knives. As he stared at the screen, the front passenger door opened and a heavy-set man in a dark suit climbed out, rotated his neck as if it was troubling him, then walked over to the entryphone that was set into one of the concrete pillars.

'Looks like an Arab,' said Crazy Boy, standing behind Two Knives.

'Maybe he thinks the Indian still lives here.'

The entryphone buzzed and Crazy Boy picked up the receiver. 'Yeah?' he said.

'Is Mr Simeon Khalid at home?'

'Who wants to know?' asked Crazy Boy.

'Mr Mamoud al-Zahrani is here and requests an audience with you,' said the man. He had a square face and a thick moustache and slicked-back hair that glinted in the security lights. His eyes were hidden behind dark glasses.

Crazy Boy looked at the small screen as he chewed his khat. The windows of the Bentley were heavily tinted so he couldn't see who else was in the car.

'I do not see visitors at my home,' said Crazy Boy.

'Mr al-Zahrani understands that but hopes that in his case you will make an exception,' said the man, his voice a dull monotone as if he had memorised a script.

'Do you know him?' asked Two Knives.

'Him I've never seen before but al-Zahrani is the guy that the Arab was talking about,' said Crazy Boy.

'How does he know where you live?'

'That's a good question,' said Crazy Boy.

'What does he want?'

'Another good question,' said Crazy Boy.

The man on the screen turned back to the Bentley. The

rear window had opened slightly and someone inside was obviously saying something. The man turned back to the entryphone. 'Mr al-Zahrani does not make a habit of visiting unannounced but he feels that this matter is of such importance that it is necessary on this occasion, and for that he offers his apologies.'

'There could be three or more assassins in a car that size,' muttered Two Knives.

Crazy Boy nodded slowly. Two Knives was right. 'Tell Mr al-Zahrani that I will receive him, but he must come alone,' he said into the intercom. 'The car and anyone else in it must remain outside.'

'I am Mr al-Zahrani's bodyguard, he goes nowhere without me,' said the man.

'Very well, you can accompany him, but no weapons of any kind are to be brought into the house.'

The bodyguard nodded and went back to the car. He spoke through the rear window and then the door opened and a tall Arab got out. He was light skinned, wearing dark glasses and a suit that fitted so well it could only have been made to measure. Al-Zahrani adjusted his cufflinks as he looked up at the security camera. He had a hooked nose and a receding hairline that he compensated for by growing his hair long at the back.

Crazy Boy pressed the button that opened the door to the side of the main entrance. Al-Zahrani pushed open the door while his bodyguard reached into his jacket and then handed something, presumably a weapon, through the window.

'You're letting them in?' asked Two Knives. He pulled his Glock from the back of his trousers and checked the action.

'Search them, but be gentle, yeah?' said Crazy Boy. He nodded at the gun. 'Keep that out of the way, we don't want to spook them.' He turned to the blonde girl lying on the sofa. 'Hey, bitch, get upstairs and wait for me in the bedroom.'

The blonde scowled at him and flounced up the stairs. She was wearing one of Crazy Boy's white shirts and nothing else and she turned and flashed him while she was halfway up the staircase but he was looking at the screen. Al-Zahrani and the bodyguard were talking, then al-Zahrani patted the man on the shoulder as he smiled and nodded. Crazy Boy looked over at the two men sitting by the window. 'Levi's, you stay in the study, keep the door open and your gun ready.' Levi's nodded and headed for the study, pulling his gun from its holster. 'Sunny, you get upstairs. Get a shotgun from the attic, stay out of sight, but if I call you come down shooting, hear me?'

'I hear you, boss,' said Sunny. Crazy Boy kept a weapons cache in the attic behind a false wall. There were half a dozen handguns, two MAC-10s, two shotguns and several tasers and plenty of ammunition. As Sunny hurried upstairs, Crazy Boy watched on one of the security screens as al-Zahrani walked slowly up the driveway with the body-guard following. The doors of the Bentley remained closed and there were no other occupied cars in the road outside.

He patted Two Knives on the back. 'Tell the kitchen staff to stay quiet.'

Two Knives hurried off to the kitchen as Crazy Boy followed al-Zahrani's progress up the driveway. It was ten o'clock at night but the halogen security lights meant that it was as bright as day outside.

Al-Zahrani reached the front door, but he waited for his bodyguard to press the doorbell. Two Knives came back into the room as the doorbell rang out.

'Remember, be gentle,' said Crazy Boy. 'He's connected to some very important people and he's got balls walking in here with no guns.'

He sat down on the sofa and used the remote to switch off the television. He heard Two Knives open the door and after a couple of minutes al-Zahrani walked into the room. His suit looked even more expensive close up and there was a gold watch on his left wrist and a thick gold chain on his right. His shirt had double cuffs and his tie was silk and perfectly tied. Al-Zahrani walked towards Crazy Boy, an easy smile on his lips, his hand outstretched. Crazy Boy realised that he had taken off his dark glasses. 'Thank you for seeing me,' he said. 'And my apologies again for arriving unannounced.'

Crazy Boy shook hands and waved at the sofa opposite the fireplace, the one where the hooker had been lying. The bodyguard had followed al-Zahrani into the room but had stayed in the doorway, his hands clasped over his groin, watching through impenetrable sunglasses.

Al-Zahrani sat down and crossed his legs. He looked around the room. 'You have a lovely home,' he said.

'Can I offer you a refreshment?' asked Crazy Boy. 'There is tea, or coffee, juice.'

'Tea would be much appreciated, thank you,' said al-Zahrani.

Crazy Boy gestured with his chin for Two Knives to go to the kitchen. 'Some cake, and fruit,' Crazy Boy said in Somali. Two Knives nodded and left the room.

'You are not what I expected,' said Crazy Boy, settling back in the sofa.

'You heard I was a Saudi and you expected a man in a dress and a towel on my head? Should I have expected you to be wearing a grass skirt because you are from East Africa?'

Crazy Boy chuckled. 'You are right, of course.'

Al-Zahrani waved a languid hand along the buttons of his jacket. 'In England I wear a suit and I belong, or at least I look as if I belong. No one can tell if I am a citizen or not. I could be a banker, a judge, a politician, a businessman, no one would know. But if I wear the *thawb* and *keffiyeh* then I am immediately marked as an outsider and treated as such.'

'Camouflage,' said Crazy Boy.

'Exactly,' said al-Zahrani. He carefully adjusted the creases of his trousers. 'I am grateful for you allowing me into your home. I had hoped that we could have met in my hotel but I gather that was not possible.'

'I have been very busy,' said Crazy Boy. 'There is much happening in my life.'

'So I understand. But at least now we can talk. You do business with Sameer Haddad, do you not?'

Crazy Boy shrugged. 'I do business with a lot of people.'

'But you buy arms from only a few. And Sameer is one of the most amenable and trusted of arms dealers in the Yemen. He is a friend of mine, and I mention it only so you know that I too can be trusted.'

Crazy Boy's eyes narrowed. 'When I do business I assume that the business I do remains confidential.'

'It is a small world, and secrets are difficult to keep at the best of times. But rest assured, Sameer did not go into specifics.'

'And what is your business, may I ask?'

Al-Zahrani smiled and shrugged. 'I have fingers in many pies,' he said. 'I move money around for people who are too busy to do it themselves, I take care of problems, I facilitate deals.'

'You are a middleman?'

'You could say that, Simeon. Or you could say that I have friends in high places.'

'And where would these friends be? Yemen?'

'I have friends in Yemen, yes. I have friends all across the Middle East. That is why I am so successful at what I do.'

'If you're here to ask me to stop what I'm doing in Somalia, you are wasting your time,' snapped Crazy Boy. 'The West has depleted our fishing stocks, used our sea as a dumping ground for its waste, treated our country as if we are less than nothing. The West owes us for what it has taken from us, and the only way to get what is owed is to take it. We take only a small fraction of what sails by our coast and it is our right.'

Al-Zahrani waited until Crazy Boy had finished speaking, then he slowly smiled and steepled his fingers under his chin. 'You Somalis have a saying, do you not? "Dogs understand each other by their barking, and men by their words." You and I are men. More than that, we are Muslim men. We can talk like men, can we not?'

Crazy Boy nodded, accepting the point. 'I apologise, brother. I should have allowed you to have spoken first.'

Al-Zahrani's smile widened. 'I appreciate that, brother,' he said. 'But let me ask you something before I tell you what is on my mind. My question to you is, are you a good Muslim?'

'Of course,' said Crazy Boy.

Two Knives returned with a silver tray on which there were two glasses of tea, a plate filled with orange segments and another plate with slices of lemon cake. He held the tray out to al-Zahrani, who took a glass of tea but waved away the cake and fruit. Two Knives put the tray down on the coffee table and then went to sit on one of the wing chairs by the window, where he stared at al-Zahrani's bodyguard.

Al-Zahrani smiled at Crazy Boy. 'And as a good Muslim you follow the five pillars of our faith?'

'Without a shadow of a doubt,' said Crazy Boy. '*Shahada, salat, zakat, sawm* and *haj*.'

There were five things that every Muslim had to do to proclaim his faith. *Shahada* was to declare one's faith to the world, *salat* was prayer, which every true Muslim did five times a day, *zakat* was the giving of alms, whereby Muslims gave at least a fortieth of their income to the poor and needy, *sawm* was fasting, which every Muslim did during the month of Ramadan, and *haj* was pilgrimage to Mecca, which every Muslim had to do at least once in his lifetime.

'That is what all good Muslims do, and praise to you for that, but a true Muslim has to do more, does he not? A true Muslim has to fight to defend his faith. As a Somali you more than anyone must be aware of that.'

'The Americans,' said Crazy Boy.

'Not just the Americans. The infidels, the infidels that think they have the right to impose their beliefs and values on our countries, on our people. These days it is not good enough just to follow the five pillars. A good Muslim, a true Muslim, has to do more.'

Crazy Boy nodded slowly. 'What you say is true,' he said.

'But if you know anything about me, you would know that I have already done more than most.'

'You are referring to Ahmed Abdi Godane, are you not?'

Crazy Boy's breath caught in his throat. He was sure that no one knew of his involvement with Ahmed Abdi Godane.

Al-Zahrani waved a languid hand. 'Please do not worry, Simeon, the information was passed to me in confidence and I am a man who guards his secrets jealously. I mention his name only so that you can assess my credibility. Your contributions have been well received and they will be long remembered.'

'So what is it you want me to do now? Am I being asked for more money?'

'Money we have in abundance, Simeon. What I want is for you to be a good Muslim, a true Muslim. And to do that you have to help us.'

'Who?' said Crazy Boy. 'Who am I helping?'

'The Lion Sheikh,' said al-Zahrani. 'The man the Crusaders seek but cannot find. The Prince in the Cave. It is he who seeks your help and I am but his messenger.'

Shepherd let himself into his flat and switched on the lights. He tossed the jacket of his suit on to a chair and took off his tie, then went through to the kitchen and took a can of Carlsberg out of the fridge, courtesy of Damien Plant. The MI5 dresser had stocked the fridge with food from the local Marks and Spencer and had thrown in half a dozen cans of beer and two bottles of Frascati for good measure. He poured the lager into a glass and went through to the sitting room. There was a Sky Plus box under the television and Shepherd grinned when he switched on the set and discovered that he'd been given the full Sky Sports package. It made sense because Oliver Blackburn wasn't married and didn't have a girlfriend.

He picked up his regular mobile and called his home in Hereford. Katra answered and she told him that Liam was out playing football with his friends. Shepherd promised to call back and returned to the kitchen. He took out a cottage pie, tossed it into the microwave and sipped his lager as he waited for it to heat up.

It had been his first day at the freight company and it had been one of the most unhappy experiences of his life. It had started badly with an early morning Tube journey to Hammersmith, crammed into a stuffy carriage with dozens of other workers who all seemed as miserable as he felt. The office was a short walk from Hammersmith Tube station. The company had two floors of a modern building, and the managing director had a corner office on the upper floor. His name was Clive Wallace and he was about Shepherd's age and clearly resentful that Shepherd had been foisted on him. After a quick chat he'd handed Shepherd over to a much more pleasant office services manager, Candice Malone. She was in her late twenties with long blonde hair and a model's walk, wearing a very short skirt and very high heels. She showed Shepherd to an office on the lower floor after giving him a quick tour, then showed him how to access the employee files on the office computer network. She was warm and had an infectious laugh and Shepherd found himself liking her after just a few minutes, which was unsettling as she was one of the suspects on Button's list.

The floor was mainly open-plan with some twenty desks surrounded by waist-high dividers, though on one side were a line of glass-sided cubicles with frosted-glass doors. Shepherd's was in the middle, and from his desk he could see pretty much everyone sitting outside. It didn't take him long to realise that work wasn't a high priority at the firm, and if he really had been an efficiency consultant he'd have happily recommended that the workforce be cut in half.

Of the twenty men and women in the main office area, eight were smokers and every hour they would all troop outside for a ten-minute cigarette break. The non-smokers appeared to compensate for the lack of smoking breaks by taking regular trips to the kitchen area, where there were tea- and coffee-making facilities. Even when they were at their desks, a large part of the day was spent chatting to colleagues or making personal calls. There was one man, overweight with a shaggy mane of unkempt hair that was peppered with dandruff flakes, who clearly spent most of his time watching pornography on his computer, because every time anyone walked by his cubicle he would hurriedly hit a button to clear his screen.

Every now and again Shepherd would take a walk around the office and more often than not he would see people with Facebook or YouTube on their screens or playing games. But just because someone wasn't working hard didn't mean that they were passing information to a group of Somali pirates, and Shepherd knew that he needed to dig deeper if he was going to identify the mole.

He'd spent the afternoon sifting through the personnel files, looking for clues, but couldn't find any red flags. The next step would be to start interviewing the members of staff individually, and it wasn't something that he was looking forward to.

The microwave pinged and at the same time his mobile rang. It was Liam. 'Homework done?' asked Shepherd.

'Will be soon,' said Liam.

'You should do your homework before playing football,' said Shepherd.

'That would mean staying out later, though, Dad. This way I'm home before it starts to get dark.'

Shepherd smiled to himself. His son was becoming quite the manipulator since reaching his teens.

'Where are you?' asked Liam, and Shepherd's smile widened as he realised that his son was using one of Shepherd's own staple techniques – whenever under pressure, change the subject if you can.

'London.'

'When are you coming home?'

'Friday night,' said Shepherd. 'And don't think I haven't noticed that you've changed the subject.'

Liam sighed. 'Dad, it'll take me twenty minutes to do tonight's homework.'

'Exactly. So you could have done it before you went out.' He closed his eyes as he realised what a nag he was becoming. 'Anyway, no problem, just get it done now. Have you had your dinner?'

'Katra's cooking now,' he said. 'Slovenian meatballs.'

'How are they different from regular meatballs?'

'Katra says that they taste better,' said Liam. 'So what are you working on?'

'Boring stuff,' said Shepherd. 'I'm in an office, mainly.'

'But you're undercover, right? You're always undercover.'

'Yes, but it's very boring.'

'So who's the bad guy?'

Shepherd laughed. His son was as good at asking questions as he was at avoiding answering them. 'It's a fraud thing,' he said. 'Very boring. So you get your homework done and I'll see you on Friday night.'

'Dad, what about boarding school?'

'I'm working on it. I'm still looking at websites and stuff.'

'But in principle, you're OK with it?'

'If it's what you really want, I don't see why it'd be a problem,' said Shepherd. 'But it's a question of finding the right school. And we'll have to look at the finances. It's expensive, you know that, right?'

'I know that, Dad. But thanks, yeah.'

Shepherd ended the call and went back to the kitchen to retrieve his cottage pie. As he sat down in front of the television with his microwaved meal and his lager he suddenly missed his son a lot. He had to fight the urge to call him back. Instead he tried to concentrate on a match between two North of England teams, neither of which he had any interest in rooting for.

Two Knives watched on the monitor as al-Zahrani and the bodyguard climbed into the Bentley. Sunny came down the stairs cradling a pump-action shotgun. 'Everything OK, brother?' he asked.

'Everything is just fine,' said Crazy Boy. He took a handful of khat leaves and chewed them as he walked over to stand behind Two Knives and watch the CCTV monitor. The Bentley reversed away from the gates and headed down the road. 'Put the gun back in the attic and send the hookers home.'

'OK if I do them first?' asked Sunny.

Levi's came out of the study, a Glock in his hand. 'Me too, yeah? That blonde is hot.'

'Help yourself,' said Crazy Boy, his eyes on the screen. 'Just put the guns away first. And don't hurt them, the agency gives me grief if we send them back damaged. No marks, you hear me?'

Sunny headed back upstairs. 'What do you think?' asked Two Knives, nodding at the monitor. 'What he wants us to do, you really OK with it?'

Crazy Boy shrugged. 'One hand washes the other,' he said. 'We help them, they help us.'

'What they want, you know what it means?'

'I'm not stupid.'

'They're dangerous people.'

'They are Muslims,' said Crazy Boy. 'The same as us. Al-Zahrani is right. These days it is not good enough to do the minimum. These are dangerous times for our people and if we don't show our strength now they will drive us from the earth.'

'Not here, not in England,' said Two Knives. 'That is why we're here. Here we have rights and laws to protect us.'

'And what about our Muslim brothers who are dying around the world? Who protects them? You can see what the infidels are doing to Muslims in Iraq, in Afghanistan. What about our brothers and sisters in Palestine? And closer to home, in France, where Muslim women are persecuted for protecting their modesty. You think that won't happen here? They hate us, brother, they hate us and they hate Islam.'

'He's a Saudi,' said Two Knives. 'You can't trust a Saudi. Everyone knows that.'

Crazy Boy put a hand on the man's shoulder and squeezed

it gently. 'He's a Muslim. And so are we. And you heard what he said, by helping him we help ourselves.'

'And afterwards? After we have done what he wants?'

'That is up to him. Our part in it will be over.'

'And all hell will be let loose.'

'We can move.' He waved his hand dismissively. 'I have no love for this place. Or this country. We can move to Germany. To anywhere in Europe. We are British citizens, and as you said there are laws to protect us.'

'I don't have my passport yet, brother. Don't forget that.' There was a buzzing sound and Two Knives pulled a Samsung mobile from his pocket. He walked away, talking in Somali.

Crazy Boy grabbed a handful of khat leaves and chewed them as he flopped back on the sofa. He picked up the Xbox controller and was just about to restart the game when Two Knives finished his call. 'I've got to go,' he said.

'What's up?'

'The two guys from the *gar*, we've got them. I'll be back in a couple of hours.'

'I'll come with you,' said Crazy Boy. His lips were tingling from the khat and he could already feel the stimulant coursing through his bloodstream. He tossed the controller to the side.

'You said you wanted me to handle it. You said you wanted to keep your distance.'

'Yeah, well, I've changed my mind. You get the car, you're driving.' He headed for the stairs.

'Now where are you going?' asked Two Knives.

'I'm gonna get me a gun,' said Crazy Boy.

*   *   *

Crazy Boy tapped his fingers on his knees in time to the Eminem track that was pounding at full volume through the speakers. He looked over at Two Knives, who was nodding his head back and forth in time with the music. 'He can rap, for a white guy,' said Crazy Boy. 'But he isn't a patch on 50 Cent.' He checked the action of his Glock and tucked it into the waistband of his jeans. Two Knives checked his rear-view mirror and then the two side mirrors. 'What's wrong?' asked Crazy Boy.

'Just checking,' said Two Knives.

'Who'd be tailing us?' said Crazy Boy. 'Nobody fucks with us in Ealing.' He patted Two Knives on the knee. 'Chill, brother, all's well with the world.' He took an envelope from his pocket. It was full of fifty-pound notes that he'd taken from the walk-in safe in his study. 'Let's swing by the bitch first,' he said.

Two Knives looked at his watch and frowned.

'Now what?' said Crazy Boy.

'I told them I'd be right over.'

'Who runs this gang, brother?'

'You do. I'm just saying . . .'

'Well, don't say. I say, you listen.' He pulled his Glock out of his waistband and pressed the barrel against the side of Two Knives' head. 'Unless something's changed. Has anything changed, brother? I'm still running this gang, right?'

'You know it,' said Two Knives.

Crazy Boy's finger tightened on the trigger. He seemed oblivious to the fact that they were driving along at almost forty miles an hour and that he hadn't fastened his seat belt.

'You're sure, because it seems to me that you're second-guessing me a lot lately.'

Two Knives kept his eyes on the road. Crazy Boy was a loose cannon at the best of times but once he started chewing khat he became almost impossible to reason with. 'This isn't Somalia, brother. This is London. And in London they put people in prison for carrying a loaded gun.'

'I ain't scared of no cops,' said Crazy Boy, tapping Two Knives on the shoulder with the gun.

'Scared or not scared don't make no difference,' said Two Knives. 'I'm just saying that we've got to be careful here. Sometimes it's better if you keep your distance when there's shit going down.' He looked across at Crazy Boy, no trace of fear in his eyes. 'I've got your best interests at heart, brother. You know that. And if anything happens to you it makes me look bad, like I didn't do what I was supposed to do, you feel me?'

'It's my gang, brother. When the shit goes down I want to see the shit going down.' He took the gun away and tucked it back in his waistband, then patted Two Knives on the knee again. 'It's gonna be good, brother. Do not worry. I'm bullet-proof.' He began nodding his head in time with the track and Two Knives nodded along with him.

The house where Crazy Boy's wife and son lived was a ten-minute drive from his mansion but he rarely visited more than once a month. He didn't feel that he was married to Haweeya Bergman, and while the boy definitely shared Crazy Boy's DNA, he had no paternal feelings towards the child. The marriage and the birth had nothing to do with feelings or emotions and everything to do with what Crazy Boy had needed – a British passport and the right to live in Europe.

Two Knives parked the car and was about to get out when Crazy Boy put a hand on his arm. 'You stay here,' he said. 'I won't be long.'

Two Knives stayed in the car as Crazy Boy went up to the front door and rang the bell. The woman who opened the door was as tall as Crazy Boy but twice his weight, with heavy jowls and a belly that looked like a late pregnancy but was only fat. She had greasy dreadlocks that reached halfway down her back and was wearing a pink tracksuit that was stretched to its limit and gleaming white trainers, even though it was clear that she never went anywhere near a gym.

'Simeon, where you been, I been calling you for days,' she said. There was a glassy look to her eyes and a line of scabs running along the vein in her left arm. 'You got my money?' There was a hint of German in her accent, a relic of the five years she'd spent with her first husband.

Crazy Boy pushed past her into the sitting room. There was a cheap plastic sofa in front of a huge plasma television which was tuned to a shopping channel. A blonde not unlike the one that Crazy Boy had back in his house was enthusiastically extolling the benefits of a food blender. The remote was sitting between two Domino pizza boxes and he used it to mute the sound.

'My money, did you bring it, honey?'

Crazy Boy took the envelope of cash from the back pocket of his jeans and tapped it against her forehead. 'Don't call my house asking for money again, do you understand?'

She grabbed at the envelope but he moved it out of her reach.

'Do you understand?'

'Yes,' she said, still trying to take the envelope from him.

He opened the envelope and threw the notes up into the air. They fluttered around her and she grabbed at them, her mouth open as if she wanted to eat them. She dropped down on to her knees, scooping up the money. Crazy Boy saw a disposable cigarette lighter and an oblong piece of silver foil that had been folded down the middle. He picked up the foil and saw the telltale residue of burnt heroin at one end.

'Why do you need this shit?' he asked.

She looked up at him on all fours. 'What do you think I do all day? I take care of your son and I watch television. Why shouldn't I have something to make me feel better?'

'You've got the khat. I can get you weed if you want to smoke weed.' He waved the strip of silver foil in her face. 'You don't need this.' Crazy Boy sniffed it and frowned. 'Who do you buy it from?'

'Here and there,' she said. She stood up, clutching the banknotes to her chest.

'Tell me,' he said.

'Down the road. A Jamaican guy.'

'You buy drugs from a Yardie?' He screwed the silver paper into a ball and threw it at her. It bounced off her head and landed in front of her big-screen TV. 'Who the fuck do you think you are, buying drugs from a fucking Yardie?'

'He's OK, he doesn't cheat me.'

'Cheat, not cheat, I don't care about that. What I care about is you buying drugs from my competition. Does he know who you are? Does he know about the child?'

'He doesn't know anything. He sells, I buy. We don't talk.'

'You don't buy from him again. Ever. Understand.'

She nodded. 'Yes. OK, honey. Whatever you say.' She began stuffing the money into the pockets of her tracksuit as if she feared that he was going to take it back.

Anger flared inside Crazy Boy and he rushed towards her, slapping her across the face, left and right, then pushing her in her chest so that she fell back on to her plastic sofa so hard that one of the legs broke. 'I'm sorry, I'm sorry,' she said, holding her hands up to protect her face. The money that she hadn't shoved into her pockets scattered across the carpet.

Crazy Boy stepped back, his hands balled into fists. He wanted to beat her face to a pulp, to feel her warm wet blood on his hands, but he took deep breaths and forced himself to calm down. Killing her or even putting her in hospital would cause him all sorts of problems, problems that he didn't need. He glared at her. 'Why do you do this? Why do you make me angry?'

'I'm sorry,' she said. The sofa had buckled at one end and she had to grab hold of one of the arms to stop herself sliding down it.

'I give you everything, I pay for your house, for your car, and you repay me by buying drugs on the street like a crack whore?'

'I'm sorry,' she said again. She wiped tears from her eyes. 'Do you want to see your boy?' she said. 'I can wake him up.'

'Why would I want to see him?'

'He's your son.'

'I have many sons,' said Crazy Boy.

'He misses you.'

'He doesn't know me.' He pointed a finger at the woman's

face. 'I mean what I say. You buy drugs from anyone else and I'll scar you for life. You want drugs, you call Two Knives and he'll hook you up.'

The woman nodded fearfully.

'Do you understand me, bitch?'

She nodded, her lower lip trembling. 'I understand.'

Crazy Boy sneered at her and let himself out of the house.

'No problems?' asked Two Knives as Crazy Boy climbed into the front passenger seat.

'Not any more,' said Crazy Boy. 'Now let's go take care of business.'

Two Knives prepared to drive them to one of Crazy Boy's restaurants in Ealing. It served Somali cuisine utilising the talents of two chefs who Crazy Boy had found working as cleaners in a Bayswater hotel. Both had claimed asylum and weren't supposed to be working but Crazy Boy paid them in cash and allowed them to live with their wives and children in a flat above the restaurant.

'We've shut the restaurant for the night,' said Two Knives, as he put the car in gear.

'What about the cooks?' asked Crazy Boy. 'I don't want them involved.'

'No problem, brother,' said Two Knives. 'They're out this evening, taking their families to the movies. They've been told not to come back before midnight.' He drove to the restaurant, which was about two miles from the house in a busy shopping street. They parked at the rear of the restaurant and went in through a back door that led straight into a large kitchen. The two teenagers were kneeling on the floor, blindfolded and gagged, their arms tied behind their backs. Four of Crazy Boy's men were standing behind them wearing black Puffa jackets and baggy blue jeans. One by one they high-fived Crazy Boy and hugged him. They were all young, three of them still teenagers, and all had been born in England, but they owed their allegiance to Somalia, and to Crazy Boy. 'Good job, brothers,' he said.

He picked up a large cleaver from one of the metal preparation tables and moved it so that it glinted under the fluorescent lights. 'Take off the blindfolds,' he said.

Two of the teenagers hurried forward and removed the strips of cloth from the faces of the bound boys. The captives blinked up at Crazy Boy. Tears were streaming down the younger one's face. They both began to try to speak but the gags were tight and all they could do was grunt.

'Shut the fuck up!' Crazy Boy shouted, waving the cleaver in their faces. 'There's nothing you've got to say that I want to hear.' He looked over at the four young men who were huddled together by one of the big stoves. 'I want you all to remember this,' he said. 'That is what happens when you cross me.' He lashed out with the cleaver and sliced through the shoulder of the older of the two captives. The boy screamed in agony but the gag muffled most of the sound. He fell to the side and tried to curl into a ball, his back to Crazy Boy. 'If this was Somalia, you know what I'd be doing?' asked Crazy Boy. 'I'd have them tied down and cut and then I'd let dogs loose on them. That's what I'd do. They've behaved like dogs so getting dogs to kill them is what they deserve. This is what happens to anyone who hurts my people. You hurt my people, you die. They need to know that out there on the streets.' He waved his cleaver at the back door. 'Those are my streets out there. Anyone fucks with me or with my people, this is what happens.'

He strode over to the younger of the two captives, who was rocking backwards and forwards with his eyes tightly closed.

Two Knives took out his phone and started videoing.

Crazy Boy swung the cleaver from side to side. 'You put my boy in hospital,' he said. 'You hurt one of my boys, you hurt me. You attack them, you attack me.' He glared at the bound and gagged teenager. 'How fucking dare you!' he screamed. He raised the cleaver and brought it down hard against the teenager's neck, slicing through the flesh as easily as cutting through a steak fillet. The teenager grunted and fell to the side as blood poured from the gaping wound. Crazy Boy raised the cleaver again and brought it down hard, carving through the back of the neck and embedding it in the spine. Then in quick succession he hit him again half a dozen times, hacking at the head, the neck and the shoulder until the body went still and blood had pooled around it on the tiled floor.

Crazy Boy straightened up. He was breathing heavily and his eyes were wide and staring and his upper lip was curled back into a savage snarl.

The second teenager was curled up on the floor, whimpering like an injured dog. The wound on his shoulder was pulsing with blood and his legs were shaking. Crazy Boy walked over and stood looking down at him. 'Look at you!' he shouted. 'You have no honour, no self-respect, no balls.' He bent down and lashed out with the cleaver, slicing the boy's thigh. 'I should castrate you, that's what I should do.' He cut the boy again, slicing a chunk out of his arm. 'Not so brave now, are you? Brave enough to attack my boy and put him in hospital, but now look at you. A snivelling piece of shit.' He growled and rained a flurry of blows down on the teenager's head until it was a mass of bloody tissue and white bone fragments.

He stood up, panting for breath, blood dripping down the blade of the cleaver. Two Knives put away his phone. He was grinning but the four men in Puffa jackets were huddled together, clearly shocked at what they'd seen. Crazy Boy walked over to them and they scattered like startled sheep. He didn't seem to notice as he walked by them to the sink, where he rinsed the blood off the cleaver, then used a cloth to wipe it clean of fingerprints. He dropped it on the draining board and tossed the cloth into the bin. 'Cut them up into pieces and toss them into the river,' he told the four men. 'If anyone asks, you can say the dogs are dead but no one must know that I was here or where it happened. Just that they're dead and they died in pain. Do you understand?'

The men nodded.

'And afterwards you wash everything down with bleach. Everything.'

The men nodded again. The youngest was staring at the bloodstained bodies on the floor, his mouth wide open.

Crazy Boy nodded at Two Knives and they walked out of the back door. As they headed over to the Mercedes, Crazy Boy held his hand out for the phone. He leaned against the car as he watched the recording, chuckling as he saw the cleaver bite through the flesh and bone. 'Nice,' he said. He gave the phone back to Two Knives.

'What do you want to do with it? Put it on YouTube?'

'Delete it,' said Crazy Boy.

Two Knives frowned. 'Say what?'

'You heard me, delete it.'

'It's a great vid, brother. Shows them for the cowards that they were.'

'Spreading the word that the dogs are dead is one thing. That makes us stronger. But a video online gives the cops something to go on. They'll start asking questions.'

'Nobody in the diaspora will talk to the cops, you know that. And anyone who does, we can take care of.' Two Knives made a gun with his right hand and pretended to fire it.

'That's as may be, but we're not going to give the cops any evidence for free.'

Two Knives nodded. 'You're right, brother.'

'Always,' said Crazy Boy. 'It was good, wasn't it? Like being back in Somalia. Not giving a shit about what we do or who we do it to.'

'I miss that, brother.'

'I miss it, too,' said Crazy Boy. He shivered. 'Still, our life is better here, no question about that.' He clapped Two Knives on the back. 'OK, drive me home. I need to talk to my uncle.'

They climbed into the Mercedes and Two Knives drove back to the house. They played a 50 Cent CD at full volume, singing along to it as loud as they could all the way home.

As soon as he was back in the house, Crazy Boy went through to the sitting room where Levi's and Sunny were watching a movie and chewing on khat leaves. 'How'd it go?' asked Levi's as he stripped leaves off a twig.

Crazy Boy grabbed a handful of khat twigs. 'Cut them to pieces, I did,' he said. 'They died like the dogs they were.'

Levi's and Sunny nodded approvingly as Crazy Boy went to the study and sat down at his desk. He switched on his laptop and as soon as it had booted up he launched Skype and watched as it logged him in. He changed his login name every two or three days, and even though he was sure that Skype was secure he still used the same sort of code words and vague terms that he used whenever he spoke on the phone.

He saw that his uncle was online and clicked on his name to connect. He heard a ringing tone and after a few seconds his uncle's grinning face appeared. Crazy Boy expanded the video to fill the whole screen as his own camera glowed red. 'Uncle, how are you?'

'Everything is good,' his uncle said. 'Roobie has been out at sea all week. He is driving his men hard.'

'Sometimes men need to be driven,' said Crazy Boy.

'Roobie keeps talking about London,' said his uncle. 'He wants to follow you. He wants to talk to you about it, he said.'

'We need him on the boats,' said Crazy Boy. 'If everyone leaves Somalia, who will bring in the money?'

'I tell him that. But he says that as soon as he gets enough money he's going to follow you and get a British passport. He talks about it all the time.'

'Keep an eye on him,' said Crazy Boy. 'I know he is your son but ambition can be a dangerous thing.'

'I will have words with him,' said his uncle.

'The magazines arrived safely?' Magazines was code for money and Crazy Boy was referring to the funds he'd sent through the Arab.

'We have them, and we will put them to good use. I have put in an order for equipment and the Yemeni says he can have it here next week.'

Equipment meant arms and ammunition. Both could be bought in Mogadishu but Crazy Boy preferred to deal with the Yemeni because his weapons were always top quality and his ammunition never jammed. Crazy Boy had plenty of rivals in Somalia and by ordering his weapons overseas there was less likelihood of other pirate gangs finding out what he was up to. Piracy was a dog-eat-dog business and Crazy Boy was determined to maintain his position as leader of the pack.

'Uncle, we are to do things differently this time,' he said. 'I have a plan.'

'Plans are good,' said his uncle. 'What do you want us to do?'

'This is too important to talk about at a distance,' said Crazy Boy. 'I will come to talk to you in person. I will fly out tomorrow. Can you meet me at the airstrip?'

'I'll be there,' said his uncle.

'I'll have your mobile number so keep it switched on in case there are any problems.'

'I understand,' said his uncle. 'May God keep you safe, son of my brother.'

'And you, brother of my father.' Crazy Boy ended the call.

As soon as he got back to his flat, Shepherd made himself a mug of coffee and phoned Button. 'Just checking in,' he said. 'I went out for drinks with the troops and heard a couple of things that might be worth looking at.'

'I'm at home, let me just get to my computer,' she said. 'How's it going generally?'

'It's as boring as hell,' said Shepherd. 'If I had to work in an office all day I think I'd top myself.'

'Well, speaking as an office worker, I have to say there are plus points,' she said.

'I didn't mean your job,' he said. 'I mean the sort of stuff they have to do. Eight hours a day filling in spreadsheets, answering the phone, photocopying and filing. I'm not surprised that they spend most of the time watching YouTube or fiddling with their Facebook pages.'

'OK, I'm in my study,' she said. 'What have you got for me?'

'First up, it might be worth taking a look at the office manager, Candice Malone,' said Shepherd. 'They call her Candy.'

'We did look at her,' said Button. 'No money in her bank that can't be explained. She's buying her own flat but the deposit came from her parents.'

'It might not be about money,' he said. 'It might be a love job.'

'I'm intrigued, tell me more.'

'She's got a black boyfriend, that's the gossip anyway. I don't know where he's from or what the story is, but she's keeping the romance low-profile.'

'So how come you're aware of it?'

'Office gossip,' he said. 'It came out over drinks.'

'Do you think you can nail down specifics?'

'Charlie, I can't start asking the staff about their sex lives,' he said. 'You'd be better off having someone watching her flat. And please don't ask me to do it.'

'I wouldn't dream of it,' said Button. 'We've got surveillance experts, I'll get her looked at. But if you find yourself chatting to her at the water cooler . . .'

'Sure, I'll ask her if she's got a thing for *Mandingo*, OK?'

'I'm sensing your cynicism again, Spider. Any other possibilities?'

'There's a guy by the name of Tim Symes, mid-twenties, bit of a Jack the lad. Plays poker and says that he wins all the time.'

'Lucky boy.' He could hear her tapping on her computer keyboard. 'Well, if he's winning big bucks he's not putting it into the bank.'

'It might be worth seeing who he's playing with,' said Shepherd. 'I might get myself invited to a game.'

'Sounds like a plan.'

'I wanted you to know in advance because if I lose I'll be looking to put the money through on expenses and I can hardly ask for a receipt at a poker game.'

Button laughed. 'Just do your best,' she said.

It had been a long flight and even though he had flown British Airways Business Class Crazy Boy was still tired when he arrived at Nairobi International Airport. There had been nothing he'd wanted to eat on the menu and he rarely watched movies that weren't pornographic so he spent most of the flight drifting in and out of sleep. He had only hand luggage with him, a black Adidas holdall with a change of clothes, so after he had cleared immigration he walked straight through customs and then left the arrivals area and caught a minibus to the General Aviation terminal. There a twin-engined Cessna was waiting for him. The Kenyan pilot had flown Crazy Boy before and he shook his hand and took his bag from him. He was in his fifties, his hair greying at the temples and his gut showing the effects of a twenty-five-year career spent sitting in a pilot's seat. His co-pilot was half his age, stick-thin with a prominent Adam's apple. Both men wore short-sleeved white shirts with black and gold epaulettes and black trousers. 'You are ready to leave now?' asked the pilot, handing the holdall to the co-pilot.

'Perhaps a visit to the bathroom first,' said Crazy Boy.

The pilot nodded. 'We'll carry out the pre-flight checks,' he said.

Crazy Boy headed for the men's room. After he'd finished freshening up he took out his mobile and called Blue. 'I am in Nairobi, I should be at the airfield in three hours.'

'We will be waiting for you,' said Blue.

'Make sure the men are less trigger-happy than last time,' said Crazy Boy. 'They nearly shot me out of the air.'

Blue chuckled. 'It was only AK-47 fire. If they had been serious they would have used a missile.'

'Hey, to you it's funny but when you're coming in to land in a small plane and someone rakes you with bullets, it's no laughing matter.'

'He was high on khat and he was punished,' said Blue. 'It won't happen again.'

'It had better not,' said Crazy Boy, and ended the call.

Nicholas Brett had no idea why he'd been knocked unconscious, then tied to a chair and gagged and had a hood pulled down over his head. He could hear two men in the room but when they talked it was in whispers so he couldn't hear what they were saying. He could feel blood trickling down the side of his head, he had a splitting headache and he had lost the feeling in both hands.

He was sure that he wasn't being robbed because his Tag

watch was still on his wrist and the two men didn't seem to be moving around his apartment. He wanted to ask them who they were and what they wanted but the gag made it impossible to do anything other than grunt.

The guy who'd hit him had been wearing the overalls of the local cable company. Brett had been watching HBO when the signal had gone and five minutes later there'd been a knock at the door and a technician was telling him that there had been a building-wide system failure and that he needed to reprogramme his box. As Brett had stepped to the side to let the man in something had slammed against the back of his head, and when he'd woken up he was tied to the chair and the hood was over his head.

Brett tried to move his feet but his ankles had been bound to the chair leg. It wasn't a robbery, and if they were there to kill him then they wouldn't have bothered tying him to the chair. If it had been the cops or the Feds then he'd have been handcuffed and taken away.

He lost all sense of time as he sat on the chair, and he had no idea how long he'd been unconscious, but he hadn't eaten since midday and his stomach was grumbling so he thought it was probably late evening when he heard a knock on the door and then footsteps as one of the men went over and opened it. He heard a woman's voice and then the click-clack of high heels walking across the wooden floor.

The hood was ripped off his head and he blinked as he tried to focus. He felt fingers tear away the duct tape from his mouth and he gasped in pain. There was a woman standing in front of him. Ginger-haired with a sprinkling of freckles across an upturned nose, long fair eyelashes, pale green eyes and skin so pale it looked as if it had never seen the sun. She was holding a photograph and she looked at it and then at his face. 'It's him,' she said, and put the photograph away. She was wearing a dark raincoat and a scarlet scarf tied loosely around her neck.

The man in the cable TV overalls tossed the hood and duct tape on to a chair. Brett looked around. There was a second man sitting at the dining table by the window, holding a bottle of beer that he must have taken from the fridge. He raised it in salute as he stared impassively back at Brett. He was a big man, well over six feet tall and broad shouldered, wearing a military-style reefer jacket, the buttons open to reveal a barrel-shaped chest in a Gap T-shirt.

'Who are you?' Brett asked the man. 'What do you want?'

'Don't talk to him, Nicholas, talk to me,' said the woman.

She had an Irish accent, Brett realised. 'What is it you want?' he asked. 'There's no money here, no drugs, you've got the wrong apartment.' He knew that wasn't true, of course. She knew his name. She knew who he was. They were in the right apartment. The question was, what did they want?

The woman sat down and crossed her legs. Her skirt rode up her thighs and she made no move to cover them. She removed her scarf, folded it neatly and placed it on the sofa next to her, then unbuttoned her coat. 'Matt Tanner,' she said.

'What about him?'

'How long have you known him?'

Brett shrugged. 'Ages.'

She reached into the pocket of her raincoat and took out a packet of cigarettes and a slim gold lighter. 'Specifically, Nicholas. When did you first meet him?'

'Five years ago. He was a Marine. I met him in a bar.'

She slowly lit a cigarette, then blew a tight plume of smoke up at the ceiling and watched as it dispersed. 'And you both being from the Old Country, you fell into conversation and became best buddies?'

'What the fuck's going on here?' asked Brett.

'You introduced Tanner to people in New York, right? Fund-raisers?'

'He wanted to know more about what was happening back in Ireland. He hated the way the Brits were behaving, and thought that the IRA had sold out.'

'A meeting of minds,' said the woman, her voice loaded with sarcasm.

'Who are you?' asked Brett.

'I'm the woman who's going to decide what happens to you next, Nicholas. You might say that your life is in my hands. And what you say to me over the next few minutes is pretty much going to determine what happens to you. You know that Tanner ended up in Belfast?'

'I didn't. Why would I? What was he doing in Belfast?'

'Winning friends and influencing people,' said the woman. 'So tell me again, where did you first meet Tanner?'

'An Irish bar in Boston.'

'Name?'

'Hell, I don't know. It was five years ago.'

She took a long drag on her cigarette before speaking again. 'You're going to have to do a lot better than that, Nicholas. There's a lot depending on this.'

'What?' said Brett. 'What's depending on this? I know Matt Tanner, sure, but I've not seen or heard from him for . . .'

He shook his head, trying to clear his thoughts. 'I don't know. Four months. Five.' He shook his head again. 'I don't know. It's been a while. Has he done something? What's he done?'

'So where were you when you saw him last?' She flicked cigarette ash on to the floor.

'We were in a bar. In Manhattan.'

'Name?'

'The Shamrock.'

'And who were you with?'

'There was a group of us. Half a dozen.'

'Give me some names, Nicholas.'

Brett shook his head again, trying to clear his thoughts. 'Mark Dawson. Tommy Crofts. Reggie McIntyre.'

The woman nodded slowly. 'Fund-raisers,' she said.

'Yeah, they send money back to Northern Ireland. For the Cause.'

The woman smiled without warmth. 'That's right. The Cause. You're a pal of Mark's, right?'

'We go back a ways, yes.'

'They're regular drinking buddies?'

Brett nodded. 'What's this about?'

'I'm the one asking the questions here, Nicholas. All you have to do is to answer them.'

'I can answer your questions without being trussed up like a chicken.'

'Who do you work for, Nicholas?'

'Handguns Unlimited, in New Jersey.'

'That's your day job, Nicholas. Your cover. Who do really work for?'

'I sell guns. That's what I do. I work in a gun store.'

The woman looked over at the man sitting at the table and nodded at him. He grinned at Brett, reached inside his jacket and pulled out a semi-automatic.

'So you won't have any problem telling me what that is,' she said.

The man held it up and waggled it from side to side.

'It's a Smith & Wesson Compact,' said Brett.

'Yes it is,' said the woman. 'So what would it sell for?'

'New? Between seven and eight hundred dollars. It's a nice weapon. Perfect for concealed carry.'

The woman nodded. 'Ten out of ten,' she said. 'Go to the top of the class.'

The man at the table took a suppressor from his pocket and slowly screwed it into the barrel of the handgun.

'Who are you?' asked Brett.

The woman held up her right hand and waggled her index finger at him. She was wearing glossy black leather gloves. They were all wearing gloves, Brett realised.

'Who told you to introduce Tanner to the guys in Manhattan?'

'It wasn't like that,' said Brett. 'I was going for a drink, Matt tagged along.'

The woman scowled, then waved at the man in overalls. He walked over and switched on the television, then used the remote to flick through to MTV. He turned the sound up, put the remote on the coffee table and then walked over to Brett and slapped him across the face, hard. Brett tasted blood as he stared at the man in horror. 'What the fuck?' he shouted but the man hit him again, this time a backhander that rattled his teeth.

'Just answer the questions, Nicholas,' said the woman.

'You supplied guns for the guys at the Shamrock, didn't you? Guns that were sent to Ireland.'

Brett shook his head. He cleared his throat and spat bloody phlegm on to the floor. 'I helped them buy guns, I didn't supply them. They were buying automatic weapons and they wanted me to check that they were fit for purpose.'

'And Tanner knew that?'

'Yes. I don't know. Maybe.'

The man raised his hand. 'Make up your mind, Nicholas,' said the woman.

Brett nodded slowly. 'Yes.'

'And Tanner knew who he was meeting, didn't he? That's why you took him to the bar. He wanted to be introduced.'

Brett shook his head and then flinched in anticipation of another blow.

'There's no point in lying, Nicholas. There's absolutely nothing you can say that's going to convince me that you didn't know who Matt Tanner was or why he wanted to get close to the guys at the Shamrock.'

Brett said nothing as he stared at the floor.

'The thing is, Nicholas, Matt Tanner killed two of our people in Ireland. He shot them in cold blood and then fled. So we know that he's bad. And you're the one who introduced him to our people. You took him into the Shamrock and then Dawson took him to Belfast. So we know you're bad, too. You're the cause of all this. You initiated it. It's your fault.'

'He just wanted a drink and I was meeting them in the Shamrock. He tagged along. I thought he was kosher.'

'Kosher? You thought he was kosher, did you?' She chuckled softly. 'You're not stupid, are you, Nicholas? You wouldn't have introduced someone to Dawson and the guys unless you trusted them. Is that what you expect me to believe? That Tanner fooled you, too?'

Brett nodded quickly. 'That's it,' he said. 'He told me he was a former Marine and that he wanted to go back to his roots, to Ireland. Said that his parents had been forced out during the Troubles and he wanted to help teach the British a lesson.'

The woman smiled at the man in the overalls and pointed at Brett's feet. The man knelt down and began removing Brett's left shoe.

'What are you doing?' asked Brett.

The woman ignored him. She stood up and walked into the kitchen and returned a few seconds later with a large carving knife which she handed to the man in the overalls.

'I'm telling you the truth,' said Brett, his voice trembling.

'No you're not, Nicholas,' said the woman as she sat back on the sofa. 'You're clinging to the hope that you're going to be able to lie your way out of this situation, but that's not going to happen. As soon as you accept that, the easier it'll be for all of us.'

The man in overalls roughly grabbed Brett's ankle and held the blade of the knife against the little toe. 'Remind me again which is the little piggy that went to market?' he said to the woman. He also had an Irish accent, Brett realised.

The woman tossed her hair and laughed. 'Was that the big one, Nicholas, or the little one? Do you remember?'

Brett struggled but there was nothing he could do. 'You don't have to do this, I'll talk,' he whimpered.

'I know that,' said the woman. 'The only question is how many toes you lose before you do.'

'OK, OK, look, I was doing my job, all right. It was nothing personal. I'm just one of the Indians and I do what the chiefs tell me.' The words came out so quickly that they were tumbling into each other.

The man with the knife sat back on his heels and looked at the woman. She waved a languid hand. 'So what are you, Nicholas? Just some rat-fink out to make a few bucks by grassing up whoever he can? Or are you a bigger rat with a salary and a pension?'

Brett took a deep breath, trying to steady himself.

'Come on, Nicholas, cat got your tongue? What are you? MI5? MI6? CIA? FBI? DEA? Which three-letter group pays your wages?'

Brett swallowed. 'ATF,' he said.

The woman nodded and took another long drag on her cigarette. 'That sounds about right,' she said. 'But I guess you weren't too concerned about the alcohol or tobacco side, were you?'

She reached into her raincoat and took out a small Ziploc bag. She extinguished what was left of her cigarette on the sole of her shoe and put the butt into the bag.

'So what were you doing, undercover?' she said, putting the Ziploc bag into her raincoat pocket. 'Tracking guns being shipped to Ireland?'

'Not just Ireland,' said Brett. 'I was watching a bunch of arms dealers in New York. One was a Russian, another was a Serb.'

'So the Irish connection was just one of several investigations?'

Brett nodded.

'And Matt Tanner. Who was he with?'

'They didn't say.'

'They being?'

'My bosses. They said I was to introduce him and that he'd do the rest. It was a rush job, I didn't have much time with him, just enough to work out how we were going to play it.' He looked at the man with the knife and back to the woman. 'I wasn't happy about it, mine was a long-term penetration operation and I didn't want to blow it by putting someone I didn't know into the mix.'

'How very unfortunate for you.'

'Look, what I'm saying is that it wasn't my fault. It was nothing to do with me. My bosses told me I had to introduce the guy and that there'd be no comeback.'

'Well, they were definitely wrong on that score, weren't they?'

'If he did something bad to your people, that's down to him.'

She nodded. 'Believe me, Nicholas, I'd much rather have Matt Tanner tied to that chair than you. But one step at a time, you know?'

'I don't know where he is,' said Brett. 'I swear on the lives of my kids.'

'You've got kids, have you, Nicholas?'

Brett nodded frantically. 'A boy and a girl.'

'So what's a good father like you doing working under-cover? Why aren't you at home tucked up with Mrs Brett?'

'She walked out on me two years ago,' said Brett. 'Took the kids with her. That's one of the reasons I took this assignment, to take my mind off it.'

The woman nodded thoughtfully. 'So Tanner, you made the introduction?'

'Yeah. I took him to the pub, we had a few drinks, he got on with them like a house on fire. I left early, he stayed with them, that was the last time I saw him.'

'That was what your bosses wanted? You introduced Tanner and then walked away?'

The man sitting at the table finished his beer. He stood up and walked slowly into the kitchen. 'Look, I was only doing my job,' said Brett. 'I didn't know what he was going to do. They didn't tell me.'

The woman nodded. 'I understand,' she said. 'Do you think Tanner was his real name?'

'I don't know.'

'Do you know who he worked for?'

Brett shook his head. 'I asked but he didn't say.'

'And he didn't tell you why he wanted to get close to them?'

'He wouldn't say word one about what he was doing, or who he was. I spent a morning with him in a motel room in New Jersey, going over our background, how we met, who he was, anecdotes, bullshit, all that stuff. He was good, I can tell you that. He'd obviously worked undercover before.'

'And he was American? Irish American?'

'Born in Belfast, he said. But moved to the States when he was a kid. Served in the military.'

'Family?'

'He said he wasn't married. No kids. We talked about my situation and he said he was glad that he'd never married.'

'And you think that was true, or just his legend?'

'I don't know. I couldn't tell. Like I said, he was good. If he was lying I'd never have known.'

Brett heard the man in the kitchen washing the bottle in the sink. There was only one reason for him to do that, Brett knew. To remove any DNA.

'I'm a Federal agent,' said Brett, his voice trembling again.

'Yes,' said the woman. 'Yes you are.'

'If you do anything to me, you'll be taking on the Federal Government.'

'I suppose that's true,' said the woman.

Brett could feel his legs start to shake and he was finding it hard to breathe.

'If you go, if you just walk away, I won't say anything,' he said, hating himself for sounding so weak.

'Now you know that's not going to happen, don't you?' she said. 'Just be quiet now. It'll soon be over.' She nodded at the man in the overalls and he came up behind Brett. Brett heard a tearing sound and then a strip of duct tape was wound around his mouth. He struggled but in seconds he was gagged and then the hood was pulled back over his head.

He tried to scream but the duct tape muffled it to a grunt and tears pricked his eyes. He wanted to plead and beg for his life, to offer them everything he had if they'd just not kill him, but even if he wasn't gagged he knew that there was nothing he could say. He jerked forwards and backwards and the chair shifted on the floor but his bonds held firm.

He heard footsteps. The man walking from the kitchen. Walking over to the dining table where the gun was. Tears streamed down his face and his breath was coming in short gasps. It wasn't fair, he'd only been doing his job and no job was worth dying for. He felt his bowels loosen and a warmth spread around his groin and he realised that he'd wet himself. He moaned like an animal in pain as he rocked back and forth, and part of him wanted to say a prayer and another part of him wanted his ATF colleagues to come charging in to rescue him even though he knew that only happened in the movies and this wasn't a movie. This was real life and he was helpless and there was nothing he could do to stop what was happening.

He heard footsteps in front of him and a metallic click and he began to moan again.

The plane banked to the right and through the window Crazy Boy saw the airfield for the first time. It had been built by the Russians in the years when Somalia had few friends among the international community. There was a single paved runway, three metal hangars and a brick barracks that had once housed Russian troops tasked with guarding the airfield. Behind the buildings was a line of concrete huts with corrugated-iron roofs. Eventually the Russians had moved out, and when the Americans had moved in they had erected a mesh fence topped with razor wire and two watchtowers. It was from one of the watchtowers that the bullets had come last time Crazy Boy had landed, a single spray of ten rounds of which two had clipped the tail.

When the Americans had moved on, various Somali warlords fought over the airfield and eventually Crazy Boy had emerged victorious. He had been magnanimous in victory, though, and allowed other gangs to use the facility from time to time, provided they paid handsomely for the privilege.

The Americans had also built a control tower but it was now only used to store food and drugs, so when the pilot called up on the radio asking for a wind reading his request went unanswered. The co-pilot spotted a windsock and pointed it out to the captain, who then set the plane up so that it would be landing into the wind. Crazy Boy peered at the watchtowers anxiously. There were two men in each, and while he could see that they had AK-47s at least they weren't being aimed at the plane.

The co-pilot twisted around to check that Crazy Boy had his seat belt fastened and flashed him a thumbs-up. Crazy Boy grinned but his stomach was churning. It was all very well for Blue to reassure him that everything was under control at the airfield but Crazy Boy knew that the majority of his men were trigger-happy teenagers who were high on khat most of the time.

The plane banked again and lined up with the runway and the undercarriage came down. It was a perfect landing, as smooth as when the British Airways jet had touched down in Nairobi. They taxied to the control tower building where half a dozen bare-chested men toting AK-47s were waiting. The pilot cut the engine. 'How long will you be staying, sir?' he asked Crazy Boy.

'An hour. Maybe a bit longer. Then back to Nairobi.'

A tanker drove up and pulled up at the side of the plane, ready to refuel it. One of the bare-chested men was smoking a cigar, and when the pilot climbed out he spoke to the man and asked him to throw it away. The man swore at him in Somali and levelled his weapon at the pilot's chest. Two of his colleagues did the same and the pilot slowly raised his hands.

Crazy Boy got out and pointed at the man with a cigar. 'Put that out, that tanker's full of fuel.'

The man kept his weapon pointed at the pilot's chest. 'I don't obey orders from him,' he said sullenly, gesturing with the barrel.

'He's responsible for the plane,' said Crazy Boy. 'But you do obey orders from me so do as you're told and put it out.'

'And who the fuck are you?' said the man, still chewing the cigar. The men either side of him had recognised Crazy Boy and they moved away, avoiding eye contact with him.

'That's Wiil Waal,' said a gruff voice from above them. 'Crazy Boy. So you show him some respect, else he teaches you some manners.'

Crazy Boy looked up and saw Blue leaning out through an open window two storeys up.

The man with the cigar took a step back as if he'd been punched in the chest. He was a teenager, nineteen years old at most, tall and scrawny with a scar running across his left cheek. He was wearing Nike running shorts and flip-flop sandals and a New York Yankees baseball cap back to front. 'Wiil Waal?' he said.

Crazy Boy turned to sneer at him. The other men had scattered, putting as much distance as possible between themselves and the man with the cigar, like a pack of zebra abandoning an infirm member of the herd to the lions.

'I didn't know,' said the man. He took the cigar out of his mouth. 'I'm sorry.' He looked around with wild eyes as he realised for the first time that he was now standing on his own.

Crazy Boy held out his hand and the man offered him the cigar, holding the wet end out towards him. Crazy Boy shook his head and pointed at the AK-47. The man put the cigar back in his mouth and held out the gun with trembling hands. Crazy Boy took it, checked the action, then lazily pointed it at the man's chest, his finger on the trigger.

The man took the cigar from his mouth again and let it fall from his fingers. It tumbled through the air and sparked as it hit the ground.

The door to the control tower building opened and Crazy Boy's uncle appeared, carrying his own AK-47. He was wearing a camouflage jacket open to reveal his bare chest, and shorts that had once been white but were now a grubby grey. He grinned when he saw the gun in Crazy Boy's hands. 'I see you've met Erasto,' he said. 'He's a new addition to the gang.'

'If he's new then he won't be missed,' said Crazy Boy, his finger tightening on the trigger.

'Blue, I didn't know,' said Erasto, tears running from his eyes.

'You do now,' said Blue. He slung his AK-47 on its shoulder strap.

'Please, tell him how hard I've worked for you, how I've pledged my loyalty to you.'

Blue chuckled. 'Tell him yourself. You have a tongue.'

Erasto dropped down on to his knees in front of Crazy Boy. 'Please, Wiil Waal, I meant no disrespect.'

'No disrespect? You asked me who the fuck I was. How is that not disrespect?' Now the barrel of his weapon was pointing at Erasto's face.

'I have only been working for Blue for a month, I had heard of you, of course, but no one told me you were coming today.' Tears were running down his cheeks. 'I am sorry for the offence.'

'And now you want to make amends?'

Erasto nodded fearfully. 'Yes, Wiil Waal. Anything.'

Crazy Boy grinned cruelly. He prodded the still-burning cigar with his shoe. 'The cigar is the problem,' he said. 'Make it go away.'

Erasto frowned, not understanding what he was expected to do.

'Eat it,' said Crazy Boy. 'Eat the whole thing. Or die. I'm happy either way.'

Erasto looked tearfully at Blue but Crazy Boy's uncle stared back impassively and shrugged.

Crazy Boy pushed the gun against Erasto's forehead. 'I don't have much time,' he said.

Erasto groped around with his hand and found the cigar. He picked it up and stared at it. It was still smouldering. He took a bite out of the wet end, chewed it and swallowed. He gagged and almost threw up.

'All of it,' said Crazy Boy.

Erasto stared at the lit end, his eyes wide and fearful. He slowly opened his mouth and put it in, then bit down hard and began to chew frantically. He whimpered and then swallowed and then crammed in the last bit of the cigar. He choked and put his hands over his lips and forced himself to swallow.

Crazy Boy grinned over at his uncle, then slammed the butt of his AK-47 across Erasto's face, breaking his nose. Erasto fell back, blood pouring over his mouth. Crazy Boy dropped the AK-47 next to the injured man and went over to Blue, his arms outstretched.

Blue hugged him, and patted him on the back. 'You're getting fat,' he said.

'But not soft,' said Crazy Boy, only slightly offended. Blue was right, he had put on weight since he had moved to the UK. The food was better and he didn't believe in exercise for the sake of it. In Somalia he had always been on the move, but in his big house in Ealing he spent most of his time playing on his Xbox or screwing hookers.

'You should come back to Somalia for a while, come back on the boats,' said Blue, slapping his washboard stomach. 'It would toughen you up.'

'Maybe one day,' said Crazy Boy. 'But for the moment I'm too busy in London.' Blue put his arm around Crazy Boy's shoulder. 'Come on in out of the sun, we can talk inside.'

The two men walked into the control tower building. There were four camp beds lined up by a window with kitbags full of clothing next to them and several dozen boxes of bottled water. Blue took Crazy Boy up a concrete staircase and pushed open the door to the main observation room, with windows on all sides which ran from knee height up to the ceiling. There were torn plastic covers over the computer equipment and radar screens.

'We should use this equipment,' said Crazy Boy.

'We don't have anyone trained to use it, and even if we did, what would be the point?' said Blue. 'We always know when a visitor is expected, and anyone who isn't expected, we shoot.' He laughed and went over to a large desk and waved for Crazy Boy to sit on one of the high-backed executive chairs there.

'The pilot didn't even know what direction the wind was blowing,' said Crazy Boy.

'That's what the orange thing is for,' said Blue. 'It points with the wind.'

'OK, OK,' said Crazy Boy, not wanting to argue with his uncle. Blue was as tough as an old boat's timbers, but like many Somalis he was naturally lazy and given the choice would always take the option that required less effort.

'Tea?' said Blue. 'Or coffee?' He laughed. 'Or something stronger?' He pulled open the bottom drawer of the desk and took out a bag of freshly cut khat leaves.

'You read my mind,' said Crazy Boy.

Blue tossed the bag to Crazy Boy, then took a second bag out of the drawer for himself.

Crazy Boy stripped off a handful of leaves and slotted them between his lips. 'So how is Roobie?'

'He's just got back. Six days at sea and nothing.'

'Still wishing he was in London?'

'That's his dream.'

'It's not that great,' Crazy Boy said. 'We're not liked there.'

'When did Roobie ever care about being liked?' Blue laughed. 'When did any of us?' He stripped off a handful of leaves.

'There is something we need to discuss,' he said. 'It's about our friend Ahmed. He requires more funds.'

'What is he planning this time?' asked Crazy Boy.

'American embassies in four different countries across Africa. Simultaneous attacks with massive car bombs. A spectacular, he says. Something that will force the Americans to react, because when the Americans react they always overreact.'

'And how much does he need?'

'As always he is vague,' said Blue. 'But I think the closer to a million dollars he has, the happier he would be.'

'Is he speaking for himself or he is part of a larger plan?'

Blue chuckled, 'You know that Ahmed always keeps his cards close to his chest. That's why he's never been caught.'

Crazy Boy nodded. 'Tell him I'll send him the money when I get back to London.' He leaned forward. 'But what we are planning to do is far more important than blowing up a few embassies,' he said. 'That is why you must follow my instructions to the letter, brother of my father.'

'You know you can trust me, son of my brother,' said Blue.

'With my life,' said Crazy Boy.

The door was thrown open and a tall man walked in, his skin as black as coal, his hair in grimy ringlets that hung down to his neck. He wore a leather necklace from which dangled a shark's tooth, and a camouflage T-shirt that was stained with sweat. 'You are back!' shouted the man, and he walked over to Crazy Boy, hugging him tightly and kissing him on both cheeks. 'We have missed you, brother.' He was in his mid thirties, some ten years older than Crazy Boy.

'Roobie, good to see you,' said Crazy Boy. '*Ma nabad baa?*'

'*Waa nabad,*' said Roobie. He released his grip on Crazy Boy and took a step back, grinning. 'You are getting fat, cousin.'

Crazy Boy shrugged. 'I don't get the exercise I used to,' he admitted.

'You should come back on the boats,' said Roobie, patting Crazy Boy's stomach. 'You would soon be in shape again. And how is Gutaala?'

'Good,' said Crazy Boy.

'He has his passport? He is a British citizen now?'

'Soon,' said Crazy Boy. He patted Roobie on his shoulder. 'It is good to see you, cousin, but I have business to discuss with my uncle.'

Roobie frowned. 'We are all in this business together, are we not?'

'This is not about the boats, cousin. This is something else.' He smiled. 'But when we are done we shall sit and talk, OK? We have many things to discuss.'

'I want to come to London, cousin. I have been on the boats long enough.'

'Later,' said Crazy Boy. 'We can talk about this later.'

Roobie slapped his cousin's chest. 'It's always later, Wiil Waal. Whenever I ask you about London you tell me later, next time, some time, but I think that you mean never. I have been patient enough.'

Crazy Boy's face tightened and he looked across at Blue, wondering why his uncle did not have better control over his son. Roobie was Crazy Boy's cousin, the son of his uncle, but that did not entitle him to question Crazy Boy's authority.

'My son, this is not the time,' said Blue, but his voice was soft, almost pleading, and it had no effect on Roobie.

'It's never the time,' he said angrily, then he turned back to Crazy Boy and smiled ingratiatingly. 'Cousin, please, I'm not asking the earth. I'm only asking for what you have done for Gutaala, and he is not your blood. And Levi's and Sunny, they are all in London, why am I still here? Why have I been left behind?' He looked over at his father as if seeking his support, but Blue studiously avoided eye contact with him.

Crazy Boy shook his head. 'Two Knives took himself,'

he said. 'He paid for his own passage, the Chinaman in Mogadishu did it for him. Levi's and Sunny, too. You can do the same. Get yourself to London and I can introduce you to the lawyer who can get you asylum. Guaranteed.'

'But you are a wealthy man, cousin. Why can you not pay for me and I will pay you back?

'Because it does not work like that, cousin,' said Crazy Boy. 'You must prove yourself, you must earn your passage.'

Roobie's eyes blazed. 'You think I haven't earned it? How can you say that? How many ships have I taken for you?'

'Ships that I have given you,' said Crazy Boy. 'I tell you which ships to take, I pay for our boats, our weapons, I pay for your food when business is slow. I take the risks so of course I take the rewards. How could it be any other way?'

'You take the financial risks, cousin, but don't forget who is taking the real risks.' He pounded his fist against his own chest. 'I put my life on the line, cousin. For you and for my father. So you're saying no? You're saying you won't help me?' He wiped his nose with the back of his hand.

'I'm saying you have to help yourself,' said Crazy Boy. His lips were starting to go numb from the effects of the khat. 'To claim asylum you have to show how you got into the country. If they find out that I brought you in there will be trouble for both of us.'

'So you can give me money and I will pay the Chinaman,' said Roobie.

Crazy Boy shook his head. 'If I did that, every man in Puntland would be beating a path to my door, and who would then be out in the boats?'

Roobie opened his mouth to argue but his father put a hand on his shoulder. 'Enough,' he said. 'We have business to discuss and you are becoming annoying.'

Roobie twisted out of his father's grasp and glared at him. He pointed a finger at his face but stopped when he heard the click of a gun being cocked. Crazy Boy was holding a revolver and pointing it at Roobie's head. 'Blood or no blood, I won't take disrespect from anybody,' he said.

Roobie immediately backed away from his father, putting up his hands and smiling his ingratiating smile. 'Cousin, I apologise,' he said. 'I have been at sea for days, the sun, the waves, I am not myself.' He took another step backwards, towards the door. 'I meant no offence, cousin.' He bowed his head.

Crazy Boy pulled the trigger and both Roobie and Blue flinched as the bullet thwacked into the wall just to the left of Roobie's head. Roobie howled and fell to his knees. He dropped and put his forehead against the floor and began to pray. Crazy Boy walked forward, his ears ringing from the explosion, and prodded Roobie's ribs with his foot. 'Get up,' he said. 'If I'd wanted to shoot you, you'd be dead.'

Roobie stayed where he was and continued to pray, rubbing his forehead against the concrete floor as he rocked back and forth.

Crazy Boy prodded him again, harder this time. 'Get up or I will put a bullet in your head,' he said.

Roobie pushed himself up into a kneeling position and looked fearfully at Crazy Boy. 'I'm sorry, cousin, I didn't mean to disrespect you,' he said.

'You forgot who I was,' said Crazy Boy. He waved the gun around. 'This is all mine. There are fifty people working for me here, every one of them owes their livelihood to me. I didn't get here by letting people disrespect me, blood or not.' He pointed the gun at Roobie's face. 'Do you understand, cousin?'

Roobie nodded.

Crazy Boy gestured at the door. 'Then get the fuck out, I need to talk to your father.' Roobie scrambled to his feet and rushed out of the door.

'I apologise for my son,' said Blue.

Crazy Boy waved away the man's apology and put the gun back on the table. 'I understand what he wants, it's what I wanted ten years ago. But he has to prove himself first.'

'I shall talk to him,' said Blue. 'What just happened will never happen again.'

Crazy Boy sat down and picked up the bag of khat leaves. 'Now let me tell you what we're going to do,' he said. 'I will need you to follow my instructions to the letter.'

Katie Cranham stretched out her legs and giggled as the bubbles from the Jacuzzi tingled against her thighs. Eric Clavier, the young Frenchman who was sharing the whirlpool bath with her, raised his glass of champagne. 'Is this the life, hey?' he asked.

'It doesn't get any better,' she said. The first time that Katie had laid eyes on Eric she'd thought that he was good looking in a male-underwear sort of way, but after four days together on the yacht she'd happily have pushed him overboard if she thought she'd get away with it. 'Are you sure you should be drinking that?'

'Champagne?' he said. 'Nectar of the gods.'

'It's the owner's champagne,' she said.

'And this is his Jacuzzi,' he said. 'What's the difference?'

Katie didn't answer. She'd already had one argument with the man since leaving Dubai and it was a long way to Sydney, Australia. She'd only been crewing for six months but one of the many things she'd learned was that boats were no place for animosity, even a yacht as big as the *Natalya*. She was a 185-foot three-masted schooner, and Katie had been told that she was worth more than twenty million dollars. It seemed a fair price for a vessel that was more luxurious than any hotel she had ever stayed in.

'You must drink a lot of champagne, surely,' said the Frenchman. 'The prime minister is your father, right? You must be as rich as God.'

'Who told you that?' said Katie.

Clavier shrugged. 'Someone.'

'Well, it's bollocks,' she said. 'He's my godfather, not my father. He went to school with my dad, that's all. They're friends.'

A figure in white appeared at the end of the Jacuzzi and Katie shaded her hand and squinted up at him. It was the captain, an Australian by the name of Graham Hooper. He was in his late twenties, and when there were no clients on board he was happy enough to be called Hoop. 'Can you take a spell on the bridge in an hour?' he asked Katie.

'No problem, Hoop.'

The captain flashed her a thumbs-up. 'It'll give me the chance to go over the charts with you. Eric, I'll need you on watch at six tomorrow morning.'

Eric saluted him lazily. 'Aye, aye, Captain.'

Hoop pointed at the bottle of champagne in the ice bucket behind Clavier. 'Is that from the owner's cabin?'

'It was in the galley, in the fridge,' said Clavier. 'You said we could eat what we wanted from the galley.'

'Eat, not drink,' said Hoop. 'That's going to come out of your wages, so enjoy it.'

Eric threw him another mock salute. 'No problem, Captain.'

Hoop shook his head as he walked away. 'You shouldn't take the piss, Eric,' said Katie. 'He's a good guy. I've been on vessels where it really is "yes sir, no sir, three bags full sir" and where we'd both be thrown off for taking a bath in the owner's Jacuzzi.'

'Hoop doesn't care, it's not his yacht. He's a hired hand, the same as us.' Clavier shifted in the water and farted. A large bubble burst to the surface. He laughed at the look of disgust on Katie's face.

'You're a pig,' said Katie, rushing out of the Jacuzzi and padding along the teak deck to a row of wooden sunloungers. A brunette in a yellow bikini was sprawled on a blue and white striped towel, her eyes hidden behind huge sunglasses that made her look like a basking insect. She was Joy Ashmore, a professional sailor and former model, and married to Andrew, another member of the crew.

'Eric's a pig, isn't he?' said Katie, as she dropped down on to the sunlounger next to Joy.

'Have you only just found that out?' Joy laughed, pushing her sunglasses up on top of her head. Her blue eyes sparkled with amusement.

'He farted in the Jacuzzi.'

'He probably had a pee, too,' said Joy. She took a tube of sunscreen and began rubbing it on her shapely legs.

Katie stretched and sighed. 'This is such a beautiful boat,' she said. 'I can imagine living on it all year round.'

'We're spoiled because the owner's not on board,' said Joy. 'We get the run of the vessel and can really enjoy ourselves. It's a different matter when we're crewing for clients. Best behaviour all the time, catering to their every whim. I tell you, sometimes my face aches from all the smiling.'

Joy and her husband Andrew had been crewing full-time for almost ten years, and between them had accrued more than half a million miles at sea, most of them under sail. They were true nomads, rarely working for the same client for more than six months, criss-crossing the world as and when the urge took them. It wasn't the life that Katie wanted for herself. She enjoyed sailing and she enjoyed travelling, but crewing was just something to do for a year before she rejoined the real world. And the real world meant a mews house in Mayfair and a job in the City and maybe, down the line, a political career. That was all ahead of her, though, and just then she was perfectly happy kicking back on a twenty-million-dollar yacht.

'You know what I hate?' asked Joy.

'Fat men in high heels?'

Joy laughed. 'Close,' she said. 'I hate men with no taste who spend millions on beautiful boats like this just so they can sail them for a couple of weeks a year. It's such a bloody waste. They don't appreciate them, they don't buy them to sail, they buy them to park in a marina somewhere so that everyone can look at them.' She squirted sunscreen on to her hand and rubbed it into her neck and shoulders.

'It is a shame,' agreed Katie.

'A damn shame,' said Joy. 'Boats like this are meant to

be sailed. Their form and function are perfectly aligned when they're under full sail. Like now.' She handed the tube of sunscreen to Katie.

Katie looked up at the massive sails above them. In all there were eight hundred square metres of white canvas billowing out from the three masts, boosted by two light-weight fisherman sails adding a further two hundred and fifty square metres. 'Why do you think he won't sail it?'

'Because he's a multi-millionaire businessman, that's why. And businessmen aren't sailors. They think that yachts are like houses, they have them dotted around the world to show how rich and important they are.' She raised her glass. 'But then if it wasn't for the likes of them, I wouldn't have the life I have, so God bless 'em, every one.' She nodded at the tube of sunscreen in Katie's hand. 'I gave you that to rub on my back,' she said.

Katie laughed. 'Sorry,' she said. She squirted more on her hands as Joy sat up and turned around.

'So how are you enjoying life on the ocean waves?' asked Joy as Katie massaged the sunscreen over her back.

'It's OK,' said Katie.

'Just OK? Most kids your age would give their eye teeth to be on a yacht like this.'

'Yeah, I know. Don't get me wrong, it's just that I tend to have more fun on dry land than I do at sea.'

Joy laughed. 'I hear that,' she said. 'But then I've got my hubby on tap whenever I need a bit of TLC. You get to choose between Hoop and Eric.'

'Oh God, no,' said Katie. She pretended to make herself sick.

'Hoop's all right,' said Joy.

'He's thirty-seven,' said Katie. 'Almost twice my age!'

'Sometimes it can be fun to have an old hand on the tiller,' said Joy. She grinned. 'That's a sailor's saying. Like red sky at night.'

'You're terrible,' said Katie. 'But seriously, this long-distance stuff isn't for me. I'm going to fly back to London as soon as we hit Sydney. A school friend can get me a chalet-maid job in Gstaad. Easy work and all the skiing I can handle.'

'And maybe land yourself a rich husband?'

Katie shrieked. 'You have to be joking!' she said. 'I'm not going to be doing the marriage-and-kids thing for years. I'm too busy having fun.'

As Crazy Boy came out of the front door, a camera clicked away in the attic of the house opposite. The clicking continued as he and Two Knives walked over to the car and climbed into the back. There were two men in the attic and they had been there for the best part of three days, eating only the food and water they had brought with them and urinating and defecating into Ziploc plastic bags which were sealed and neatly packed in a rucksack.

'Wonder how much was in the case?' asked the man who was taking the photographs. His name was Michael Franklin and before joining MI5 he had worked for an advertising agency. When the agency had run into financial problems and dispensed with his services he had applied for more than fifty jobs, and the only organisation which had asked him along for an interview was MI5. The interview had gone well, the two men and one woman who had grilled him had been interested more in his technical knowledge of photography than his portfolio, and a week later he had joined the Secret Service. It was a big change from photographing models or plates of food or electrical appliances, not least because he no longer worked in studios. Usually he was in an attic or in the back of a van and once in the steeple of a church overlooking a Turkish café where he had had to stay for more than a week. On that occasion Franklin didn't know who he was photographing or why, which was more often than not the case with the Secret Service work, but the officer he was working with on the Crazy Boy case was chatty and more than happy to tell Franklin about the man he was following.

Franklin's digital camera was linked to a MacBook laptop which his colleague was operating.

'A million, could be more,' said the man, studying the computer. 'Depends on whether he was carrying fifty-pound notes or five-hundred-euros.' His name was Robert Splaine, a twenty-year veteran of MI5.

'And what happens to it?' asked Franklin.

'It stays in the house until someone else comes to get it.'

'Like a bank?'

'More like Western Union,' said Splaine. 'Al-Faiz will be giving that cash to someone in London totally unconnected to Crazy Boy. But someone in Somalia or maybe Yemen or Kenya will go in and pick up cash from another man and somewhere along the line the books will be balanced. Crazy Boy was in Nairobi a couple of days ago so it'll be connected to that. Maybe funding a new wave of pirate attacks.'

'How come he can just come and go like that? He's a pirate warlord, right?'

'He's a British citizen now, with a British kid. That trumps anything else.' He shook his head. 'We're in the wrong business. Do you ever think how long it would take you or me to save a million quid?'

Franklin laughed. 'Two hundred years, maybe.' He swung the long lens to the side so that he could capture the number plate of the Mercedes as it drove away, then turned to look at his colleague. 'You don't mean that, about being in the wrong business,' he said. 'You like being one of the good guys.'

'Yeah? Well, you tell me why all the bad guys get to screw the best-looking girls and drive the best cars? Have you seen Crazy Boy's house? It's a bloody mansion. I couldn't even get a mortgage to buy his garage.' He screwed up his face as if he had a bitter taste in his mouth. 'He's got a Ferrari that's worth more than my house.'

'Now you're sounding all bitter and twisted. The difference is that what he has is temporary. We'll get him eventually and then he'll lose everything and end up in a six-foot-by-ten-foot cell.'

'Yeah, but here's the thing,' said Splaine as he looked at the images on the laptop. 'If he does go down, the cell we'll put him in will be a hundred times better than the shithole he came from.'

'You ever been to Somalia?' asked Franklin.

Splaine nodded. 'Several times. It's the shithole of all shitholes.'

'I guess you can understand why they do what they do,' said Franklin, detaching the long lens from the body of the camera. 'You'd probably do anything to get out, if you were born in Somalia.'

'No argument there,' said Splaine. 'And to be honest, if he stayed in Somalia I'd probably not give him another thought. But he's come to my country, my city. That's what pisses me off.' He smiled. 'But we'll get him. We always do. Once MI5 gets you in their sights, it's all over.'

Shepherd walked past the Pizza Express restaurant where he was supposed to meet Button, then stopped and doubled back, a last-minute check to see if he was being followed. She was sitting at a corner table and had already ordered a bottle of Pinot Grigio and two glasses.

'How's office life?' she asked.

'It's hardly life-threatening,' he said.

'Anyone else fit the bill other than Malone and Symes?'

Shepherd grimaced. 'They all bitch and moan about money so if he's throwing big bucks around I think there's a few possibilities.' He sipped his wine. A waitress with badly dyed blonde hair came over and in an East European accent asked them if they wanted to order.

'Are you hungry?' Button asked Shepherd.

'I can always eat,' said Shepherd. She ordered a Margherita pizza and Shepherd asked for an American Hot. He waited until the waitress was out of earshot before continuing. 'I can't help wondering if this is a sensible use of my time,' he said.

'Crazy Boy is a legitimate target,' said Button. 'He's taking millions in ransoms and his uncle has terrorist connections. How is putting together a case against him not a productive use of your time?'

Shepherd sighed. 'I'm not good in offices,' he said. 'It's not what I'm best at. Hanging around the water cooler talking about *EastEnders* and *Coronation Street*, chipping in for birthday cakes, it's all a bit . . . normal.'

'And you can't do normal?'

'Of course I can. But they're nice people, Charlie. They're not villains.'

'One of them almost certainly is.'

'But not in a . . .' He shrugged. 'I hear what you're saying, but I feel bad lying to a group of people who are basically nice. I know that sounds soppy, but it's the way it is. They try to include me in their conversations, they ask me to go to the pub at lunchtime. They're civilians, Charlie, regular people trying to earn a living. And I'm in there, lying through my teeth.'

'And you're feeling guilty?'

'Usually when I'm undercover I'm lying to career criminals or terrorists, people who deserve whatever they get,' said Shepherd. 'I don't give it a second thought. But with these people, yeah, I feel guilty. I really do.'

'It's a necessary evil,' said Button.

'The ends justify the means?' He shook his head. 'That doesn't make me feel any better about what I'm doing, Charlie.'

'Well, if it makes you feel any better, things are starting to move. Crazy Boy is just back from Somalia. And he's started to move money in anticipation of something.'

'Who did he go to see?'

Button grimaced. 'We're not sure.'

'You're not sure? I thought he was under surveillance?'

'It caught us all by surprise,' said Button. 'We had no idea that he was planning to go. He didn't make any calls to Somalia that we're aware of, he just got into the car with a small bag and the next thing we knew he was at Heathrow getting on a plane. It's getting harder to monitor his phone calls as well. We've just found out that he's opened a Skype account and we think he's using that to talk to his uncle out in Somalia.'

'But you had him followed, right?'

'He went straight to the General Aviation terminal in Nairobi,' said Button. 'That much we know.'

'You lost him?'

'Our people in Kenya lost him,' said Button. 'The point is, he's obviously getting ready for something because almost as soon as he got back he paid a visit to this man.' She took a surveillance photograph out of an envelope and slid it towards Shepherd. An Arab man was sitting at a café table sucking on a hookah pipe as he listened to a bearded man wearing dark glasses. Button pointed at the man with the pipe. 'This is Muhammad al-Faiz. He's a Saudi national but is also now a British citizen. How much do you know about Halawa?' asked Button.

'It's the Arabic word for sweet,' said Shepherd. He grinned when he saw the frown flash across her face. 'I know, it's the underground system of transferring money, it's been around for a thousand years or more. It's used for trading but various terrorist networks are known to use it.'

Button nodded. 'The 9/11 conspirators were funded through Halawa, as were the London Tube bombers.' She tapped the photograph. 'We've no reason to think that al-Faiz is involved with terrorists, but Crazy Boy is a regular visitor to his house, and he usually arrives with a suitcase.' She showed Shepherd another surveillance photograph, this one of two black men entering a terraced house, one of them carrying a large suitcase. The waitress returned with their pizzas and Shepherd passed the photographs back to Button, face down. She slid them back into the envelope.

The waitress offered them black pepper and chilli oil before heading back to the kitchen.

'Al-Faiz has been handling Halawa transactions for Crazy Boy for at least five years. Crazy Boy sends money out to Somalia to fund his gang and he brings some of his profits back the same way. He then runs the cash through his legitimate businesses and the money ends up in his accounts here.'

'So why hasn't SOCA done something about it? Their brief is to recover the proceeds of criminal enterprises, right? And I can't think of an enterprise more criminal than holding ships to ransom, can you?'

'Knowing and proving are two different things, Spider. The Halawa system is almost impossible to break, which is why it's the banking system of choice of al-Qaeda and pretty much every terrorist group there is.'

Shepherd nodded at the envelope. 'Presumably the suitcase in that photograph is full of money. Why didn't the cops just go in and take it? Get him to prove that it wasn't the proceeds of crime?'

'Because at best we'd only get the one suitcase. A million pounds, two maybe. Crazy Boy would probably deny it was his and walk away. Al-Faiz won't have any records, the Halawa players never do. There are no receipts, no electronic trails, it's all in their heads. Maybe a few scribbled figures that will mean nothing to outsiders.'

'But you must be able to follow the money, right? If he's paying off pirates in Somalia, that's a crime, right?'

'The problem with Halawa is that more often than not money doesn't move between countries. Crazy Boy gives the money to al-Faiz. Al-Faiz makes a call or more likely sends an email, probably not even to Somalia. To a middleman in Dubai, maybe. The middleman in Dubai sends an email to his contact in Somalia. The contact in Somalia pays the money to Crazy Boy's uncle. But Crazy Boy's cash never leaves London. It stays with al-Faiz. But everybody in the chain remembers their debt. At some point money will come back from the pirates to Crazy Boy. It all works on trust. Crazy Boy probably doesn't know the middleman in Dubai. He doesn't have to. He trusts al-Faiz and that's all that matters. The player in Mogadishu doesn't know Crazy Boy, but he trusts his contact in Dubai. Each step in the chain works on trust, and the end result is a system that is cheaper, faster and more secure than the banking system.'

'Cheaper?'

'Al-Faiz takes five per cent of any money that he transfers, but he offers an exchange rate that is at least five per cent better than the banks. And a Halawa transfer is almost always same-day, often virtually instantaneous. The banks take three working days or longer. It's an almost perfect system, Spider. And it's not one that we can crack by seizing one suitcase.'

Shepherd nodded reluctantly and sipped his wine.

'So here's the thing, Spider. Crazy Boy went to see al-Faiz yesterday, along with what we assume is a suitcase full of money. At least one million pounds by the look of it. That money will now be in the hands of his uncle in Somalia, which means that he's preparing another operation. If someone is feeding him information then it's either happened or it's about to. If you can nail down who it is and we can tie the informant into the next ship seizure then we can bring Crazy Boy down.' She cut into her pizza. 'Did I say how good you look in a suit, by the way?'

Katie put the binoculars to her eyes and scanned the waves, but she couldn't see anything but water. She took the binoculars away and squinted out to sea. The two dots were larger, and definitely heading their way. 'There's something out there, Hoop,' she said.

Hoop narrowed his eyes and looked where she was pointing, then looked at his radar. 'Nothing on the screen.'

'Could be whales,' she said. She handed the binoculars to him. 'Have a look yourself.'

Hoop put the binoculars to his eyes and stared out to sea for several seconds. 'No, not whales. They're moving way too fast.' He looked over his shoulder. 'Fishermen, maybe. Andrew, what do you think?'

Andrew walked over with his own high-powered binoculars. It took him a while to spot what they were looking at. 'Boats,' he said. 'Skiffs with outboards. Doing forty knots, maybe. They're definitely not out fishing.'

'Terrific,' said Hoop.

'And they're heading this way,' said Andrew, lowering his binoculars. 'What do you want to do?'

'What is it, what's happening?' asked Katie.

'Pirates,' said Hoop.

'What?' said Katie. She laughed nervously. 'You're joking, right?'

'They could be fishermen but it's doubtful in boats like that,' said Andrew. 'We won't know until they get closer.'

Katie took her binoculars back from Hoop and put them to her eyes. The dots had become bigger and were clearly boats with men on board.

'Andrew, get the guns, will you?' said Hoop calmly.

'Guns?' said Katie. 'We've got guns on board?'

'For self-defence,' said Hoop. 'These waters can be problematic at times.'

Andrew left the bridge. Katie put the binoculars to her eyes and scanned the waves again. She found the boats easily this time, and they were a lot closer. There were five black men in the first boat, all young with red scarves tied around their necks.

'Where've they come from?' she asked Hoop. 'They can't have a range of more than a hundred miles or so; they've only got outboards.'

'There'll be a mother ship somewhere, on the horizon, maybe.'

Katie saw one of the men talking into a transceiver. She moved the binoculars to the right and focused on the second boat. There were four men in it, wearing similar red scarves. One of them had something strapped to his back. It was a gun, she realised.

'We can't outrun them, can we?' she said, her voice shaking.

Hoop shook his head. 'They can do thirty, maybe forty knots,' he said. 'We can't do much more than ten. Less with this wind.'

Andrew reappeared with two shotguns and a box of cartridges.

'We're not going to shoot them, are we?' asked Katie.

Hoop smiled and took one of the guns from Andrew.

'They're just for show,' he said. 'To demonstrate that we're not a pushover. They're not after vessels like us. Generally they go for oil tankers or big freighters, vessels where they can get a big ransom.'

'This is a twenty-million-dollar yacht,' said Katie.

'They'll just see us as a sailboat,' said Hoop. 'Don't worry.' He smiled reassuringly.

'You've dealt with pirates before?' asked Katie.

Hoop shook his head. 'First time for everything,' he said. 'Look, we'll just show that we're no pushover and they'll move on to easier pickings,' he said. 'Katie, take the wheel. Andrew and I will go up on deck. They might be on their way somewhere else and go right past us, we could be worrying about nothing.'

Katie held the wheel. 'And what if there is something to worry about?' she said.

'No point in counting chickens,' said Hoop. He patted her on the shoulder. 'It'll be OK.'

Katie forced a smile but she could see from the look in his eyes that Hoop was worried.

Hoop pointed at the compass. 'Stay on that course,' he said. 'Come on, Andrew.'

Hoop and Andrew left the bridge and went to stand by the middle mast. The two skiffs were definitely heading towards them. Hoop swore under his breath and Andrew looked over at him. 'What's the game plan, Hoop?'

'One step at a time,' said Hoop.

Andrew put his binoculars to his eyes and focused on the closest skiff. 'They've got guns, Hoop.'

'So have we. There's a dozen reasons they could be coming this way. They might need water, medicine, they might want to borrow a radio. Just stay calm.' He gestured towards the bow. 'Move forward so that we're not too close. OK?'

Andrew nodded. 'OK.' He moved to stand by the forward mast. The skiffs got closer. One of the men in the leading boat was cradling his weapon. It was a Kalashnikov, Andrew realised. He didn't know much about firearms but he knew that a Kalashnikov was a much more effective weapon than the shotgun he was holding. The skiff was about a hundred yards away and had cut its engines to idle. The second skiff was farther away, to the right of the first one.

Hoop held the shotgun with his right hand and waved with his left. 'Smile,' he said to Andrew. 'Smile but make sure they can see your gun.'

Andrew did as he was told. 'Shouldn't we fire a warning shot?' he said, waving at the two skiffs.

'We're outgunned,' said Hoop. Three of the men in the nearest skiff were now holding Kalashnikovs.

The yacht veered to starboard and Hoop had to hold on to the railing to steady himself.

'Katie! Hold your course!' he shouted.

The skiff to the right had slowed and was heading towards the bow of the yacht. Andrew was holding the shotgun with one hand and grasping the forward mast with the other.

Hoop waved at the men in the closest skiff. 'What do you want?' he shouted.

The men didn't reply. The engines blipped and the skiff moved closer.

'What do you want?' shouted Hoop again.

The three Kalashnikovs were all pointing at the yacht. A fourth man was bending down, doing something at the bottom of the skiff, while a fifth was holding the tiller.

'What do you want to do, Hoop?' shouted Andrew. 'They're getting closer and the shotguns don't seem to be worrying them. Do you want me to fire a warning shot?'

Before Hoop could reply, the man in the skiff straightened up, holding something in both hands. 'Oh shit,' said Hoop when he saw what it was.

'That's an RPG,' said Andrew. 'We are so fucked.'

'They won't fire it,' said Hoop. 'Why would they fire it?'

'Because they're fucking pirates,' said Andrew. 'Shit. What do we do?'

'There's nothing we can do,' said Hoop. 'If they shoot us with that the yacht sinks in seconds. Then what? We're fifty miles from land.'

Andrew said nothing. The blood had drained from his face.

'We're going to have to let them board us,' said Hoop quietly.

'We can shoot their boats, they're pretty fragile by the look of it.'

Hoop shook his head. 'Shotguns are useless beyond fifty feet,' he said. 'The shot spreads out too far.'

'So we wait until they get close and let them have it.'

'There's five in that boat, four in the other. We can't shoot all nine. And even without the RPG they've got us outgunned.'

'I'm going to fire a warning shot!' shouted Andrew, raising the shotgun to his shoulder.

There was a short burst of fire from one of the men in the skiff. He'd fired over the top of the masts but he slowly took aim at Andrew.

'Put the gun down, Andrew!' shouted Hoop.

Andrew slowly did as he was told.

'Start taking the sails in,' said Hoop.

'We can't just surrender,' said Andrew.

'We can't fight them and we can't outrun them. And the longer we leave it, the more we're going to piss them off. Now put down the gun and bring in the sails.'

Hoop ran back to the bridge.

'What's happening?' said Katie.

'We're going to have to let them board us,' said Hoop. 'They've got an RPG.'

'A what?'

'A rocket-propelled grenade launcher,' said Hoop. 'It'd blow right through the hull, we'd be matchwood.'

'What do they want?' asked Katie. 'Are they going to rob us?'

'I don't know,' said Hoop. 'They might just take our food and valuables but they might . . .' He tailed off. The yacht was slowing as Andrew pulled in the sails.

'They might what?' said Katie, her voice trembling.

'They're pirates, Katie. They might want to take us hostage. For ransom.'

'No,' said Katie, hugging herself.

'It'll be OK, there's no need for them to hurt us, we're too valuable as hostages. Just smile and don't offer any resistance.'

'This can't be happening,' said Katie. 'Can't we call someone? I thought the navy was out here.'

'It's a big sea, Katie,' said Hoop. 'By the time anyone can reach us it'll all be over. I'll call it in but go down and get Joy and Eric up on deck.'

Hoop reached for the radio as Katie rushed below deck. He tuned it to Channel 16 and clicked the microphone. 'Mayday, mayday, mayday,' he said. 'Mayday, this is the *Natalya*. Mayday, mayday, mayday. We are about to be boaded by pirates.' He read his position off the GPS. 'We have a crew of five and no passengers, repeat five souls on board. The *Natalya* is a 185-foot three-masted schooner.' He gave their position again. 'Mayday, mayday, mayday, is anyone receiving me?'

He took his finger off the transmit button and listened. There was nothing but static.

He heard the rattle of gunfire off the port bow and flinched. He looked over to the left and saw that one of the pirates was standing up and brandishing his AK-47. He looked through the window and saw Andrew standing up, his hands held high.

Hoop pressed the transmit button. 'This is the *Natalya*, we're about to be boarded by pirates, can anyone hear me?'

Katie hurtled down the wood-panelled corridor and banged on the door to Eric's cabin. 'What?' he shouted.

'Pirates!' she shouted. 'We're being attacked!' She banged on the door again with the flat of her hand. 'Get the hell out, now!'

Eric threw open the door. He was wearing only tartan boxer shorts and his hair was unkempt. He was blinking as if he'd just woken up. 'What are you talking about?' he asked, rubbing his eyes.

'Hoop wants you on deck. There're pirates trying to board us.'

'You're joking, right?'

Katie grabbed his arm, her fingers biting into the flesh. 'Get on deck now!' she yelled.

Joy opened her cabin door and peered down the corridor, wondering what the noise was.

Outside there was a burst of gunfire, followed by angry shouts.

'Katie, what's happening?' shouted Joy.

'Pirates!' Katie shouted back. 'There are pirates with guns and they want to board us.'

Joy hurried down the corridor. There were more shouts from above deck. It sounded like Andrew. 'Are you serious?' she said.

'Dead serious,' said Katie. 'They've got an RPG.'

'Oh my God,' said Joy. 'What's Hoop doing?'

'He's calling for help on the radio but he says we can't stop them boarding.'

'Why are they boarding us?' said Eric. 'We're a yacht, we haven't got anything they want.'

'We're what they want,' said Joy. 'Don't you watch TV? They kidnap people.'

'Not yachts,' said Eric.

'Yes, yachts,' said Joy, nodding. 'They take anyone hostage, they don't care. And this boat is worth millions.'

'Hoop wants us all on deck,' said Katie.

'Maybe he can talk to them,' said Eric.

'Eric, Hoop says now. Everyone up on deck now!'

They heard Andrew shouting again and the tat-tat-tat of automatic gunfire.

'Oh my God, Andrew,' gasped Joy, and she headed down the corridor and up the stairs that led to the deck.

'Did you see them, the pirates?' asked Eric as he grabbed a pair of jeans from his bunk and pulled them on.

'They were in two boats. They had guns and the RPG. Hoop said they can outrun us.'

'I thought we had guns on board?' said Eric. He picked

up a T-shirt and stepped out of the cabin. 'Are you going up?'

'I need the bathroom,' she said.

Eric nodded and padded down the corridor in his bare feet. Katie watched him go up the stairs to the deck, her mind in a whirl. Her heart was pounding and she felt as if she was close to fainting. She'd seen the look of hatred on the faces of the men in the boats and she doubted that there'd be any reasoning with them. She could tell that Hoop was scared, too. He had tried to put a brave face on it but he couldn't hide the fact that he knew what a dangerous situation they were in. She ran down the corridor to the master cabin and threw open the door. It was a huge room, panelled in light oak, with a king-sized four-poster bed, a walk-in closet and a marble-lined bathroom with a massive shower and a roll-top bath. She closed the door and leaned against it, panting like a racehorse that had been ridden too hard. She wanted to hide, to be somewhere they wouldn't find her, and then after they'd done whatever it was they wanted to do they'd leave and she'd be OK. She rushed over to the bathroom. The shower walls were glass, and the bath was in the middle of the room. There was a porthole beyond the bath and she peered through it just in time to see one of the boats whizz by, the men in it shouting and screaming and waving their guns. She jumped back as if she'd been stung.

'OK, OK, OK,' she muttered to herself. 'It's going to be OK. Stay calm, Katie, come on. It's a game. Hide and seek. We're playing hide and seek. Now think.'

There was room to hide behind the bathroom door so she stood there but realised immediately that she could be seen in the mirrored wall of the cabin. She went back into the cabin and opened the closet doors. The rails and shelves were empty. There was a shoe cupboard at the far end but it was lined with shelves with no room to hide. She could stay in the closet but anyone who opened the doors would see her immediately.

'Coming ready or not,' she whispered to herself. 'It's only a game. All you have to do is to find somewhere to hide.'

There were drawers underneath the bed, two on one side and one on the other that ran the full length of the bed. She pulled open the large one. It was filled with a duvet. She pulled it out. The drawer was about the size of a coffin. Big enough for a body. Big enough to hide in. There was another burst of gunfire from the starboard side, and more cheering. She could hear Hoop shouting but couldn't make out what he was saying.

There was a silk bedspread on the bed and she pulled it off, then threw the duvet on and smoothed it out. She heard footsteps running across the deck above her head and her heart pounded. She threw the bedspread over the duvet then rushed around the bed straightening it, and ran to the side with the drawer. She pushed it halfway in, which left just enough room for her to slip inside. She lay down on the floor then slid her left arm and leg into the drawer, grunting as she pushed up with her right arm and eased herself inside. There was plenty of room to slide in and then she rolled over on to her back, breathing heavily. She placed the palms of her hands flat on the wood above her head and pushed hard, levering the drawer into the bed. It barely moved and she tried again, panting with the effort. It moved a couple of inches. Katie was drenched in sweat and the third time she tried it her hands slid across the wood. 'It's OK, it's OK,' she muttered. 'You can do this, Katie.' She wiped her hands on her shirt and tried again, this time bucking her body up with her heels and shoulders. It worked and the drawer slid in two inches. The gap was now less than six inches. She kept pushing and gradually the gap closed. Five inches. Three inches. Two inches. An inch. Katie gasped and put her hands on her stomach, her chest rising and falling as she sucked in air.

She heard more footsteps on the deck, and shouts. She forced herself to breathe slowly. 'Coming ready or not,' she whispered.

Joy hurtled on to the bridge. 'Where's Andrew?' she shouted. 'Where is he? What's happening?'

Hoop was standing with one hand on the wheel, the radio in the other. 'By the forward mast,' he said. 'He's OK, they're just firing to make us stop.' He clicked the transmit button. 'This is the *Natalya*. Mayday, mayday, mayday. Can anyone hear me?'

'I thought the navy was out here, protecting ships?'

'We're not near the secure corridor,' said Hoop.

'Why the hell not?'

'Because we're a yacht, Joy, and we'd be asking for trouble trying to sail among freighters and tankers. The corridor isn't for pleasure craft.'

Joy headed for the deck. 'Stay here, stay on the bridge,' said Hoop.

'Screw you, Hoop, I'm going to my husband.' She pushed open the door and rushed forward. Andrew had placed the shotgun on the deck and had one hand in the air while he used the other to balance himself against the mast.

'Joy, go back inside!' Andrew shouted.

She ignored him and hurried along the deck. When she reached him she put her arm around his waist and pressed her face against his shoulder. That was when she saw the pirates for the first time, four black men with guns while a fifth sat at the back of the skiff with his hand on a tiller that connected to two huge outboard engines. He was gunning the engines, edging the skiff towards the yacht. 'What do you want?' Joy screamed at them. 'We haven't got any money! This isn't our yacht, we're just hired hands!'

'Joy, don't antagonise them,' hissed her husband.

Joy saw the RPG, a bulbous shell at the end, the pirate holding it so that it was pointing at the bow. His finger was on the trigger mechanism, she realised. All he had to do was pull it and the yacht would be destroyed. The skiff was close enough for her to see the manic gleam in the man's eyes.

'Go back to the bridge, Joy,' said Andrew.

She shook her head. 'I'm staying here with you.'

She heard the roar of engines and she looked to the left and saw a second skiff, this one slightly smaller with four pirates on board. One of the pirates was reaching out to grab the handrail and he locked eyes with her. He was tall with greasy dreadlocks and he sneered at her as he hauled himself on board. His bare feet slapped on to the deck and then he swung his Kalashnikov from around his shoulder and aimed it at her.

Katie flinched as she heard a door to one of the cabins bang shut, then there were footsteps and another loud bang. She was soaking wet and rivulets of sweat were running down her neck and between her breasts. She heard shouts in a language she didn't recognise. She closed her eyes and clenched her hands.

A man laughed and then she heard the door to the cabin burst open. She heard bare feet on the wooden floor as he went over to the bathroom, and then a second voice and feet padding over to the closet. She heard the closet doors opening and a man laughing, then the bed shook and she realised that someone had climbed on to it. There was more deep-throated laughter and then the bed began to shake. He was jumping up and down on the bed, she realised. Playing like a child.

The bed shook with each jump, harder and harder, then there was a loud thump and the bouncing stopped.

Katie squeezed her eyes shut tighter. She bit down on the knuckle of her right index finger and concentrated on the pain.

She heard the sound of wood scratching against wood and the bed vibrated. They were pulling open one of the drawers on the other side of the bed.

She placed the palms of her hands against the wood above her face and pressed. Maybe if she pressed hard enough she could stop them opening her drawer.

She heard a crash as the drawer was thrown across the cabin, then a scraping sound as the second drawer was pulled out.

She began to tremble as footsteps padded around the bed. She pushed harder. The drawer shook but it didn't move. The man who was trying to get it open said something and she heard a second man join the first and they both began to pull at the drawer. She felt her palms slide across the wood above her head and she pushed up with all her might but it made no difference.

She heard whoops of triumph and she opened her eyes and gasped as she saw two black men staring down at her. Their eyes were wide and they were grinning, their teeth white slabs. Katie began to scream as they pulled out the drawer and hauled her out. She tried to kick one of them but he seized her wrist and twisted it around her back and then threw her on to the bed. She rolled over on to her back, panting. She held up her hands. 'Please, don't hurt me,' she said.

The two men looked at each other and said something in their language and then laughed.

The younger of the two was a teenager, tall and lanky, wearing a sweat-stained Nike T-shirt and raggedy denim jeans that had been hacked off above the knees. He was barefooted, as was his companion, a stocky man with a shaved head and pockmarked cheeks who was wearing a white string vest and cargo pants with a rope belt. The younger one had a machete tucked into his belt and his companion had an AK-47 hanging over his back from a webbing strap. They both turned to look at Katie, laughing.

Katie scrambled backwards until she banged against the headboard. 'Do you speak English?' she said, her voice trembling. 'French? *Parlez-vous français?*'

The younger man pulled out his machete and waved it menacingly at her.

Katie drew up her legs. Tears were streaming down her cheeks. 'Please, just take me to the others,' she said, wiping her nose with the back of her hand.

The man with the machete jumped on to the bed and

straddled her. She tried to push him away but he jammed the machete under her chin and screamed at her.

'OK, OK,' she said. 'Don't hurt me.'

The teenager laughed and ran the tip of the machete down between her breasts and across her stomach, then slipped it under the bottom of her T-shirt and used the blade to rip it down the middle. He grinned as he saw her breasts rise and fall, then he used the blade to cut her bra.

Katie wailed like an animal in pain, her eyes wide with terror.

The second man took off his AK-47 and leaned it against the wall of the cabin, then pushed the younger man to the side and started pulling off Katie's shorts.

She screamed and tried to stop him but stopped struggling when the machete was thrust under her chin again.

The man ripped off her shorts and tossed them to the floor. The younger man used the machete to cut away what was left of her T-shirt and bra. Katie tried to cover her breasts with her hands as she sobbed.

The older man slid his fingers inside her pants and slowly pulled them off.

'Please, don't do this,' sobbed Katie, as the man untied his rope belt and pulled down his cargo pants. He was already erect as he got on to the bed.

The younger man said something but the older one shouted at him. They were arguing over who was going to rape her first, Katie realised.

'I've got money,' she said. 'I can pay you.'

The older man forced her legs apart as he climbed on top of her. She struggled but the man with the machete waved it menacingly over her head and screamed at her.

He made a chopping motion with the weapon and the message was clear – if she fought, he'd kill her.

She lay still and turned her head away from him. 'Please,' she begged, 'won't you at least wear a condom?' She screamed as the man entered, his foul-smelling mouth just inches from hers as he grunted with every thrust.

There was a knock on the door and Charlotte Button looked up as it opened. A tall Asian man in his early thirties popped his head around the door. 'You wanted a chat?' he said.

'More than a chat, Amar, come in,' said Button. She waved him to a sofa that had been shoehorned into her cubicle of an office. Thames House was full to capacity and the office she'd been allocated was about half the size of the one she'd occupied when she'd worked for the Serious Organised Crime Agency.

Amar Singh worked for MI5's technical support section, and had moved with Button when she had transferred from SOCA. From the moment that Button had first met Singh she had been impressed with his technical knowledge and positive attitude. Singh never saw problems, only challenges, and he would work as long and as hard as it took to overcome any obstacle in his way. He was wearing a soft brown leather jacket that glistened under the office lights, Armani jeans and a grey silk shirt, with a thin gold chain around his neck, and he sat with the straight spine and confident poise of a male model waiting for the camera to start clicking away.

'How's the family?' asked Button.

'A handful, as always,' said Singh, and he flashed a Bollywood-star smile. 'Being the only man in a family of women is getting tiring. But Mishti is pregnant again so we're hoping to redress the balance.'

'Congratulations,' said Button. 'Give Mishti my best. And the job, everything is OK? They're looking after you?'

Singh had been reluctant to leave SOCA and its gold-plated pension and it had taken a large jump in salary to convince him to move to MI5. 'It's been a blast so far,' he said. 'I can't believe the toys I'm getting to play with. They're using stuff I never even heard about with SOCA. You know, we've got cameras here that can pretty much look through walls? They use infrared detectors but they are so sensitive that we can make out the sort of detail that you get with regular cameras. Had a job last week where we needed the combination of a target's safe and we were able to pick out the keyboard code as the target tapped it in. And we were sitting in a van outside his house.' He leaned forward, his eyes sparkling. 'How cool is that?'

'Amazing,' said Button, amused as always by Singh's enthusiasm for all things technical. 'Let me tell you about a problem I've got that needs your talents. We're looking at a guy in Ealing who's running an operation out in East Africa. Up until a few months ago he was using phones all the time but then he switched to a computer.'

'He probably figured out that it's not enough just to change Sim cards these days. We can listen in on phones no matter what Sim card is in.'

'Whatever the reason, he's started using mobiles a lot less. We were able to monitor his email traffic through GCHQ and all was good but now he's using Skype. We haven't been able to access his Skype account so we need to get something in the house that will let us monitor his Skype conversations.'

'Not a problem,' said Singh. 'How many computers does he have in the house?'

Button shook her head. 'I don't know,' she said. 'We haven't been able to get inside.'

'Does he use dongles or does he have wifi in the house?'

Button shrugged. 'Sorry, Amar. All we know is that he opened a Skype account three weeks ago. I don't know anything about the equipment he uses.'

'I'll check our databases,' said Singh. 'If he has wifi in the house it's just a matter of getting our own router in there. We can do that in minutes – we just arrange for his service to go down and when he rings up to complain we take in our own equipment. It's a bit more complicated with dongles but the principle is the same.' He grinned and stood up. 'I thought you were going to ask me for something difficult.'

'Always a pleasure doing business with you, Amar, thanks.'

The boat powered across the waves, bucking and lurching like a living thing. Katie held on to the side of the skiff and narrowed her eyes against the wind. Tears were dragged across her cheeks and she sniffed and spat saliva over the side.

Hoop was sitting opposite her but he kept avoiding her eyes. He felt guilty, Katie knew, because he was the captain and she had been his responsibility and he hadn't been able to prevent what they'd done to her. Hoop's left eye was almost closed where he'd been struck with the butt of an AK-47 when he'd argued with them about leaving the yacht. The pirates had screamed at them and pointed at the two skiffs moored alongside the *Natalya*. Hoop had said that there was no reason for them to be taken off the yacht and one of the pirates had smashed him across the face.

The pirates didn't speak English or French and Joy had even tried a few words of Arabic but there didn't seem to be any way of communicating with them. That was what made it so frightening, they had no idea where they were being taken or what the pirates planned to do with them.

Katie shifted on her seat and grimaced as she felt sperm trickle down her thigh. They hadn't let her shower after raping her, just thrown her off the bed and tossed her clothes at her. The T-shirt had been ruined but she had managed to grab another one from the laundry basket. She tried to blot out what they'd done to her but images kept flooding back. The machete. The foul smell of their breath. The hatred in their eyes as they'd pounded into her and the way they'd laughed afterwards. She was nothing to them, they knew nothing about her and they didn't care, they'd just wanted to use her.

She sniffed and wiped her eyes with the back of her hand. The man who'd been the first to rape her was standing at the front of the boat, looking out over the sea. The second man who'd abused her was in a second boat, following them across the waves.

Eric and Joy were in the second boat. The pirates hadn't tied them up or gagged them. There was no need. The pirates had guns and knives and they were all lean, hard men with the scars to prove that they were no strangers to violence.

Katie flinched as a hand touched her on the shoulder but then she realised it was Andrew. 'Are you OK?' he mouthed.

Katie shook her head. No, she wasn't OK. She'd never be OK again. She wasn't a virgin, she'd had two serious relationships at university and several flings, but the men who had raped her had changed her for ever. She closed her eyes and wished that she was dead.

Andrew squeezed her shoulder again but she shook him off. She didn't want anyone to touch her.

The sound of the engines faded for a few seconds and Katie opened her eyes. One of the pirates at the back of the boat was standing up and talking into a transceiver. He was the oldest of the group, in his mid-thirties maybe, with jet-black skin and greasy ringlets almost down to his neck. He was wearing a photographer's vest with dozens of small pockets on it and jeans that had been cut off at the knees, and around his neck was a leather necklace with a single shark's tooth hanging from it. The pirate saw that Katie was looking at him and he grinned at her, showing blackened teeth as he pressed the transceiver to his ear. As he stared at her he slowly licked his lips and widened his eyes. Katie shuddered and looked away.

Crazy Boy used an Uzi to spray bullets at a passing Porsche and the car spun off the road and burst into flames. The driver climbed out, screaming in pain as he tried to extinguish his burning shirt with his hands. Crazy Boy switched to his sawn-off shotgun and blew off the man's head with one shot. 'That's the way to do it!' he shouted. He reloaded and ran down the street towards a group of drug dealers. They looked his way and reached into their jackets, where he knew they had MAC-10s. He switched back to his Uzi as he ran and blew them away.

The entryphone buzzed. 'Who the fuck's that?' he shouted.

Levi's walked over to the bank of CCTV screens, stripping leaves off a khat twig and popping them into his mouth. He picked up the receiver. 'Yeah?' he said, through a mouthful of khat. 'What do you want?' He listened, then replaced the receiver. 'Internet guy at the gate,' he said.

'Yeah, they said they'd be here today,' said Two Knives.

'About bloody time,' said Crazy Boy. 'What the fuck are we paying for if it keeps going down? I wanna play Halo online and I can't do that with no internet. And I need to talk to my uncle and can't trust the fucking phones.'

'Buzz him in,' Two Knives said to Levi's. He pointed at the two Glocks on the table by the window. 'And hide the guns upstairs.'

Levi's did as he was told.

'Don't forget to frisk him,' said Crazy Boy.

'He's the internet guy, how can I frisk him?' asked Two Knives.

'Same as you frisk anyone who comes into this house,' said Crazy Boy. 'He could be anyone.'

'I called the internet company, they said they'd send a guy. This is him.' A blue van pulled up outside the house.

Crazy Boy looked over his shoulder. 'Just do it,' he said.

Two Knives nodded, knowing that to argue would only provoke an angry outburst. Crazy Boy never reacted well to criticism, even when he was in the wrong, and especially when he was high on khat. Two Knives had learned the hard way that the best way to handle his boss was to agree and smile and to do as he was told. They heard the van door open and slam shut and footsteps heading for the front door. Two Knives got there just as the doorbell rang and he opened the door to see a tall Asian man in dark blue overalls carrying a plastic toolbox in one hand and a clipboard and cardboard box in the other. He had a company ID pinned to his chest pocket. He smiled at Two Knives. 'Simeon Khalid?'

'This is the right house,' said Two Knives. 'I need to look in your toolbox.'

The Asian frowned. 'My what?'

Two Knives gestured at the box. 'Can you open it for me?'

The Asian's frown deepened. 'It's just my tools.'

'Just open it for me, please.'

The Asian sighed, then gave the clipboard and box to Two Knives so that he could use both hands to open the toolbox. Two Knives saw only tools, wire and insulation tape. 'Happy?' said the Asian. He closed the toolbox and took the clipboard and cardboard box back.

Two Knives lifted his hands and touched the Asian on the hips. The Asian stepped back. 'What the hell are you doing?'

'I need to check that you're not carrying a weapon.'

'A weapon? Are you crazy? I'm a technician. You called us, remember?' He looked at the clipboard. 'Simeon Khalid?' He showed the clipboard to Two Knives. 'And this is the right address?'

'It's the right address,' said Two Knives patiently. 'But we have had security problems in the past and my boss insists.'

The Asian laughed. 'What do you think, I'm carrying a gun?'

'Look, just let me pat you down. There's a tip in it when you're done.'

The Asian nodded. 'That's more like it,' he said, putting down the toolbox and raising his arms. 'Pat away.'

Two Knives ran his hands up and down the overalls but didn't find anything out of the ordinary.

'You should think about installing a metal detector, the sort of thing they use at airports,' said the Asian as he picked up his toolbox.

'Through there,' said Two Knives, nodding at the sitting room. The Asian walked down the hall and Two Knives could smell his aftershave, sweet with a hint of oranges and something else. He closed the door and went after him.

'Manhunt, huh?' said the Asian as he looked at the screen. 'Cool game.'

'You play?' said Crazy Boy.

'Yeah, but I'm a fan of PlayStation 3. I prefer the graphics.'

'Yeah? Same games, though, right?'

'Pretty much. But I prefer the PlayStation controller. Better feel.' He looked around the room. 'So your internet connection died, yeah?'

'It was intermittent yesterday and went completely last night,' said Crazy Boy.

'Where's the router?' asked the Asian.

'Study,' said Crazy Boy, still watching the screen. 'Show him, yeah?' he called over to Two Knives.

Two Knives pointed at the door to the study. 'In there,' he said, and he took the Asian through. The study had been furnished by the Indian businessman who'd owned the house before Crazy Boy in the same garish style as the rest of the house. There was a huge gilt desk with ornate legs like Grecian pillars and behind it the window was covered by thick red velvet drapes hanging from a gold pole that had a gilt lion's head at either end. On one wall was a large

LED television and facing it a six-foot-square painting of the Taj Mahal at sunset.

'Nice,' said the Asian, looking around.

'You like this crap?' asked Two Knives.

'I mean the computer,' said the Asian, nodding at the Sony computer on the desk. 'Latest model. It's only been out a few months.'

'Yeah, my boss changes his computer every few months.'

'Yeah? Why's that?'

'He just does,' said Two Knives. He pointed at the black box on a side table next to a Hewlett-Packard printer. 'That's the internet thing.'

'The router,' said the Asian. 'It's called a router.'

'I don't give a fuck what's it called, I just want it fixed.'

The Asian smiled so condescendingly that Two Knives was tempted to punch him in the face. 'We don't fix them these days. They're sealed units made in China so if they break we just change the whole thing.' He picked up the router and examined the back. 'Did you try switching it off for ten seconds and then switching it on again?'

'We did that.'

'And rebooting your computer?'

'We did everything.'

'It's Plan C, then.'

'Plan C?' repeated Two Knives.

The Asian grinned and opened the cardboard box. 'I give you a new one,' he said. He unplugged the old router and put it in the box, then attached the power cable and the phone line to the new unit and switched it on. He nodded at the computer on the desk. 'Mind if I reboot it?'

'Let me talk to the boss,' said Two Knives. He went to the door. 'He wants to use the computer, is that OK?'

'No it's not fucking OK!' shouted Crazy Boy. 'How the fuck could that be OK?' He paused the game and grabbed a handful of khat leaves before joining Two Knives and the Asian in the study. He pointed at the computer. 'What do you want?'

'Just to check that it's working,' said the Asian. 'Reboot and then check that the existing password still works. If it doesn't we'll have to reset it.' He gestured at Two Knives. 'Your friend here didn't want me to touch it.'

'Yeah, he's right,' said Crazy Boy, sitting at the desk. 'There's personal stuff on it.'

'I hear you,' said the Asian. 'I wouldn't want anyone looking at my internet history either.'

Crazy Boy switched off the computer and then switched it back on.

'You should think about getting a Mac,' said the Asian. 'Faster boot-up, zero viruses, none of that "not responding" crap.'

Crazy Boy ignored him and waited for Windows to start working, then launched Internet Explorer. He visited a few pages and then nodded. 'It's working,' he said.

'We aim to please,' the Asian said. 'So you're Mr Khalid?'

'What's it to you?' Crazy Boy scowled.

The Asian smiled amiably as he held out his clipboard. 'I need your signature.'

Crazy Boy scrawled his signature and went back to his computer. Two Knives took the Asian back into the hall and opened the front door.

'What about my tip?' asked the Asian.

'Go fuck yourself,' said Two Knives, and slammed the door in his face. He went back to the study, where Crazy Boy was still sitting at the desk. 'I hate Indians,' said Two Knives.

'Yeah, you and me both,' said Crazy Boy. 'But he did the job. I need to talk to my uncle tonight. Things are starting to move.'

Robbie Fox prodded the burning logs with the brass poker and stood back as a shower of sparks rushed up the chimney. He waited until the logs had calmed down before giving them a final prod and putting the poker back on its stand. He sat down in his easy chair and picked up his glass of Laphroaig. 'How's your drink there, Lisa?' he asked, nodding at the glass in O'Hara's hand.

'I'm fine, Uncle Robbie,' she said. 'Just fine.' They were sitting in Fox's farmhouse on the outskirts of Newry. Fox's two spaniels were sitting by the door, their ears pricking up every time they heard a word that sounded like 'walk'. She looked around the large room with its fireplace big enough to walk into, its oak dining table that could sit ten people with ease, and the massive wood-burning stove where Robbie Fox's wife used to produce the best stews and casseroles that O'Hara had ever eaten. She'd died five years earlier after a long battle with cancer, but O'Hara still expected her to walk in at any moment, rubbing her hands on her apron before giving her a big, floury hug. She smiled over at her uncle. 'You're never going to leave here, are you, Uncle Robbie?'

'They'll have to carry me out in a box, love,' he said, swirling the whisky around his glass.

The farmhouse had once been the centre of five hundred

acres of farmland, but after his wife had died Robbie had signed it over to his sons, Padraig and Sean, and left them to the farming. But the two men had disappeared and were believed to have been murdered and buried somewhere on the land that Fox had given them. Despite extensive searches the bodies had never been found, but Robbie Fox was sure that he knew who had killed them, an SAS major who was now himself dead and buried. Major Alan Gannon had been killed by a car bomb outside his London home and it was Robbie's niece, the pretty red-haired woman sitting in front of him, who had arranged it.

'So how did it go in the States?' asked Fox.

'The guy who introduced Tanner was an ATF agent working undercover. The ATF guy doesn't know who Tanner works for. Of course, Tanner isn't his real name. He was deep undercover. MI5 or PSNI or maybe SAS.' O'Hara took a still photograph taken from a CCTV camera and gave it to him. 'Recognise him?'

Fox shook his head.

'I got this from one of the Irish pubs in New York. It'll give us something to go on because Nicholas Brett was a dead end.'

'Literally, I hear,' said Fox.

O'Hara looked surprised. 'What big ears you have.'

'Aye, and I keep them to the ground,' he said. 'You did a good job there, Lisa.'

'I had a good team with me,' she said. She took back the photograph. 'What do I do now, Robbie? He killed Connolly and Hughes. He blew our operation wide open. Because of him Maguire and the rest are behind bars. But he's gone to ground, and he'll be well protected.'

'What do you think you should do?'

O'Hara sighed. 'They need to be taught a lesson,' she said. 'They need to know that if they use spies then there's a price to be paid.'

Fox nodded. 'I don't think that the Army Council will see it any other way,' he said.

'But he's gone, Robbie. It's like he was never there. His flat's empty, his car registration number no longer exists, his phone number has just disappeared. Every trace of him has gone.' She held up the photograph. 'Except for this.'

Fox nodded. 'He'll be out of the country by now, for sure. There's no chance that he was working for the Yanks?'

'Almost certainly not. Brett was ATF and he was looking at several groups there. But Tanner or whoever he was used the New York connection as a way of getting into the cell in Belfast. The Americans wouldn't have any interest in Northern Ireland, not in that way. It was the Brits, Robbie. The Brits or the Belfast cops.' She sighed. 'I'm not sure where to go next.'

'You need someone on the inside,' he said. 'Inside the PSNI or MI5.'

'Do you have someone, Robbie?'

Fox chuckled. 'That would be need-to-know, Lisa,' he said.

'I've heard that we have, that's why I'm asking. Sleepers, in so deep that no one will ever find them, burrowing away to be used at some point in the future.'

'Now that would be a fine thing, wouldn't it?' said Fox, his eyes twinkling.

'It's true, though, isn't it? It makes sense. The cops have been bending over backwards to hire Catholics and MI5 has been recruiting like crazy at Loughside.'

'Lisa, if we did have sleepers like that, I wouldn't be told about them. I wouldn't want to be told, either. A secret like that could be a dangerous thing.'

'But there must be someone on the Council who would know, right?' She held up the photograph. 'If there was someone with access to the MI5 and PSNI databases, they could get us a name. Couldn't they?'

Fox shrugged. 'Maybe.'

'Can you ask, Robbie? Can you raise it with the Council?'

Fox took the photograph from her and stared at it. He nodded slowly. 'Aye, let's give it a go,' he said.

Amar Singh parked his van in the car park next to the McDonald's outlet and called Charlotte Button on her mobile. 'It's all done,' he said. 'Everything he does on any computer connected to the router will be copied to our database. You can access it at the URL I gave you from anywhere in the world in real time, and you'll be automatically emailed a report every six hours with a list of all the sites he has visited and copies of all emails that he sends and receives.'

'And the Skype?'

'If you're online when he's Skyping you can watch it real-time, otherwise you can watch and hear any transmissions at your leisure. They'll be stored for ever, or at least until you delete them.'

'Excellent, Amar. Thanks.'

'I'm sure I don't have to tell you that anything we get from the router won't be admissible in court because we didn't have a warrant,' said Singh.

'Not a problem, Amar. We just need the intel.'

Singh ended the call and got out of the car. His daughters were big fans of Chicken McNuggets and ever since she'd fallen pregnant his wife had developed a craving for McFlurries. He smiled to himself, knowing that he was going to win some serious Brownie points when he got home.

The cabin door opened and Katie moaned. She rolled on to her back and opened her legs, knowing that there was no point in struggling. If she lay where she was with her eyes closed, then she was raped and it was usually over quickly. If she fought, then they'd beat her and she would still be raped and it would take longer. They seemed to enjoy it more when she put up a fight so now she just let them do what they wanted.

The cabin was small, barely eight feet long and six feet wide, with a porthole less than a foot across which had been opened to allow in some fresh air. Katie lay on a single bunk and across from her was a built-in cupboard and a small sink. They had run a chain from her ankle to the hinge of the porthole and given her just enough play on the chain to reach the sink. She drank water from the tap when she was thirsty and washed herself as best she could, though they hadn't given her a towel and she was still wearing the T-shirt and shorts that she'd had on when they took her off the yacht.

She was on a fishing boat, no more than sixty feet long, with four small cabins at the bow and a large hold for the catch at the stern. The skiffs had moored next to the boat and she'd had a quick glimpse of half a dozen Somali men and a pile of nets and then she'd been dragged to the cabin and shackled. Katie tried to remember how long ago that had been. Two days? Three? She couldn't remember.

They'd fed her, she remembered that much. They'd fed her several times, soggy rice on a plastic plate, usually with a piece of rancid meat and once with a fish that was more bone than flesh, and once they'd given her a bunch of green bananas.

'You are British?' said a voice. It was the first time she'd been spoken to in her own language since the pirates had boarded the yacht. She opened her eyes. The man standing in the doorway was holding her passport. He was tall, with skin so dark that it glistened like wet coal. His hair hung down to his shoulders in greasy dreadlocks. Around his neck was a white shark's tooth hanging from a leather necklace. It was the man from the skiff that had brought her to the fishing boat.

'British?' he asked. He jabbed a finger at the passport. 'You British?'

'You speak English?' said Katie.

The man grinned, revealing a row of blackened teeth. 'London?' he said. 'You know London?'

Katie nodded. 'Yes, I know London.'

The man tapped his chest. 'My cousin live in London. Son of the brother of my father. Rich man.'

Katie nodded tearfully. 'OK,' she said.

The man waved the passport in front of her face. 'One day I go to London,' he said. 'Have passport, same you.'

'What?' said Katie, squinting at the man. 'What do you mean?'

'I go stay London,' he said. 'Anyone can live in London. Anyone can have passport.'

Katie suddenly realised what he meant. 'What's your name?' she asked. She pointed at herself. 'I am Katie.'

'Roobie,' he said.

'That's great, Roobie,' she said. 'Look, I can help you.' She nodded encouragingly. 'My father knows the prime minister. Understand? The prime minister. The big boss of England. He can get passport for you.' She smiled and nodded. 'OK? You understand? I can help you get a passport.'

Roobie sneered at her. 'I not need help from you. Need money.' He took out a key and used it to unlock the padlock that fixed the chain to the porthole. 'Come with me,' he said, yanking the chain and heading for the corridor. There were two more pirates there, holding machetes. They were both teenagers and they had both raped her the previous day. They grinned at her and one of them made an obscene gesture.

They bundled her along the corridor and pushed open the door to another cabin. Joy was sitting cross-legged on her bunk. 'Katie!' she gasped. She stood up and they hugged. She too had been chained to her porthole. She was wearing a T-shirt and had a towel wrapped around her waist. She sobbed as she hugged Katie and then Katie started to cry.

'Sit!' shouted Roobie. He thrust Katie's passport at her and took Joy's passport from his back pocket. 'Hold these,' he said.

The two women sat together on the bunk, wiping away their tears. Another pirate appeared at the door. It was the man in the vest, the first man to rape her. He was holding a small Sony video camera. He leered at Katie and licked his lips suggestively but stopped when Roobie flashed him a warning look.

'We make movie,' said Roobie. 'Make movie put on internet so we get money.'

'Ransom?' said Katie. 'You want a ransom?'

'Just let us go, please,' said Joy. 'We're not anybody impor-tant, we're just sailors. We were just taking the yacht . . .'

Roobie stepped forward and slapped her across the face and she fell back on the bunk, sobbing.

Katie put up her hands. She felt surprisingly calm now that she had someone she could talk to. 'Roobie, please, just listen to me. I can help you get what you want. But you have to stop hurting us. If you hurt us, no one is going to help you, do you understand?'

Roobie pointed a finger at her face. 'You talk to camera. Say you want them pay ransom or we kill you.'

'You're not going to kill us, though, are you?' said Katie. 'That wouldn't make sense, would it?'

Roobie raised his hand to hit her and Katie scurried back on the bunk until she was up against the wall of the cabin. 'OK, OK,' she said.

'Hold up passports and talk to the camera,' he said.

Katie nodded. 'OK,' she repeated. She put her arm around Joy. 'Come on, babe, we have to do what he says.'

'They're going to kill us, I know they are.' Joy sniffed. 'They're not going to let us go, not after what they've done to us.'

'They just want money,' whispered Katie. 'If they get a ransom, they'll let us go.'

'Who's going to pay money for me?' asked Joy. Tears streamed down her face. 'Me and Andrew, we haven't got a penny to our name. He hasn't spoken to his parents in ten years and my dad died when I was a kid. My mum lives in a council house in Milton Keynes.' She began to sob and Katie hugged her.

The pirate with the camera pressed the 'record' button and a red light glowed. Katie held up her passport. 'My name is Katie Cranham,' she said. 'This is Joy Ashmore.

We were crewing the *Natalya*, from Dubai on the way to Sydney. We've been kidnapped by pirates and they say that they'll kill us if you don't pay what they want.' The words caught in her throat and she began to cry. 'Mummy, Daddy, please, I want to come home.' Tears streamed down her cheeks and she covered her eyes with her passport. More than anything in the world she wanted to be back with her parents, sitting in their farmhouse kitchen in front of the Aga with the family Labrador at her feet.

Roobie said something to the man with the video camera and he stopped filming. Roobie took the camera from him and checked the recording as Katie and Joy hugged each other on the bunk. They were both crying softly. Roobie gave the man back the camera then grabbed the passports from the two women.

'Roobie, please, we need decent food,' said Katie. 'And we need to be able to wash properly. Otherwise we're going to get sick.'

Roobie shoved the passports into the back pocket of his jeans. 'You talk too much.'

'I did what you wanted,' said Katie. 'Can't you at least let us shower?'

'Please, can I see my husband?' asked Joy.

Roobie handed Katie's chain to one of the teenagers and said something to him in Somali. He laughed and pulled the chain, dragging Katie off the bunk.

'I want to see my husband,' begged Joy. 'Please.'

'Today I am your husband,' said Roobie, unzipping his jeans.

'Please, no, don't,' said Joy. She curled up on the bunk, sobbing.

The teenagers dragged Katie along the corridor as Joy began to scream.

'You bastards!' shouted Katie.

One of the teenagers thumped her in the back and she staggered into her cabin and crashed against the bunk. Before she could turn they were on her, slapping her and pulling off her clothes. Katie went limp. There was no point in fighting. She closed her eyes and let them get on with it.

Robbie Fox tore the slice of bread into small pieces and tossed them to the waiting ducks, which were urging him on with a series of rapid quacks. He was standing by the lake in Stephen's Green, the twenty-two-acre park in the centre of Dublin. He was on the O'Connell Bridge and he was early. Fox was always early to meetings, even when he was seeing someone he trusted as much as he trusted Kieran FitzGerald. It was a habit that had saved his life on at least two occasions.

The ducks gobbled up all the bread and began quacking for more.

It was FitzGerald who had wanted to meet in Dublin and it made sense to do it south of the border so Fox hadn't argued. Northern Ireland was crawling with undercover cops and spooks but none of them had the authority to carry out any sort of investigation in Eire. If the authorities in the North wanted to monitor a conversation or meeting in the South they would first have to liaise with the Garda Síochána and the Irish police force was not renowned for its efficiency.

Fox had driven down and had parked in a multi-storey

car park close to the Stephen's Green shopping centre. He'd bought the small loaf of sliced bread at the food section of Dunne's department store and then walked across to the park, checking for a tail, even though he knew that there was more chance of a donkey winning the Grand National than of somebody following him in the Irish capital.

He saw FitzGerald walking across the grass, coming from the Shelbourne Hotel, where no doubt he'd been having a pint of Guinness or two while waiting for the appointed time. FitzGerald had two bodyguards that Fox could see, a big man in a long coat who was walking ahead and to the left carrying a newspaper, and a smaller man in a dark suit wearing sunglasses who hung back at the entrance to the park and was trying unsuccessfully to look inconspicuous.

FitzGerald never went anywhere without protection, and with good reason. As Operations Director of the Real IRA there were any number of Loyalist groups who would happily kill him and dance on his grave.

FitzGerald was in his mid-fifties, more than a decade younger than Fox, but his hair was greyer and thinner than Fox's and his hands were mottled with liver spots. He walked on to the bridge and stopped next to Fox, but made no move to shake his hand, and stood looking at the ducks. 'How are things with you, then, Robbie?'

'Fine,' said Fox. 'Yourself?'

'Not so bad,' said FitzGerald, holding the railing of the bridge with both gloved hands.

Fox threw another handful of bread at the quacking ducks.

'You know the story of the ducks, right, Robbie? During the Easter Rising?'

Fox shook his head.

'There were more than two hundred of the boys, holed up in the park, with Commandant Michael Mallin running the show. They'd blocked the streets with cars and carts and dug trenches in the park. Big mistake, because the Brits moved into the Shelbourne and started shooting at the Volunteers. Bloody trench warfare in the middle of the city. Bloody madness. Went on until the Volunteers pulled out and took refuge in the Royal College of Surgeons.' He gestured at the quacking ducks. 'Thing is, all through the shooting, there were ceasefires so that the groundsman could feed the ducks. I kid you not. Out he went with a white flag and they stopped shooting while he fed them.' FitzGerald shook his head. 'People are funny, right enough.'

'They are that,' agreed Fox. 'As funny as fuck.'

'So how's it going, Robbie? How's the knee?'

'Hurts more in the winter than the summer, but I can walk on it OK.'

'No fun getting older, is it?'

Fox shrugged. 'Not many advantages to it, right enough.'

'And young Lisa, quite the rising star.'

'Aye, she's committed, and she's got a good head on her shoulders.'

'Took care of that bastard SAS major for us, did a great job there.'

Fox nodded and threw another handful of bread pieces out to the quacking ducks. 'Well, it was personal. She was close to Padraig and Sean, like brothers they were.'

'Aye, that was a terrible thing. But he's dead now.'

'It was a quick death, though, and that he didn't deserve. I'd have preferred to have had him screaming in pain and begging for mercy.'

'Dead is dead, Robbie,' said FitzGerald.

'That's what they say,' agreed Fox.

The man in sunglasses had moved to sit on a bench from where he had a good view of the bridge.

'So where do we stand?' asked FitzGerald.

Fox looked around to check that no one could overhear them. Two nuns walked over the bridge deep in conversation and a middle-aged woman was pushing a stroller with a toddler munching on a bar of chocolate.

'We're not that much farther forward,' said Fox. 'Tanner killed Connolly and Hughes to protect O'Leary, who was undercover for the cops. Lisa went to the States and interrogated the ATF agent who introduced Tanner to the New York fund-raisers but that was a dead end. The thing is, if Tanner was a cop, he'd have known about O'Leary and it wouldn't have gone as far as it did. He was surprised to hear about O'Leary, so he must have been with another agency. MI5, maybe. Or Sass. We think Five.'

'He was bloody good with a gun, so I can't see he'd be with Five,' said FitzGerald. 'Took out Connolly and Hughes without them firing a shot, I'm told.'

'The thing is, Sass aren't great at undercover work. They're not the sharpest knives in the drawer, you know that. And this Tanner, he was good. He was bloody good. Barely been in Ireland for a few months and we had him on an execution squad with Connolly and Hughes, and those two didn't suffer fools gladly.'

'So maybe Sass working for Five?' suggested FitzGerald.

'If he had been with Sass there'd have been a dozen men with MP5s there and there weren't,' said Fox. 'Tanner was alone.' Fox threw more bread to the ducks. 'Not that Tanner is his real name, of course.' He sighed. 'I've got a horrible feeling he's going to get away with it, Kieran. The bastard is going to walk.'

'So what do we have on this Tanner?'

'We have a picture taken from a CCTV camera in the States. Lisa's passing the photograph around Belfast, see if anyone knows him.'

'That's not much of a plan, is it?'

'Here's the thing, Kieran. If he's with Five, one of our Loughside people could maybe get a look at his file.'

FitzGerald didn't say anything as he watched the ducks bobbing for bread.

'I know it's a risk, right enough,' said Fox.

'Damn right it's a risk,' said FitzGerald. 'We've precious few resources there and we need to take care of those that we have.'

'Sure, they're too valuable to squander. But this Tanner, he killed two of our men in cold blood. And blew a major bombing operation.'

The two men stood in silence for a while, looking at the ducks but their minds elsewhere.

'The people we've got at Loughside, they're gold, Robbie. They've passed positive vetting and their Republican sympathies are well hidden. If they keep their noses clean, who knows where they'll be in ten years. We can't put assets like that at risk for one man.'

'It's the long fight that matters, I see that,' said Fox. 'But there's a point of principle here. If we strike back, they're less likely to use undercovers in the future. And it shows that we're serious about defending our Volunteers.'

FitzGerald's eyes narrowed but there was no hint of

annoyance in his voice. 'You're saying this is a PR exercise, are you, Robbie?'

'I'm saying that perception matters,' said Fox. 'And that by letting this pass we might look weak. But if we show strength, if we show that we can strike at our enemy when they hurt us, it can only help our image.'

FitzGerald frowned. 'Image? Is that what it's come to?'

'In the battle for hearts and minds, sometimes perception is more important than the reality of the situation,' said Fox. 'It's a brave new world, right enough.'

FitzGerald said nothing for almost half a minute as he considered his options.

'You see the guy on the bench, wearing sunglasses,' said FitzGerald eventually.

'Sure,' said Fox.

'Give him the photograph,' said FitzGerald. 'I'll see what can be done.'

Fox nodded. 'I appreciate that, Kieran.'

'And if we find this Matt Tanner or whatever his name is, will Lisa take care of it?'

'That's the plan.'

FitzGerald smiled. 'We need more like her, Robbie.'

'We'll get them,' said Fox. 'People can see that Martin and Gerry sold us out, that the only way we'll get our country back is to fight for it. *Tiocfaidh ár lá.*'

'*Tiocfaidh ár lá,*' echoed FitzGerald.

Shepherd wandered over to the kitchen area, carrying his mug. Everyone on the floor had their own cup or mug and on his second day he'd bought one from a gift shop in Praed Street with a cartoon of a policeman on it. Shepherd

knew it was a silly thing to do but no one paid it any attention. There was a coffee fund and Shepherd had put a
ten-pound note into the tin when it was first pointed out
to him.

Over the two weeks he'd been in the office he'd become
a familiar face and everyone either nodded or said something
to him. He chatted about football with the Spurs fan, the
weather with the middle-aged lady who was going through
an ugly divorce and listened to the office Romeo's latest
adventure. Shepherd was all smiles and nods, playing the
nice guy. It was a total contrast to his regular undercover
work, where more often than not he was in hard-man mode,
intimidating those around him and getting physical when
needed. His role as a human resources consultant wasn't a
part that he enjoyed playing and for most of the time he
was bored rigid. At least when he was undercover in criminal gangs he had to be on his toes and the adrenalin rush
kept him going. It was all he could do to stay awake during
his eight-hour shifts at the company.

Candy Malone was pouring hot water over a tea bag
when he walked up. She smiled at him over her shoulder.
'Hi, Oliver, how's things?'

'Hopefully getting to the end of it,' said Shepherd, and
that was the truth.

'Any hints as to what's going to happen?'

Shepherd shrugged. 'I just file a report,' he said.

'You don't make recommendations?'

She turned to face him and he noticed bruising around
her left eye. She'd done a good job of concealing it with
make-up but it was still visible. And there was bruising on
her right wrist, and scratches.

'Someone in a different pay grade makes those decisions,' said Shepherd, pouring coffee into his mug. 'Are you OK? That's a nasty bruise you've got there.'

Her hand instinctively went up to her eye but she stopped herself and smiled. 'Stupid accident,' she said. 'Stumbled getting out of the shower, almost knocked myself out.' She hurried away and Shepherd watched her go. A slip in the shower might have explained the bruised eye but not the scratches on her arm.

He added a splash of milk to his coffee. One of the clerks appeared at his shoulder. It was Danny Kelly, a rabid Arsenal fan. 'You play poker, Oliver?' asked Kelly.

'I've been known to,' said Shepherd.

'Tim's putting together a game at his place. You up for it?'

'Could be,' said Shepherd. 'Who's playing?'

'Group of guys from the office and a few friends of Tim's.'

'You're not hustling me, are you?'

Kelly laughed and patted Shepherd on the back. 'A quid to open, it's not going to break the bank, Oliver.'

Shepherd headed back to his office, nodding hello to Annie Yorke, one of the women on Button's list of suspects. She was in her early thirties and as far as Shepherd could tell there wasn't a criminal bone in her body. A red flag had been raised because of a payment of twenty thousand pounds that had gone into her account but it had taken only a few minutes for Shepherd to find out that the money had been from the estate of an uncle who had died in Malaga. Annie was a pretty brunette who reminded Shepherd of Charlie Button, and she'd made it clear that she was interested in him, dropping hints about restaurants she wanted to try and films that she wanted to see. Shepherd was tempted but knew that as soon as the job was over Oliver Blackburn would have to vanish so he kept her at a distance.

He sat down at his desk and was just about to sip his coffee when his mobile rang. It was Button. 'Are you busy?' she asked.

'Worked off my feet.'

'When can you get away?'

'Five thirty.'

'You don't have flexitime?'

'I have an hour for lunch and I finish at five thirty.'

'Sounds wonderful. Do they do luncheon vouchers?'

'Sadly, no. What's up?'

'Best explained face to face,' she said. 'Let's have a drink. Where's quiet near you?'

'Rose and Crown,' he said. 'Buckingham Street, around the corner.'

Charlotte Button was sitting at a corner table by the fruit machine, whose lights were flashing continuously. She had a bottle of Pinot Grigio in a stainless-steel bucket and two glasses. Shepherd walked up and sat down opposite her. 'Is wine OK?' she asked, holding up the bottle.

'Wine's fine,' he said.

She sloshed some into his glass. 'Had a good day at the office, dear?'

'It's doing my head in, frankly.' He took a couple of gulps of wine. 'That's good,' he said. 'Someone's knocking Candy around. Bruises on her face and scratches on her wrist.'

'Well, she's seeing a Somali guy, I can tell you that much. He lives in Ealing. He's married with two kids but it doesn't look as if Candy knows that. We've checked his phone records and he hasn't called Crazy Boy but our surveillance boys are watching out for him.'

'Maybe she's just found out about the wife,' said Shepherd. 'So it looks as if she's the mole?'

'We need hard evidence so we're putting a tap on her phone but it looks like it, yes.'

'I'll knock the poker game on the head, then,' he said. He sipped his wine. 'So that's me out of the office, right? I have to say it's about time. I don't think I could have taken much more.'

'To be honest I'd have been pulling you out anyway,' said Button. 'We've managed to get a bug into Crazy Boy's house and we can monitor all his email and Skype communications and eavesdrop on anything that's said in his study, so as soon as he targets a ship we should know about it.' She leaned forward and lowered her voice. 'Anyway, everything's changed. A yacht was seized by pirates three days ago sailing from Dubai to Sydney. Five people on board. They're being moved to Somalia where they'll be held until a ransom is paid.'

Shepherd frowned. 'What does that have to do with us?'

'One of Crazy Boy's cousins seized the yacht. And one of the crew is the god-daughter of our own prime minister.'

Shepherd's jaw dropped. 'Wow,' he said.

'Yes, exactly,' said Button. 'Wow. She finished her degree at Oxford a while back and took a year off. She joined the crew sailing the yacht to its new owner in Australia.'

'This hasn't hit the papers, has it?'

Button shook her head. 'We know about it because Crazy Boy's uncle tipped him off. We only have the cousin's first name, Roobie, but apparently he's trying to make the big time now that Crazy Boy's in the UK.'

'Do they know about the PM connection?'

'Not yet. As far as they're concerned they've got an expensive yacht and the crew. They'll be contacting the owner and asking for a ransom.'

'But Crazy Boy's not involved? Not personally?'

'He's talked to his uncle about it so if nothing else we can already get him on conspiracy.'

Shepherd sighed and sat back in his chair. 'The shit's going to hit the fan when it gets out who their VIP prisoner is,' he said.

'Hopefully not,' said Button. 'Downing Street has contacted all the editors and everyone's playing ball, but I agree, it's going to get out eventually.'

'And when it does, what then? Presumably the price goes up?'

'Presumably,' agreed Button.

'So what's going to happen? Will they pay the ransom?'

'Who? Most of the crew are regular sailors. The girl's parents own a farm but I doubt they've got five million pounds.'

'The owner of the yacht?'

'That's where it gets complicated, unfortunately. The yacht was being delivered to the new owner in Sydney. It's a twenty-million-dollar yacht but he's only paid a deposit. He's sympathetic but doesn't see that it's his problem.'

'Nice guy.'

'You can see his point, Spider. The yacht isn't his until it arrives in Sydney. You can't expect him to pay a five-million-dollar ransom for something that doesn't belong to him.'

'What about the builders?'

Button nodded. 'They're in Turkey and they've got cash-flow problems. The yacht was being built for a Russian oligarch who ended up in prison, and a broker in Dubai did a deal with the guy in Sydney. The builders are depending on the Australian's money to keep their business afloat.' She smiled. 'No pun intended.'

'So neither the builder nor the owner is prepared to pay a ransom?'

'The intended owner won't and the builder can't. The kidnappers don't know that, of course. And they mustn't.'

'So what happens? Is the PM going to put up the money?'

'The PM doesn't have Tony Blair's money,' said Button. 'Not yet, anyway. But there are political considerations.'

'There always are.'

'There've been other British citizens seized by pirates over the years and the government has always taken the view that we can't negotiate.'

'Yeah, like they said they'd never negotiate with the IRA,' said Shepherd bitterly. 'It seems they only refuse to negotiate when it suits them.'

'I hear you, but in this case the PM really is caught between a rock and a hard place. His god-daughter is an only child, he can't let anything happen to her. But he can't be seen to be giving her favourable treatment either.'

'So what happens?'

Button sipped her wine. 'We've been asked if there's anything we can do. Unofficially.'

'Five?'

Button shook her head. 'No, I've been asked unofficially. It's bloody awkward, actually.'

'You mean the PM wants you to do this off the books?'

'It wasn't the PM who approached me, obviously. But that's the way it is, yes.'

'It's a poisoned chalice,' said Shepherd.

'That's one way of looking at it,' said Button. 'The request was made behind closed doors and that's the way it's going to stay. We're going to see if we can find the crew.'

'And if we can?'

'One step at a time,' said Button. 'But we've been asked if we can facilitate a rescue.'

'An unofficial rescue? With what? Mercenaries?'

'It's been done before,' said Button. 'SAS members have been given compassionate leave for one reason or another while they've gone off to places where they shouldn't be.'

'That's the plan? To use off-duty members of the SAS?' Shepherd shook his head. 'That could get very messy.'

'Like I said, we take this one step at a time.' She took another sip of her wine. 'What would be helpful is to have you on board the ship that Crazy Boy is planning to seize. First we need to know which ship that is. If you were there when the ship is taken, you could give us intel on what's going on. We can then follow the pirates back to shore and that should lead us to Crazy Boy's uncle and hopefully the hostages.'

'Two birds with one stone?'

'If it works, yes. No one is going to query the government putting resources into protecting one of our ships, and no one is going to complain if the crew of the yacht is rescued at the same time.'

'And you want me on board this ship? As what? A stow-away?'

'As a member of the crew, obviously. With the officers. We'll talk to the shipping company and clear it with them but no one on board will know who you are, not even the captain.'

'And I let myself be taken? Bloody hell, Charlie, you're not asking much, are you?'

'Generally the pirates don't kill their hostages, Spider, not if they think there's a payout at the end of it.'

'Just so long as you have my back.'

'As always,' said Button. 'Just one more thing.'

'Oh dear.' Shepherd sighed. 'I guess the other shoe is about to drop, isn't it?'

'I need your help putting the team together.'

'What happened to one step at a time?'

'If we do need to go in it'll be at short notice, so we have to get the team primed now.'

'And you want to share the poisoned chalice with me, is that it?'

Button smiled and brushed a lock of hair behind her ear. 'I've no right to ask, I know that. But you do know people who can help.'

'Sure, I know people. But this is more than a favour for a friend. They're going to need paying.'

'I have a budget,' said Button.

'Off the books?'

'It's complicated,' she said. 'But I can put it through the expenses for the piracy investigation.'

'So why not just pay the ransom and put it through as expenses?'

Button laughed harshly. 'If only life was that simple,' she said. 'See who you can bring on board.'

'No pun intended, again?'

'I was thinking your pal Martin.'

Shepherd nodded. 'So was I.'

'And I've fixed you up with a briefing from a naval intelligence officer who's been out in the Gulf of Aden with the multinational task force that's fighting the pirates. Just so you know what you're letting yourself in for.'

Hoop reached out to steady Katie as she stepped off the skiff and on to the walkway that led to the harbour wall. She was so weak that she could barely stand, never mind walk. 'Are you OK?' he asked.

Katie glared at him. 'No I'm not fucking OK,' she said, and pulled her hand away.

'I'm sorry,' he said.

Katie felt suddenly ashamed for snapping at him but she knew that what she and Joy were going through was far, far worse than what was happening to the men. She'd lost count of the number of times that she'd been raped on the boat, and it had been clear from the screams and cries from Joy's cabin that she was being attacked just as often. All the men had to put up with was the bad food and the lack of washing facilities. So far as she could tell they weren't even being beaten, whereas the men who came to her cabin seemed to get as much enjoyment out of hitting her around as they did raping her. 'I just want to go home,' she said.

'We all do,' said Hoop.

Roobie pulled Joy along the walkway. Her hair was matted

with what looked like dried vomit and her shirt and shorts were spotted with blood.

Two teenage pirates jumped out of the skiff and jabbed their AK-47s at Hoop and Katie, screaming at the top of their voices.

Katie and Hoop stepped off the walkway on to the sandy beach. In the distance there were a dozen or so single-storey cement buildings with corrugated-iron windows. Farther down the beach was a much larger jetty made of scaffolding and wooden planks where two small fishing boats with peeling paintwork were moored. The sky above was cloudless and the sun was blisteringly hot.

Katie shaded her eyes with her hands. 'Where are we?' said Joy, joining her. Beyond the beach was a strip of road where half a dozen pick-up trucks were parked, and on the other side of the road was a line of market stalls tended mainly by women with colourful dresses and black head-scarves.

'Puntland, probably,' said Hoop. 'That's where most of the Somali pirates are based. There are hundreds of fishing villages all down the coast.'

A second skiff roared up to the wooden jetty and then settled back into the water as the engines cut out. Huddled in the middle of the boat were Eric and Andrew, surrounded by half a dozen AK-47-toting pirates.

They had been taken off the fishing boat at gunpoint and forced on to the skiffs. Joy had tried to get into the same boat as her husband but had been slapped across the face and pushed into the boat with Hoop and Katie. The two boats had roared across the sea at full pelt, heading west, for the best part of two hours until they'd seen land. Roobie had a hand-held GPS unit which had helped guide them to the jetty.

He walked over to them, cradling his AK-47.

'Where are you taking us?' Katie asked Roobie. 'Have they paid the ransom?'

'No, no ransom,' said Roobie.

'But you're letting us go?'

Roobie pointed his AK-47 at a truck parked next to a steel-sided warehouse. 'In truck,' he said.

'Where are we going?' asked Katie, but she flinched as Roobie raised the Kalashnikov as if he was going to strike her. 'OK, OK,' she said.

Joy put her arm around Katie's shoulder and the two of them headed for the truck. The rusting wings were flecked with reddish mud and there was a piece of rope holding the bonnet shut. The rear of the truck was covered with a dirty green tarpaulin that flapped in the breeze that blew off the sea. There were two gleaming black SUVs parked to the left of the truck. The teenage pirates fell into step either side of the two women, laughing and talking in their own language.

The one walking next to Katie reached over and stroked her breasts and she twisted away from him.

'Leave her alone!' screamed Joy. 'Keep your filthy hands off her.'

The pirate next to Joy punched her in the back of the neck and she pitched forward on to her knees. She scrabbled to her feet and spat at her attacker. 'Fuck you!' she screamed. 'Fuck all of you.'

'Easy, Joy,' shouted Hoop. 'Don't give them an excuse.'

'Fuck you too, Hoop!' shouted Joy, her eyes blazing.

'You've no idea what the fuck we've been going through.' She pointed her finger at the man who'd hit her. 'You fucking keep away from me, do you hear me?'

The pirate snarled at her and then shouted something to her in Somali as he raised his machete.

Joy stood her ground and stared at him with narrowed eyes. 'Yeah, you want to kill me, do you? Go on, then. Big man with a knife, yeah? Well, fuck you!' She spat at him again and phlegm splattered across his face.

Katie sank to the ground, sobbing, her hands over her face.

Joy's husband jumped out of the skiff he was in and waded through the waves, screaming her name. Two pirates jumped out and chased after him, lifting their legs high and jumping through the waves. He reached the beach ahead of them and ran across the sand to his wife.

'Come on, you bastard, do it!' shouted Joy. 'You think I'm scared? You think dying is worse than what you scum have been doing to me?'

'Joy!' screamed Andrew, but Roobie whirled around and slammed the butt of his AK-47 into his stomach. Andrew doubled up, gasping for breath, and Roobie swung the butt again, this time bringing it crashing down on the back of his neck.

'Please, Joy, don't!' cried Katie through her tears.

'I don't care!' screamed Joy. 'I don't fucking care any more!'

Everyone on the dock had stopped what they were doing and were staring at Joy. There were fishermen squatting over nets, beggars, bare-chested and shoeless children, women in brightly coloured dresses with baskets of fruit and vegetables balanced on their heads. Katie even saw two men in what she assumed were scruffy police uniforms and half a dozen lanky teenagers in military fatigues with rifles standing by an open jeep. 'Why doesn't somebody do something!' Katie screamed up at the sky, but no one looked at her, all eyes were fixed on Joy and the pirate who stood in front of her, slowly swinging his machete.

Andrew tried to get up and he reached out to her with one hand but then he fell back, face down, his chest barely moving.

'Come on, you bastard, do it!' shouted Joy. 'Put me out of my fucking misery, why don't you.'

'Joy, no!' yelled Katie. 'Stop it, please!'

The pirate took a step towards Joy, a cruel smile on his face. He said something in Somali, and sneered at her. Joy stared at him, her chest rising and falling, her hands bunched into fists at her side. 'Come on, you piece of shit,' she said scornfully. 'You're man enough to rape, are you man enough to kill?' She raised her chin and then turned, exposing the left side of her neck to him.

'Joy! No!' screamed Katie, pulling at her own hair. 'Stop!'

The pirate raised the machete high in the air and it glinted under the fierce African sun. Joy seemed to relax, her face slowly went blank and her hands unclenched. Her eyes remained open, staring at the pirate.

The man screamed at the top of his lungs and brought the machete down hard, towards the exposed neck, but at the last second he stopped, the blade less than an inch from Joy's neck. Joy didn't so much as blink. The pirate threw back his head and roared with laughter.

The soldiers standing by the jeep were laughing and

pointing. Katie looked over at them, wondering why they hadn't done anything to help. Everyone on the dock could see that they were being held prisoner and were being forced from the boats to the truck at gunpoint, so why didn't they step in? The two policemen were leaning against a dirt-streaked white car and one of them was drinking from a bottle that looked as if it contained whisky. 'How can you let this happen?' she screamed. 'Why won't anybody help us?'

Two obese women, one in a bright yellow dress, the other in a dress with dark blue and light blue checks, laughed at her, and a boy who couldn't have been more than eight years old picked up a stone and threw it at her. It smacked against her bare shoulder and drew blood, and he ran away laughing.

Roobie walked over to Joy, who was still staring at her tormentor. Without breaking his stride he slammed the butt of his AK-47 against the side of her head and she went down without a sound. He bent down, grabbed her under the arms and picked her up in one smooth movement, then swung her over his shoulder and carried her over to the truck.

The pirate with the machete seized the back of her shirt and pulled her to her feet. She folded her arms and walked slowly towards the truck, mumbling to herself.

Two more pirates picked up Andrew, who was moaning incoherently, and dragged him after Roobie.

Hoop and Eric were marched at gunpoint from the dock to the truck. They were followed by half a dozen children who were chanting in Somali as they marched like soldiers, their bare feet kicking up clouds of dust around them.

Roobie dumped Joy in the back of the truck and turned

around to shout at the rest of the pirates. The pirate behind Katie pushed her in the middle of the back and shouted at her. She climbed into the back of the truck and crawled over to Joy. She was breathing heavily, her mouth wide open and her eyes closed. Katie sat down next to her and lifted her head on to her lap.

There was a thump at the end of the truck and Andrew was tossed in. He landed heavily and lay face down. The back of his head was matted with blood. Tears ran down Katie's face as she cradled Joy.

The tarpaulin was pulled back and Hoop climbed in. He cursed when he saw the state of Andrew's scalp. 'Bastards,' he said.

Eric climbed in after Hoop and sat down at the far end of the truck, with his back against the cab, his head in his hands.

Hoop gingerly moved Andrew's hair to get a look at the wound. 'It's not bleeding too much,' he said.

'He could be bleeding in the brain and we wouldn't know,' said Katie. 'He needs a scan.'

'Yeah, well, that's not going to happen any time soon, is it?' said Eric, sitting back on his heels.

The tarpaulin was pulled back and Roobie looked in.

Hoop scowled at him. 'We need water,' he said. 'And I need a cloth to clean his wound after you caved his skull in.'

The tarpaulin closed and they heard Roobie shouting. Two minutes later and Roobie reappeared, and he tossed two plastic bottles of water and a piece of dirty cloth at Hoop. Then he pulled the tarpaulin shut and threaded a rope through a series of holes to tie it closed.

The truck engine coughed and spluttered and the entire

vehicle started to shudder. It jerked forward and picked up speed. Through a gap in the tarpaulin Katie could see the two SUVs fall in behind them.

'Why didn't anyone help us?' asked Katie. 'How could they stand by and let it happen?'

'Most of them depend on the pirates for money,' said Hoop. 'The fishing industry has been in decline for years. If it wasn't for the pirates most of them would be starving.'

'So they let them beat us up and rape us and treat us like animals?'

'Katie, look at us. In case you haven't noticed we're the only white people here. We're the outsiders, we mean nothing to them, we're just a source of income.'

'But the police? You saw the police?'

'Yeah,' said Eric. 'And they saw us. The pirates pay them off like they pay everyone in Puntland. The cops aren't going to help us and neither are the army.' He drew his knees up to his chest. 'That's why they haven't bothered tying us up or gagging us. They don't have to. Even if we get away from this lot anyone who finds us will hand us straight back. The whole bloody country is corrupt.'

Katie stroked Joy's cheek. 'She wanted him to kill her, you know? She meant it.'

'It's going to work out all right in the end,' said Hoop. 'They always hand their hostages over alive once the ransom has been paid.'

Katie shook her head. 'Joy was right,' she said. 'We'd be better off dead.'

Captain Peter Giles flopped down into his chair and waved for Shepherd to sit down on one of the two chairs facing the teak-effect desk. 'Take a pew,' he said. They were in a nondescript office in the old War Office building in Whitehall. There were bomb-proof curtains over the windows and two of the fluorescent light bulbs were missing from the fittings in the ceiling. Giles was a few years younger than Shepherd, with blond hair cut very short and skin that was so white it suggested he spent more time in submarines than on the deck of a ship. 'I appreciate you coming in,' said Giles. 'A lot of the info I have is classified and can't leave the building.' He flicked his hair from his eyes.

'In case it gets left on a train?' said Shepherd.

'You can mock but it has happened, several times,' said Giles. 'Not to me, I hasten to add. Now, can I get you a coffee or tea or water? The coffee and tea are from a machine, I'm afraid – they did away with the tea ladies years ago.'

'I'm fine,' said Shepherd. 'My boss says you're just back from Somalia.'

'Not quite,' said the captain. 'I was at sea all of the time but we did get to within about twenty miles of the Somali coastline a few times. I was out with the task force that patrols the MSPA within the Gulf of Aden.'

'I'm really bad with initials,' said Shepherd. 'MSPA?'

'Sorry,' said Giles. 'Maritime Security Patrol Area. It was set up by CTF-150 in August 2008, basically a secure corridor between Somalia and Yemen. Ships know that within that area they are under our protection, though between you and me the bloody pirates don't pay it much attention. What tends to happen now is that ships gather at either end of the corridor and group into convoys that are then guarded by warships. Safety in numbers and all that.'

'CTF-150?'

Giles shrugged apologetically. 'CTF. Combined Task Force. Strictly speaking it's the CJTF-HOA, Combined Joint Task Force – Horn of Africa, but it's generally accepted that that's too much of a mouthful. We advise shipping to stick to what we call the IRTC, the Internationally Recommended Transit Corridor, which runs down the middle of the Gulf of Aden, bisecting the MSPA. Provided ships stick to the IRTC, they're pretty much safe, especially if they're in a convoy. The danger areas are in the Arabian Sea before they get to the IRTC. There's a lot of sea out there so it's harder to patrol. If they encounter a problem out at sea then they have to radio for assistance, and if there's one available we'll send out a chopper.' He stood up. 'Look, I'm going to need a coffee. If I don't put caffeine into my system every few hours I get a blinding headache. You sure you don't want anything? I've a lot of info to get through and this could take a few hours.'

'Coffee with a splash of milk and no sugar,' said Shepherd.

'No sugar's easy enough but the machine isn't programmed for a splash,' said Giles as he headed for the door. 'Frankly, I'm not even sure it's milk.'

He left the office. Shepherd sighed and looked around the room. There was nothing of a personal nature, no photographs, no certificates, no books, just a computer on the desk along with an empty in-tray and out-tray. There had been no name on the door, just a number, and Shepherd realised that the office was probably one that Giles was using temporarily.

The captain returned with two white plastic cups. He put one down in front of Shepherd and walked around the desk to sit down. 'Just a few ground rules before we start,' he said. 'Feel free to take notes but I can't let you take photocopies or print-outs from the building, and we can't give you any thumb drives or disks.' He grinned. 'Though your boss tells me that you've got some sort of trick memory, right?'

'It's pretty much photographic,' said Shepherd. 'I can remember anything I see and most of what I hear.'

'Lucky you.'

'Yeah, it comes in handy.'

'So you'd be a good card counter?'

Shepherd frowned. 'What do you mean?'

'In a casino. Blackjack. You'd know what cards are still in the deck.'

Shepherd chuckled. 'It doesn't work like that,' he said. 'If you showed me a deck of cards one by one I'd be able to recall the order you showed them to me. And if you asked me to tell you what card followed the ace of diamonds, I could tell you that. But if you showed me fifty cards and asked me which two I hadn't seen, I'd have to think about it for a long time.'

'What about languages?'

Shepherd grinned. 'You sound like a psychiatrist,' he said.

'I'm just fascinated by it,' said Giles. 'My job is all about information and I find it a real pain to remember most of it. But I'm great at languages. I can speak French, Italian, Arabic and Russian almost fluently and can make myself understood in half a dozen more. I've never had a problem remembering vocabulary but I can't remember numbers, for instance.'

'Then we're opposites,' said Shepherd. 'I can memorise

numbers without trying, and I'm good with vocabulary, but I can't follow a conversation in another language.'

'But faces you can remember? And names?'

Shepherd nodded. 'That's where it comes in really handy,' he said. 'Once I've seen a face I never forget it.'

'Well, I've plenty of faces to show you,' said Giles. He tapped at the keyboard on his desk, then he sat back and steepled his fingers on his chest. 'OK, how are you on the background to this whole piracy thing?'

'Only what I've read in the papers,' said Shepherd. 'Illegal fishing destroyed their livelihoods so they turned to piracy instead.'

'That's pretty much what happened,' said Giles. 'Though fishing declined during the civil war, the Somali fish stocks were reduced to almost nothing by overfishing. Plus European companies have been dumping hazardous waste offshore for years. With the government in disarray there was no one to stand up to the big companies and between the toxic waste and the commercial overfishing, the Somali fishermen saw their livelihoods destroyed. Some three-quarters of the population exist on less than two dollars a day, so you can understand why they took up piracy.'

He sipped his coffee. 'During the 1990s they tended to stick to their shoreline and only seized vessels close to the Horn of Africa. Usually small freighters, but they seized yachts, fishing boats, whatever they could board. Initially they just robbed the ship, taking money and valuables, sometimes food and equipment. Then they realised that they could ransom the vessels and the crew. Ransoms were usually of the order of tens of thousands of dollars and more often than not they were paid. Once they realised how easy it was, they started to roam farther afield and now anywhere in the Gulf of Aden is fair game. These days there's no limit to the size of vessel they're capable of seizing, from massive container ships to supertankers laden with oil. What we've seen recently is the pirates heading out to sea in skiffs to seize small freighters or fishing boats which they then sail out into deeper waters so that they can board larger vessels. They have supply ships loaded with food, water and weapons so they can stay at sea for months at a time. They've struck as far as eight hundred miles off the Somali coast.'

'And the ransoms went up, right?'

'Through the roof,' said Giles. 'Last year alone the pirates got more than eighty million dollars. Five million for a single ship isn't unusual but the shipping companies tend to keep quiet about how much they pay. It's a major industry now, and even with CTF-150 on patrol, they're still making millions. The thing is there's no real incentive for the shipping companies to do anything. The chances of an individual ship being seized are remote. Some thirty thousand ships a year sail through, accounting for eight per cent of world trade and twelve per cent of the world's oil.'

Shepherd chuckled. 'You are okay with numbers, after all.'

The captain smiled and jerked a thumb at the computer monitor. 'I told you, I've got a crib sheet,' he said. 'But with the pirates taking around seventy or eighty ships a year, the shipping companies know that the chances of one of their ships being taken are small. Considering the billions of dollars of goods and oil that are shipped through every day, they can afford to pay a ransom if and when they have to.

Or they can take out insurance. Taken as a whole, the cost of ransoms probably works out at about three thousand dollars per ship. Which in the grand scheme of things is barely a drop in the ocean.' He grinned. 'Pun intended. The shipping companies could avoid the area by sailing around Africa, but that would add weeks to any voyage and they'd be stuck with extra fuel and wage costs. They can take out insurance, or they can carry a protection squad. But insurance premiums for piracy are going through the roof and a decent protection squad will cost five thousand dollars a day.'

'Who pays the ransom?' asked Shepherd.

'If the shipping company has taken out insurance then it's all covered. The insurance company will pass it over to a hostage negotiator and they'll try to cut the best deal they can and then arrange to pay the money. Always in cash. Any shipowner running his vessels around the Gulf of Aden has to pay an extra premium for the privilege. A ship worth a hundred million dollars a few years ago would pay twenty thousand dollars for insurance from Asia to Europe, but that's now gone up to a hundred and fifty thousand or so. If the ship isn't insured then the cost of the ransom will generally be shared between the shipowner and the cargo owner. I think most companies have been waiting to see if CTF-150 will deal with the problem.'

'And will it?'

Giles shrugged. 'That's why I was out there this month, getting a sit-rep for my bosses. The thing is, we've got all the technology we need, but at the end of the day we're sailing around in warships and they're fishermen in inflatables and skiffs. We can hardly blow them out of the water.

And if we do manage to catch them, what do we do with them? The days of clapping them in irons or hanging them from the yardarm are long gone. We took a group of six earlier this year, caught them red handed with Kalashnikovs and RPGs. You know what they did? Demanded to see the captain and said they wanted asylum.'

'No way,' said Shepherd.

Giles nodded. 'They were in international waters on a British ship and they were claiming that they were being persecuted by the government in Somalia. The captain was stuck between a rock and a hard place. He was supposed to hand them over to the Somali authorities but once they had claimed asylum the human rights legislation kicked in.'

'I guess this never made the papers?'

'Complete media blackout,' said Giles. 'The captain ended up giving them back their weapons, plus extra food and water, and letting them go on their sweet way.'

'Madness,' said Shepherd.

'What was the alternative? Taking them back to the UK so that they could claim housing benefits? We can't shoot them out of the water because then we become the imperialist bullies that everyone says we are. The only thing we can do is fire a warning shot across their bows, but they're starting to realise that we're not going to hit them.'

'So you can't stop them taking ships?'

'We can scare them off, that's about it. And if they do take a ship, there's not much we can do. Our orders are not to try to retake the vessel.'

'Because?'

'Because of the risk to our forces and the risk of losing hostages. We can't be seen to be responsible for any casualties.

And the simple fact is that ninety-nine times out of a hundred the hostages are released in good health once the ransom's been paid. The Russians and the French have sent in their special forces to release ships and we could do the same with the SAS and SBS if the powers-that-be wanted us to.'

Shepherd sighed. He hadn't realised that the country's armed forces had become as politically correct as its law enforcement agencies. 'So we just wait for the ships to be released, is that it?'

Giles nodded. 'There's a whole industry geared up for the ransom business,' he said. 'The cash is raised and flown out, usually to Kenya first and then into Somalia. From there it's more often than not flown out to the ship and dropped using special parachutes. The pirates divide up the cash and leave, usually in several groups heading in several directions. And like I said, generally the hostages aren't harmed. There have been some killings and a few rapes but they're the exception. The pirates talk tough but really they know that they gain nothing by killing hostages.'

'And the pirates, do we know who they are?'

'We've got a lot of photographs and video, and some intelligence,' said the captain. 'There are up to a thousand or so men involved, mainly from the Puntland region in north-eastern Somalia, which is where the fishing industry was concentrated. There are at least six major gangs and several dozen other smaller ad hoc groups.'

'Can you run the photographs by me, and any details you have?'

'Are you planning to go out there?' asked the captain.

'Looks that way,' said Shepherd.

'Well, I can guarantee you won't be bored,' said Giles.

He gestured at his side of the desk. 'Pull your chair over here and I'll show you what we've got.'

'So you're telling me that the fragrant Charlotte Button has authorised an off-the-books operation?' said Martin O'Brien. He sipped his lager. 'I must have woken up in some alternative reality this morning.'

'I was as surprised as you,' said Shepherd.

'Remember when you went AWOL in Dubai and Iraq?'

Shepherd nodded. 'The Riot Act was read,' he said.

'So now we're in a pot calling the kettle black situation.'

Shepherd raised his glass of Jameson's and soda. 'We are indeed,' he said, and stretched out his legs. They were sitting in the Dancers Bar in the atrium of the Hilton Hotel close to Heathrow Airport's Terminal Four. 'And she even asked for you by name.'

O'Brien's eyebrows headed skywards. 'Now I know I'm dreaming,' he said. He looked at his watch, a Rolex Submariner with a black bezel. 'My flight's in an hour,' he said, 'and I'm guessing you need a decision now?'

'It's a rush job,' said Shepherd. 'I'll understand if you can't do it.'

O'Brien ran a hand over his shaved head. 'The job I'm on is management, mainly. I've a good team and they can practically run themselves.'

'Bodyguarding?'

'Taking care of a Russian oligarch who's moved to Cyprus. He made a lot of enemies in Moscow and thinks they're out to get him. I think he's paranoid but his money's good.'

'Can you get away?'

'Sure,' said O'Brien. 'He's getting on my nerves anyway.'

He nodded. 'I'm up for it. Basically you need an extraction team, right?'

Shepherd nodded. 'Ten guys. Maybe twelve.'

'And Charlie's OK with all this? Because it won't be cheap.'

'She says she'll find the money from the operation she's running.'

'We'll need some sort of fixer in Somalia, someone who speaks the language.'

'Can you get people?'

'Sure. But it'll take a few days and I'll have to be out there. Probably set up in Nairobi. I'll need a few Kenyans on board.'

'What about the Bradford boys?'

'Jack's on leave, I think he's in Bristol. Billy's out in Iraq but they're both on short-term contracts so I'm pretty sure I can sign them up. Let me put my thinking cap on. What about kit?'

'Buy what you need. Give me a bank account number and I'll see about getting funds transferred.'

'That's going to leave a trail.'

Shepherd grinned. 'Charlie's with Five now, not SOCA. She's got access to all sorts of offshore accounts.'

'What about intel?'

'I'll be your conduit while I'm in London. If I leave, we'll fix up someone else. You'll have everything we have, satellite imagery, phone taps, money movements, surveillance pictures.'

'And for the extraction, are we going for the whole crew or just the girl?'

Shepherd chuckled. 'I can just imagine what the press'll

say if she gets rescued and everyone else gets left behind.
It's a three-musketeers job. All for one and one for all.'

'And what about getting into Somalia?'

'Good question.'

'It would mean a decent-sized plane or two helicopters.
And if we go the chopper route we'll need two pilots and
two mechanics.'

'Not necessarily,' said Shepherd. 'It depends where
they're being held. If they're close to the sea you can take
them out by sea. A fast boat, and straight out to one of
the Royal Navy's, God bless 'em. Or get them to the
Somali government forces. Maybe even let them take the
credit.'

O'Brien nodded thoughtfully. 'Might work,' he said. 'But
we'd have to be sure of whoever we hand them over to. It'd
be a nightmare if the government gave them back to the
pirates.'

'The government hate the pirates. There won't be a
problem.'

'We're going to need weapons – the pirates have everything from AK-47s to RPGs.'

'You'll have to arrange your own supplies, but you'll have
the money. Nothing traceable to the UK, obviously.'

'That's not a problem, Africa's awash with ordnance.' He
leaned towards Shepherd. 'What are the chances that we'll
go in?' he said. 'The ransom's definitely not being paid, is
that right?'

'Not specifically for the crew of the yacht. Neither the
owner nor the builder will stump up the cash and the
government can't be seen to be negotiating with the pirates
just because one of the crew is the PM's god-daughter. I

think Charlie's hoping that the pirates will accept one payment for two groups.'

'Which ship have they taken?'

Shepherd chuckled. 'They haven't yet.'

'Bloody hell, Spider, this is seat of the pants stuff, isn't it?'

'We've got the pirates under surveillance and we're pretty sure they're ready to move. When they do, Charlie's going to put me on the ship.'

O'Brien laughed. 'They do like to put you in the firing line, don't they?'

'Yeah, well, in Plan A I was just there to make sure that nobody gets hurt. Charlie's Plan B is a bit more complicated.'

'I bet,' said O'Brien.

'She thinks we can track them from the freighter to their base. Then if the ransom negotiations don't pan out you go on in and pull them out.'

'There'll be casualties,' said O'Brien. 'It could get very messy.'

'You're always the pessimist, Martin.'

'Just so you know, Spider. If the shit hits the fan, I'm guessing that Charlie is going to wash her hands of us all.'

'She'll have our backs.'

O'Brien raised his glass. 'She's a bureaucrat, she'll cover her own arse first.'

'I trust her,' said Shepherd. 'And like I said, it could all turn out well. We'll send in negotiators and they'll try to do a deal for all the hostages they've got. The ship they'll be targeting will be worth hundreds of millions and the shipping company will be keen to pay. The price of a few sailors should get lost along the way.'

'But with my pessimist's hat on, I've got to point out that if we have to go in, people are going to get hurt.'

'I don't think anyone's going to cry over a few dead pirates,' said Shepherd. 'They've been a thorn in the Somali government's side for years. But hopefully it won't come to that.'

'We still haven't decided on choppers or a plane.'

'I'd go for fixed wing. But keep your options open until we know exactly what we're going to be doing.'

O'Brien looked at his watch again. 'I've got to head off,' he said. He stood up and the two men hugged. O'Brien patted Shepherd on the back. 'Be careful, pal,' he said.

'Always,' said Shepherd.

Shepherd phoned Katra from the train and she was waiting at Hereford station with the CRV. They drove to Liam's school, where he was standing outside, looking at his watch. He scowled when he saw the CRV but grinned when he saw that Shepherd was in the front passenger seat.

'Sorry we're late. Katra had to pick me up,' said Shepherd as Liam climbed into the back seat.

'How long are you back for?'

'Not sure. A few days. Maybe longer.'

'Great,' said Liam. 'Can we go to McDonald's?'

'I don't see why not? Unless Katra has cooked.'

Katra grinned. 'McDonald's is fine,' she said.

'McDonald's it is. Even though your old dad prefers Burger King.'

'You're not old, Dad,' said Liam.

'No need for flattery, kid, I've already agreed to McDonald's.'

Katra drove them to McDonald's and they picked up a takeaway and ate it at home in front of the television.

The following day Shepherd took Liam to school in the CRV, then went home and changed into his running gear – an old sweatshirt that had once been white but which had greyed over the years, a pair of baggy tracksuit bottoms and two pairs of wool socks. He went downstairs and fetched his boots and a battered old rucksack from the cupboard under the stairs. The rucksack was heavy, packed with half a dozen bricks wrapped in newspaper, and the boots were more than ten years old. Shepherd didn't run for fun, he ran to make himself stronger. He took a plastic bottle of Evian water from the fridge and headed out of the front door.

He had half a dozen routes starting from his house, varying from three miles to twelve, and he decided to run for a while in the fields not far from his home on a route that would include a small wood and take him the best part of forty-five minutes.

He ran the first mile at full speed to get his heart beating fast and then he settled back to a more solid pace to give himself a good cardio workout. The rucksack bounced against his hips and shoulders with every stride but he ignored the pain, just as he ignored his aching feet. Shepherd had long ago learned to ignore pain and discomfort, he simply gritted his teeth and got on with the job in hand.

By the time he was halfway around his circuit he was sweating freely but his breathing was still steady and even. He cut through woodland and slowed down to avoid over-hanging branches and grasping brambles. His boots slapped through mud and twigs cracked like gunshots and his lungs started to burn. He took deeper breaths, increasing the amount of oxygen he was taking in, and pumped his arms back and forth as he ran.

He heard a twig crack to his left and he looked over but didn't see anyone or anything so he increased his pace.

He emerged from the woodland on to a recently ploughed field and turned left, running between the furrowed soil and a high hedge. A group of crows scattered from the branches of a tree overhanging the field, then re-formed as Shepherd continued on his run. At the end of the field he cut left, following another hedge, then jumped over a ditch into a field of sheep that turned to watch him run.

Shepherd checked his watch and smiled grimly. He was thirty seconds slower than the last time he'd run the route. He ran all the way around the pasture and jumped the ditch back into the ploughed field. As his boots hit the ground he realised that there was somebody standing by a five-bar gate. A man. A big man in a black tracksuit.

'You're slowing down in your old age, Spider,' said the man.

Shepherd's jaw dropped and he took a step back, almost falling into the ditch behind him. He was in total shock because the man in front of him was dead and buried. Shepherd tried to speak but his mouth worked soundlessly.

The big man smiled. 'I'm not a ghost,' he said. 'Not yet, anyway.'

Shepherd shook his head. 'You're dead,' was all he could manage to say. And that was the truth. Major Allan Gannon had been killed in a car bomb almost a year earlier. But the man in the black tracksuit was no ghost, and there was no mistaking the wide shoulders, the jutting lantern jaw and the oft-broken nose.

'That was then,' said the Major. 'This is now.' He took a step towards Shepherd. 'I'm sorry to spring this on you, but there's something you need to know.'

'This doesn't make any sense,' said Shepherd. 'What the hell's going on, boss?'

'Not here,' said the Major. 'There's a lot to talk about. Go home, get changed, and come on over to the barracks. The indoor range.'

Shepherd opened his mouth to argue but before he could say anything the Major had turned and run off, heading towards the trees. Shepherd ran a hand through his hair, unable to come to terms with what had just happened. It was impossible. The Major was dead, blown to bits outside his London home. The Real IRA had claimed responsibility, and revelled in his death. Shepherd had been at the funeral. So had Charlotte Button and more than a hundred members of the SAS, past and present. And the Major's name was on the clock tower in the Stirling Lines barracks, where the Regiment made sure that its dead were never forgotten.

Shepherd started to jog home, his mind in a whirl.

After he'd showered and changed his clothes, Shepherd climbed into his BMW X3 and drove to the Stirling Lines barracks at RAF Credenhill. He showed his MI5 identification card at the gate and a uniformed guard told him where to park. As he approached the indoor firing range he heard a handgun being fired in bursts of two. Rat-tat. Rat-tat. Rat-tat.

He opened the door and the acrid tang of cordite assailed his nostrils. The Major was reloading a magazine and he grinned when he saw Shepherd.

'Fancy showing me what you can do?' he said, holding

out the gun. 'Never met a spook who could shoot to save his life.'

'What's going on, boss?' said Shepherd. He was in no mood for making small talk with a man he'd thought was dead.

'It's been a funny old year,' said the Major, putting down the gun. 'I've had to lie low, for obvious reasons. They almost got me, Spider.'

'I went to your funeral, boss. We all did. How the hell could you do that to us? How could you put us through that?'

'No one could know,' said the Major. 'If they thought I was still alive then they'd keep coming after me. By letting them think they'd killed me, they lowered their guard and we could find them.'

Shepherd pointed at his own chest. 'What about me? How the hell could you not tell me?'

'I couldn't tell anybody,' said the Major.

'Bollocks,' said Shepherd. 'The Regiment must know for a start.'

'And only the Regiment,' said the Major. 'I'm here full-time now. Hardly ever leave the barracks.'

Shepherd shook his head. 'You could have trusted me, boss.'

'It's not about trust, Spider. I had to go ghost, I had no choice.'

'But the bomb?'

'They were careless. There was a smudge on the bonnet, and the bomb was rigged to the ignition. I got out and made a call and the Increment did the rest.'

The Increment was the Government's best-kept secret,

an ad hoc group of highly trained special forces soldiers used on operations considered too dangerous for Britain's security services. The Increment could call on the resources of the SAS and its naval equivalent, the Special Boat Service, and the Major had run it for almost five years.

'Including coming up with a body?'

'There wasn't much left after the bomb went up.'

'In a residential area?'

'It was controlled. Damage was kept to a minimum and the area was immediately cordoned off by the MoD and the Met were kept well away.' He shrugged his shoulders. 'I wasn't happy about it, about any of it. But it has to be this way, at least until I'm sure that all the leaks are plugged, and frankly I'm not sure that's ever going to happen.'

'Does Martin know?'

'As of today, you're the only person outside the Regiment who knows I'm alive.'

'So what are you doing?'

'I'm based here. I stay in the barracks, which is just about the safest place in the world for me. I do some work with the Increment but obviously I'm not running it any more. Also, I'm heading up X-Squadron.'

Shepherd frowned. 'X-Squadron?' he repeated. 'I haven't heard of them.'

'I should bloody well hope you haven't,' said the Major. 'Come on, let's get some fresh air.' They walked outside. 'X-Squadron is all secret squirrel. Made up of volunteers from the SAS and SBS, held in reserve for black operations approved by the Joint Intelligence Committee. Really hush-hush. Automatic D-notice if it's even mentioned by a journalist. We're about to send an X-Squadron team to

Sangin in northern Helmand province to take out a sniper that the Taliban have paid to kill our boys. Never a dull day.'

'I hate snipers,' said Shepherd.

'You and me both. I rank them alongside car bombers.' The Major grinned. 'Mind you, we've got personal reasons for hating both, haven't we?'

'It's a coward's way of fighting, striking from a distance.'

'Yeah, well, this one is a pro. We think he's a former Marine.'

'A Yank?'

'Born-again Muslim. Rumour has it that the Taliban are paying him ten thousand dollars for every soldier he kills.'

'It's a sick world, isn't it?' said Shepherd. 'I can understand killing for what you believe in, but killing your own for money, I don't get that.'

'He probably sees himself as fighting the infidel and that every hit is a step closer to his seventy-two virgins.'

'Do you think anyone actually believes that crap?'

The Major shrugged. 'Who knows? But the one thing I'm sure of is that if we don't stop him he's going to carry on killing our boys.' He looked at his watch. 'Well, the sun's over the yardarm. Fancy a drink?'

'You still haven't told me why you've come back from the dead.'

The Major put an arm around Shepherd's shoulder. 'Let's do it over a drink in the officers' mess,' he said. 'You're going to need one.'

'To crime,' said the Major, raising his glass of lager and clinking it against Shepherd's Jameson's and soda. 'Or at least the fighting of it.' They both drank. They were sitting in easy chairs in the officers' mess. The Major had poured the drinks himself and they were sitting at a window overlooking the clock tower. Shepherd looked over at the tower and the Major read his mind. 'Funny seeing your own name listed among the dead,' he said.

'Yeah, it must be,' said Shepherd. 'As funny as being pall-bearer at a funeral only to see the deceased come back to life a year later.' He sipped his whiskey. 'So no one at MI5 knows about this?'

'The lovely Charlie, you mean?' Gannon shook his head. 'We've got a problem with Five.'

'In what way?'

'The Real IRA found my home. How could they have done that? It's not as if I'm in the phone book. And I'm sure the Regiment wouldn't play fast and loose with my information.'

'But Five? The Secret Service?'

The Major laughed. 'Secret Service? They've got a website and the director general is always in the papers. How secret is that? But it's the Irish situation that's thrown the cat among the pigeons. The second-largest MI5 centre outside London is in Loughside in Northern Ireland. It's not just running local intelligence operations, it's now the back-up HQ in the event of a national emergency. If something goes wrong at Thames House, operations are switched to Loughside and five hundred key staff will be straight over. Loughside is already handling a big chunk of Five's international counter-terrorism operations as well as the local stuff.'

'So?'

'So they're recruiting locally. And just like the cops, they're bending over backwards to sign up Catholics. They're now as politically correct as the rest of the Establishment so they can't afford to be repeating the mistakes of the old regime.'

'But everyone is positively vetted, right?'

'Sure. But suppose they get a Belfast graduate with a PhD in Arabic studies applying, and a Catholic to boot. Are they going to care overmuch if he's got a couple of cousins who are known Republican sympathisers? Probably not. But what if down the line he gets an approach from someone pointing out that the fight against Islamic fundamentalism is one thing but that his loyalty to his country is another.'

'His country? But we're talking about Brits.'

'They're both, Spider. They're British but they're Irish too. Everyone born in the North of Ireland is entitled to British citizenship and Irish, don't forget that. And I'm not saying that the barrel is full of rotten apples but it's only got to happen once for it to be a problem.'

'And you think that's happened already?'

The Major nodded. 'I'm sure of it.' He grinned. 'You know, the SAS is one of the few organisations left where we can say we don't want to take someone on because we don't like the look of them. Doesn't matter if he's as fit as fuck, if we don't think he's got what it takes we can just say no and there's not a damn thing anyone can do about it.'

'It can't be any other way, can it?' said Shepherd. He remembered his own selection, almost fifteen years earlier. One of the hardest parts of the gruelling process was the Fan Dance, where the soldiers had to run up Pen y Fan, the tallest peak in the Brecon Beacons, fully loaded with kit and weapons, run down the far side, and then run back up and down again. It was the most demanding physical exercise on the course and could break the fittest soldier. Shepherd did the Fan Dance with fifteen other men in a winter rainstorm, and it was the weather that did for three of the men. One slipped and broke his ankle on the first ascent, one collapsed from exhaustion the second time they reached the summit, and the third managed to get separated from the group and turned up a full eight hours after everyone else. All three were sent home. Shepherd's time was respectable and he finished the Fan Dance about half an hour after the leader, a black Liverpudlian called Frankie, who'd done five years as a paratrooper before applying to the SAS. He was tall but wiry with a runner's build and he powered through all the stamina and endurance tests. He was probably the fittest on the course, but in the end he wasn't accepted because he had the wrong attitude. He took every opportunity to belittle the others on selection, mocking them when they got tired or struggled to finish a section, and laughing at anyone who made the smallest mistake. Frankie was dropped because he wasn't a team player, and the SAS was all about teamwork.

'No, but in any other organisation if someone gets turned down for a job for pretty much any reason they can sue. Wrong sex, wrong colour, wrong disability, wrong religion – the world has gone so politically correct that you can't risk offending anybody. And Northern Ireland is now as politically correct as it gets. So even MI5 can't be seen to be rejecting someone just because they drink the blood of Christ on a Sunday.' He held up his hands. 'I know, not every Catholic supports the IRA, Real or Continuity, but I'm damn sure that there are no Protestants among them.' He took another pull on his pint before continuing. 'It's not just an Irish problem,' he said. 'I know of at least four al-Qaeda sympathisers who are working in Thames House as we speak. They're being watched and they won't be able to do any damage, but that's not the point. What about the ones we don't know about? By throwing its doors wide open in the way it has, it's left itself wide open to penetration by the very forces it's supposed to be combating.'

'The world's gone crazy,' said Shepherd. He knew the Major was right – if Frankie had applied to the Met or MI5 or pretty much any government department, he'd probably have launched a racial discrimination lawsuit and walked away with a healthy pay-off.

'No argument here,' said the Major. 'But the bottom line is that I'm running out of people I can trust. And if I were you, I'd be careful too.' He took a long pull at his pint. 'So I guess you're well out of SOCA.'

'Yeah, it was a disaster from day one,' said Shepherd. 'Too many chiefs and not enough Indians. I don't know what idiot thought that you could push cops into the same organisation as taxmen, accountants and customs officers and expect them to become a crime-fighting organisation. It was supposed to be intelligence-led but most of the analysts wouldn't know a criminal if he stuck a gun in their face and asked for their wallet.' He sipped his drink. 'You know, when they set it up in 2006 they drew up a list of the one hundred and thirty most-wanted criminals, the men and women they really wanted to put behind bars. Why a hundred and thirty and not a hundred or two hundred?

Who the hell knows? It was probably left up to some desk jockey with a spreadsheet. Anyway, they come up with this list of one hundred and thirty villains who are supposed to be responsible for most of the organised crime in this country. Four years later do you know how many of them we'd put away? Eight. Bloody eight. And of the one hundred and thirty, it turns out that more than ten of them were dead. And half the names on the list weren't even major criminals.' He sighed. 'Most of the decent cops packed it in within the first two years and went back to proper policing.'

'Your timing was perfect,' said the Major. 'You'd only been gone a few months when they announced they were bringing the shutters down and folding it into the National Crime Agency.'

'You make it sound like I was a rat deserting a sinking ship,' said Shepherd. 'It wasn't like that. Charlie offered me the move to Five long before they announced that SOCA was being wound up.'

'I just hope it's not out of the frying pan and into the fire.'

'Yeah, I'm starting to wonder that myself,' Shepherd said. 'I thought I'd be getting bigger and better jobs, but it's not working out that way. To be honest, if it hadn't been for Charlie Button I'd probably have applied to rejoin the cops.'

'Ah yes, the lovely Charlotte. How is she?'

'No problems. She's a good boss. Gives me free rein when I need it.'

'Yeah, but does she have your back?'

Shepherd pulled a face. 'You heard what happened over the water?'

'I'm in the loop for all things Irish,' said the Major. 'You slotted two terrorists, so well done you.'

'I blew my cover because the right hand didn't know what the left was doing,' said Shepherd. 'It should never have happened.' He frowned. 'Is that why you're here? It's nothing to do with the Somalia thing I'm working on?'

The Major shook his head. 'I'm here because you're in deep shit, Spider. The same sort of shit I was in.' He paused to make sure that he had Shepherd's undivided attention. 'Nicholas Brett.'

'You know Nick?'

'I know that he's dead,' said the Major. 'They fished him out of the Hudson three days ago. Shot in the face at close range.'

'And I'm guessing it wasn't a robbery, right?'

The Major smiled thinly. 'I'm pretty sure that he was killed because he helped introduce you to the IRA cell at the Shamrock,' he said. 'Dawson, Crofts and McIntyre.'

'How do you know about the cell?' asked Shepherd. 'And how come you know that Brett's dead and Button doesn't?'

'Because my contacts are better than hers,' said the Major. 'She's MI5 and the CIA don't trust them, special relationship or not. But my contacts trust me, and they know I've a vested interest in things Irish.' He shrugged. 'Either that or the lovely Miss Button doesn't want you worrying.'

'What, you think she knows and hasn't said anything?'

'I've no idea how she operates, but I've always said that she's a spook first and foremost. If she doesn't think you need to know then I'm damn sure she'll be giving you the mushroom treatment.'

Shepherd sat back and folded his arms. That was the last

thing he wanted to hear, especially from a man he trusted as much as the Major. Working undercover was all about faith. The handler had to trust the undercover agent, but just as important the agent had to trust his handler, literally with his life. The agent was often so busy dealing with the job at hand that he wasn't able to see the big picture, so it was up to the handler to watch out for problems on the horizon and to deal with them as necessary. The agent had to have absolute faith in his handler, and if Charlotte Button had been withholding information, for whatever reason, then it meant she no longer had his best interests at heart.

The Major leaned forward. 'Don't get me wrong, Spider, I'm not saying she's playing fast and loose with your safety. She might not know, she might have her eye on another ball now.'

Shepherd shook his head. 'She should be monitoring the Irish situation. I killed two of their people and if they get the chance they'll hit back at me. It's not good enough to say that she's busy with other things. She knows how dangerous those people are.' He sighed. 'This job is hard enough without worrying about whether or not your boss has your back.'

'Well, you've got your friends behind you, no matter what,' said the Major, raising his glass.

Shepherd picked up his glass and clinked it against the Major's. 'So what happened to Brett? Was he tortured?'

'Doesn't look like it,' said the Major. 'But that probably means that he told them everything he knows. When an IRA enforcer and interrogation team turn up on your door-step it's your call as to how much punishment you want to take. All you can do is postpone the inevitable.'

'Unless the secret's worth taking to the grave,' said Shepherd.

'Agreed,' said the Major. 'But I'm guessing it was just a job for him and that protecting you would be pretty low on his list of priorities.'

'So they got what they wanted and then they killed him?'

'That's how I read it, yes. How much did he know about you?'

'Next to nothing,' said Shepherd. 'He thought I was a Yank, name of Matt Tanner. I can do a passable accent and they gave me a watertight legend. I was born in Belfast, moved to the States when I was a kid, served seven years in the military, served in Iraq, two tours. All of it will stand up to any checking.'

'So the Americans were in on your investigation?'

'The ATF were liaising with MI5. But Brett wouldn't have known that.'

'You can't be sure of that, can you?'

'After what happened, I'm not sure of anything any more. But Brett wouldn't have any personal details that would give me away.'

'OK, but look at it from their point of view. The ATF introduces you to fund-raisers in the States and you use that to infiltrate a Real IRA cell in Belfast. You shoot two of their people to protect an undercover cop. They've got to put it down as either a PSNI or a UK operation, right?'

'You're not exactly cheering me up here, boss.'

'I'm just being realistic,' said the Major. 'Your cover might well have been watertight and Brett might not have known anything, but that doesn't mean that they don't know where to look for you.'

Shepherd drained his glass then went to the bar and made fresh drinks. He carried them back to the table. 'So who do you think killed him?' he asked as he sat down.

The Major reached into his jacket pocket and pulled out a surveillance photograph, of a red-haired woman getting into a New York taxicab. 'Lisa O'Hara,' he said. 'Real IRA but with family links to Continuity. She left New York the day before Brett's body was pulled out of the river. Flew to Dublin but is probably back in the North by now.'

'She's known?'

'By those in the know, yeah, but it's not public knowledge. She's an enforcer, interrogator, and isn't averse to the occasional wet job.'

'Unusual in a woman,' said Shepherd, looking at the picture. 'I've known women bombmakers and the IRA uses them as decoys and the like, but she's the first female enforcer I'm aware of.'

'It's in her blood,' said the Major, taking back the photograph. 'Her dad was with McGuinness back in the day, shot by the SAS during an attack on a police station in Londonderry two years before the ceasefire. Her uncle had a big bust-up with the Provos and moved to Continuity, taking a big stock of Gaddafi's Semtex with him.'

'What's her uncle's name?'

'Robbie Fox.'

'Robbie Fox? Please don't tell me that he's related to the Fox brothers.'

The Major exhaled through pursed lips. 'Guilty as charged. He was their father.'

Shepherd groaned. 'Hell's bells, boss. Do you think she knows what happened?' Padraig and Sean Fox were dead, killed by the Major after they'd mown down a group of off-duty soldiers in a Chinese restaurant. One of the murdered soldiers had been the Major's nephew and his retaliation had been swift and final. Only Shepherd and the Major knew what had happened and where the bodies were buried.

'I think it's worse than that, Spider. I think she might have been the one behind the bomb in my Jag.' He rubbed his chin. 'Problem is, I've no way of proving it. The technical boys went through the wreckage with the proverbial fine-tooth comb but didn't find anything in the way of a signature. And there's no passport control between London and Dublin so we don't even know if she was in the country at the time.'

'But she's related to Padraig and Sean? She'd have been close to them?'

'Not closely related . . . what would they be, first cousins, second cousins? They lived in different counties but you know what Irish families are like, they'd have been at the same wedding or funeral at some point.'

Shepherd ran a hand through his hair. 'This is getting serious, boss,' he said. 'Is it possible she knows I helped you take care of the Foxes?'

'I don't see how,' he said. 'My name would obviously be in the frame because of what they did to Tommy, but they wouldn't know about you. We covered our tracks well, Spider.'

'Clearly not well enough,' said Shepherd.

'They might have guessed it was me, and not cared about proof. The fact that I headed up the Increment would be good enough reason for them to target me.'

'The Real IRA released a statement claiming responsibility

for your death,' said Shepherd. 'And they specifically mentioned the Fox brothers.'

'That doesn't mean they know about your involvement. But whether or not they do know isn't really the issue. Either way she's going to be looking for you.'

Shepherd put his head in his hands. 'This is a bloody nightmare,' he said. 'My job's hard enough without me having to spend the rest of my life looking over my shoulder.'

'It might not be as bad as that,' said the Major. 'They'll be looking in the North, and their first port of call will be the PSNI.'

'They don't know who I am and there'll be nothing on the police computer,' said Shepherd.

'So it might end there,' said the Major.

'They found you,' said Shepherd.

'But I was high profile,' said the Major. 'You've been undercover for years, first for the cops, then for SOCA, now for Five. You've had professionals covering your tracks every step of the way. And I can make sure that O'Hara and anyone she's connected to are red-flagged.'

'You know it's not as easy as that, boss,' said Shepherd. 'The England–Ireland border is a border in name only most of the time. We've both crossed the water incognito loads of times.' He shrugged. 'Anyway, there's no point in crossing bridges or counting chickens.'

'*Que sera, sera*,' said the Major, raising his glass in a silent toast.

'Yeah, well, at least I know what's coming.'

'What might be coming,' corrected the Major.

Shepherd nodded and clinked glasses with the Major. 'Thanks for the heads-up, anyway.'

'That's what friends are for.'

'And I'm glad you're back in the land of the living.'

The Major grinned. 'You and me both,' he said. 'So what's the lovely Charlie got you working on these days?'

Shepherd drove from the barracks to Liam's school just in time to see him arrive at the gates with two of his friends. Liam waved goodbye to them and climbed into the passenger seat. Shepherd's mobile rang just as he was parking in front of the house. It was Charlotte Button and Shepherd felt a sudden surge of adrenalin. Did she know that he'd just met the Major? He forced himself to relax. Button was good but there was no way that she could know what he was doing in Hereford.

'Hey, how's it going?' he asked as Liam disappeared inside the house.

'Are you busy?'

'School run,' he said. 'What's up?'

'We're ready to move,' said Button. 'Can you come to London tomorrow? Same place as before?'

'No problem,' said Shepherd, locking the car and walking towards the house.

'How did it go with the navy?' asked Button.

'Yeah, he's a good guy, that captain. He showed me a dozen or so photographs of pirates working for Crazy Boy.'

'I've just heard back from our people in Mogadishu, and Crazy Boy's uncle has collected the money.'

'You've got people in Mogadishu?'

Button laughed. 'We've got people everywhere, Spider. That's what we do.'

'How do you go about getting a spy in Somalia? I'm assuming you don't advertise in the *Guardian*.'

'We screen the refugees that arrive here and some of them are prepared to go back for us. Plus we recruit people *in situ*.'

'For money?'

'More often than not, yes. So I'll see you tomorrow. As close to noon as you can make it, OK?'

'I'll be there,' said Shepherd.

'Are you OK?' she asked.

'Sure, why?'

'You sound a bit tense, that's all.'

Shepherd screwed up his face. Button was good, all right. He took a deep breath. 'One of the mums cut me up outside the school,' he said. 'Pulled right in front of me.'

'Oh dear,' she said. 'School runs can be brutal. That's one of the great things about boarding school, of course. No more acting as a free taxi service.'

'I'm looking forward to that,' said Shepherd.

'You've decided, then?'

'Yeah, I think we're going to go for it. It's just a matter of finding the right school.'

'I'm sure you're doing the right thing,' said Button, and she ended the call.

Shepherd had to juggle the tea and coffee he was holding to press the buzzer for the office but he managed it and the lock clicked and he pushed the door open. He took the two cups upstairs, where Button already had the door open for him. She took the tea from him with a smile of thanks and sat down at the desk. There were several aerial photographs of a yacht next to her Gucci handbag and she pushed them over to him. 'Things have started moving,' she said. 'This is the yacht. It's been taken to a place called Eyl, an old fishing town in northern Puntland. That's where Crazy Boy's family is from. It's a Wild West place and anyone in authority is in the pay of the pirates. As we speak there are nine hijacked vessels moored at Eyl.'

'Do we think that the crew are being held there?'

'They were taken off the yacht so they weren't on board when it moored at Eyl. We don't have an exact location for them but they'll be in Puntland and probably won't be too far away from Eyl.'

'And why aren't we just going in and taking the yacht back?'

'Because it's not about the boat, it's the crew we want.'

'Any chance of us getting a location? It'll make our life a lot easier if we can go in now and pull them out.'

Button shook her head. 'We've got our man in Mogadishu but he can't suddenly pop up in Eyl. It's a small place and they're wary of strangers.' She pushed another photograph towards him, this one an aerial shot of a large container ship. 'We've got a line on the ship that Crazy Boy is planning to take,' she said. 'It's a cargo ship that left Tianjin in China a few days ago. The *Athena*. It's one of the largest cargo ships in the world, a shade under three hundred and fifty metres long with several thousand containers on board.' She handed him a large colour photograph of a fully laden container ship, its deck piled high with containers of different colours. 'It cruises at about twenty-four knots and spends most of its time ferrying cargo between China and Europe.'

'Any idea why they've chosen this one?'

'It's a valuable vessel, obviously. But there's some interesting cargo that might be the reason. Chinese arms destined for the Yemen. They'll be offloaded in Jeddah and taken overland from Saudi.'

'What sort of arms?'

'Guns, RPGs, ammunition. Nothing big and all legal, they're showing on the ship's manifest and all the paperwork's in order. But the shipping company isn't going to want a cargo like that delayed for any longer than necessary, and the Chinese will almost certainly start to apply pressure to get it resolved.'

'And you think Crazy Boy knows that?'

'I think he's a lot smarter than the average pirate,' said Button. 'He probably realises the publicity value of a British ship carrying Chinese weapons to the Yemen. No one is going to want that information in the public domain, so everyone is going to want to see the ransom paid and the ship back on its way.'

'And this is connected to the shipping company? Did Candy tip them off?'

'That's the strange thing, no. None of their containers are on the ship. This is a departure from his normal way of operating. Maybe there's a problem with Candy. Maybe she had a bust-up with the Somali boyfriend.'

'The bruising and the scratches? Maybe.' Shepherd frowned. 'But we're sure that he's going to go for this ship?'

'Straight from the horse's mouth,' said Button. 'Or at least his uncle's mouth. We heard him on a mobile in Somalia referring to the *Athena* by name. And we have Crazy Boy on Skype with his uncle talking about a ship leaving China. The uncle is taking delivery of weapons and GPS equipment as we speak. Two and two together make five.'

Shepherd looked at the photograph of the *Athena*. It was huge. 'I'd have thought the really big ships would be harder to seize,' he said.

'It's certainly way bigger than anything he's taken before,' said Button. 'But he was on Skype to his uncle and told him to get ready for the ship, the week after next. The ship's stopping at Malaysia before heading through the Suez to the Mediterranean and then to Jeddah and Southampton. We then monitored phone traffic between the uncle and an arms dealer in Yemen. It's definitely on.'

'And I'm guessing you're telling me this because you want me on board?'

'That's the plan, yes. You can monitor what's happening on the ship and then we can work out some way of following the pirates to their base and locating the crew of the yacht.'

'Some way? I'd hope we have something more specific than that.'

Button smiled thinly. 'There's going to have to be an element of playing it by ear, that's true. The *Athena* is a big ship so it's unlikely that they'll take it to Eyl. They might well insist on the ransom being paid to the ship. We'll be insisting that the ransom is paid on land, and that we get sight of the hostages there. Once we know where the hostages are, your guys can go in and get them.' She sipped her tea. 'OK, so far as your legend goes, we thought we might as well continue with the Oliver Blackburn legend. The consultancy thing holds together, you've already got a passport in that name, and we've got confirmation from the company that owns the *Athena* that you're going on board to do a time and motion study. That way you'll be able to move around the ship without the crew wondering what you're doing.'

'Wouldn't it be better to put me on as security? That way at least I could be armed.'

'The shipping line doesn't have armed security,' said Button, 'so it would look suspicious if you suddenly turned up with a gun.'

'I thought the shipping lines used private security firms for protection when they sailed near the Gulf of Aden?'

'Some do,' said Button. 'But this one doesn't. I'm not sure why, but I'd guess that it's to save costs.'

Shepherd sat back in his chair and folded his arms, then realised that he was adopting a defensive posture and tried to relax, putting his hands on his knees. That felt uncomfortable so he folded his arms again. He saw a look of amusement flash across Button's face and he realised that as always she was assessing his body language and drawing her own conclusions. 'And the shipping line is OK with me being on board?' he asked.

'They weren't crazy about the idea,' she said. 'They don't see why they should be putting one of their ships in harm's way.'

'Not to mention the crew.'

Button smiled. 'Actually, I got the impression that they were more concerned about the vessel and its cargo than they were about the men. They were all for taking the Jeddah and Karachi cargo off and rerouting the ship around the Cape.'

'But you managed to persuade them otherwise?'

'I explained that if they pulled the *Athena* from the Gulf of Aden the pirates might target another of their ships and that next time we might not have advance warning. At least this time we know what's happening.'

'And the ransom? That's what the pirates are after. They'll pay. Right?'

'That's where it got complicated. They have insurance, but the insurance company isn't going to be pleased if they find out that the company knew that the hijacking was on the cards.'

'Understandable,' said Shepherd.

'So they won't do it through the insurance company, they'll come up with the ransom themselves and we'll provide the negotiator.'

'That's very public-spirited of them.'

Button looked uncomfortable. 'I did sort of promise that we'd recover any ransom that was paid.'

Shepherd raised his eyebrows. 'How exactly can you make a promise like that?'

'Because we're going to catch Crazy Boy in the act of piracy and we'll hopefully get the ransom back.'

'All's well that end's well?'

'Something like that. I also mentioned that there might be someone on the ship passing information to the pirates.'

'Is that likely? Or even possible?'

'No and yes,' said Button. 'We've no evidence that there is an inside man but it would make Crazy Boy's life much easier if there was. I just put it forward as another reason why the shipping company shouldn't pull the vessel.'

'And would my presence on the ship have something to do with them accepting that deal?'

'Let's just say that they'll be happier knowing that we have an operative on board and that the SAS are on stand-by.'

'The SAS? Not the SBS? The Special Boat Service has the edge when it comes to naval matters.'

'I've already talked to the Increment,' said Button. 'They'll have a unit standing by on one of the navy ships in the area, ready to go in at a moment's notice.'

'The Increment?'

Button nodded. 'There's a new head, now that Major Gannon's . . .'

'Dead?'

Button smiled sympathetically. 'No longer with us, I was going to say. I met his replacement two days ago. He's putting together a team.'

'Who is he? The replacement?'

'Another major, six years with the Regiment. Andy Johnson. Did you ever come across him?'

Shepherd shook his head.

'He's very professional. But then all you guys are. Must be the training.'

'It's more to do with the selection,' said Shepherd. 'It weeds out anyone who is less than professional. So this Major Johnson sets up a crack team to do what exactly?'

'To a large extent that depends on you, Spider. You'll be the man on the inside.'

'But I'll be held hostage, along with the crew?'

'That's right, making sure that they're safe. The ransom will be paid, the pirates leave the ship and the Increment moves in to secure the vessel.'

'And at the same time on dry land Martin moves in and rescues the PM's god-daughter? Hell's bells, Charlie, shove a brush up my arse and I'll sweep the floor while I'm at it.'

'It's a lot of balls in the air, Spider, I can't argue with that. But if we pull it off we come out of it covered in glory.' She leaned forward. 'I know it's all a bit seat of the pants, but we know what the target is, we know who the bad guys are, and we know pretty much what they're planning to do. We'll have full satellite coverage, we can put a GPS transmitter in the ransom, and the Increment won't be far away. And from what I know about Martin O'Brien, I'm confident we'll get Katie Cranham and the rest of the yacht crew back as well.'

'I wish I was as confident as you,' said Shepherd.

'I'm looking at the bigger picture,' said Button. 'And it looks just fine to me.' She reached down for her briefcase and swung it up on to the desk. She clicked open the locks and took out an A4 manila envelope. She pushed it over to him. 'A few extras for you,' she said. 'There's correspondence from the owners of the ship to our consultancy company in the Midlands and a yellow fever vaccination certificate that's valid for another seven years. You'll need that to get on board. If you haven't actually had the jab then you should.'

'It's OK, I had it a couple of years ago. I'm up to date on all my vaccinations.' There was a small grey thumb drive on the desk and Shepherd picked it up.

'I've put schematics of the ship on there along with full details of the officers and crew,' she said. She reached into her briefcase again and took out a plane ticket. 'You can board in Malaysia. Port Klang. From there it makes a stop in Karachi and then passes through the Gulf of Aden on the way to Jeddah and then through the Suez into the Mediterranean.'

'Why don't I board in Pakistan, save myself a few days at sea?'

'Because there are visa issues with Pakistan, and you'll

attract less attention going through Malaysia. Port Klang is one of the ports the company uses for crew changes and Karachi isn't.'

Shepherd slipped the thumb drive into his pocket. 'When do I board?'

'As soon at it docks at Port Klang,' said Button. 'It'll be departing within twelve hours of arriving so you'll need to liaise with the shipping line's representative in Kuala Lumpur. He'll handle all the clearances for you.' She took a Motorola satellite phone from her briefcase. 'Communications on board are going to be a problem,' she said. 'Most of the time you're at sea you'll be out of phone coverage. There's a ship's phone but obviously that's not secure. There's email through the ship's computer system but no wifi and no personal internet access.' She handed him the sat-phone. 'You can use this, but you're going to need to keep it away from prying eyes,' she said. 'It's not the sort of phone that a company official would usually have.'

Shepherd took the sat-phone from her. It was the size and shape of a regular handset. 'I remember when these came in a suitcase,' he said. It didn't weigh much more than his Nokia.

'It's synced to the Iridium satellite system. Amar has been tinkering with it so now it gives you almost sixty hours on stand-by and six hours' talk time. It's got GPS so we'll know to about twelve feet wherever you are in the world, even while you're at sea.'

'What about the captain?' he asked.

'What do you mean?' asked Button, passing him the charger that went with the sat-phone.

'I've known a few captains in my time and they're all very protective about their vessels. And I'm damn sure they wouldn't allow an undercover agent on their ship.'

'The captain won't know,' said Button. 'No one will know. It has to be that way, just in case something goes wrong. If no one knows, no one can give you up.'

'Like Nicholas Brett?' said Shepherd quietly.

Button's eyes narrowed. 'Now why would you say that, Spider?'

'Do you know what's happened to him?'

'I know he's dead, if that's what you mean.'

'It's a bit more than dead, isn't it? Shot in the face.'

'America's a violent country. More than thirty thousand gun-related deaths a year. Now if you don't mind me asking, how did you hear about his death?'

'More importantly, Charlie, why didn't I hear it from you?'

'He was a contact, nothing more. I was told that he'd been murdered but there's nothing to suggest that it was anything to do with what happened in Belfast, assuming that's what you're concerned about.'

'You don't think it's more than a coincidence that he was murdered after my cover was blown?'

Button shrugged. 'He was an ATF undercover agent working on several cases, he was up against a lot of dangerous people. If I had any reason to believe that it was connected to you, of course I'd have told you.'

'But you didn't want to worry me, is that it? You didn't want me taking my eye off the ball?'

Button leaned forward across the desk. 'Spider, I always have your best interests at heart. You should know that. Yes,

I was told that Nicholas Brett had been killed and the New York cops are investigating it, but as things stand it could just as easily have been a mugging. His wallet and watch were taken. Did you know that?'

Shepherd shook his head. 'No, I didn't.'

'So I didn't want you to worry over nothing. And that still stands. As soon anything changes, I'll tell you.'

Shepherd stared at her, trying to get a read on her. Her eyes were wide, suggesting honesty, there was no tightening of the jaw or pulse at her temple indicating unusual stress levels, no licking of the lips to suggest nervousness, no awkward swallowing to suggest a dry mouth; her hands were relaxed on the desk with no instinctive upward motion to touch her nose or cover her mouth. All the indications were that she was telling the truth, but then Charlotte Button knew as much as he did about body language, maybe more, and she would be able to fake it if she had to. 'You didn't answer my question,' she said. 'Who told you that Brett was dead?'

He forced himself to appear relaxed and kept smiling amiably. He could see that she was studying him as carefully as he was watching her. He opened his hands, showing his palms, trying to make it a casual gesture. Palm-showing suggested honesty and openness, but done too aggressively it was a sign of deceit. He was about to lie to her and there weren't many people harder to lie to than Charlotte Button. 'Old friend of mine in the DEA,' he said. 'I'd asked him for background on Brett when I first went over.'

'I didn't know you had friends in the DEA.'

'A friend,' said Shepherd, maintaining eye contact and keeping his breathing steady. 'Brett was an unknown so I asked my guy and he said he didn't know him. When Brett turned up dead he gave me a call.'

Button nodded slowly as she studied Shepherd's face. 'OK,' she said finally, sitting back in her chair and linking her fingers. 'This isn't a problem, is it?'

Shepherd shrugged. 'Of course not.'

'You're sure? I get the feeling that you think I should have told you straight away. But believe me, Spider, it was just one of a thousand pieces of intel that pass across my desk every day. I'm far more concerned about what's coming out of Northern Ireland than the States. If there are going to be any repercussions about what happened in Belfast, they're more likely to come from there than from across the pond.'

'And Belfast is quiet?'

'Lots of chatter, and obviously Matt Tanner's name keeps coming up, but so far nothing to even suggest that they know who Tanner really was.'

Shepherd flashed her a confident smile. 'Let's hope it stays that way, then.'

Katie had lost all track of time and she no longer knew how many days she'd been held captive. They were kept together, which was something, and the rapes had stopped. They were being held in a village, and when they'd dragged her into the concrete-walled hut from the truck she'd seen women in headscarves watching, so maybe the pirates didn't want them to know about the sexual assaults.

There was no furniture in the hut and they all sat on the bare mud floor with their backs against the wall. There was a zinc bucket in one corner with a piece of sacking. That was where they went to the toilet. The bucket was emptied once a day, if they were lucky.

Katie was sitting between Eric and Joy. Andrew and Hoop sat together on the opposite side of the hut. Joy and Andrew had barely spoken since they had been taken off the boat. Katie didn't know if it was because Joy blamed her husband for not protecting her or if it was because Andrew was ashamed of what had happened. Either way they behaved as if they were strangers and not husband and wife.

They all smelled bad. Worse than bad. They hadn't showered or had a proper wash since they'd been taken off the yacht and they hadn't been given any toilet paper. And they had to eat with their hands because their meals came without any cutlery.

They were fed three times a day, always rice and a piece of fish, and occasionally a bowl of watery soup. The dishes never seemed to be washed and the water they were given to drink came in a plastic bucket and there were always insects floating in it. Katie's stomach had been playing up for the past three days and she was having to use the bucket every hour or so, much to her embarrassment.

Katie put her head in her hands. She was beyond crying. She had no more tears left inside her. She wished that she was dead, and if there had been any way of killing herself she would almost certainly have done it there and then.

The door scraped open and Roobie walked in. He was wearing a camouflage T-shirt and baggy shorts and had a machete tucked into a thick leather belt.

'The owner won't pay,' said Roobie. Everyone looked at him fearfully.

'What do you mean, he won't pay?' said Hoop.

'He says the boat isn't his. He says the boat is his when it gets to Australia.'

Hoop cursed.

'Is that right?' asked Roobie.

'Maybe,' said Hoop, getting to his feet.

Roobie stepped forward and slapped Hoop across the face, hard enough to split his lip. 'Maybe!' he shouted. 'You say maybe to me!' He brought his knee up into Hoop's groin and he pitched forward, clutching his private parts, then fell to the ground.

Hoop lay on the floor, curled up into the foetal position and whimpering. Roobie turned to glare at the rest of his prisoners. Joy and Katie huddled together and Eric was trembling. Andrew clenched his fists but knew that if Roobie attacked him there'd be nothing he could do. Even if he were to try to defend himself Roobie's men would come piling into the hut.

'Someone must pay for you!' Roobie shouted, spittle spraying from his lips. 'If no one pays, you die.' He pulled the machete from his belt. 'You understand me?' he screamed. He lunged for Joy and grabbed her hair. She wailed in pain as he pulled her across the mud floor and thrust the blade against her neck. 'No money, you all die!' Tears were streaming down Joy's face. Andrew roared and ran towards Roobie, his hands curved into claws, but Roobie lashed out with the machete and cut him across the chest. He released Joy and lashed out again at Andrew, hacking at his arm. Andrew fell back, bleeding from his wounds.

Roobie raised the machete, ready to bring it crashing down on Andrew's head, but then he held himself back. His chest rose and fell as he stared down at Andrew, but then he relaxed and stepped back. Two of his men came through the door, Kalashnikovs at the ready. Roobie snapped at them in Somali and they went out.

'This is what you do,' said Roobie, tapping the machete against his leg. 'You will give me the telephone numbers of your families. We will call them and if they pay, you live. If they not pay, you die.'

Shepherd used his Oliver Blackburn mobile that Button had given him to call the number of the shipping line's representative in Malaysia. He had only been given the man's first name – Jamal.

Jamal answered on the third ring and Shepherd introduced himself as Oliver Blackburn. 'I'm supposed to be joining the *Athena* when it gets to Port Klang.'

'Yes, Mr Blackburn, we are expecting you,' said Jamal in clipped BBC English.

'So how does it work, Jamal? When is the *Athena* due in?'

'The vessel has already left China and we have an estimated arrival date three days hence,' said Jamal. 'I will know more in another twenty-four hours.'

'When would be the best time for me to get there?'

'The day after tomorrow would be fine.'

'Is there a hotel I can use while I'm waiting?'

'There is the Crystal Crown Hotel in Port Klang,' said Jamal. 'If you like I can make a reservation for you. Where are you flying from?'

'London, Heathrow,' said Shepherd.

'You can take an airport taxi to the hotel,' said Jamal. 'A word of advice, buy your ticket before leaving the terminal. The airport taxis don't take cash. Call me when you've arrived and I will hopefully have a boarding time for you.'

Shepherd thanked him and ended the call, impressed by Jamal's efficiency. Then he took out the business card that Captain Giles had given him when he'd left his office and called his mobile number.

Shepherd walked into the Waterstones branch in Trafalgar Square and spent ten minutes browsing in the science fiction section and another five minutes in the children's section before he was satisfied that no one was following him, then he went upstairs to the Costa Coffee outlet on the first floor and ordered himself a large cappuccino. He looked at his watch as he sat down in an easy chair facing the stairs. It was just after 4.30 and he was fifteen minutes early. He took out his mobile and phoned Liam. 'Have you done your homework?' he asked.

'Dad, I've only just walked in through the door. I need some down time.'

'Hard day?'

'It's school, Dad. It's never easy.'

'So get Katra to make you a sandwich and get stuck in to it.'

'I want to check my Facebook page first.'

'OK, but then homework, right?'

Liam sighed. 'OK, Dad.'

'Everything all right at home?'

'Sure. When are you coming back?'

'I'll try to get back tonight but then I'm flying out to Malaysia.'

'On a job?'

'Of course on a job. Do you think I'd go on holiday without you?'

'How long this time, Dad?' Liam's voice had gone cold and flat and Shepherd winced.

'I'm not sure. A week or so. Maybe a bit longer.'

Liam sighed again. 'It's like you're never here these days,' he said.

'I'm sorry. It's been a busy few months.'

'Years, Dad. It's been a busy few years.'

Shepherd saw Captain Giles walking towards him and he waved him over. 'Liam, I've got to go.'

'Tell me something I don't know,' said Liam, and the line went dead. Shepherd cursed under his breath and put his phone away, then stood up to shake hands with Giles.

'Good choice,' said Giles, looking around. 'I much prefer Costa to Starbucks though either of them is ten times better than the dishwater we get at the MoD.'

'I'm sorry about the short notice,' said Shepherd. 'I'm heading out of London and I wanted to pick your brains before I go.'

'Pick away.'

'What can I get you?'

'A mocha would be great,' said Giles. He patted his stomach. 'Low-fat milk and no whipped cream.'

Shepherd chuckled. 'Watching your weight?'

'I'm either at sea or sitting at a desk,' he said. 'And the hours I work I don't get much gym time.'

He sat down while Shepherd went to get his coffee.

'I know the type of ship that's going to be attacked and I wanted to know what I should expect,' said Shepherd after

Giles had taken his first sip of mocha and wiped the foam from his upper lip. 'How the pirates would board and so on.'

'You know they're going to target a particular ship?'

'Yeah, we've got pretty good intel.'

'So what are you going to do? Put an SBS team on board and catch them, is that it?'

Shepherd looked pained. 'I can't say, I'm afraid.'

'Well, if that's what you're planning it'll be a first,' said Giles. 'But it's about time somebody did something.'

'So we think they're after a container ship, just under three hundred and fifty metres long.'

Giles nodded and took another sip of his coffee. 'That's big,' he said. 'Eleven thousand TEUs, I'd say.'

'More initials,' said Shepherd. 'You nautical types do like them, don't you?'

Giles grinned. 'Twenty-foot equivalent units. A standard container is twenty foot long. But a lot of them are double that length, forty feet. So to calculate the storage space we convert it to single units, or TEUs. So the ship that you're talking about would be able to carry eleven thousand single containers or five and a half thousand doubles, or a combination of the two.'

'You know the sort of ship I'm talking about, then? I'm told it has a cruising speed of twenty-four knots.'

Giles nodded. 'Yeah, it's a standard type, one of the biggest in service. The only bigger container ship would be thirteen thousand TEUs, though there are plenty of larger oil tankers. Probably built in Korea.' He frowned. 'You're sure about the intel on this?'

'I'm told it's gold,' said Shepherd. 'Why?'

'Because that's a bloody big ship and the pirates tend to go for easier pickings.'

'I'd have thought that the bigger the ships, the bigger the profits?'

'That's not really the case, because the ransoms are a small fraction of the value of the ship and the cargo,' said Giles. 'Ransoms run from a million to five million, but doubling the value of the ship doesn't necessarily double the ransom.' He leaned forward. 'The thing is, the deck is some fifteen metres above sea level, so that is a major hurdle for the pirates. If they're in skiffs or inflatables, they can't be handling ladders that long.'

'Grappling irons and ropes?'

'In rough seas? Could you climb a fifteen-metre rope up the side of a moving ship?'

Shepherd grinned because he had done exactly that as part of his SAS training, but Giles was right, the pirates were enthusiastic amateurs and not highly trained soldiers. 'I hear you,' he said.

'To stand any chance of getting on board they'd have to be at the stern. The displacement at the bow and sides is way too much to allow any sort of boarding.'

'Now you've lost me,' said Shepherd.

'OK, look, this is one huge ship. I'm guessing it would be displacing maybe a hundred and seventy thousand tonnes. That means as it moves through the sea, it pushes that amount of water away, and most of that water is pushed to the side. Any small vessel would be swamped. So the pirates couldn't pull up next to the ship if it was moving and toss up a grappling hook. They'd be capsized before they even got within throwing distance.'

'So they wait until the ship has stopped.'

'But they don't stop, not unless they're in port. The ships are always moving because any time they're not moving they're losing money.'

'What about the stern, then?'

'In theory that's possible, there isn't as much wash directly behind the ship, but then they'd be right over the propeller and that's ninety tonnes of brass and steel whirling around. One mistake and it's mincemeat.'

'But possible?'

'I've never heard of pirates boarding a ship that size while it's moving,' Giles said. 'And remember that twenty-four knots is its cruising speed, it could probably get up to thirty-five knots with the engine full ahead.'

'I'm told that there's no security on board. Can that be right? The ship alone must be worth millions and there's the cargo on top of that.'

'Shipowners are always trying to cut costs, but they're obviously not going to risk losing a ship,' said Giles. 'They'll simply be taking the view that the chances of a ship that size being taken are so remote that there's no reason to pay for extra security.'

'You said it was only five thousand dollars a day.'

'Sure, but they'd have to be on board all the time they were in pirate waters. Four or five days, maybe. But they might have a dozen ships that size. And they might all be passing through the Suez Canal every couple of months. It soon mounts up, and as in all big businesses there are always accountants sniffing around looking to cut costs. Don't get me wrong, security is a good idea for the smaller ships, but a ship that size is in a whole different league.'

Shepherd frowned as he sipped his cappuccino. 'So talk me through what could happen if a group of pirates were to go after a ship like this.'

Giles nodded. 'OK, well, first of all the vessel will be in open sea, miles from shore, so the pirates will have to have a mother ship, a base from which they operate. Often that's a ship that they've seized in the first place. They'll tie their inflatables or skiffs to the mother ship and then head out to sea. The mother ship will have radar so they can use that to spot bigger prey.'

'So they're not targeting specific ships?'

'Generally not, it's usually opportunistic. When they spot something on the radar they head off on the smaller boats for a look-see. If it looks like a reasonable catch then they'll try to get on board. Their boats are usually fitted with powerful outboards which means that they burn fuel like nobody's business, so if they haven't managed to board within forty minutes or so they'll usually give up and go back to refuel. If they can, they'll run alongside and use ladders to get aboard, so they want ships that are low in the water.'

'And what do the crew do? Presumably they don't just sit and wait to be boarded.'

Giles laughed. 'No, I don't think anyone wants to be held by pirates for months at a time, do they?' He stretched out his legs. 'OK, the first line of defence is vigilance. On a clear day you can see to the horizon, so twenty miles or thereabouts. You keep an eye out for any traffic visually and on the radar, and you use the ship's identifiers to see who's close to you. Anything without an identifier, or even if they have an identifier but seem to be heading in the wrong direction, is a red flag. You have to remember that pretty much all traffic is going from port to port, so anyone not going with the flow is either a tourist or up to no good.'

Giles sipped his mocha. 'So you stay vigilant, that's basically your first line of defence. If you see something untoward, you can take evasive action. Steer away from the trouble and up your speed. Say you spot a skiff heading your way and it's doing forty knots. You head away at full speed, maybe thirty knots. At a ten-knot difference it's going to take him the best part of an hour to reach you and that means if he doesn't board you he's going to run out of fuel with no way back to the mother ship.'

'So they'll give up?'

'Yeah, probably. They know that if the mother ship doesn't come for them then they'll die on the ocean. Fuel isn't a problem for the big container ships, they carry enough to be able to go right around the world without refuelling. But the pirates can't run at full speed for more than an hour or so, even with extra fuel tanks on board.'

'What about at night? Can't they get closer without being seen?'

'Radar still works at night and the pirates are carrying guns and radar reflects off anything metallic. Also it's harder for the pirates at night. Boarding at sea is dangerous enough in daylight, it's a hell of a lot harder in the dark.'

'So they don't attack at night?'

'That's not a hard and fast rule, but it's certainly a lot easier during daylight. And if the crew know they're under attack they can use the searchlights to dazzle the pirates. Sounds simple, I know, but it works. Ships have very powerful searchlights and they'll temporarily blind anyone who gets too close. In the daytime the crew can use the fire hoses to keep them at bay.'

'What about guns? The crew have access to guns, right?'

'Absolutely not,' said Giles. 'There are no guns on merchant vessels. There might be the odd rogue master who keeps a weapon hidden away for a rainy day but it'd be a sackable offence to have a gun on board.'

'But searchlights and hoses, it all sounds very basic.'

'It is, mainly. But so are the pirates. Most of them are teenagers, some of them are fishermen, but we're not talking Mensa members here. They're looking for easy pickings. Think of them as street muggers, prowling around for victims. If they see a big guy who looks like he can take care of himself, they keep well clear. If they come across a group of guys, they walk on by. But when they see an old lady or a kid with an expensive mobile, that's when they strike. That's why I was asking you about the quality of your intel. They don't usually pick their targets in advance.'

'Like I said, the intel's good, or at least I'm told it is,' said Shepherd. 'Maybe we're looking at this the wrong way. I'm asking you how the pirates operate when what we should be doing is asking ourselves how they would seize a hundred and thirty thousand tonne vessel.'

Giles ran a hand through his blond hair. 'It's a toughie.'

'I guess I'm asking you to think like a pirate,' said Shepherd. 'If it was you out there, how would you take a vessel of that size?'

Giles sighed and sipped his mocha. 'OK, well, first of all you need to get the vessel to stop. Or at least to slow right down.' He nodded slowly. 'Stand and deliver would probably work. Pull a Dick Turpin.'

'Hold them up at gunpoint?'

'The pirates have RPGs. AK-47s. I've heard tell of hand grenades.'

'But an RPG or a hand grenade isn't going to destroy a ship that size, is it?'

Giles smiled. 'They don't have to destroy the ship, just threaten to damage it. You've got to remember, this is all about money. A damaged ship is as useless to the owner as a hijacked ship. In fact a damaged ship is worse because it's got to be taken away and repaired, whereas a seized ship is on the move again as soon as the ransom has been paid.' He leaned forward, an eager glint in his eyes. 'OK, this is how I'd do it. I'd use a pincer movement, come in from two directions to cut down on his options. Off the starboard bow and the port side simultaneously. It wouldn't be easy and it would take some planning but it's doable. Once the two skiffs are in close he can't outrun them. All he can do is to keep on going at full speed and hope that they give up. So if I was a pirate I'd fire a few warning shots at the bridge, just to show him that I mean business. Then I show him the RPG. Might even call him up on the radio, if he'll talk to me.'

'And then he'll stop?'

'Probably not,' Giles said. 'By this stage the master's looking at his watch and trying to work out how much fuel I've got left. He's hoping that I'll give up if he doesn't show any signs of stopping. So then I fire an RPG across his bow and then he stops looking at his watch. He knows that an RPG isn't going to sink the vessel, but it could disable the bridge, or if a shell hits the right container it could start one hell of a fire. But he's weighing against that the fact that if the pirates damage the ship too much then they're not going to be able to move it. Then they're stuck on a drifting ship and by then the master has already put out a mayday call so help is probably on its way. He has to work out in his own mind if the pirates really are prepared to damage the ship so much that it becomes inoperable. So then I reload my RPG and point it at the bridge. Maybe he thinks I'm getting angry, maybe angry enough to shoot whether or not it makes him stop. And then he starts to wonder what the shipowner is going to say, because by not stopping the master is putting the lives of his crew and the safety of his vessel on the line. It's a tough decision for anyone to have to make.'

'So what does he do? What would you do?'

Giles grinned. 'Me, I'm navy through and through. I'd never give up my ship, but then I'd like to think that I wouldn't have got my ship into that position in the first place. But the captain of a container ship isn't in it for queen and country, he's in it for his salary and his pension so he's not going to fight just for the sake of it. Every decision he makes is based around cost. And the point might be reached where he realises that the cheapest option is to surrender his vessel and wait for the company to pay the ransom. If he does that, he doesn't get blamed, the company will just write it down to bad luck. But if he tries to run and the ship is damaged, then the company is likely to blame him for making the wrong decision and that could be the end of his career. Like I said, it's a tough decision.'

'And what happens then? Once he's stopped the ship?'

'Then the pirates board, which is simple enough if the ship's not moving. Not without its dangers, mind, but it's doable. The first thing they'll do is to secure the vessel. They'll probably keep the captain in the bridge but everyone else will be locked away below decks. If they know what they're doing they'll switch off the ship's AIS.' Giles grinned when he saw Shepherd frown. 'AIS, Automated Identification System, the device that identifies the ship for what it is. If they switch it off then the ship will still be visible on radar, obviously, but no one will be able to identify it. If they're really smart they might change their AIS details and pretend to be a different sort of vessel. Then they'll move it from its present position. If it was a smaller ship then they'd maybe take it into Somali waters and maybe even dock it, but that's not an option for a ship the size of the one you're talking about. They'll take it away from the shipping lanes, somewhere quieter, while they start negotiations.'

'They can't make the ship invisible, though,' said Shepherd. 'Even if they switch off the AIS planes can spot it, satellites, radar.'

'Yes, but they're not hiding,' said Giles. 'Once they've taken a vessel it's very difficult to reclaim it by force. It's happened, the Americans did it once, so did the French and the Russians, but any show of force puts the lives of the hostages at risk. At the end of the day it's all about money. Provided the ransom is paid then the ship and the hostages are released unharmed. And generally the ransom is affordable.'

'But what about the CTF you talked about in your office?'

'They're prevention rather than cure,' said Giles. 'Their job is to stop the pirates taking vessels, not to drive them off a ship they've already seized. They're not geared up for that. It's also a legal minefield because the seizures take place in international waters most of the time. The ship you're looking at, what flag is it flying under?'

'British.'

'So if anyone would take on the pirates it would have to be the SAS or SBS. Now, they could do it, of course they could, but with the hostages down below decks under armed guard there'd be risks. And just to make it more complicated, even though the ship is flying under a British flag there's every chance that the officers and crew would be from other countries. The crew would almost certainly be Filipino, the officers could be Polish, Croatian, French, who knows? So if the SAS do go in with guns blazing and people get hurt, how's that going to look? British special forces try to rescue a British ship but foreigners get caught in the crossfire.'

'Messy,' said Shepherd.

'Very messy,' said Giles. He raised his eyebrows as he thought of something. 'There's one way that special forces can go in,' he said. 'That's if the ship has a panic room. That changes everything. Does the ship you're talking about have one?'

'I don't know. I'll check. How do they work?'

'Same as they do in a house. A secure room that the occupants can retreat to in case of attack. Some of them have duplicate controls so that the ship can be run from the room, others are just safe places and the crew disable the engine before they lock themselves in. If special forces know that all the crew are out of harm's way they can go in and basically shoot everything that moves. The Russians did it a while back, killed all the pirates and retook the ship.'

'But you're saying if there's no panic room, they won't go in?'

'It's too dangerous, too many ways that the crew can end up dead. It would be a different ballgame if this was happening out in South-East Asia and it was Chinese ships being taken. The Chinese would just blow the pirates out of the water and to hell with public opinion. Once a ship is taken the CTF will monitor what's going on but it's up to the shipping company to negotiate and pay. And that's what they do.'

Shepherd nodded thoughtfully.

'Is that any help to you?' asked Giles.

'It gives me an idea of how this is probably going to play out,' said Shepherd.

'This might sound like a stupid question, but if you know that the pirates are going to target a particular ship, why don't you just warn the shipowners?'

'That's a good question,' said Shepherd.

'But I get the feeling you don't have an answer.'

'It's complicated,' said Shepherd.

Martin O'Brien joined the immigration queue, put his bag on the floor and stretched. He was a big man and even a British Airways business-class flat bed didn't offer much in the way of comfort, not compared with the king-size bed that he normally slept in.

Ahead of him in the line were two of the men he'd hired for the operation, and there were another four somewhere behind him. They would rendezvous outside the terminal once they'd collected their bags and gone through customs, but until then they acted as if they didn't know each other.

It took twenty minutes for O'Brien to reach the front of the queue. He handed his Irish passport and landing card to a chubby Kenyan woman with bright red lipstick and wire-framed spectacles. She studied the card, flicked through the passport and examined his photograph, then looked at him. 'What is the purpose of your visit?' she asked, a redundant question because O'Brien had already ticked the box that said 'Tourism'.

He showed no annoyance at the question, though, and he flashed the woman a beaming smile. 'I'm here to hunt,' he said. He mimed firing a gun.

'Big game?' she asked.

O'Brien's smile widened. 'Oh yes,' he said. 'The biggest.'

Shepherd drove back to Hereford and arrived home just after ten o'clock at night. Katra was in the kitchen working on a Sudoku puzzle when he walked in. 'Are you hungry?' she asked. 'I made a stew and there's plenty left. I can do some mashed potatoes.'

'Sounds great,' he said, dropping his bag on the floor. 'When did Liam go to bed?'

'Not long ago,' she said. 'He was on the computer.'

Shepherd took a white box out of his bag, went upstairs and pushed open the door to Liam's bedroom. His son opened his eyes as the light from the hallway cut across his bed. 'Dad!' he said.

'Hi, Liam,' said Shepherd. He sat on the edge of the boy's bed. 'I just wanted to say good night.'

Liam sat up, rubbing his eyes. 'Where were you?' he asked. 'Still London?'

'Yeah, the Big Smoke.'

Liam laughed. 'I don't think anyone calls it that any more, do they? It's a hangover from Victorian times, right? When they had smog and stuff.'

'I know plenty of people who call London the Big Smoke,' said Shepherd.

'When are you going to Malaysia?' asked Liam.

'Tomorrow,' said Shepherd. 'I'll get the train back to London and fly out from Heathrow.'

'What's in Malaysia that's so important?'

'A ship. I'm going on board.'

'Why?'

'Just to protect it.'

'Why does a boat need protecting?' asked Liam.

Shepherd didn't like lying to his son, but working for MI5 brought with it a new set of rules. As an undercover police officer he was usually able to tell Liam the bare bones of the cases he worked on, and even when he was employed by SOCA he could discuss his work, but MI5 wasn't called the Secret Service for nothing and there were limits to what he could tell his son. He hadn't even told Liam that he worked for MI5. Button had explained when he'd joined that it was theoretically acceptable for close relatives to be told who he worked for, but that whenever possible it was best to be circumspect. If Shepherd had told Liam then the boy would have had to have been sworn to secrecy and Shepherd figured that it was a burden best not shared.

'It's got a valuable cargo,' he said, which was fairly close to the truth.

'What sort of boat is it?'

'A container ship. And it's a ship, not a boat.'

'What's the difference?'

'Basically anything that weighs more than twelve tonnes is a ship. Below that it's a boat.'

'How do you know that?'

'I studied hard at school,' said Shepherd. 'Speaking of which, how's the homework going?'

'All done,' said Liam.

'And everything's going well at school?'

'Sure.'

'When's the next PTA meeting?'

'They haven't said yet.'

'I don't want to miss it.'

Liam sighed. 'Dad, it's been years since you went to a PTA meeting.'

'Two years ago.'

Liam shook his head. 'No, Dad. Two years ago you were in Northern Ireland, and last year you were in London. Three years ago I don't know where you were but you were too busy.'

'I was in the school last year to talk to Miss Claire, your teacher.'

'That was different, Dad. That wasn't a PTA meeting.' There was a glass of water on his bedside table and Liam reached over for it. He saw the white box in Shepherd's hand. 'What's that?'

Shepherd grinned and held out the box. Liam put down his glass of water. 'Is that what I think it is?' he said.

'I don't know, what do you think it is?'

'An iPad? Did you get me an iPad?'

'Nah, I found the box, I put your new dictionary in it.'

Liam's face fell but then he grinned as he realised that his father was joking. He opened the box and took out a brand-new iPad. 'Oh my God,' he said. 'I'm the first in my class to get an iPad. I can't believe it.'

'Yeah, but no taking it to school,' said Shepherd. 'That's

a valuable piece of kit. I don't want someone taking it off you.'

Liam hugged it to his chest. 'I'll guard it with my life.'

Shepherd ruffled his hair. 'There's no need to go to extremes,' he said. 'And no playing with it now. You've got school tomorrow.'

'Can I at least switch it on?'

Shepherd laughed as he realised that he should have waited until morning before giving him the present. 'OK. But half an hour and then sleep.'

'Thanks, Dad,' said Liam. 'You're amazing.'

'Yeah,' said Shepherd as he stood up. 'That's what they tell me.'

Shepherd stayed up late as he studied the information on the thumb drive that Button had given him. Katra had gone to bed soon after he got back and he ate his chicken stew in the kitchen in front of his laptop.

The ship was huge. Built by the Daewoo shipbuilding company in South Korea, it had been delivered in 2008. It was a shade under 350 metres long and 45 metres wide and weighed more than 130,000 tonnes. The engine had been built by Hyundai-Man and was capable of almost a hundred thousand horsepower, and was fitted with a 4,000-horsepower bow thruster allowing the ship to be moved sideways when in port.

The bulk of the *Athena* was given over to container storage, with space for 11,040 TEUs. Shepherd tried to visualise that many of the massive containers in one place but he couldn't do it. But he was starting to realise how valuable a fully loaded ship would be. The vessel alone would have cost close to one hundred and fifty million dollars, and if each container held just five thousand dollars' worth of goods then the cargo would be worth another fifty-five million dollars. And that would be a conservative estimate – each TEU was equivalent to more than 1,500 cubic feet and could be packed with all sorts of valuable goods or raw materials. But even using two hundred million dollars as a benchmark, a five-million-dollar ransom was a bargain, and that was even before the lives of the crew were taken into account.

There was a full schematic of the ship showing all the different levels, from the bridge at the top to the engine room at the bottom. Shepherd studied every inch of the vessel but couldn't find a panic room.

The bridge ran the full width of the vessel with huge windows providing all-round visibility and exterior sections port and starboard each with a set of duplicate controls allowing the master to manoeuvre the vessel from either side if necessary.

Below the bridge was G-Deck, where the captain and chief engineer had their cabins and offices. Then there was F-deck with cabins for the chief officer, the second engineer, and any passengers who were being carried on board, and the owner's cabin in case one of the company bosses decided to visit the ship.

On E-Deck were the bulk of the officer cabins, with the crew cabins just below them on D-Deck, along with a gymnasium, swimming pool and sauna.

Cabins for the crew were also on C-Deck, with the ship's mess rooms, galley and pantry on B-Deck.

A-Deck was the ship's hospital and laundry and the main

food storage areas, with a fish room, meat room, vegetable room and drinks storage area able to hold enough provisions to feed the officers and crew for a year.

The Upper Deck was the main working area with various storerooms and workshops and below it was the vast engine room, four floors deep.

The entire structure was the size of a small hotel and serviced with a lift that ran between the floors. Shepherd's trick memory effortlessly filed away the floor plans.

There was also a list of the officers and crew on board, including their personnel files and photographs. The captain was Polish, as were all the officers except for an officer cadet who was Slovenian. The crew were without exception Filipinos.

There were twenty-two men on board – the captain, the chief officer, a second and third officer, a chief engineer, a second and third engineer, an electrician, a bosun, a deck fitter, five seamen, three engine-room workers, a cook, a messman and two cadets, one of whom was an engineer. It seemed a small number of men considering the size of the vessel, and Shepherd doubted that they would be thrilled to hear that a company man was on board who might want to downsize them even further.

Button had included several PDF files on seamanship and shipping and he skimmed them, knowing that the more information he had the easier it would be to pass himself off as an employee of the shipping company. Button's choice of legend had been a good one because a human resources executive would be an outsider and no one would want to get too close to him, but at the same time it would give him an excuse to wander around the vessel and to ask questions.

He finished reading the files on the thumb drive at just before two o'clock in the morning, then he went upstairs, showered and slept.

Liam was already in the kitchen eating cheesy scrambled eggs and toast and drinking orange juice when Shepherd went downstairs the following morning. Katra made him a cup of coffee as he poured cornflakes into a bowl and added milk. 'I'll drive Liam to school, and then can you take me to the station,' Shepherd said to Katra. 'I'll get the train to London.'

'When will you be back?' asked Katra.

'Hopefully not too long, a couple of weeks maybe. It's open ended.'

Liam sighed theatrically but didn't say anything.

Shepherd finished his coffee and cereal and nodded at Liam. 'Ready?'

Liam picked up his school bag and walked with Shepherd to the black BMW SUV. 'A couple of weeks?' he groaned as he climbed in.

'It's a ship,' said Shepherd. 'They move slowly.'

Liam fastened his seat belt. 'Did you do anything about boarding school?'

'Yeah, I thought about it,' said Shepherd, fastening his belt and starting the engine. 'I'm starting to think that it's not a bad idea. I've looked at a few websites already. Are you sure that's what you want?'

'Yeah, I think so,' said Liam. 'There's no point in me being at home all the time if there's only Katra there. At least if I was boarding I could hang out with friends and stuff.'

'I'll talk to a few schools, get some brochures,' said Shepherd. 'We can go and look at a few when I get back.

And if you see somewhere you like and the fees aren't too extortionate, you can give it a go.'

'That'd be great, Dad, thanks.'

'Hopefully we'll be able to find somewhere not too far away so that when I am back I can drive over or you can come back for weekends.' He drove away from the house.

'Dad, what about Katra?'

'What do you mean?'

'If I go to boarding school, you won't need an au pair, will you? She won't have to look after me.'

'We'll still need someone to take care of the house,' said Shepherd.

'I don't want you to send her back to Slovenia.'

Shepherd laughed. 'No one's going to send her anywhere,' he said. 'Even if you do go to boarding school you'll still be home at half-term and holidays and if it's close to Hereford then you'll be back at weekends as well. And don't forget that Katra does all sorts of other things around the house, not least the ironing. Because believe me, son-of-mine, I am not going to start ironing my own shirts.'

'Good,' said Liam.

'You'd miss her, wouldn't you?'

'Wouldn't you?'

Shepherd nodded. 'Of course.'

'So let's not lose her. OK?'

'Deal,' said Shepherd.

He dropped Liam outside the school gates, then drove back to his house and spent the next half an hour packing a kitbag. He hadn't been on a ship for any length of time before but he knew that if he forgot anything he wouldn't be able to pop down to the shops. He put a large can of shaving foam and two disposable razors into his washbag along with a bottle of shampoo. According to the crew list there wasn't a doctor on board so he added a bottle of aspirin and some antibiotic tablets. It wasn't going to be a holiday but there wouldn't be any television at sea so he put half a dozen paperbacks into his kitbag, including the new John Grisham and Stephen King and a couple of Andy McNabs that he'd had by his bed for the past three months but never had time to read. He kept his clothes simple – half a dozen polo shirts, a couple of sweatshirts and two pairs of jeans, plus some gym clothes and a pair of trainers. Shepherd preferred to run in boots with a heavy rucksack on his back but he didn't see that happening on board a container ship, no matter how big it was.

Katra was waiting for him in the kitchen. 'I'm hoping I won't be away too long, but if I'm not back for the PTA meeting, can you go in my place?'

'Of course,' said Katra. 'You know, last time I went they thought I was his mum?'

'That's crazy,' said Shepherd. 'You're not that much older than him.'

'Dan, I'm twenty-six.'

'OK, so you're twice his age, but you're still not old enough to be his mum. And you don't look twenty-six.'

She grinned and curtsied. 'Thank you, kind sir.'

'At this point you're supposed to tell me that I don't look thirty-eight.'

She narrowed her eyes as she scrutinised his face. 'No, you look thirty-eight,' she said.

'That would be the famous Slovenian bluntness,' he said. Her jaw dropped and she put her hand up to cover her mouth. 'I'm sorry,' she said. 'I was supposed to say you looked younger, right? I am so stupid.'

Shepherd laughed. 'No, honesty is the best policy,' he said, 'especially when people are fishing for compliments.'

'Fishing?' she said. 'Who is fishing?'

Shepherd laughed again. 'It's an expression. Fishing for compliments. It's when someone is looking for someone else to say something flattering.'

She nodded. 'OK, I understand,' she said. 'In that case, you only look thirty-five. Is that better?'

'Much better,' he said. He looked at his watch. 'Can you drive me to the station?'

Katra dropped him outside the station, and ten minutes later he was on the train to London. He wanted to phone Charlotte Button but the train was packed and he didn't want to be overheard so he waited until he got to Paddington before heading upstairs to Starbucks, where he bought himself a regular coffee. He found a quiet table and called her. 'I'm at Paddington, about to go to Heathrow,' he said. 'I just wanted to check that the *Athena* is definite.'

'Why the concern?' she asked.

'I had a chat with the navy guy, Giles. He gave me all sorts of reasons why pirates wouldn't take a ship that size.'

'Crazy Boy gave his uncle the name of the ship, its call sign and route,' she said. 'There's no mistake.'

'It's just that I'm going to look pretty damn stupid if nothing happens and I sit there like an idiot all the way to Suez.'

'You and me both,' she said.

'Crazy Boy's people haven't taken a ship that big before, have they?'

'They've taken some big ships, but I'll have to check if any of them are as big as the *Athena*. You're telling me that size matters, are you?'

'Giles said that the big ships are hard to board, that's all. And that the ransom isn't really dependent on the size of the vessel. There are easier ships around. I was just wondering why they'd chosen the *Athena*.'

'All right, I'm on it,' she said. 'We're keeping tabs on Crazy Boy and his people and if it looks as if we're on a bum steer we'll pull you off.'

'That's not as easy as it sounds,' said Shepherd. 'You can't just pull in at the nearest port.'

'We'll send a helicopter.'

'I'll hold you to that,' he said.

Shepherd's Malaysia Airlines flight left Heathrow at 10 p.m. and he arrived at Kuala Lumpur International Airport at just after five o'clock the following afternoon. There was a long queue at immigration and by the time he reached the luggage carousel his bag was already there. He slung it over his shoulder and walked through customs and bought his taxi ticket at a kiosk where there was another long queue. By the time he got into the back of a Suzuki taxicab it was after six. Port Klang was a forty-five-minute drive from the airport along a motorway. The speed limit was showing as 90 kilometres per hour but the driver kept it at a steady 120.

The Crystal Crown Hotel was a nondescript block next to a main road and his room on the eleventh floor smelled of stale cigarette smoke. There was an arrow painted on the ceiling with the word 'Kiblat' on it, which Shepherd knew was showing the Muslim faithful which way Mecca was. As he stared out of the window at a row of drab houses he heard an amplified call to prayer, but the hotel appeared to be hedging its bets as there was a Gideon Bible on the bedside table.

To the right was a fire station and several mustard-coloured blocks of apartments, and in the far distance were a line of dockside cranes looking like spindly birds perched at the water's edge. He shaded his eyes with his hands but couldn't see any ships.

He opened the minibar and popped open a can of Coke, then took out his mobile and called Jamal.

'You are here, Mr Blackburn, excellent,' he said.

'What about the ship, Jamal? Has it docked yet?'

'We have an ETA of nine o'clock tomorrow,' said Jamal. 'I shall collect you after eight if that is convenient?'

Shepherd thanked him and ended the call. He showered and ordered a club sandwich and coffee. The sandwich was barely edible and the coffee bland, but the food on the plane hadn't been much better so he ate it all and then fell asleep with the television on.

He woke early to the sound of the mosque, but drifted back to sleep and woke again when the phone rang. It was 8.30 and it was Jamal, saying that he was down in reception. Jamal was in his late twenties, dark skinned with a beaming smile. He took Shepherd's bag for him and hefted in on to his shoulder before taking him out to a black van standing in front of the hotel.

Shepherd sat in the front passenger seat while Jamal drove to the port, and like the taxi driver from the night before he had a total disregard for the posted speed limit on the motorway. For much of the time he talked in Malay on his mobile phone.

There was a large building on the outskirts of the port with what looked like an observation tower at the top. Jamal stopped the van and took Shepherd into the building but had him wait outside the immigration office while he went in and dealt with the paperwork necessary to get him on to the ship. Then they got back into the van and Jamal drove to the port entrance. Jamal showed his port ID to a policeman. Three young customs officers in uniforms several sizes too large for them peered curiously at Shepherd and one of them said something to Jamal in Malay. Jamal replied and they waved him through.

'What was that about?' asked Shepherd.

'They were just asking who you were. They said you didn't look like a sailor.'

'I'm not,' said Shepherd. 'I work in an office usually.'

They reached the quayside and Jamal turned left. Half a dozen huge ships were lined up under rows of blue and white cranes that ferried containers back and forth. Trucks were driving away from the ships with containers on their back, and others were queuing up to have their containers unloaded.

They drove alongside the ships and for the first time Shepherd realised just how big they were. He had to tilt his head back to see even the bottom rows of the containers. The top levels were as high as a ten-storey building.

The *Athena* was at the far end of the dock. There were four massive cranes above the vessel and they were all whizzing backwards and forwards, loading containers at a dizzying speed.

Jamal brought the van to a stop and helped Shepherd out with his bag. There was a metal stairway leading up the side of the ship to the deck, some three storeys above them. 'I leave you here,' said Jamal. 'Enjoy your voyage.' He shook hands with Shepherd and climbed back into the van. Shepherd shouldered his bag and started up the stairway. Above his head the massive cranes moved back and forth, the operators sitting in plexiglass cubicles, looking down between their legs to guide the containers into place.

As he reached the deck a Filipino in blue overalls and wearing a yellow hard hat looked up from a clipboard and frowned. 'Oliver Blackburn,' said Shepherd. 'From the company.'

'The master said he wasn't sure if you were coming or not,' said the Filipino. There was a badge sewn over his heart that identified him as the third officer.

'Well, I'm here,' said Shepherd. 'Bright eyed and bushy tailed.'

'I'll show you your cabin,' said the officer. He led Shepherd through a hatch and down a wood-lined corridor to a lift. 'The master said to put you on F-Deck; it's where the passenger cabins are.'

'No problem,' said Shepherd.

The officer took Shepherd up to F-Deck and opened the door to a cabin facing the lift. Shepherd was pleasantly surprised. It was about twice the size of the hotel room he'd slept in the previous night, and a good deal cleaner. There was a bathroom to the left with a double bunk beyond it, and to the right of the cabin was a seating area with two sofas and two easy chairs around a large coffee table. Against one wall was a desk with a reading lamp and a telephone.

There were three windows but the view was limited to a line of containers, though he could look up to see the crane operators still hard at work. Two of the windows were sealed but the one closest to the bed could be opened, with five large removable bolts and two hinges.

'If you let me have your passport and your yellow fever paper I'll take them to the master,' said the officer.

Shepherd gave him his Oliver Blackburn documents. 'When do I get to see the master?' he asked.

'He's ashore at the moment. He'll call down for you when he's back on board,' said the officer, pointing at the phone. He was wearing a transceiver on his belt and it crackled with static.

'I'll be needing a radio,' said Shepherd.

'The chief officer can arrange that for you,' said the officer. There was a clock on the wall behind the sofas. It was just after ten o'clock in the morning. 'You've missed breakfast, that's between seven thirty and eight, but the cook does tea and coffee in the galley on B-Deck between ten and ten twenty. Lunch is from twelve to one and dinner is from six to seven. There's a passenger recreation room across the corridor.'

'Got it,' said Shepherd, dropping his bag on to the coffee table. 'Are there any other passengers?'

'Just you, so you've got the room to yourself.'

'And what time do we leave?'

'About four, maybe five,' said the officer, looking at his watch. 'Depends how quickly they finish the loading.' His transceiver crackled again. He took it off his belt and began speaking into it as he left the cabin.

Shepherd unpacked his bag, hung up his shirts and

trousers and put his socks and underwear into one of the drawers. The bathroom was a good size with a toilet and a large shower. He put his washbag on a shelf and cleaned his teeth and then went across the corridor to check out the recreation room. It was slightly bigger than his cabin with a sofa that curved around one corner facing a flatscreen television and DVD player, and half a dozen blue easy chairs and a couple of coffee tables. The television was on a sideboard that ran almost the full length of the outside wall of the cabin. Next to the television was a stack of DVDs in cardboard folders, most of which appeared to be Chinese counterfeit copies of recent Hollywood blockbusters, including all the *Pirates of the Caribbean* films.

He figured that the best way of meeting his shipmates would be at lunch, so he slotted in one of the Johnny Depp DVDs, dropped down on to the sofa and swung his feet up on to the coffee table, figuring that it was entirely appropriate that he should pass the time watching a pirate movie. He smiled to himself as he realised that actually he was watching a pirate pirate movie, which made it doubly appropriate.

Shepherd went down to the officers' mess at midday on the dot. The *Pirates of the Caribbean* movie had been something of a disappointment and it had nothing to do with the quality of Johnny Depp's performance. The printing on the cardboard had been professional enough and the disc looked right, but the film had clearly been shot on a video camera by someone sitting in a cinema, probably somewhere in China. The soundtrack was barely audible, though he could clearly hear people coughing and rustling sweets and laughing whenever anything funny happened on screen, and every now and again he'd see the head and shoulders of someone sitting in front of the lens.

He walked down the stairs to B-Deck and along to the officers' mess, which was on the port side of the ship. A note next to the door said that overalls and workboots weren't allowed. He pushed open the door. Facing him was a long table running the width of the room, with just one man sitting at it with his back to the door. He looked over his shoulder. He was in his fifties, grey haired and with a couple of days' stubble on his chin, and he looked at Shepherd over the top of horn-rimmed spectacles. In front of him was a plate of steak and green beans.

'Hi,' said Shepherd, holding out his hand. 'Oliver Blackburn.'

'Hainrich,' growled the man, ignoring Shepherd's outstretched hand. 'Chief officer.' He turned his back on Shepherd and went back to eating his steak.

Shepherd looked around the room. There was a long sideboard against one wall that seemed to be the twin of the one in his recreation room, and two circular tables each with six chairs around it. The chairs also matched the ones in his recreation room. The people who had outfitted the vessel had obviously brought in a job lot of furniture. A place had been set at one of the round tables.

A Filipino messman in a white uniform and a black and white checked apron came out of the galley and smiled at Shepherd. He motioned for him to sit at the single place setting but Shepherd pointed at the table where the chief officer was sitting. 'OK if I sit there?' he asked. The messman looked confused and scratched his head. 'Chief, is it OK if I sit with you?' There were six other places set at the long table.

The chief officer shrugged without looking up from his meal. 'You're a company man, I guess you can sit where you want,' he growled.

Shepherd sat down at the head of the table, farthest from the door, and the messman hurriedly transferred the place setting. To Shepherd's left were two windows, identical to the ones in his cabin, but instead of a view of the containers he could see a red lifeboat. In between the two windows was a framed poster of a gloomy Van Gogh painting of a church at night, and on the wall behind the sideboard was a larger print, also by Van Gogh, of a wheat field on a summer's day.

Through a door at the far end of the mess room Shepherd could see the stainless-steel cupboards and cooking stations of the galley, where a Filipino in grubby whites was standing with his arms folded, a spatula in one hand.

'Soup?' asked the messman as he finished resetting Shepherd's place.

'Soup would be great,' said Shepherd, and the man hurried off to the galley.

'So you're a time and motion man, are you?' said Hainrich, his head bent down low over his plate as he worked on his steak.

'Human resources,' said Shepherd.

'Looking to cut back the crew even more, huh?' He had a Polish accent that reminded Shepherd of Katra when she had first arrived in England. 'The bloody owners won't be happy until they've got computers running the whole ship and done away with human beings completely.'

'I'm just here to see how things run,' said Shepherd. The last thing he wanted on his first day on board was to have an argument with the chief officer. 'I file a report and that's me done.'

Hainrich shook his head. 'You accountants are killing the job, you know that?' He thrust a chunk of steak into his mouth and chewed noisily.

'I'm not an accountant,' said Shepherd.

The messman returned with a stainless-steel tureen that he put down in front of Shepherd. Shepherd thanked him and asked him what his name was, even though he knew from the file that he was Jimmy Aguallo. 'Jimmy,' said the messman, flashing a wide grin. Shepherd lifted the tureen lid and used a stainless-steel spoon to pour watery minestrone soup into his bowl.

'Ten years ago the food allowance was fifteen dollars a day,' said Hainrich. 'It's half that now.' He pointed at his plate with his knife. 'This is probably horsemeat.'

'It's beefsteak,' said the messman, clearly offended.

'It tastes like horse,' said Hainrich.

The messman snorted and headed back to the galley.

'I don't see how you accountants can cut costs any more than you have,' said Hainrich, putting another forkful of steak into his mouth. 'There's only twenty-two officers and crew on the ship. How do you expect us to work with any less?'

'Like I said, I'm not an accountant,' said Shepherd. 'I'm human resources.'

'You know, we're not even allowed to send personal emails any more,' said Hainrich. 'And no wifi for personal use. If you're human resources, don't you think humans need to be in contact with their families when they're away for months at a time? Don't you think Skype is a basic human right?'

Shepherd used his soup as an excuse to avoid any further conversation with the chief officer. He was just finishing it when the door opened and a man with unkempt jet-black hair wearing a New York Yankees T-shirt and baggy grey shorts with button-down pockets came in. At first Shepherd thought it was a deckhand but when he sat at the head of the table he realised it was the captain. Dominik Kaminski. Shepherd knew from the file that the captain was forty-seven years old but he looked a good ten years younger.

The captain poured himself a glass of water, then looked up and noticed Shepherd for the first time. He peered over the top of his round-lensed spectacles with a slight frown, and then he grinned. 'The man from the company, yes?'

'Oliver Blackburn,' said Shepherd. He stood up and offered his hand and the captain shook it. He had a firm grip and nicotine stains on his first and second fingers.

'Dominik,' he said. 'You are with us until Suez?' His accent was more pronounced than the chief officer's.

'Yes,' said Shepherd, even though he was fairly sure that the ship wouldn't be reaching the Suez Canal, not as planned, anyway. He sat back down and picked up a bread roll.

'And you're here to decide who to sack?' The messman reappeared with another tureen of soup that he put down at the captain's elbow.

'It's not like that,' said Shepherd.

'The company is always trying to cut costs,' said the captain, ladling soup into his bowl.

'I told him that already,' growled the chief officer. He looked over at Shepherd. 'Do you know how many television sets there are on this ship?'

Shepherd shook his head.

'Three,' said the chief officer. 'I was talking to a head office guy last year and I asked him why we didn't all have televisions and DVD players in our cabins. Why are they only in the recreation rooms? You know what he said?'

'Tell me.'

'He said that the company wanted us to socialise, and not to just stay in our cabins. It's bullshit, of course. The company doesn't care about socialising, all it cares about is the bottom line.' He shrugged and hacked away at his steak.

'Well, anyway, I hope you enjoy your time with us, Mr Blackburn,' said the captain.

'Oliver,' said Shepherd. 'Please call me Oliver. And do I call you master? Or captain?'

The captain chuckled. 'You can call me what you want,' he said. 'We don't stand on ceremony here.' He reached for the bottle of water and poured himself a glass. He raised it to Shepherd. 'To management,' he said. 'Fuck them!'

Hainrich raised his glass. 'Fuck them all!' he said. The two men clinked their glasses and then drank until they were empty and slammed them down on the table.

There were two bottles of wine on the table, red and white, both untouched.

'Not drinking?' said Shepherd.

Dominik laughed. 'We're leaving port in two hours,' he said. 'If the pilot smells alcohol on my breath I'll lose my job. But you go ahead.'

'Pilot?' said Shepherd.

'Yes, pilot. He comes on board to help us leave the port.' He narrowed his eyes. 'You've been on a ship before?'

'Not this big,' said Shepherd.

'You're in the office all the time?' said Hainrich.

'Pretty much, yes.'

'That's the problem with this company,' said Hainrich. 'The people who make decisions have never been to sea.'

'I'm not a decision-maker,' said Shepherd. 'Like I said, I just compile a report, that's all.'

'Just following orders,' snorted Hainrich. 'Like the Nazis.'

Shepherd kept his head down as he finished his meal, while Hainrich and the captain chatted away in Polish.

After lunch, the captain went up to the bridge and the chief officer disappeared down to the Ship Office on the Upper Deck. Shepherd finished the coffee that Jimmy had brought him and then spent the time before departure getting a feel for the layout of the structure. All the decks, from the Upper Deck where he'd first arrived to G-Deck, which was directly below the bridge, were all laid out the same way. There was a central corridor that stretched the full width of the ship, lined with wood-effect plastic and with a chrome handrail at waist height. The floor was grey, the ceiling made of cream-coloured metal sections, dotted with smoke detectors and emergency lights. Cabins and rooms led off both sides of the corridor, fore and aft. In the middle of each floor was a central stairway that also functioned as an emergency exit, and next to it was a lift big enough to hold six people. The lift ran from G-Deck and down through the Upper Deck to the engine room.

At either end of each corridor was a hatchway that led out to the green-painted outside deck. The metal stairways and decks ran from the wings of the bridge all the way down to the Upper Deck. White metal stairs linked the outdoor decks and provided an escape route in the event of an emergency but also allowed the sailors to move between decks outside the superstructure.

There were two large chrome levers on either side of the hatch doors so that they could be closed securely and made watertight, and a third regular handle for opening and closing. Most of the hatches were locked. Shepherd went down floor by floor, walking back and forth along the corridors and taking the stairs. He didn't pass anyone else as he wandered around the superstructure but through the windows he occasionally saw seamen in overalls climbing up and down the exterior stairways as they went about their work.

When he reached the Upper Deck he went along to the Ship Office. Hainrich was sitting at one of three computers, comparing a spreadsheet on the screen with a computer printout. 'Busy?' asked Shepherd.

'I'm always busy,' said Hainrich, looking at Shepherd over the top of his spectacles.

Shepherd sat down on a chair. 'I was wondering about the locked hatches,' he said. 'The ones that give you access to the outer decks.'

'What about them?'

'Are they always locked? If so, I'd like a key.'

'They're always locked while we're in port,' said Hainrich. 'The stevedores will steal anything. You should keep your cabin locked, too. It's different at sea, nobody steals, but we have a lot of strangers on board.'

'But you can give me a key, right?'

Hainrich shrugged. 'Sure, but why?'

'I'd just like to have access to all areas, that's all. It's my understanding that's how it should work.'

'But not the cabins?' said Hainrich. 'There'll be an uproar if a company man starts going through personal belongings.'

Shepherd shook his head. 'Just the hatches, and any doors,' he said. 'I saw the doors on this floor that lead outside have combination locks. I'll need the combination.'

'That's easy,' said Hainrich. 'One six two seven. The key I'll have to get from the master's safe.'

'Thanks.'

'Is there anywhere in particular you want to go?' asked Hainrich.

'I just want to be able to move around the ship.'

'To spy?'

'To see how things work. To see what people do. You'll hardly be aware that I'm here.'

'I doubt that very much,' said Hainrich, turning back to his computer.

At four o'clock Shepherd went up to the bridge. There was a numerical keyboard to the side of the door handle but the door wasn't locked. He pulled it open and walked in. The bridge ran the full width of the ship with huge windows giving full all-round visibility. To the right of the door were two desks each twelve feet long, and behind them a bookcase filled with folders and manuals. On the desk closest to the door were two computer screens, two printers, a line of transceivers in their charging docks and a sat-phone; on the other was a large Admiralty chart on which the ship's course was marked every hour, in pencil, so that it could be rubbed off for the next voyage. Below the second desk were lines of drawers filled with charts for every part of the world. Separating the desks from the front of the bridge were thick green curtains that could be closed at night so that officers could look at the charts without disrupting the night vision of the men on watch.

A four-foot-wide green non-slip rubber mat ran the full width of the bridge leading to a hatch at either end that gave on to the port and starboard outside wings.

The main instruments of the ship were housed in a chest-high green metal structure that curved in a semicircle in the centre of the bridge, a twenty-foot-long console with six large computer screens and a variety of dials and controls. Facing the screens and dials were two large black leather chairs with armrests and footrests that wouldn't have been out of place in a dentist's surgery, and between them were the controls that directed the ship, including the ship's wheel, which was barely eight inches across. Loose items such as transceivers and binoculars were placed on white mesh non-slip mats to stop them sliding around in rough weather.

Dominik was sitting in the right-hand chair, his foot up on the console, and he nodded at Shepherd. 'We're just loading the last few containers. The pilots are on their way,' he said. He looked up at the ship's clock. 'Half an hour and we should be moving.'

'You don't mind me being on the bridge?' asked Shepherd.

'I'm not sure that I can stop you,' said Dominik, lighting a cigarette. 'The company said you were to have the run of the vessel.' He leaned forward and brushed ash off the console.

'I'll try not to get in your way,' said Shepherd. At either side of the bridge were wooden chairs with high legs and Shepherd went to sit in the starboard one as he watched the last of the containers being loaded. The *Athena* had looked big when he'd arrived at the port, but from his vantage point on the bridge he could see the entire deck of containers stretched out in front of him, and he realised for the first time what a true leviathan it was. At the bow was the forward mast, a white metal tower topped by one of the radar scanners. From where he was sitting the mast seemed quite small, but he knew from the plans he'd studied that it was more than thirty feet tall.

Containers filled every part of the deck, and while they were all one of two sizes, either forty feet or twenty feet long, they were in a multitude of colours – dark blue, light blue, dark green, pale green, white, orange and red. Some were obviously brand new, others were dented and spotted with rust, suggesting that they had been around the world several times. Overhead were the giant cranes sending containers whizzing from the dockside to the ship, and lowering them into place with a confidence and speed that belied their bulk.

There were three cranes loading the ship, moving independently of each other, each with its own operator shuttling backwards and forwards in a small plexiglass cabin. Thick wires snaked down from the overhead gantries to a metal slab some forty feet long and ten feet wide which had locking catches that gripped the corners of the containers and held them fast. The slab could hold either one forty-foot or two twenty-foot containers with equal dexterity.

Shepherd ran his eyes from port to starboard, counting the containers in a single row. He counted sixteen, but on the plans that Charlie Button had given him there had been eighteen. He counted the number of rows forward between the bridge and the bow. There were twelve, and that wasn't right either. On the plans there had been sixteen. Sixteen containers long and eighteen across.

'Captain, can I ask you a question?' he said, looking over his shoulder.

Dominik looked up from his instruments. 'I thought that's why you were on board,' he said.

Shepherd grinned. 'It's a technical question. About the ship.' Shepherd pointed at the containers stretching ahead of them. 'I thought there were eighteen bays across but I can only see sixteen. And I thought there were sixteen rows between here and the bow. But I can't see sixteen. More like twelve.'

Dominik took a drag on his cigarette before blowing smoke across the console. 'You're quite right. But the stacks are tapered to give us better visibility. The outer sides are one container less and they decrease in height as you go towards the bow. The stacks below you are seven above deck, with another eleven below in the holds. At the bow the upper stack is five deep. But when you look forward the eye is fooled, it makes the ship look shorter than it really is.'

'An optical illusion?'

'Exactly,' said Dominik. 'I'd have thought that someone from head office would have known how we stack our containers.'

'I'm not based at head office. I'm an outside consultant hired to do this particular report, so shipping isn't really my field.'

'That's becoming painfully clear,' said Dominik. He pointed at the door that led to the outdoor starboard wing of the bridge. 'If you go out there you'll see the containers on the outside.'

Shepherd did as the captain suggested. From the outside deck he could look down on the side of the ship and see that the stack on the outside did indeed contain one container fewer than the one next to it. There were six in the stack while there were seven in the middle.

Down below on the dockside there was a line of trucks waiting to have their containers picked up by the cranes.

'Happy now?' asked Dominik as Shepherd went back inside. 'I can see how important numbers are to you.'

'It was just confusing me,' said Shepherd. He went to the window and looked again over the stacks of containers. He understood now what the captain meant. The fact that the stacks sloped towards the bow meant that several of the rows were hidden from the bridge.

'Even with the slope we still have a huge blind spot in front of us,' said Dominik. 'When we're at sea we can't see the five hundred metres directly in front of the ship.'

Shepherd got out of his chair. The bridge was actually an L shape, with the bottom leg of the L on the starboard side pointing to the stern. The leg offered a view of the rear of the ship, and it was a rest area with a sofa, a sink and tea- and coffee-making facilities.

Shepherd looked out of the rear window where a fourth crane was loading containers. There were another five rows of forty-foot containers stretching to the stern.

Shepherd joined Dominik at the controls. The captain was blowing smoke at the window as he watched a container zip across the ship, suspended from one of the massive overhead cranes. The containers arrived on the back of trucks at the dockside, the crane lifted them up on to the ship and lowered them into place, where stevedores made sure that they were fixed securely in place. The workers were so skilled they made the job look as easy as a child assembling a fort from wooden blocks, but Shepherd knew that any error of judgement would be catastrophic, especially for the stevedores on the deck.

'How many containers do we have on board?' asked Shepherd.

'Just over five thousand, including three hundred and twenty reefers.'

'Reefers?'

Dominik frowned. 'You don't know what a reefer is? A refrigerated container. The white ones are reefers.' He shook his head. 'You guys in head office have no idea about shipping, do you?'

'I told you, I'm a consultant,' said Shepherd. 'And I'm more concerned about personnel.'

'Well, I'm more concerned about cargo,' said Dominik, 'which is what pays your fees and my wages.'

Two Malaysian pilots came on board at 4.30, escorted by the second officer. They were both dark skinned and had matching thick moustaches and were wearing white shirts and black trousers and carrying identical briefcases. The pilots shook hands with the captain and then went outside with him on to the starboard wing of the bridge. The captain stood at the controls, a transceiver in his hand. Shepherd went out to watch them. The loading had finished and the gantries of the cranes were now upright, as if saluting the soon-to-be-departing vessel.

On the bridge wing was a magnetic compass in a chest-high grey housing on a wooden circular plinth, and a large pale green metal box that looked as if it might have been a barbecue, but when the captain pushed back the retractable cover Shepherd saw a duplicate set of controls, including a small steering wheel and a throttle lever.

On the deck at the side of the compass was a black mat about six feet square on which had been painted a two-foot-high letter P in a yellow circle. Dominik saw Shepherd looking at it. 'You're wondering what that is, Company Man?' said the captain.

'It looks like a miniature helicopter landing pad,' said Shepherd. 'But they have an H and not a P.'

Dominik laughed. 'It's for when the pilots land by helicopter,' he said. 'Usually they arrive by boat but at some ports they fly them in.' He pointed at the mat. 'They winch them down and that's where they land. Hopefully.'

Three tugs had appeared, two at the stern and one at the bow. Far below on the dockside, Shepherd could see five men in overalls and hard hats gathering around the bollard at the front of the ship. One of the pilots said something to Dominik, who spoke into his transceiver, and a few seconds later two of the men down below pulled the rope loop off the bollard and it began to snake back into the bow of the ship. Shepherd smiled at the realisation that a ship the size of the *Athena* worth a hundred and fifty million dollars still had to be let loose by a couple of seamen pulling on a rope. And as was the case in almost every workplace the world over there were two men doing the actual work and three men supervising them.

The seamen slowly walked the length of the ship and after the pilot gave new instructions to Dominik, which were relayed over the transceiver, the men released the two ropes that were tethering the stern. The two ropes slowly withdrew into the ship.

The tugs began to ease the giant ship away from the dock, and then start to gradually turn it clockwise. Shepherd was amazed that the tugs, tiny in comparison with the 130,000-tonne container ship, could move it so easily and with such grace. Once they had moved fifty feet or so from the dock, the pilots asked Dominik to turn on the bow thruster, which increased the rate of turn. The ship smoothly turned through a hundred and eighty degrees as it backed away from the dock, and within fifteen minutes the bow was pointing towards the port entrance. The pilot asked for the main engine to be at slow ahead and again Dominik operated the engine at his console. Once the ship was moving towards the port entrance, the two pilots and Dominik walked quickly back to the main bridge.

The chief officer was watching the radar screens. There were three, the one on the right giving a view of one nautical mile, the middle one three nautical miles and the one on the left six nautical miles.

Dominik took a quick look at the screens as the main pilot sat in the left-hand chair. The second officer was now standing at the ship's controls.

The pilot gave a heading and Dominik relayed it to the second officer, who repeated it as he turned the ship's wheel.

'How does this work?' Shepherd asked Hainrich. 'Who's in charge of the ship right now?'

'The master is in charge, but he has to take the advice of the pilot,' said Hainrich. 'That's how it works in most ports. The pilots know these waters, but the responsibility still falls on the master.'

The pilots helped Dominik guide the massive ship out of the port, westwards towards the Malacca Strait, then they

shook hands with Dominik and left the bridge, accompanied
by the second officer. Dominik sat down on the right-hand
chair and studied the radar screens.

'This might seem a stupid question,' Shepherd asked
Hainrich. 'But how do they get back to land?'

Hainrich looked at him curiously. 'You really don't know
anything about shipping, do you?'

'I'm human resources,' said Shepherd. 'This is my first
time on a ship like this.'

Hainrich shook his head sorrowfully. 'That's what the
world is coming to,' he said. 'Our futures are being decided
by people who have no idea what they're doing.' He sighed.
'They leave by one of the pilot hatches. There are two, one
port, one starboard, about two metres above the waterline.
They go to the hatch and the pilot boat comes alongside.'
He waved at the starboard wing of the bridge. 'You can see
it for yourself, out there.' Hainrich reached into his pocket
and pulled out a key. 'Here's the key you wanted, for the
outside hatches.' He held it out, but as Shepherd reached
for it he pulled it away and held it just out of reach. 'This
key you must not lose,' he said. 'If it is lost it's a major
breach of security and you'll be thrown in the brig.'

Shepherd grinned. 'Hainrich, I've been all over this vessel,
there is no brig.'

'You lose this key and I will personally build one,' said
Hainrich, finally giving him the key.

Shepherd went out on to the wing and peered over. Far
below he could see the pilot vessel running alongside the
Athena. A man in a dark blue uniform was standing on
the deck of the pilot ship, holding on to the railing with
one hand. Two metal doors in the hull were open and as

Shepherd watched the two pilots took it in turns to step across on to the pilot boat, where they were helped on to the deck by the uniformed seaman. Once they had gone inside the boat peeled away and headed back to the harbour.

Shepherd let himself back into the bridge, shutting the door and closing the two chrome levers, and went over to stand behind Dominik. There were only three other vessels on the central radar screen, showing as small white triangles.

As Shepherd watched, Dominik moved a cursor on to the closest of the triangles and clicked on it. On the right of the screen the details of the ship flashed up. It was an oil tanker en route to Singapore. 'That's the AIS, right?' asked Shepherd.

Dominik grunted. 'Most of the bigger ships have it,' he said. 'It gives us the call sign and any other details that the master decides to put in.'

'But they can switch it off, right?'

'They can do, but once they switch it off they can't see anyone else's AIS.'

'But if you do switch it off, you disappear, right?'

Dominik laughed. 'No, you still show up on radar. But no one will be able to see your details.'

'And smaller boats don't have AIS?'

'It's not required and it's expensive, so small yachts and fishing boats tend not to have it,' said Dominik. 'It's a big help for navigation and useful if we need to talk to another ship. If it's got AIS we can get their call sign rather than just sending out a general hail.'

'What about pirates?' said Shepherd. 'Can't they use it to track ships?'

'Pirates?' repeated Dominik. 'I've never heard of pirates using AIS.'

'But if they wanted to, couldn't they use it to target a particular ship?'

Dominik frowned. 'I suppose they could.'

'But it'd be easy, right? Say they wanted the *Athena*. All they would have to do is to use the AIS and they'd see where you were and where you were heading.'

Dominik threw back his head and laughed. 'You've got a funny idea about the way the pirates work, Company Man,' he said. 'They're not high-tech villains, they're simply bloody fishermen in skiffs. They don't have GPS, never mind AIS.' He laughed again. 'Don't worry, Company Man, no one is going to mess with us. Least of all some scrawny fishermen.'

Shepherd left the captain on the bridge and went down to his cabin, where he showered and changed into clean clothes before going down to the mess room at six o'clock. The chief officer was already there, halfway through a bowl of fish soup. Sitting opposite Hainrich was a middle-aged man with curly black hair and a square chin with a dimple in the centre. He stood up and formally shook hands with Shepherd. 'Feliks Dudek,' he said. 'I'm the electrician.' He had a strong grip and his biceps bulged as if he spent a lot of time working out.

Jimmy appeared from the galley with a bowl of soup for Shepherd, and just as he raised his spoon the captain appeared and took his seat.

The three Poles shared a bottle of red wine and began talking in their own language. They made no attempt to include Shepherd in their conversation. Shepherd wasn't offended; he realised that he was the outsider and the fact that he was supposedly there to report on them added to their suspicions. He kept his head down and ate in silence.

Hainrich finished his soup and turned around in his seat. 'Jimmy!'

The messman appeared at the galley door. 'Yes, sir?'

'My salad,' said Hainrich, and the messman nodded and disappeared. Hainrich twisted back in his seat and a few seconds later Jimmy reappeared with a large glass bowl filled with lettuce, chopped green pepper and cucumber, and what looked like the contents of a can of tuna.

Hainrich saw Shepherd looking at the bowl and he pulled a face. 'I used to be a hundred and five kilos,' he said. 'Then the company brought in a new rule that says we have to weigh less than ninety kilos. More than ninety kilos and you can't sail. Also you have to meet their body mass index targets. I scraped the last medical but they only signed me off for six months. They said if I don't lose more weight then I lose my job.' He nodded at the bowl of salad. 'Now I eat like a rabbit.'

'You had steak for lunch,' said Shepherd.

'Protein,' said Hainrich. 'A man has to have some protein.'

'And you use the gym?'

Hainrich made a barking sound that was half contempt, half amusement. 'Have you seen our gym? The company doesn't want to waste money on equipment so we have a treadmill and an exercise bike and a punchbag and that's it.' He jabbed his fork into the bowl and shoved salad into his mouth.

Jimmy took Shepherd's soup bowl away and took it to the galley, returning almost immediately with a pork chop that glistened in fat, greasy carrots and French fries.

'You play ping-pong?' asked Hainrich.

'Ping-pong?' repeated Shepherd.

Hainrich made a sweeping motion with his hand. 'Table tennis,' he said.

'I haven't played since I was a kid.'

'The chief likes ping-pong but he can never find anyone to play him,' said Dominik. 'We're too busy and the crew prefer their beer and karaoke when they're off duty.'

'I'll give you a game sometime,' Shepherd said to Hainrich.

'Be careful,' said Dominik. 'He doesn't like to lose.'

'Who does?' said Shepherd.

Just before he went to bed, Shepherd called Charlotte Button on the sat-phone. 'All aboard,' he said. 'We've just left Port Klang. We'll be in pirate waters in four or five days.'

'How is it?'

'There are rumblings of mutiny among the officers but all's good.'

'Gin and tonic on the poop deck, is it?'

'Chance'd be a fine thing,' said Shepherd. 'They're not happy about having a company man on board, they think I'm there to sack them.'

'Well, I just hope they don't make you walk the plank.'

'Don't even joke about it,' said Shepherd. 'If anything were to happen at sea, nobody would ever know. It'd be the captain who'd handle any investigation and I don't think he'd be shedding any tears if I fell overboard.'

'I'm sure you'll win them over, you always do,' said Button. 'They'll be your new best friends in no time.'

'Any news on the yacht crew?'

'The kidnappers have made contact with the relatives, including Katie's parents. We've made sure that there's no publicity and we've put minders with all of them. I'm running negotiations from here. They're asking for five million and I've said I'll get back to them.'

'You've got a number to call?'

'They phoned us but only to give me an email address. It's being done by email now.'

'Charlie, what if I'm on a wild goose chase? What if Crazy Boy doesn't take the *Athena*?'

'Let's cross that bridge when we come to it,' said Button.

'What about proof of life?'

'They've emailed photographs and put a video up on a website. We've managed to block visitors to the site so no one else can see it. They look the worse for wear but they're alive.'

'OK, I'll check in tomorrow. Send me a text message to this phone if anything breaks.'

'Sweet dreams,' said Button, and sounded as if she actually meant it.

Shepherd tapped in Martin O'Brien's number. The phone clicked several times and then rang out and O'Brien answered almost immediately. 'Hey, how's it going?' he asked.

'We've just left port. You?'

'Nairobi,' said O'Brien. 'Just waiting for the Bradford boys to put in an appearance and then we're moving to Ethiopia.'

'Ethiopia?' repeated Shepherd. 'Where's that come from?'

'It's closer to Puntland than Kenya and it's easier to move around. It's full of white men in SUVs working for all the

NGOs there. No one will pay us any attention. I've got contacts with a business that handles cash transits for the Ethiopian government and they've let me use a small airfield near the border with Somalia. We've scouted a base and we have the ground transport in place and I've a plane arriving tomorrow. I've arranged a short-term lease on a C-23 Sherpa.'

'The money's coming through OK?'

'Your Charlie Button's a magician,' said O'Brien. 'Money just appears in the account. Never more than ten grand at a time and from all sorts of places.'

'Yeah, she'll be making sure it can't be traced, keeping below the notifiable limit and washing it through multiple accounts.'

'She's a smart cookie, all right. Have you given her one yet?'

'Hell's bells, Martin, she's my boss.'

'Yeah, but she's fit, right enough.'

'And I'm not sure how secure this sat-phone is either.'

O'Brien laughed. 'You think she's listening in?'

'I wouldn't put it past her. I'll check in with you tomorrow.'

'Give the Bangladeshi cabin boy my best.'

'There are no cabin boys, idiot,' said Shepherd, and ended the call.

Shepherd woke at eight o'clock in the morning, showered and went down to the mess room. The long table had been set for breakfast with boxes of cereal and jugs of milk, but there was nobody around. Jimmy the messman appeared from the galley, smiling apologetically. 'Sorry, sir, breakfast at seven, finished already.'

There was a bowl of fruit on a side table and Shepherd helped himself to two large green apples. 'No problem, Jimmy.'

'If you want I can ask the cook to make you eggs.'

'No thanks, no special treatment for me, Jimmy, I'll be on time tomorrow.' Shepherd took the stairs up to the bridge on the top floor and pushed open the door. The second officer was standing by the controls and looking at the radar screen on the left.

Shepherd introduced himself and the second officer shook his hand. 'I didn't see you at dinner last night,' said Shepherd.

The second officer shrugged. 'We eat with the crew, the third officer and me.' He grinned. 'We prefer Filipino food. We get withdrawal symptoms if we don't eat rice every day.'

Shepherd took a bite out of one of his apples and looked out of the windows. The sea appeared as smooth and flat as glass, with barely any flecks of white on the wave crests. 'Is it always as smooth as this?' he asked.

'It's not that smooth,' said the second officer. 'Those waves down there are probably a metre or two high. You don't notice it because we're such a big vessel. If you were in a twenty-footer you'd be finding it very rough going.'

Shepherd looked port and starboard but couldn't see any other vessels, just sea and sky. 'I thought there'd be more traffic,' he said.

'The Bay of Bengal is a big sea,' said the second officer. 'We probably won't see many other vessels until we round Sri Lanka. Then we're into the Arabian Sea which isn't much busier. There'll be traffic in and out of Karachi but once we get to the Gulf of Aden and Suez, that's when we'll be busy.'

'Pirate waters,' said Shepherd.

'Yes,' said the second officer. 'It can be dangerous. The Gulf of Aden, anyway. And maybe the Red Sea.'

'Have you ever had a problem there?'

The second officer shook his head. 'This ship is too big,' he said. 'Too big and too fast.'

Shepherd spent the next couple of hours sitting on the bridge, getting a feel for what went into operating a ship that was the size of a tower block that had been placed on its side. The autopilot took care of the steering and speed; the job of the officer on duty was to monitor the radio, check the three radar screens and keep an eye out for traffic that didn't appear on the radar.

There were three radar scanners, one on the forward mast and two on the roof of the bridge. While they were at sea they were set for six miles, twelve miles and twenty-four miles, but as accurate as they were they still didn't pick up small wooden vessels and there was no substitute for a pair of human eyes, albeit helped by powerful binoculars. Also on the console was a screen showing the *Athena*'s position and course on a satellite map of the area.

Every hour the officer would go to the chart desk and plot the ship's position on the Admiralty chart. On the desk were two screens giving the GPS coordinates of the ship and the ship's clock, but despite the high-tech wizardry the distances on the charts were measured with an old-fashioned pair of brass compasses.

At 10.30 Shepherd went back to his cabin and changed into a T-shirt, shorts and training shoes, and then went down to the gym. Hainrich was right; it was a big disappointment, a room not much bigger than his cabin with a treadmill, an exercise bike, a table tennis table and a dartboard on one wall. There were three square portholes looking out over the sea. There was a door to the left that led through to a small blue-tiled swimming pool, barely fifteen feet square, but there was no water in it and it was covered with a white rope net.

Shepherd climbed on to the treadmill and programmed it for an hour at a small incline. He began to run but the action was jerky and he had trouble getting into a steady rhythm. He tried slowing it down but that wasn't any better, and the only way he could maintain any sort of pace was to hold on to the handrails as he ran, and doing it that way meant he couldn't manage much more than a jog. He gave up after thirty minutes and had barely worked up a sweat.

He began to hit the punchbag. There was a pair of boxing gloves on top of a cabinet by the dartboard, but he ignored them. He'd always regarded boxing gloves as a waste of time, like high-tech running shoes. When he needed to fight for real there was never any time to put on gloves. Fights came unexpectedly and when they came he had to be able to hit with his bare hands and to hit hard. There were a lot of small bones in the human hand and they were easily broken so it was crucial to know how to punch properly.

He ran through various combinations of punches, and then began to use his legs, striking with his knees and feet. He worked the bag hard and fast and after fifteen minutes he was bathed in sweat, but he pushed himself for another ten minutes, by which time every muscle in his arms and legs was screaming in pain. He stopped and steadied his breathing as the bag carried on swinging from side to side.

When his breathing and pulse had returned to normal

he dropped down and did a hundred press-ups and then rolled over and did fifty quick crunches followed by fifty slow ones. By the time he had finished his T-shirt and shorts were soaking wet. He headed back to his cabin, showered and changed and at twelve o'clock on the dot he went down to the officers' mess.

Lunch was vegetable soup with pasta in it followed by roast chicken, fried courgettes and mashed potato. Dominik was there with Hainrich when Shepherd walked in, and when he was halfway through his soup the door opened and a big man in a company polo shirt walked in and sat down heavily. He had bulging forearms, hands as big as shovels and hair that had been shaved close to the skull. 'You're the spy?' said the new arrival. Like Dominik and Hainrich he had a strong Polish accent.

'Spy?' said Shepherd, wondering what he meant.

'The company spy? The man who decides who to fire to cut costs.'

'Oliver Blackburn,' said Shepherd, offering his hand. 'Human resources.'

The man's hand dwarfed Shepherd's and stopped just short of being painful. 'Tomasz Gorski,' he said. 'Chief engineer.' He grinned, showing slab-like grey teeth. 'You can't sack me, without me the ship would grind to a halt.'

'Unless the second engineer is around,' said Dominik, smearing soft cheese across a hunk of French bread.

'Which he isn't because he's always in his cabin watching porn on his laptop,' said Tomasz. His eyes widened in mock horror and he put his hand over his mouth. 'Have I said too much?' he said. 'Will you report me to the company?'

'Guys, I'm not a spy, really. I'm just here to file a report on how the crew functions, who does what and when, and then someone at a higher pay grade will make any decision that needs to be made.'

He finished his soup and Jimmy replaced Shepherd's empty bowl with his main course. The messman asked Tomasz if he wanted soup and he shook his head. 'Just the chicken and the courgettes,' he said, helping himself to salad, scooping lettuce, cucumber, green pepper and tomato from a bowl on to his side plate. He sighed as he looked at the salad, then at Shepherd. 'This is the company's fault,' he said. 'They said I have to lose weight.' He pointed his fork at Hainrich. 'Him too. So now we have to count calories like a couple of supermodels.' He gestured at Shepherd's plate. 'I see you don't have to watch your weight.'

'I exercise,' said Shepherd.

'Yeah? Pilates? Yoga?' He chuckled and said something in Polish to Hainrich. Hainrich laughed and nodded.

'I run,' said Shepherd. 'When I can.'

'Yeah, well, I work with engines and that's real work, my friend, not like sitting at a desk all day.' He poured olive oil over his salad and then added a splash of vinegar. 'These company medicals are a joke,' he said. 'Who's the most famous sailor of all time?' He waved his fork at Shepherd. 'Answer me that, can you, Mr Human Resources? You're English, you must know.'

'Nelson?'

'Exactly,' said Tomasz. 'Admiral Horatio Nelson. A man with one eye and one arm. How do you think he'd have fared with the company's medical? Do you think they'd have passed him as fit to sail?'

'Probably not,' said Shepherd, making a mental note to

tell Charlotte Button to never again use human resources as a legend.

'So there you go,' said Tomasz. Jimmy placed a plate of roast chicken and courgettes down in front of him and the engineer grunted his thanks. 'So why the hell does it matter if I'm a hundred kilos or ninety or eighty? I'm as good at my job now as I've ever been. My weight's got nothing to do with it.'

'I get it,' said Shepherd, and kept his head down as he ate.

Dominik, Hainrich and Tomasz switched into Polish and spent the rest of the meal talking and joking in their own language. Shepherd couldn't tell whether or not they were talking about him, but he was pretty sure that they were, especially when Tomasz looked over at him and scowled.

Jimmy brought Shepherd a cup of coffee once he'd finished his meal. The door opened and a man in his twenties entered. He was well over six feet tall and thin but with broad shoulders. He had a boxer's nose and a shaved head, but he smiled pleasantly and stuck out his hand. 'You're the company man?' he said, with only a trace of an accent. 'I'm Janko. Deck cadet.'

'Oliver Blackburn.'

As Shepherd sipped his coffee, Dominik left with the chief officer and the chief engineer. On the way out, Hainrich pointed at Shepherd. 'Tonight, ping-pong? Five past eight after I finish my watch, OK?'

Shepherd nodded. 'I'll be there.'

'He'll beat you,' said Janko as the door closed. Jimmy asked the cadet if he wanted soup and Janko nodded.

'How come?'

'He beats everyone. He's been playing since he was a kid.'

'You're from Slovenia, right?' said Shepherd.

Janko looked surprised. 'How do you know? Most people think I'm Polish or Croatian.' He sat down and grabbed a chunk of French bread and smeared butter on it.

Shepherd knew because he'd read the man's details on the crew manifest that Button had given him. 'You sound like my au pair,' he said. 'Katra. She's from Slovenia.'

'What part?'

Shepherd frowned. 'Good question,' he said. 'I've never asked.'

'I'm from Koper,' said Janko. 'My father was a sailor, and his father. And probably his father's father too.'

'It's in the blood,' said Shepherd.

'I think it'll end with me,' Janko said. 'In fact first chance I get it'll be off the ships and into the head office. You should give me your card, maybe you can help me some-time.'

'Sure. I've no cards on me but I'll give you one before I leave,' lied Shepherd. 'But why would a cadet not want to be on a ship?'

Janko laughed. Jimmy put a bowl of soup down in front of him and went back to the galley. 'My dad wanted me to be a sailor, and I'm happy enough to work in shipping, but the job's changed since he was at sea.' He waved his hand in the air. 'This isn't a ship, not really. It's . . .' He shrugged. 'I'm not sure what it is. A floating warehouse, maybe. It's not about the ship, it's about the cargo, and the cargo is just boxes. Thousands of identical boxes. And the boxes are nothing to do with us. Most of the time we don't even know what's inside them. We go from port to port and someone takes boxes off and puts more boxes on. That's all we're doing, moving boxes around.'

He dunked his bread into his soup. 'In my dad's day, he got to spend days in port, sometimes weeks. That's the sailing that he remembers, when sailors would be a week in Shanghai then three days in Hong Kong and then two days in Colombo and then a week in Tangiers. They got to see the world.'

'A girl in every port?'

'Sure, several girls in every port if you believe my dad's stories. I sometimes wonder how many siblings I've got scattered around the world. He sowed a lot of wild oats before he met my mother. And maybe afterwards, too.'

Shepherd sipped his coffee. He wasn't a fan of instant but Jimmy had made it good and strong and it was surprisingly drinkable.

'But it's not about the girls,' said Janko. 'It's about seeing the world. That's what my dad and grandfather did. Can you imagine how great it must have been to have had a week in Shanghai? Once the ship's sorted you could just go ashore and hang out. Meet the people, look around. Sleep ashore if you wanted. Hang out with sailors from other ships, swap stories.' He shrugged. 'You joined us in Port Klang, right?'

Shepherd nodded.

'We were there for six hours. During that time the amount of cargo they transferred would have taken three days back in my dad's day and probably two weeks when my grandfather was sailing. Our next port of call is Karachi and we'll be there eight hours, maybe ten, then after Suez we'll be in Tangiers for five hours, max.'

'So you never get to spend any time ashore?'

'In some ports you might have enough time to get a cab into the nearest city but that's about it, just time enough to grab a quick coffee and then back to the ship. Most guys don't bother.'

'So you just stay on board, yeah?'

'Exactly,' he said. 'My contract this time is four months and I probably won't set foot on land once. Same for most of the guys.' He grinned and dunked his bread in his soup again. 'Don't get me wrong, I'm not always complaining like Hainrich and Tomasz. But I'm not planning a life on the ocean waves. I'll do this for five years so that I understand how the ships work, but then I'll look for a job in head office. The shipping companies make millions and I want to be part of that. Who knows, maybe one day I'll have my own shipping company.' He shrugged again and continued to eat his soup.

Shepherd was pulled from a dreamless sleep by a loud alarm. He rolled on to his back and opened his eyes, then frowned as he realised it wasn't his portable alarm clock, it was the insistent blast of a siren coming from the corridor outside. The short blast became a much longer blast, then there was a silence lasting just a few seconds before the short blasts started again. He counted the blasts. Seven short ones followed by a much longer one. Shepherd's heart began to race; it was the ship's general emergency alarm. He cursed, threw on the jeans and polo shirt that he'd been wearing the previous day and raced up the stairs two at a time to the bridge. He threw open the door and burst in. Dominik was alone on the bridge, a mug of black coffee in one hand and a half-smoked cigarette in the other. 'Good morning, Mr Oliver,' he said. 'Is everything OK?'

'What's the alarm for?' asked Shepherd.

Dominik pulled a face. 'A drill,' he said. 'Didn't anyone tell you?'

'Does it look like anyone told me?' said Shepherd.

The alarm stopped mid-blast. 'It's our monthly drill,' said Dominik. 'That was for an emergency spillage. There'll be another in a few minutes for fire. Then we'll have a boat alarm followed by an abandon ship.'

'Should I be involved?'

'It's only a drill,' said Dominik. Ash fell from his cigarette on to the control desk and he cursed and wafted it away. 'You can if you want to. But it's for the crew really. They're usually done separately but the chief's put together a scenario that allows us to run them all at the same time.'

His transceiver crackled and Shepherd heard the chief's voice. 'This is the chief officer on the Upper Deck. We have a container leaking liquid. I am sending in a clean-up crew. Over.'

Dominik put the transceiver to his mouth and clicked the transmit button. 'Master to chief officer. Keep me informed. Over.' He grinned over at Shepherd. 'It starts with a leak. That's the first alarm, when it's spotted. Then the cleaning crew go in dressed for dealing with hazardous waste. Then the liquid catches fire, which will be when he'll sound the fire alarm. Then the fire gets out of control and we move to abandon ship. You can go and watch if you like. They're on the Upper Deck now and the lifeboats are on B-Deck. You'll be on the port side.' He took a drag on his cigarette. 'If you do go then take your immersion suit from your cabin, and your hard hat.' He shrugged. 'But it's up to you, it's only a drill.'

'I'll give it a miss,' said Shepherd. He looked at the three radar screens on the console. They were all completely clear.

Dominik waved to his right. 'There's coffee and tea stuff over there, help yourself,' he said. 'And we have cookies.'

Shepherd padded over in his bare feet and picked up a mug. There was a water dispenser with two taps, red for hot and blue for cold, and he half-filled the mug with hot water and then stirred in two spoonfuls of Nescafé and added a splash of long-life milk.

'Do you want a coffee?' he asked the captain.

Dominik looked over at him, surprised. 'The company man offering to make me coffee? What is this, are you offering the condemned man a last request?'

'Last request?' repeated Shepherd. 'You think the company would want to get rid of a captain?'

'If they could, sure,' said Dominik. He gestured with his thumb at the controls to his left. 'We're on autopilot right now, we are most of the time when we're at sea. And when we arrive at and leave port, we have a pilot on board. It wouldn't take much for the company to realise that with a combination of autopilot and port pilots, do they really need a captain on board? But as you are offering, a black coffee with one sugar would be nice, thank you.'

Shepherd spent the best part of an hour chatting to the captain about the various ships he'd sailed on during a career that spanned more than twenty-five years and the ports that he'd visited. Shepherd liked the man; he had a quiet confidence and a gentle sense of humour and patiently answered any questions that Shepherd asked, explaining how the various instruments worked and the rules of the sea that had to be followed by every vessel.

At nine o'clock Shepherd went back to his cabin, changed into a T-shirt and shorts, pulled on his training shoes and headed down to D-Deck. He opened the door to the gymnasium but his heart fell when he saw the running machine. He looked through the windows at the containers on deck, then had an idea. He went back to the stairs and down to the Upper Deck, then along the corridor to the starboard hatchway. The sea was calm and there wasn't much of a wind so the vessel was fairly stable. He looked left and right and grinned. It would be a bit cramped in places and he'd have to watch out for the valves and pipework dotted around, but the deck still made a half-decent running track.

He started off at a slow jog in a clockwise direction until he was familiar with the motion of the ship, then he upped the pace. He couldn't go anywhere close to his top speed because of all the equipment and fittings around, but it was still much more satisfying than running on the treadmill. He did five laps and after the fifth lap he stood at the bow doing stretching exercises. As he looked out to sea he saw a grey shape in the water, then another, then one arced into the air and within seconds there were more than a dozen dolphins, leaping and splashing back into the water. Shepherd moved to the front of the bow and watched them for a while, but couldn't work out if they were feeding or just playing.

He looked port and starboard but there was nothing to see other than the dolphins. No land. No ships. And above, not even a cloud in the sky. And no sound other than the wind whistling by his ears and the deep throbbing of the *Athena*'s massive engine.

As Shepherd headed back to the superstructure he looked up at the containers, towering above him and blocking out the sky. Those on the bottom were raised up off the deck. To get to them he had to climb a metal ladder up to a passageway that ran between the rows of containers. Those on the lower levels were locked into place with metal fasteners that criss-crossed the doors like shoelaces in sneakers. Metal gangways ran across the ship, giving access to the lower levels of the containers, but from the third level upwards there were no gangways or lashings and the containers simply rested on top of each other.

At the top of the ladder were waist-high metal railings, and Shepherd spotted that they were perfect for doing arm thrusts. He stood between the railings, grasped one in each hand and let his arms take his weight. He crossed his legs at the ankles and did fifty rapid press-ups until his muscles were burning. When he'd finished he walked down the passageway to the far side of the ship.

Some of the bottom containers had thick metal legs that meant they were standing some eighteen inches above the deck. It was, he realised, a great place for a stowaway to tuck themselves away.

Halfway along the gantry there were fewer lashings and he saw that most of the containers weren't locked. There was a bright yellow seal on most of them but there didn't seem to be any locking mechanism, though several did have large brass padlocks. He found one without a seal and grabbed the two levers that operated the opening mechanism. The two doors swung open. The container was empty, though there were wooden boards on the floor. He climbed in and walked around, realising that it was actually bigger than the first apartment that Sue and he had shared. It made his head spin to think that the container was one of more than five thousand, most of which were packed with goods and materials.

He climbed out and closed the doors, then walked back along the deck, passing two Filipino seamen in overalls and hard hats who looked at him curiously and then talked in their own language. He heard them laughing as he went back into the superstructure and started climbing the stairs two at a time. He went up to the gym and spent half an hour hitting the punchbag and half an hour on the exercise cycle and then did a hundred sit-ups and three sets of fifty press-ups. By the time he'd finished he was aching all over and bathed in sweat, but feeling better.

He went back to his cabin, showered, changed into clean clothes, and went up to the bridge. Hainrich was there, in shorts and a sweatshirt, and there was a Filipino seaman scanning the horizon with binoculars.

'Did you see the dolphins?' asked Hainrich as he checked out a tanker on their starboard bow.

'Yeah, amazing,' said Shepherd.

'You only see them in good weather,' said Hainrich. 'They don't like too much spray, it gives them pneumonia. Today's perfect for them, good weather and lots of fish.' He looked across at Shepherd. 'You take your life in your hands, running on the deck,' he said.

'You saw me?' Shepherd looked down through the bridge windows but all he could see was containers. There was no way that anyone on the bridge could see anything happening on the deck far below.

Hainrich laughed. 'I had three seamen radio me to tell

me there was a crazy man running around. What would we do if you fell overboard?'

'Come back and get me?'

Hainrich laughed again. 'Come back for a company man? In your dreams. Do you have any idea how many health and safety regulations you're breaking by running around the deck?'

'I hate treadmills,' said Shepherd, shrugging. 'I always feel like a hamster on a wheel.'

'Everyone hates treadmills,' said Hainrich. 'What's to like?' He patted his waistline. 'But exercise and diet, you have to do both or the weight stays on.'

Shepherd stood looking out over the vast sea ahead of them. There was a large container ship off to the left, almost on the horizon, and an oil tanker to his right, just behind them, but other than that the sea was empty. There was something calming about the way the ship was just carving through the water, the only sound the throb of the massive engine far below his feet. The sky above was also empty, not a single bird and not even a vapour trail from a passing jet.

Shepherd realised that although the ship was totally stable, with barely any sense that they were travelling across water, it was leaning to the side. It was only a few degrees but it was definitely not level.

'Answer me a question, Hainrich,' said Shepherd.

'If I can,' said the chief officer.

Shepherd pointed to the bow. 'See how we're listing there,' he said. 'The port side is higher than the starboard side, so we're leaning to the right. Is that because of the wind?'

'It's because of the ballast in our tanks,' Hainrich said. 'We are slightly heavier on our starboard side.'

'Why's that? Why aren't we level?'

Hainrich sighed. 'The captain's shower,' he said.

Shepherd turned to look at him. 'Huh?'

Hainrich shrugged. 'The outlet for the captain's shower is on the starboard side. So if we are higher on the port side the water in his shower drains away. My shower, however, is on the port side, so I have to use a squeegee to push the water towards the drain.' He waved at the bow. 'That, my friend, is why we list to starboard. And why every time I use the shower, I have to use the squeegee.'

'You're joking, right?'

Hainrich looked at Shepherd over the top of his spectacles. 'Do I look as if I am joking, Mr Blackburn?' he said solemnly.

Robbie Fox hurled the stick as far as he could and his two spaniels ran after it, barking happily, their tail stumps wagging furiously. Fox smiled as the two dogs play-fought over possession of the stick. It was a game they never tired of.

He heard a car driving down the track and he turned to see Lisa O'Hara at the wheel of her Land Rover. She parked and climbed out, dressed sensibly in a Barbour jacket and green wellington boots. 'Hi, Uncle Robbie,' she called.

She walked over and hugged him, kissing him affectionately on both cheeks. The dogs came running back, sharing the branch between them. Fox took it and threw it again.

'I've good news for you, Lisa,' said Fox, walking towards a copse of trees, the wind at his back.

She walked by his side, her hands deep in the pockets of her jacket. 'I'm all ears,' she said.

'Your man, Matt Tanner. You were right, he's MI5.'

O'Hara smiled. 'You know who he is?'

'He's been identified, but I had to do some string-pulling. And it goes without saying that no one must ever know how you got this information.'

O'Hara put her arm through Fox's. 'It's me, Uncle Robbie. You know you can trust me.'

Fox chuckled. 'Aye, lass, that I can. But I've had to vouch for you, so don't go letting me down.'

'That'll never happen,' she said.

'And they want him dead. Same as you killed that bastard major.'

'That's the plan,' she said. 'So who is he?'

'His name's Shepherd. Daniel Shepherd. Former SAS. We don't have an address but we have a date of birth so it won't be difficult to find him.'

'Excellent,' said O'Hara.

'The fact that he was in the Sass set alarm bells ringing,' said Fox. 'Gannon couldn't have acted alone when he killed my boys.'

O'Hara nodded slowly. 'And you think Shepherd might have been involved.'

'I don't expect we'll ever know for sure,' he said.

'We could interrogate him.'

Fox sighed. 'The Army Council made it clear they want a clean kill, Lisa. And they're calling the shots.'

'Either way he's dead, Uncle Robbie.'

Fox put his arm around her and gave her a hug. 'Aye, that's the truth,' he said. 'I just wish I knew where my boys were so that I could give them a proper burial.' There were tears in his eyes and he turned his head away from her as he blinked them away.

★   ★   ★

Shepherd was having trouble sleeping and after an hour of tossing and turning he pulled on some clothes and went up to the bridge. It was just after midnight and there was a Filipino seaman standing at the side of the bridge scanning the waves with a pair of binoculars. Dominik was standing on the port outdoor wing of the bridge, blowing smoke up at the stars. He grinned when Shepherd walked out on to the wing. 'Can't sleep, Company Man?' he asked. He offered his pack of cigarettes but Shepherd shook his head.

'Don't smoke,' he said.

'Have you tried?'

'I gave it a go,' he said. 'Didn't like it.' Actually he'd taken up smoking several times during his undercover career. It was often the quickest way of getting into conversation with a stranger. 'So we don't slow down at night?'

'There's no need,' said Dominik. 'We've got the radar and the AIS and any vessel out there should have their lights on. If they don't it's their own fault.' He blew smoke into the wind. 'Fishing boats are the problem because we've got to give way to them. But this far from shore there's not too many about.' He pointed off the port bow. 'See the small yellowish spot, just above the horizon?'

Shepherd looked to his left. Even without binoculars he could see the small yellow circle, a few degrees over the horizon.

'That's Venus,' said Dominik. He turned around and looked to the rear of the vessel. 'And the bright one over there? That's Jupiter.'

Shepherd looked over at the second planet. 'That's something, isn't it?'

'People in cities, they never get to see the stars or the

planets,' said Dominik. He took a long drag on his cigarette and then blew more smoke up at the stars. 'Too much light pollution.'

Shepherd looked up. It was an amazing sight, the heavens seeming to go on for ever, dotted with an infinity of stars. A small light moved high overhead, little more than a pinprick moving in a straight line. Too slow to be a meteor, it was almost certainly a satellite. Shepherd wondered if there were cameras on the satellite and if somewhere in London Charlotte Button was watching him on a screen. He smiled to himself. There were hundreds of satellites circling the Earth and the chances were slim in the extreme that the one he'd seen was even involved in surveillance.

'Over there is the Big Bear,' said Dominik, pointing to the right. 'See the four stars there, with the three leading away from it?'

'The Plough,' said Shepherd. 'We call it the Plough.'

'And the two stars at the back, you follow them up and there we have the North Star,' said Dominik. 'And there,' his hand moved across the sky, 'there's the Little Bear.'

He leaned back and pointed directly overhead. 'And there's the Milky Way. Have you ever seen a more beautiful sight than that?'

Shepherd looked up. It was an awesome sight, the stars appearing to be so close together that they formed a foamy white band that stretched across the night sky.

Dominik pointed out half a dozen stars in quick succession, his finger moving confidently around the heavens.

'You know your stars,' said Shepherd.

'It's just a hobby these days,' said Dominik. 'They don't even teach celestial navigation any more. GPS has done away with it. Show a sextant to the cadet and he probably wouldn't know what it was, never mind how to use it.'

'Really? I'd have thought that sailors would need to know how to navigate by the stars.'

Dominik laughed and flicked the butt of his cigarette over the side. 'Maybe fifty years ago. But not any more. It's all done by computers and before long they won't need men on ships any more. Or maybe just one man monitoring a computer screen back at head office. But I'll have retired by then.' He sighed. 'The world's changing, Mr Blackburn, and it's changing for the worse.'

'It's hard to argue with that,' said Shepherd. 'And you can drop the "mister". Just Oliver is fine.'

'Have you got children, Oliver?'

'No,' said Shepherd, and felt the involuntary twinge of guilt that always came when he denied the existence of his son. Liam was the most important thing in his life but he wasn't part of the Oliver Blackburn legend. Blackburn didn't have a wife either, even one who had died in a senseless car accident. Dan Shepherd wasn't Oliver Blackburn; Oliver Blackburn was the figment of someone's imagination, someone in MI5 who had created a fiction that would allow him to complete his mission, and once that mission had been completed Oliver Blackburn would simply cease to exist. 'You?'

'Two boys, two girls,' said Dominik. 'Perfect balance.'

'Are any of them into sailing?'

Dominik shook his head. 'My elder boy wants to be a doctor, the elder girl is already a teacher. The other two are still at school and they hate the sea.'

'Because?'

'Because it takes their father away from them. Four months on and two months off, they get to see me for just one third of the year. I've missed big chunks of their lives. And for what? Do you know how much I get paid?'

Shepherd shook his head.

Dominik's eyes narrowed. 'You're a company man, you surely know how much I earn.'

'I keep telling you, Dominik, what people earn doesn't have any bearing on what I do. I'm only concerned with what people do.'

'Well, I'll tell you. Five thousand euros a month, that's what they pay me. And for that I spend months away from my family and my kids grow up without knowing their father.' He looked out over the waves. 'My brother-in-law is a plumber in London and he earns twice what I earn. My wife keeps telling me I should go and work with him.'

'Why don't you?'

Dominik shrugged, then waved his arm at the night sky above him. 'Because I'd miss the stars. And the sea. I'm a master, that's what I do. It's in my blood. Yes, I miss my family, I miss being away from them, and there are easier ways to earn a living, but this is my life and it always will be.' He shrugged again. 'You wouldn't understand.'

Shepherd smiled. 'Actually, what you say makes perfect sense to me,' he said.

Shepherd stayed on the bridge for an hour talking to the captain, then went down to his cabin. This time he fell asleep as soon as his head touched the pillow. His alarm woke him at seven and he went down for breakfast. Hainrich was already there, along with Tomasz, the chief engineer, and Konrad Krol, the Polish second engineer. It was the first time that Shepherd had met Konrad so he introduced himself and shook hands.

Hainrich said something in Polish and they all laughed.

'I guess he's telling you that I'm the company man and I'm not to be trusted,' said Shepherd as he sat down. Hainrich was eating toast and marmalade, but the two engineers both had fried eggs and bacon in front of them.

'Actually, the chief was saying that I should show you the Burma Road,' said Konrad. He was quite small, probably under five feet eight, with close-cropped wiry hair and a tattoo of a mermaid on his left forearm. He had a thick gold wedding band but no watch. Shepherd had noticed that most of the officers and crew didn't wear wristwatches, probably because the time on board ship was always being changed as they moved across time zones.

'Burma Road?'

'You'll understand when you see it,' said Hainrich. He said something to Konrad and all three of the Poles laughed.

Jimmy appeared at Shepherd's shoulder and asked him what he wanted to eat. Shepherd asked for an omelette and toast as he poured himself a glass of orange juice.

Hainrich, Tomasz and Konrad chatted away in Polish as Shepherd ate his breakfast. It wasn't a language he was at all familiar with and very few of the words they used had any resonance. They made no effort to include him in the conversation, which suited Shepherd just fine because pretty much every conversation that he did understand seemed to involve the officers taking verbal potshots at him.

When they had finished, Tomasz ordered a coffee but Konrad pushed his plate away, burped, and grinned at

Shepherd. 'So, do you want to see where the real work's done?'

'The engine room? Sure.'

'Get your hard hat from your cabin and I'll meet you in the Ship Office on the Upper Deck.'

When Shepherd got to the Ship Office, Konrad had pulled on a pair of white overalls and was holding two pairs of orange and black ear-defenders. 'You'll need these,' he said. Shepherd took a pair and Konrad picked up his hard hat. 'Let's go,' he said. He led Shepherd down the corridor to the lift and took him down to the engine control room. There was a large green metal console peppered with computer screens and dials, and a set of engine controls that matched the one up on the bridge, including a throttle lever. The third engineer, a Filipino, was studying one of the screens.

Shepherd pointed at the controls. 'You can run the engine from here?' he said. 'You can use the throttle and everything?'

'It's not a throttle, it's the telegraph,' said Konrad. 'In the old days it was a way of communicating with the engine room but these days it's all computer controlled. The captain uses the telegraph on the bridge to set the speed but with the control switches on that panel we can bypass the bridge completely.' He nodded at Shepherd's ear-defenders. 'Put them on and we'll go through to the engine room.'

Shepherd put the ear-defenders on and then his hard hat and followed Konrad through a hatchway into the main engine room. Even with the ear-defenders on he could hear the throb of the massive engine, and felt the vibration running up his legs.

Konrad took him first into a large room which was very hot, filled with thick pipes, most of which were lagged with bulky silvery insulation. Konrad put his mouth close to Shepherd's right ear and by shouting loudly he could just about make himself heard. 'This is where we heat the fuel,' shouted Konrad. 'It's thick, almost solid, at room temperature so we have to heat it before it goes to the engine.'

The heat was stifling, and after just a few seconds Shepherd's face was bathed in sweat. He followed Konrad back into the main engine room and they went down a flight of metal stairs to the second level, from where they could get a view of the entire engine. It was huge, the size of two double-decker buses, and seemed to be in two parts, two large steel cylinders stuck end to end at the back, and in front of them twelve massive green piston units that reminded him of spark plugs, with metal pipes connecting them all. Even from twenty feet away the vibrations of the engine ran through his body from his feet to his head.

Shepherd looked at the engineer, lost for words. The sheer power of the engine was breathtaking.

'Almost one hundred thousand horsepower,' shouted Konrad.

'Awesome,' shouted Shepherd.

Konrad nodded. 'There are twelve pistons,' he said. He pointed to the left, where there were two giant pistons hanging from a gantry. They were more than twenty feet from top to bottom. 'Those are spares.'

'They're huge,' said Shepherd.

'A man could stand in one of the cylinders,' said Konrad. 'If he wanted to.' He took Shepherd down another flight of metal stairs and they walked around the engine. It was spotless, not a drop of oil or soot anywhere, and all the surfaces gleamed as if they were in a chemical processing plant and not the engine room of one of the biggest container ships in the world.

At the back of the engine were huge steel cowlings that led from the engine up into the roof of the engine room. 'Turbochargers,' shouted Konrad. 'They heat the air before it's mixed with the fuel.' He pointed to one of the huge pipes that slanted up to the ceiling, four storeys overhead. 'That takes the exhaust to the funnel.'

'How much fuel does the engine burn?' shouted Shepherd.

Konrad shrugged. 'At full speed, about two hundred and fifty tonnes a day,' he shouted. 'Cruising, like now, about a hundred and fifty tonnes.'

Konrad took him to the rear of the engine, where the massive driveshaft emerged. It was about four feet across, a tube of gleaming metal that whirred around, driving the propeller at the stern. A metal gantry ran above the shaft and the two men stood on it looking down. 'And this is what it's all about,' said Konrad. 'All the fuel, all the power, it's all about turning this piece of metal around so that the propeller pushes us through the sea.' Konrad clapped him on the shoulder. 'OK, we'll go back now,' he shouted. On the way to the engine control room Konrad showed Shepherd the desalination plant that converted sea water into drinking water, the sewage plant, and the generators that provided power for the ship.

When they reached the engine control room, Tomasz had joined the third engineer and they were studying one of the computer screens. On it was a computer schematic showing the twelve pistons and the temperature at which they were operating. 'What do you think?' asked Tomasz, removing his ear-defenders.

'It's huge,' said Shepherd. He took off his helmet and ear-defenders.

'It has to be,' said Tomasz. 'It has to move a hundred and thirty thousand tonnes from a dead stop to twenty knots. And it has to sail around the world no matter what the weather. You need a lot of power to do that.'

'A hundred thousand horses,' said Shepherd. 'And that's one hell of a lot of horses.'

'You see how they have twelve pistons?' said Konrad. 'The old engines were six pistons, now they have twelve.' He grinned. 'Twice as much work but the same number of people. Tell that to head office when you get back. Tell them that engineers are working twice as hard as they used to.'

'I will,' said Shepherd, though he knew that he'd never be saying anything to the company bosses.

Konrad clapped him on the back. 'Make sure you do,' he said. 'Now, come with me, this way.' He led Shepherd through a door to the right of the lift, a tool room with dozens of tools and pieces of equipment on the walls. A seaman wearing dark blue overalls was filing away at a piece of metal. At the far end of the room was a metal hatchway with a wheel lock in the middle. Konrad turned the wheel and pulled the hatch open with a grunt. 'This is what the chief said I should show you,' he said.

Shepherd followed Konrad through the hatch into a tunnel that stretched left and right, running the full length of the ship. It was painted a pale yellow and was about five feet wide and maybe ten feet high. Konrad gestured with his thumb. 'That way's the bow, it runs right up to the Bosun's

Store and then back along the port side.' He pointed to the right. 'And it goes all the way to the stern and around. It's the Below Deck Passageway,' said Konrad. 'It runs all around the ship, between the engine room and holds and the hull of the ship.' He grinned. 'The crew calls it the Burma Road.'

'What's it for?'

'Mainly for checking the tanks,' Konrad said. He kicked the floor with the heel of his steel-tipped boots. 'They're underneath us. The oil tanks and the water ballast tanks, for adjusting our trim. And we use it to gain access to the pilot hatches; the pilots usually come on board through them from their ships. I'll show you.'

He took Shepherd along to the middle of the ship and showed him a hatchway in the floor with a locking wheel in the middle of it. He kicked it with his boot. 'You open that and it leads down to a waiting area where you can open the hatch in the hull. The pilot comes up through here, through into the engine room, and then we take him in the lift up to the bridge.'

Shepherd looked around the metal corridor. It was about five feet wide and every few feet there were metal buttresses, presumably to add strength to the structure, though the metal floor was clear of any obstructions. He frowned, wondering what he was missing. 'Why did the chief want you to show me this?' he asked.

Konrad laughed. 'He thought you could run here. All around the ship, it's more than seven hundred metres.'

'Are you serious?'

Konrad nodded. 'Sure. This way there's no chance of you falling overboard.'

*   *   *

Two tugs were gently easing the *Athena* towards the dock-side, like tiny birds pecking away at an elephant. Harry Kamal couldn't work out where all the power came from to move the massive ship sideways. 'How much does it weigh, the ship?' he asked.

The man sitting in the driving seat of the rusting Nissan Sunny shrugged. 'Who knows?' he said. 'Who cares?' Kamal only knew the man's first name. Ishan. Ishan was morbidly obese with rolls of fat around his neck and always appeared to be suffering from the heat and humidity of Pakistan, even though he had been born there forty-five years earlier.

Kamal, on the other hand, had been born thousands of miles away in a suburb of Birmingham and had been brought up with the chilly winters and rainy autumns of the Midlands, but he had never found the heat or humidity of Pakistan to be a problem. 'I didn't realise they were so big.'

The tugs were pushing the ship into a gap between two other freighters, with perfect precision.

'Eleven thousand and forty TEUs,' said Ishan, mopping his brow with a damp handkerchief. 'There's not many bigger, but they've got ships twice that size on the drawing boards.'

'Unbelievable,' said Kamal, shaking his head.

'To be honest, a ship is a ship,' said Ishan. 'A hull, and an engine, and that's it. The only restriction on the size is whether or not the ports can handle them.' He took out a silver pocket watch and flipped it open. 'They're late,' he said. 'They're always late.'

Containers were being picked up by the cranes and whipped off the ships that were tethered to the dockside and on to waiting trucks. As soon as one truck drove off with its load another moved to take its place. The cranes were the height of ten-storey buildings, massive metal structures that reached the full width of the ships, controlled by operators sitting in small plexiglass cubicles who whizzed to and fro above the grabber units that picked up the containers as easily as if they were a child's building blocks. Kamal had never seen anything like it. 'You can hardly believe that men could build things as big as this,' he said. 'It's breathtaking. Literally breathtaking.'

Ishan squirmed uncomfortably as he put his watch away, then wiped the back of his neck with his handkerchief. 'It's just a port,' he said. 'They're the same the world over.'

The car was parked between two stacks of containers, facing the sea. They had been there for the best part of an hour, wearing cheap suits with port IDs clipped to their breast pockets. Kamal didn't know if Ishan had been paid to get him on board the *Athena* or if he was doing it because of his beliefs. He didn't care so he didn't ask; all that mattered was that he got on to the ship and had time alone with the vessel's computer.

Computers were Kamal's speciality. He'd always been good with computers, ever since his father had bought him a Sony laptop for his tenth birthday. Kamal preferred computers to people. Computers didn't steal his lunch money or punch him in the school toilets or call him 'Paki' or make jokes about his name. Kamal was a good Pakistani name. It meant water lily. But at school he was Kamal the Camel. The more he was bullied the more time he spent in his bedroom with his computer. But unlike most teenagers he didn't fool around with computer games and chat rooms, instead he devoted himself to programming. He was fifteen when he designed and released his first computer virus, which resulted in all the teachers in Birmingham schools seeing their wages cut by half. His second virus was aimed at one of the country's largest banks and transferred almost a million pounds to a charity helping children in the poorest areas of Pakistan before the bank's security people neutralised it.

Kamal was readily accepted at a top London university after getting A-level results that were so impressive that he was featured in the local newspaper. It was as a student that he began to become more involved with Islam. His first step was a small one. A pretty girl in a headscarf had asked him to sign a petition protesting against a shop's decision not to serve Muslim women wearing the burka. Kamal had been more interested in the girl than the petition, but he began to attend Islamic meetings and for the first time found people who seemed to be happy in his company. For the first time in his life he had real friends.

Before long he was attending several mosques and taking lessons in the Koran, learning Arabic so that he could read it in its original form. The more he learned about Islam the less he wanted to work in the Western world. Kamal had wanted to leave university in his second year, but his imam had persuaded him to continue his studies. Education was the key to everything, the imam had told him. Without education man is no better than an animal. Kamal realised that the imam was right, but that didn't stop him from attending a training camp in northern Pakistan during his summer break after his second year. Three members of his mosque were going and he needed little persuasion to join them. He'd paid for his ticket on his credit card and was told that all his expenses in Pakistan would be taken care of. The four young men had flown out together on the pretext of attending the wedding of a close friend but they were met at Islamabad Airport by a grizzled man in his fifties with an eye patch and three fingers missing from his left hand. His name was Salim and he showed them to a waiting coach before heading back into the arrivals terminal and returning an hour later with four more young Pakistani men, who sat together at the back of the coach and spoke with Scottish accents.

Kamal spent six weeks in a training camp, and he was never precisely sure where it was. They'd driven in the coach for the best part of eight hours and then they'd been transferred to a truck, where they'd sat facing each other on wooden benches, the sides of the truck covered with flapping tarpaulin, for another four hours. The camp was in a dry, dusty valley, little more than four wooden cabins next to an obstacle course and a firing range. As they'd driven up to the camp on the first day, Kamal had flinched at the sound of automatic gunfire, but after just a week he was able to strip and fire a Kalashnikov as if it was the most natural thing in the world.

His training was made up of three parts. He was schooled in Islam in a way that he'd never been schooled before. His eyes were opened to the true meaning of the Koran and it was explained to him what Allah expected from his followers. He was taught history, too. Not the British imperial history that he'd learned at school, the history of fat kings and holocausts and wars and Roman conquests, but the history that mattered, the history of Islam and how the most holy and pure of religions had been persecuted throughout the ages. He studied the Crusades and the Spanish Inquisition and studied the way the European colonial powers had invaded countries across Asia and Africa, from Morocco in the west to Indonesia in the east, killing Muslims wherever they went. The killings had continued to the present day, with Muslims dying in Egypt, Syria and Palestine, and then in Bosnia, Afghanistan and Iraq, and Kamal was taught that there would be no stopping the Crusaders until the Muslim world met the violence with violence.

The third leg of his training was physical. He was made to run, to jump, to crawl and to shoot. He was taught how to fire the workhorse of the oppressed, the AK-47, and to strip it and reload it blindfold, he was taught to make Molotov cocktails and how to throw them, he was shown how to fire an RPG though never actually got to pull the trigger himself, and he was schooled in the use of knives and clubs. In the final week he was shown how to make basic explosives and how to put together IEDs, the improvised explosive devices that were so successful in Iraq and Afghanistan.

Three of the men on the course were taken off for special training, to a separate hut where they studied, ate and prayed independently of the rest of the group. Kamal knew that they had been selected as *shahid*, an Arabic word that literally meant witness but which had come to mean glorious martyr, a Muslim who gave his life in the name of jihad.

Kamal had asked his instructors if he could join the *shahids* but he was told that the computer skills he had were far too valuable to be thrown away. Kamal had been surprised that they knew about his talent for programming, but he listened to what his instructors told him and returned to his degree studies and waited for the call. When it came he was asked to design a very specific computer virus and to take it to Pakistan. That is how he came to be sitting in the car with Ishan, watching the giant container ship being nudged into position.

Men in overalls and hard hats were soon pulling on ropes fore and aft; the ship was tied up and about twenty minutes later the gangway was lowered into place.

'Right,' said Ishan, opening the car door. 'We can go on board now. Say nothing until we are in the Ship Office. It is possible that we may be searched but don't worry, they are looking for guns, not what you are carrying.'

Kamal nodded. They got out of the car and Ishan took two fluorescent jackets out of the boot and gave one to Kamal. They put them on as they walked over to the ship. Kamal had to crane his neck to see the top of the super-structure and he could just about make out two figures standing there, looking down. He had a childish urge to wave up at them but he lowered his eyes. He wasn't there for fun, he was there to further jihad. He followed Ishan up the gangway, keeping his eyes fixed on the other man's legs and fighting the urge to look down. He'd never liked heights and he hadn't expected to have to climb up to the ship. Ishan's fat thighs rubbed against each other.

Ishan reached the top and turned to look at Kamal, whose forehead was beaded with sweat. 'Are you OK?' he whispered.

Kamal waved away the man's concern. 'I'm fine,' he said.

The ship's second officer was standing with a hand-held metal detector and he slowly ran it up and down Ishan, and then did the same with Kamal. Kamal smiled as the detector passed over his body without making a sound. Ishan was right, they were looking for guns or knives or maybe a bomb, but what he was carrying in the pocket of his jacket would cause far more damage than any weapon.

The second officer gave the two men ship IDs, which they clipped to their fluorescent jackets, and then he called up the chief officer on his transceiver. 'Planner is on board, two persons, on their way,' he said, then pointed to the hatch that led to the corridor. 'Straight down, on the right,' he indicated, then he noticed the deck cadet coming along from the bow and asked him if he'd take the two men along to the Ship Office.

The deck cadet led them through the hatchway and tapped in the four-digit code to open the door and showed them where the office was. The chief officer looked around as he heard the door opening. 'Planner's here,' said the deck cadet. He held the door open for the two men and then went back outside.

'Hello, Chief,' said Ishan, offering his hand. They shook and Ishan introduced Kamal as his assistant.

'You have the files?' asked the chief officer, holding out his hand.

Kamal took the thumb drive from his jacket and gave it to him. On it were all the details of the containers that were to be loaded on and off the ship. The planner's job was to ensure that the loading was as efficient as possible, and that the containers were stacked correctly. The heavier containers had to go at the bottom, containers with explosives or with flammable liquids inside had to be kept well away from the engine room, certain chemicals had to be stored away from other chemicals. And the destination of the container also played a part in where it was placed on the ship. In all it was a complicated jigsaw that required computers to monitor and check that every container was in the right place.

The chief officer slotted the thumb drive into one of the USB slots and sat back in his chair as he waited for the computer to open the files. 'Chief, do you have an aspirin or paracetamol or something?' asked Ishan, putting a hand to his head and playing the wounded soldier. 'I've got a throbbing headache.'

The chief officer looked up from the computer. 'Now?' he said.

'I wouldn't ask but I feel really bad. Bad enough to throw up. It's been bad since I woke up this morning.'

The chief officer sighed and pushed himself up out of his chair. 'I'll have to get it from the Sick Room,' he said.

'I'm so sorry,' said Ishan, massaging his temples with his podgy fingers. 'I appreciate your kindness.'

As soon as the chief officer had left the room Kamal sat down at the computer. He temporarily disabled the anti-virus program, even though he doubted that it would have detected the virus that he had created, then transferred the program to the computer's hard drive. From there it was a matter of seconds to send the virus across to all the computers on the ship's network.

By the time the chief officer returned with two aspirins and a glass of water for Ishan, Kamal was sitting by the door, his arms folded.

'You are a lifesaver, Chief,' said Ishan. As Ishan swallowed the tablets and gulped down the water, the chief officer sat down and began checking the planner's spreadsheets.

*   *   *

The *Athena* left Karachi less than nine hours after it had arrived. Shepherd stood with Dominik on the starboard wing and watched as two tugs helped to move the leviathan away from the dockside. Its departure was as smooth and effortless as its arrival. The pilots who supervised the operation weren't the same ones who'd brought the ship into the port, but they wore similar black trousers and short-sleeved white shirts and had the same unsmiling faces, as if they somehow resented having to spend their time helping the captain. With careful nudges from the tugs, the *Athena* slowly reversed away from the dock and then headed out to sea. The pilots left through the starboard hatch, stepping nimbly on to the pilot vessel and disappearing into the darkness. By the time the ship was passing through the last buoys marking the harbour entrance Dominik was sitting in the right-hand chair staring at the radar screens. There were more than a dozen vessels showing, all with AIS identification. It was as if the captain was playing a complex video game, assessing the speed and course of each ship and working out how best to weave a way through them. At one point he had the giant engine in reverse, bringing the ship to a stop as an oil tanker crossed in front of them.

Shepherd stood behind Dominik, watching him work. He had a quiet, unflustered confidence, though he did chain-smoke throughout the procedure. After forty-five minutes they were in clear sea and all the traffic was behind them. Dominik blew smoke up at the ceiling. 'So, Company Man, do you think I am worth one hundred and seventy euros a day?'

Shepherd grinned. 'I don't think I could have done what you just did,' he said.

Dominik shrugged and flicked ash on to the floor. 'It's all about predicting the future,' he said. 'You know where a vessel is, its speed and its direction. So you know where it will be in ten minutes' time, or fifteen, or twenty. The trick is to make sure that your future doesn't coincide with another vessel's.'

Shepherd went down to his cabin, locked the door, and called Charlotte Button on the sat-phone. 'We've just left Karachi,' he said. 'Another twelve hours or so and we'll be in the area where the pirates operate.'

'And everything's OK?'

'They seem to have got bored of the office spy routine,' he said. 'And they don't seem to be over-worried about the threat of pirates. The consensus seems to be that the *Athena* is too big and too fast to be boarded at sea.'

'Well, they did say that the *Titanic* was unsinkable, didn't they?'

'I'm serious,' said Shepherd. 'They've got contingency plans for a pirate attack but no one seriously thinks we're at risk.'

'Let's see what happens,' she said. 'Crazy Boy definitely has his sights on it, no matter what the crew there think. He was talking to his uncle on Skype and he told him that the ship was in port and would be leaving soon.'

'Did he mention Karachi?'

'He's careful not to use names. But he told his uncle to make sure that he had a spare GPS. It sounds as if they have a specific location in mind.'

'Any news on the yacht crew?'

'Stalemate, but they're talking. Emailing, anyway. Lots of threats but we've been sent new photographs and they've posted another video on an Islamic website. Luckily the media haven't picked up on it yet and we've got our technical boys blocking access to the site.'

'And no idea where they're being held?'

'Almost certainly in Puntland, but we don't know exactly where as yet.'

Shepherd ended the call, then phoned O'Brien to fill him in on what was happening. 'What's your situation?' he asked.

'We're about ten miles south of the border with Somalia,' said O'Brien. 'We're posing as hunters on safari. We've block-booked a small game farm, which gives us an excuse to get in some firing practice without upsetting the neighbours, and it's got its own airfield. But I'm scouting for places in Ethiopia. It's a fair bit closer to Puntland.'

'How are you for equipment?'

O'Brien chuckled. 'Buying arms in Africa is like buying chocolate bars in a sweet shop,' he said. 'It's all available here – longs, shorts, heavy artillery. We've got everything we need.'

'And the plane?'

'Yeah, it's arrived. Jack Bradford's got his pilot's licence and he's current for the Sherpa. He's made a few recon flights along the border.'

'Charlie still hopes to get this sorted through a ransom. If that pans out, it'll just be a matter of flying in and picking them up.'

'Yeah, well, the best-laid plans and all that crap.'

'O ye of little faith,' said Shepherd. 'What about manpower?'

'Still hiring, but so far so good. Six experienced guys. With at least another six on the way. And one girl.'

'A woman?'

O'Brien chuckled. 'You know her.'

'What?'

'Carol Bosch. Your mate from Iraq.'

'You're not serious.'

'She's a pal of one of the pilots and she was between contracts. Thought that would get your juices flowing.'

'I'm on a ship with twenty men, Martin, flowing juices is the last thing I need right now.'

'So how is Roger the cabin boy?'

'He sends his regards.' Shepherd ended the call.

Early on Saturday morning, just after five o'clock, the *Athena* officially sailed into pirate waters. Nothing changed, they merely crossed a line that had been drawn in pencil across the Admiralty chart. To the left of the line, written in neat capital letters, also in pencil, were the words 'Risk Of Piracy, Anti-Piracy Procedures To Be In Effect'.

The chief officer spent the morning fixing fire hoses at the stern so that plumes of water could be sprayed over the vessel in the event of pirates attempting to board. The only other change was that there was always an extra seaman on the bridge during the daylight watches.

Shepherd spent a lot of time on the bridge, scanning the sea through binoculars. There were plenty of small vessels travelling between Yemen in the north and Somalia in the south, usually with just one or two men on board and more often than not ferrying boxes or bales. According to Dominik they were almost certainly smugglers, though he had no idea what they might be smuggling. They saw the occasional fishing boat, and whenever one came into view there was increased tension on the bridge until they were able to satisfy themselves that they weren't pirates. The problem was that the only difference between a fisherman and a pirate was a weapon and the weapons would be concealed until the last moment.

One fishing boat passed within half a mile of them and there were three men on deck but there were also mounds of nets at the stern and the men didn't even look towards the *Athena*.

Once darkness fell everyone was more relaxed. It was hard enough to board a moving ship at the best of times but it would be next to impossible at night. After dinner Shepherd spent an hour playing the chief officer at table tennis. He lost every game. Hainrich took his ping-pong seriously and whenever it looked as if Shepherd might take the lead he played with a fierce intensity until he had regained the advantage. Shepherd didn't mind losing, he was just happy to be exercising, and he was surprised at how quickly he worked up a sweat.

When they'd finished, Hainrich slapped him on the back. 'There are only two ways you will beat me, Company Man,' he said. 'You can kill me or I can let you win. Neither is going to happen.'

Shepherd woke up early on Sunday morning and got to the mess room at exactly 7.30. There was nobody else there. Jimmy came out of the galley and Shepherd asked him if the cook could make cheesy scrambled eggs. Deep furrows appeared in Jimmy's brow as if Shepherd had asked him to solve a quadratic equation. 'Get him to make scrambled eggs and add cheese,' explained Shepherd. He made a stirring motion with his hand. 'Just mix cheese in with the eggs. Cheesy scrambled eggs. And toast. And coffee.' Jimmy nodded and went into the kitchen and returned five minutes later with Shepherd's order. The eggs were quite good, but not as good as when Katra made the dish. He'd ordered the scrambled eggs because he missed home and he missed his son and cheesy scrambled egg was Liam's favourite food. Shepherd was used to being away from home, that came with the turf when working undercover, but at least his son was only just a phone call away, most of the time. There had been no signal on his mobile phone since they'd left Karachi and he was reluctant to use the sat-phone to call him. Being at sea meant that there was no contact at all, no way that Liam or Katra could get in touch in the event of an emergency. Dominik had said that he could let Shepherd use the ship's email if he wanted but that wouldn't be any good because the captain would receive any replies and Oliver Blackburn didn't have a son.

After he'd finished his breakfast Shepherd went up to the bridge. Hainrich was there, along with the third officer, who was just about to take over the watch.

'Been for your run yet?' asked Hainrich.

'Just about to,' said Shepherd.

'You'll need to be fit if you want to beat me at ping-pong,' said Hainrich. He grinned over at the third officer.

'It would be a help if I had my own bat,' said Shepherd.

'A bad workman always blames his tools,' said Hainrich. 'It's not about the bat, it's the skill.'

'So I can use your bat tonight?'

Hainrich looked offended. 'Of course not, it's mine,' he said.

Shepherd looked at the right-hand radar screen, where two masses of triangles seemed to be about to meet some eight miles ahead of them. 'What's happening?' he asked.

Hainrich looked at the screen. 'Convoys,' he said. 'The one on the port side is heading to the Suez Canal, the one to starboard is from the canal, heading to the Arabian Sea. Forty vessels in all. You should just be able to make them out ahead.'

Shepherd picked up a pair of binoculars and scanned the horizon to starboard. He could just about make out a line of grey shapes. He walked over to the port side and through the binoculars he could see the back of a tanker, heading west.

'You'll get a better view in about half an hour,' said Hainrich. 'They're only making eleven knots.'

'How do the convoys work?' asked Shepherd.

'The slower ships wait at either end of the corridor and then they go through together under the supervision of navy vessels. The ones to starboard are being guarded by two Japanese warships, and there's a Chinese warship to port.'

'So will we join the convoy?'

Hainrich shook his head. 'There's no need, we're too big and too fast.'

'But there's safety in numbers, right?'

'We don't need no stinking warship,' Hainrich said, and laughed. 'Seriously, the convoys are for smaller, slower ships, or for tankers that are lower in the water. We'd be wasting our time slowing down. And besides, the warships are no bloody use anyway.'

'How so?'

'Because they can't shoot the pirates out of the water.

Until they've actually boarded a ship they're just fishermen with guns. If they try to arrest them they'll just throw the guns overboard and then they're just fishermen.'

'So what do they do?'

'That's a good question.'

'So? What's the answer?'

Hainrich threw up his hands. 'They observe, they file reports, they collate information. They offer advice. They might send out a helicopter to buzz pirate skiffs. But other than that, they're no use at all.'

'So what's the point of the convoys?'

'They can be more vigilant. But if pirates head towards the ships, all they can do is take evasive action. The warships won't fire on the pirates while they're trying to board and they won't do anything once they have boarded. They're a waste of time.'

Shepherd stayed on the bridge and watched through the binoculars as they gradually overhauled the convoy on the port side. There were three oil tankers, longer than the *Athena* but moving at almost half her speed, half a dozen cargo freighters of various shapes and sizes, and seven small container ships. They were following a grey Chinese warship, like ducklings struggling to keep up with their mother. As Shepherd watched, a helicopter took off from the back of the warship and did a slow circuit around the convoy at about a thousand feet. The barrel of a machine gun poked through an open door.

Shepherd walked over to the starboard side of the bridge. There were more ships there but farther away and more spread out than the convoy, some of them so far away that they were just smudges on the horizon. The eastbound ships were being guarded by two Japanese warships, each slightly smaller than the Chinese version. As Shepherd watched, the radio crackled and a Japanese voice identified itself as the lead warship and requested that the *Athena* alter its course slightly.

Hainrich acknowledged the transmission and altered their course accordingly. 'Best not to argue,' he said to Shepherd. 'They're carrying a lot more firepower than we are.'

It took almost twenty minutes before the eastbound convoy disappeared from sight and a further fifteen minutes before they left the westbound one behind.

'It's like Dunkirk must have been,' said Hainrich. 'That many ships in one place.' He laughed. 'All that fuss over a few fishermen with guns, huh?'

Shepherd went to his cabin and locked the door and took out the sat-phone. He looked at the clock on the wall. It was eleven o'clock, which meant that it was nine o'clock in the morning in London. He sat down on one of the sofas and called Button's mobile.

'How's life on the ocean waves?' she asked.

'It's starting to look like a waste of time,' said Shepherd. 'I can't help wondering if the intel you got was just plain wrong.'

'How so?'

'We rounded the Horn of Africa last night, the bit of Somalia that sticks out in the sea, and now we're in the Gulf of Aden.'

'Which is where most of the pirate attacks are, right?'

'Before the safe corridor, yes. But now it's heavily patrolled. This morning we sailed through two convoys, thirty-seven ships between them, guarded by Chinese and Japanese warships.' He rubbed the back of his neck. 'The thing is, I don't see pirates attacking anybody here.'

'Well, I'm looking at the latest Admiralty reports and they say that a group of pirates with automatic weapons attacked a cargo ship close to the Somali coast yesterday, chased it for half an hour and sprayed the bridge with bullets. And a mother ship towing skiffs was reported just a hundred miles from your present position.'

'I'm not saying there aren't pirates around, and I'm not saying that they're not taking ships. I don't see them taking anything in the secure corridor.'

'But you're not in convoy, are you?'

'No, the convoys are for the slower ships. Anything that does above eighteen knots goes it alone. What I'm saying is that if we were going to be hijacked, it would have happened while we were in open sea. But even then, it wouldn't be easy. This ship is huge, Charlie. Boarding her at speed would be like trying to climb a three-storey building in an earthquake. An SBS or SAS unit could maybe manage it but they're trained for it and they've got the right equipment. We're talking about teenagers with ladders and grappling hooks.'

'All I can tell you is that the intel we have seems good and that nothing has changed to make me think otherwise. Crazy Boy and his uncle are definitely about to do something. And all the signs are that it's the *Athena* they're after.'

Shepherd sighed. 'Well, tomorrow we enter the Red Sea. Have Crazy Boy's people ever taken ships that far west?'

'No, they haven't. But other pirates are active in the Red Sea. It's still a risky area for shipping.'

'But it's Crazy Boy we're interested in. Charlie, cards on the table, this is a waste of time.'

'So what are you suggesting? You can hardly swim ashore, can you? And you're due into Jeddah in two days.'

'I suppose so.'

'There's no suppose so about it. You can disembark at Jeddah and fly back from Riyadh. I'll arrange to have someone from the embassy meet you there and organise the transfers.'

'Back to London?'

'You've got somewhere else to go?'

'I was thinking that I should stay close to Somalia. You know Martin is in Ethiopia?'

'Near the border, yes.'

'I could go there,' said Shepherd. 'Or I could wait in Nairobi. Do we have any idea where the yacht crew is being held?'

'It's gone quiet. The kidnappers have asked for five million and the negotiator has said he'll get back to them. What we're looking for is a phone in Puntland that we can home in on. Look, I've no problem with you joining Martin. At some point we're going to want to go in and get the yacht crew, no matter what happens to the *Athena*. I'll get our man in Riyadh to make the arrangements.'

'And if I were you, I'd check the intel again,' said Shepherd. 'So far as I can see, there's no way that Crazy Boy is going to be taking the *Athena*.' Shepherd ended the call and changed into his running gear. He went down to the engine room. Tomasz and Konrad were in the engine control room and they both laughed when they saw what he was wearing. 'Do you want to do a few laps with me?' Shepherd asked.

'We work for a living,' said Tomasz. 'That's exercise enough.'

He went through into the workshop and opened the hatch that led to the Below Deck Passageway. He closed it behind him, then did a couple of minutes of loosening-up exercises, then a circuit of the ship at a slow jog. It was a good place to exercise, though the air smelled of oil in places. He had to be careful of the occasional obstruction, but he could run a lot faster than on the Upper Deck. He increased the pace for his second lap, then did a third at almost full speed, then alternated between fast and medium pace for another six circuits. By the time he'd finished he'd run almost seven kilometres and he was drenched in sweat. He dropped down and did press-ups and sit-ups until his muscles burned.

When he went back into the control room heading for the lift, Konrad had gone but the chief engineer was still there. 'Good workout?' he asked.

'Not bad,' said Shepherd. He rubbed his face on the bottom of his T-shirt.

'You lift weights?'

'Sometimes. There's none in the gym, though.'

The engineer grinned. 'Come with me,' he said. He took Shepherd back into the tool room and opened a steel cabinet. He took out a pair of dumbbells and handed them to Shepherd. They were each about ten kilos and as Shepherd held them he realised that they had been handmade from a screw thread and hefty metal bolts.

'You made these?' asked Shepherd.

'Sort of. I always get the engineer cadets to make them to practise their metalworking skills. The crew has to fly to meet the ship and you can't really fly with a suitcase full of weights. Take them.'

'You're sure?'

Tomasz opened the cupboard door and showed Shepherd that there were half a dozen dumbbells of various sizes inside. 'I've got plenty,' he said.

Shepherd thanked him and took the weights up to his cabin. He showered, changed into clean clothes and put a load of washing into one of the machines, then read a book until it was time for lunch. He went downstairs to the officers' mess. Dominik was the only one there and he nodded when he saw Shepherd.

The soup was vegetable and pasta with little in the way of taste, and it was followed by grilled tuna steak, boiled potatoes and overcooked spinach. It was as bad as anything Shepherd had eaten in the army, but he hadn't complained then and he didn't even think about complaining now. Food was fuel, pure and simple, and provided he was given protein, carbohydrates and the vitamins and minerals he needed, he was happy.

As he was finishing his tuna, Hainrich arrived. He smiled at Shepherd and sat down, reaching for a chunk of French bread. He said something to Dominik in Polish and they both laughed. Shepherd looked up expectantly but neither of them seemed prepared to tell him what the joke was.

'So Jeddah in two days?' said Shepherd.

Dominik nodded. 'No time to get off for sightseeing, though, we're only in port for six hours, maybe seven. Then we're off to the Suez.'

'I'll be getting off,' said Shepherd.

Dominik put down his knife and fork. 'You've finished your work?'

'All done and dusted.'

'And what have you decided?' asked Hainrich.

'I don't decide anything,' said Shepherd. 'I just compile a report. Someone higher up the food chain makes any decisions that need to be made.'

'But what will be in your report?' asked Dominik.

Shepherd was trying to think of something non-committal to say but before he could reply the alarm went off and a red light flashed on the console by the door. Hainrich grunted and hauled himself out of his chair and went over to peer at the console. He said something to Dominik and shrugged.

'What's wrong?' asked Shepherd.

'Engine overheating warning, one of the turbochargers,' said Dominik. 'It's nothing. It happens sometimes.'

Hainrich pressed a button and the alarm stopped. He ambled back to his seat but just as he was sitting down the alarm started up again. He went back to the console, looked at the screen. 'Second one's overheating now,' he said. He pushed a button to silence the alarm.

'Now what?' asked Shepherd.

'The sensors say that the turbochargers are overheating,' said Dominik. 'That does happen sometimes but it's more likely to be a computer glitch or a faulty sensor.' He shrugged. 'It's unusual for two to go at the same time.'

Jimmy came out of the galley and asked Shepherd whether he wanted coffee, but Shepherd waved him away as he listened to Dominik call up the chief engineer on the transceiver. They spoke in Polish back and forth and then Dominik sighed and slid out of his chair. He left the room without saying anything and Shepherd followed him. Dominik pressed the button to call the lift. 'The chief engineer is going to check the engine now,' he said. 'It's probably nothing.'

'But you're slowing the ship down?' said Shepherd.

'It's procedure, until we know for sure that the engine is OK,' Dominik said. 'If the turbochargers are overheating we could do major damage. If it carries on like this they'll shut down automatically.'

The lift arrived and they rode up to the bridge together. The second officer was standing behind the left-hand chair, looking flustered, and Hainrich was sitting in the right-hand chair, one hand on the telegraph, which was in the half-speed position. Dominik said something in Polish and the chief officer frowned at the controls.

The alarm went off again and Hainrich hit a button to silence it.

'What's happening?' asked Shepherd.

'The alarm keeps going off,' said Dominik. His transceiver crackled and he put it to his ear. The chief engineer spoke in Polish and Dominik replied.

'The engine is fine, so are the turbochargers,' Dominik said to Shepherd.

Again the alarm went off, and again Hainrich hit the button.

'So it's the computer?' said Shepherd.

'Seems to be,' said Dominik.

'Fixable?'

Dominik laughed. 'We're at sea, we have to be able to fix everything,' he said. 'We can't wait for a tow truck.' He said something to Hainrich in Polish and they both laughed. They both stopped laughing suddenly when all the screens went blank. The second officer jumped back as if he'd been stung.

Dominik frowned and put a hand on Hainrich's shoulder. 'Computer's down,' he said. 'We've lost all electrical power.'

The screens flickered on again but the ship was visibly slowing.

'Now what?' asked Shepherd.

'I don't know,' said Dominik. 'We just lost power and the emergency generators have kicked in. But they don't supply power to the main engine so we're stopping.'

'We're stopping? How can that be?'

'The emergency generators power the lights, the radar, the radio, but that's all.'

'Is it a major problem?'

Dominik ran a hand through his unkempt hair. 'It's never happened before. This is a relatively new ship, most of this equipment is still under guarantee, it shouldn't happen.'

His transceiver crackled and the chief engineer spoke in Polish. Dominik barked back and then looked at Shepherd. 'The engine's shutting down,' he said.

'So what happens?'

'We can reboot the software, same as if you had a problem with a laptop.'

'How long?'

Dominik shrugged. 'I don't know, the chief engineer's going to handle it. An hour. Maybe longer. I've never known anything like this happen before.'

'It's a first for me,' said Hainrich.

One of the Filipinos was standing at the starboard side of the bridge, scanning the sea with his binoculars. The water was almost flat, differences in shade marking the various currents that swirled ahead of them. There was no mist and Shepherd could see clear to the horizon. Other than a group of dolphins playing a mile off the port bow, the sea was empty.

Shepherd walked away from the controls and around to the chart area. The ship's last position had been marked at noon. They were midway between Yemen and Somalia with another couple of hundred miles or so to go before they reached the Red Sea.

As he walked away from the chart desk he saw movement in the sea at the stern of the ship, on the starboard side, not much more than a small dark dot on the horizon. He went back to the main section of the bridge, picked up a pair of binoculars, and went back to the rear. It took him a few seconds to focus the binoculars. The dot was a skiff, moving fast and moving towards the *Athena*. He took the binoculars away from his face and squinted at the horizon. There was a second dot, to the left of the first. He focused the binoculars on the second dot. It was another skiff. He could make out half a dozen figures in the boat. And guns.

'Dominik!' he shouted. 'I think we might have a problem.'

The skiff cut across the waves, bouncing over each crest as it hit the bow, sometimes hitting the wave so hard that the boat left the water completely and hung in the air before slamming back into the sea in a shower of spray. There were two powerful Yamaha outboards at the stern linked to a single control. Blue looked over at the man holding the tiller and grinned. The tillerman was in his fifties and knew the waters well and was able to keep the engines at full throttle without damaging the hull.

There were five men with Blue in the front of the skiff, in three rows of two. They all had AK-47s hanging on their backs and machetes in scabbards on their belts. The man sitting next to Blue was called Marlboro, after his favourite brand of cigarettes. He was in his twenties but had already been involved in four hijackings. He was tall and wiry and had spent days practising climbing and strengthening his arms with press-ups and pull-ups. He would be the first to board the *Athena*.

In Blue's hand was a portable GPS unit, but he no longer needed to look at it. Ahead of them was the *Athena*. It was drifting in the currents, its stern swinging slowly to starboard. Blue looked at his watch. Crazy Boy had been right, to the second. The *Athena* was dead in the water. Everything was going exactly to plan.

Dominik joined Shepherd at the rear of the bridge. 'I see two skiffs,' said Shepherd. 'Seven men in one, five in the other. Armed.' The captain put his binoculars to his eyes and cursed. 'Heading this way, right?' said Shepherd.

'Yes, it looks like it,' said Dominik calmly. He looked over his shoulder. 'Chief, come here, please,' he called. There was just a hint of tension in his voice.

The chief officer hurried over and Dominik gave him the binoculars. 'Two skiffs, heading straight for us,' said Dominik.

'What are our options?' asked Shepherd. 'Can we restart the engine?'

Hainrich shook his head. 'We're dead in the water.'

'Can they board us?'

Dominik took back the binoculars and focused on the skiffs. 'I don't see any ladders.'

'They could have ropes,' said Hainrich. 'Ropes and hooks.'

'Turn on the fire hoses,' said Dominik. Hainrich hurried away.

'Will the fire hoses stop them?' asked Shepherd.

'They'll make it harder, but with the engine stopped they'll be able to board at the stern, hoses or no hoses.'

'So can we fight back with something?'

'What, throw rocks at them?'

'Have you got any weapons? Any guns?'

Dominik shook his head.

'So what's the plan?' asked Shepherd.

'There is no plan, not to fight them off anyway,' said Dominik. He put the binoculars back to his eyes. 'The plan is to take evasive action, but with the engine down that's not possible. The company says that in the event of us being boarded, the crew and officers should gather together on the bridge.'

'Then what?'

Dominik shrugged as he looked at the skiffs in the distance. 'Then we wait. We cooperate. And the company negotiates for our release.'

Shepherd looked at the skiffs through his binoculars. He could see the men and their weapons more clearly now. Kalashnikovs. The skiffs were about fifty feet apart and moving at the same speed. 'This was planned,' said Shepherd. 'It has to be. It can't be sheer luck that they're turning up just as we break down.'

'They can't have known,' said Dominik. 'The computers going down like that, it's a one-in-a-million shot. No one could have predicted it. It's just a coincidence.'

'I don't believe in coincidences,' said Shepherd. 'How long before they get here?'

'They're about six miles away, probably doing twenty knots,' said Dominik. 'Between fifteen and twenty minutes.'

'And how long to board?'

'While we're drifting like this? Five minutes, at most. Then it's all over.' Dominik took his binoculars with him as he walked across the bridge to the radio. He picked up the telephone receiver. 'Mayday, mayday, mayday, this is container ship *Athena*, call sign Alpha Delta Tango Two Four Six, we are under attack by pirates.' He gave his position.

Hainrich walked up to the captain. 'Fire hoses are on,' he said. 'Not that they'll do any good.'

'I need you to call the company's emergency number,' said Dominik. 'Tell them we're under attack and that we're following the anti-piracy procedures but that we've lost our engine.'

'They're not going to help, are they?' said Hainrich.

'Maybe not, but they need to know what's happening,' said Dominik. 'Once you've phoned the company, put in a call to UKMTO Dubai.'

He repeated his mayday broadcast, then sounded the general emergency alarm as Hainrich went over to the sat-phone.

Dominik let the alarm cycle twice then he announced over the public address system that all members of the crew should muster on the bridge immediately.

Shepherd stood and watched the captain as he repeated his mayday message for a second time, then looked over his shoulder at the two approaching skiffs. Shepherd knew that he could do one of two things. He could stand and wait with the crew for the pirates to board, or he could act.

He knew that Button's instructions were to stay with the crew, but he had a bad feeling about the way the hijacking was going down.

The door to the bridge opened and three Filipino crewmen walked in, followed by the second officer. The officer hurried over to the seaman on watch and took the binoculars from him. All the Filipinos started chattering in their own language.

Dominik put the transceiver to his mouth and called up the chief engineer. For the first time Shepherd saw a look of panic in the captain's eyes. More seamen came up the stairs and on to the bridge. Dominik was talking to Tomasz in Polish.

Shepherd went out on to the port wing of the bridge and looked at the skiffs through his binoculars. They were close now. One of the men was holding something. The skiff was bucking up and down so it was difficult to focus but Shepherd was fairly sure it was either a radio or a GPS unit. He went back on to the bridge, where Dominik had finished talking to the chief engineer and was staring helplessly at the controls. Hainrich was talking on the sat-phone.

'What's happening?' asked Shepherd.

Dominik shrugged. 'The computer says the turbochargers are overheating.'

'And are they?'

Dominik shook his head. 'Tomasz has checked them himself. They're fine. But so long as the computer says there's a problem, the engine shuts down.'

'That can't be a coincidence, can it?'

'What do you mean?'

Shepherd pointed at the approaching skiffs. 'We're a long way from land. They can't just have stumbled across us.'

'You think they killed our engine?' He screwed up his face. 'Impossible.'

'Maybe not,' said Shepherd.

Feliks appeared on the bridge and shouted over to Dominik in Polish. The third officer and three more seamen rushed in.

Shepherd came to a sudden decision, and without saying anything he rushed off the bridge and down the stairs to F-Deck. He burst into his cabin and grabbed the sat-phone. He tapped out Button's number and she answered almost immediately. 'Everything's changed,' he said. 'We're about to be boarded by pirates. Two skiffs heading our way and we're at a full stop.'

'How come?'

'Some sort of computer fault, the engine just died.'

'Are you OK?'

'I'm not sure,' said Shepherd. He looked at his watch. There were another five minutes before the skiffs would be there. 'This doesn't feel right.'

'Explain?'

'I can't. It's a hunch. A feeling.'

'What do you want to do? I assume it's a bit late to abandon ship?'

'Charlie, the crew and officers are gathering on the bridge. That's the company policy. If it looks like they're about to be boarded they stay together.' He took a deep breath. 'I can't do that,' he said. 'I can't just roll over and die.'

'I know you don't mean that literally,' she said. 'It's your call, Spider. Whatever you want to do, I'll back you. You're the one on the spot.'

'It's about observing the situation, and I think I'd be better placed to do that elsewhere on the ship.'

'You can do that?'

'It's a big ship, Charlie. Bloody huge. Lots of places to hide.'

'For how long? You'll need food and water.'

'I was trained for escape and evasion, I can handle it. And these aren't highly trained soldiers. Most of them are kids. Look, there're twelve pirates on two boats. I figure that two of the pirates will stay with the skiffs and head back to the mother ship. That leaves nine on board. Most of them will be guarding the crew or on the bridge so I reckon I can avoid them. I can watch what's going on. And report back to you.'

'And if it takes weeks?'

'Then I'll stick it out for weeks. Rather that than be locked in some storage area for the duration.' He looked at his watch again. He was running out of time. 'I'll phone you when I can,' he said. 'I'll have the sat-phone off to conserve power. If I can I'll try to call on the hour and I'll only call your mobile. I've got to go.'

'Good luck,' she said.

Shepherd ended the call and looked around the cabin. He opened the fridge and grabbed three bottles of water and shoved them into his bag, threw in some of his clothes and the sat-phone and then dashed along the corridor to the stairs. He hurtled down the stairs to B-Deck, passing Jimmy the messman on the way, then ran along to the officers' mess. The bowls of fruit were still on the sideboard and he tipped them into his bag, then ran into the galley. There were two baskets of French bread left over from lunch and he threw them into his bag, followed by three plates of cheese that had been covered with cling film. Outside he heard the tat-tat-tat of a Kalashnikov being fired.

The skiffs had been approaching from the starboard side so he ran down the stairs to the Upper Deck and along the corridor to the port door. He opened it and then opened the metal hatch that led to the outside. He looked left and right but the sea was clear. He heard more automatic fire, louder now that he was outside.

They'd probably be boarding from the rear so he had to move quickly. He bent low and began running towards the bow, his bag held tightly against his chest.

The second officer ducked and backed away from the window as one of the pirates on the larger skiff let loose a burst of fire, spraying bullets over the top of the bridge. The other skiff had disappeared around the stem.

'Bloody idiots,' said Hainrich. 'Why are they shooting?'

'Because they're morons,' said Dominik. 'Everybody, listen to me!' he shouted. 'Stay away from the windows. Don't show any aggression and do exactly as they say. The company will handle this, everything will be OK. All they care about is money, they've nothing to gain by hurting us.'

'They've got guns!' shouted one of the seamen. 'They're going to kill us!'

'They're only firing to scare us,' said Dominik. 'If they wanted to hit us they could. They're firing into the air. Now just relax and keep calm.'

The third officer came from the rear of the bridge. 'Can't see them, they're at the stern.'

'It won't take them long to board.' Dominik turned to the chief officer. 'Is everybody here?'

'Twenty, with two still on the engine room,' said Hainrich. 'But the human resources guy is missing.'

'Mr Oliver? Where is he?' said Dominik, looking around. 'He might have panicked.'

'He doesn't look the type to panic,' said Hainrich.

Dominik held up his hands. 'Did anyone see Mr Oliver?' he shouted. 'The company man? Did anyone see him?'

Jimmy the messman raised his hand. 'I saw him on the stairs. Going down.'

'When?'

'When the alarm was sounding. He had a bag.'

'He had a what?'

Jimmy mimed holding a bag.

Dominik looked over at Hainrich. 'What the hell's going on?'

The chief officer shrugged. 'Do you want me to go and look for him?'

'It's too late,' said Dominik. 'They'll be here any minute. He'll have to take care of himself.'

Dominik raised his hands again. 'Can I have everyone's attention!' he shouted. Half a dozen of the Filipinos continued to chatter over on the starboard side of the bridge so he clapped his hands and shouted again. 'Please, everyone, listen to what I have to say.'

The seamen went quiet and everyone looked at the captain.

'We're about to be boarded by pirates, and there's nothing we can do to stop them. They have guns and as you know our engine has stopped. We've informed the company and there's a warship on its way but by the time they get here the pirates are going to be on board.'

'Why don't we fight them?' shouted the deck fitter, a well-built Filipino in his thirties who had once been a semi-professional boxer and had the nose to prove it.

'Because they've got guns and we haven't and if we put up any sort of fight we're just going to make them angry,' said Dominik. 'Our best chance of coming out of this without any injuries is to cooperate and to comply with any instructions they give us. That's company policy.'

'The company doesn't care about us!' shouted one of the younger seamen.

'Listen, I understand you feel worried, scared even, that's natural,' shouted Dominik. 'But as scary as these men might appear, they're only interested in money. Just do as they say, don't give them any excuse to get violent, and we'll all get through this.'

'We should lock ourselves in the engine room,' said one of the seamen. 'If they can't get the engine started they'll just leave.'

'And what if they don't?' said Dominik. 'How long could we stay down there with no food or water? Then when we eventually come out they're going to be very angry and that's when people get hurt. I'm telling you what the company is advising; they have experts who draw up their plans so we should follow them.'

'It's easy to be an expert when you're sitting at a desk,' said another seaman.

The tillerman took the skiff in to the rear of the ship, turning at just the right time so that it was parallel to the stern. Marlboro was standing at the bow of the skiff, swinging the grappling iron. He let go of it too late and it clanged against the stern and fell into the sea. Blue cursed him, then flinched as one of the men in the second skiff let rip with his Kalashnikov.

'I told you, no shooting!' he shouted, but his words were lost in the crashing of the waves against the hull.

Marlboro pulled the grappling hook out of the water and began to whirl it again, a look of grim determination on his face. He allowed the wet knotted rope to slide through his fingers and then he yelled as he launched it skywards. It spun through the air and then hooked over the safety rail. Marlboro yelped in triumph and pulled the rope tight. He began to pull himself up, using his hands and bare feet to grip the knotted rope. Blue could see the muscles in the boy's arm tensing like steel cables as he hauled himself up, his AK-47 banging against his shoulders.

'Go on, boy, faster!' shouted Blue.

The tillerman grinned as he worked the rudder to keep the skiff close to the ship's stern. 'Like a monkey after bananas,' he shouted.

'Yeah, but this banana is worth millions of dollars,' said Blue.

Marlboro reached the rail and rolled over it on to the deck. One of the men behind Blue came forward with a rolled-up chain ladder and attached it to the end of the rope and Blue waved up at the teenager. As he pulled up the rope the ladder unwound and snaked up the side of the ship, the metal rungs rattling against the stern. Marlboro hooked the ladder over the rail and waved at Blue.

Blue grabbed the ladder with his left hand and adjusted the strap of his AK-47 with the other, then started to climb. He was heavier than Marlboro and not as nimble but he was soon at the top, though his arms and legs burned as if they were on fire and his knuckles were bleeding from where he'd scraped them against the hull. He rolled over the rail and his bare feet slapped on the deck. He shouted for the rest of the men to climb up and he swung his AK-47 around so that the butt was snug against his hip.

One by one the pirates climbed the ladder and assembled behind Blue. As the last one came up, the tillerman edged his skiff away from the ship and accelerated away, back towards the mother ship, now just visible on the horizon. The second skiff moved in to take its place.

'Right,' shouted Blue, pointing at three men in quick succession. 'You go up to the bridge on the starboard side. Don't shoot unless they give you a problem. I'll come with the rest up the port side. Go!'

The three men raced along the deck to the superstructure, cradling their weapons. Blue shouted down at the men in the second skiff, telling them to get a move on.

Shepherd jogged along the Upper Deck, his bag against his chest. He knew that no one could see him from above as the deck was hidden by the containers, but if either of the skiffs was to come around the port side it would probably spot him. With the engine stopped the ship was being buffeted by the waves so every few steps he banged against the railing. He slowed to a fast walk, looking over his shoulder. There was no sign of the skiffs; he guessed that they would be coming up to the stern. Now that the propeller was no longer turning it would be the easiest and safest place to board.

He reached the metal ladder that led up to the passageway and he climbed up quickly then jogged along to the middle. He reached up and opened the container he'd already picked out, threw in his bag and then crawled in after it. He pulled the doors shut behind him and sat with his back to the wall of the container, breathing slowly and trying to steady his heart rate. The adrenalin was coursing through his system, the flight-or-fight response, but it was wasted because he wasn't in a position to do either. All he could do now was wait.

'There, look!' shouted Tomasz. He pointed at the starboard exterior bridge where a black man in a Nike vest and baggy khaki shorts had appeared, an AK-47 in his hands. He had a red bandana tied around his neck. He waved the weapon and screamed at them. A second pirate appeared behind him, older but with a similar Kalashnikov.

'Everybody lie down on the floor!' shouted Dominik. 'Lie face down and put your hands behind your neck.'

One by one the Filipinos dropped down on to the floor and did as Dominik said. Hainrich looked over at him. 'Are you sure about this?'

'It's procedure,' said Dominik, getting to his knees. 'We cooperate, we comply, we assist. We do nothing to antagonise them.'

Hainrich got down, as did Tomasz and the rest of the Poles.

The port door opened and two pirates rushed in waving AK-47s and shouting. One of them was wearing a mesh vest and cut-off jeans. 'Which one captain?' he shouted, revealing two gold teeth at the front of his mouth.

The seamen flinched as the starboard door was flung open and more pirates flooded in. One took a machete from his waistband and waved it around.

'Which one captain?' shouted the man in the mesh vest

again. He had a thick scar running across his neck and what looked like an old burn on his left calf.

Half the heads swivelled to look at Dominik. He got to his feet as the pirate walked towards him. He jabbed the barrel of his Kalashnikov into Dominik's chest, so hard that the captain gasped and took a step back. 'Safe?' said the pirate. 'Where is safe?'

'The admin office,' said Dominik. He pointed at the floor. 'G-Deck. Look, there's no need to hurt anyone, we'll do whatever you want.'

'If you do not, you die.'

Dominik nodded. 'It's not a problem. I just work for the company, I don't care what you do with the ship.' He tapped his chest. 'My name's Dominik. What's your name?'

'Blue.'

Dominik held out his hand. 'We can be friends, Blue. We don't have to fight.'

Blue ignored the outstretched hand. 'You radio the Americans already?'

'We put out a mayday call, yes.'

Blue nodded. 'Go on radio now, tell them if they try to board the crew will die.'

Dominik knew that there was no point in arguing. He picked up the radio and broadcast a brief message.

'Now turn off AIS,' said Blue.

Again the captain did as he was told.

'Which one chief officer?' Blue asked.

'That's me,' said Hainrich.

'Get up,' said Blue.

Hainrich got to his feet. 'You stay on bridge,' Blue shouted at him. He turned to Marlboro, who was waving his machete at the terrified seamen. 'Watch him.' Blue pointed his gun at Hainrich. 'You do anything, we kill you,' he said. He pointed at Marlboro. 'He kill you good. Maybe with gun, maybe with knife, but he kill you for sure.'

Hainrich raised his hands. 'Whatever you want,' he said. 'You're in charge.'

Blue nodded. 'Yes,' he said. 'Do not forget that. If you do as we say, you will be OK and soon back with your family.' He prodded Hainrich's chest with the AK-47. 'But you try anything, you die.'

'I understand,' said Hainrich.

Blue stared menacingly at the Filipinos, who were huddled together like frightened sheep. 'All of you, understand this. We do not want to hurt you, we want only money. Money not worth dying for. Be calm, be quiet, do as we say and everything will be OK.' He gestured with his AK-47. 'But you cause any problem, you try to do anything, we shoot you for sure.'

Blue saw the list of officers and crew on the wall and he ripped it out of its perspex frame. He quickly counted the photographs, then did a head count of his prisoners before waving the list in Dominik's face. 'Two missing,' he said. 'Where?'

'The engine room,' said Dominik. 'We have a problem with the engine, that's why we stopped. The ship can't go anywhere.'

'Both in engine room?'

Dominik nodded.

Blue waved over two of the pirates. 'Go down to the engine room and bring the engineers up,' he told them in Somali. 'Any problems, hurt them.'

The two pirates nodded eagerly and headed for the stairs.

Blue jabbed Dominik in the chest with his AK-47. 'Show me safe.'

'Whatever you want,' said Dominik. 'But you don't have to keep pushing me with that thing. We'll do whatever you want.'

Blue pushed the captain out of the bridge and down the stairs. 'It's down here,' said Dominik, pointing at G-Deck. 'The office and my cabin.'

'OK, go,' said Blue. Dominik took him along to his cabin. The safe was in the outer working area, next to his desk. A door led to his cabin and from there another door opened into his bathroom.

Blue gestured at the safe with his AK-47. 'Open it but don't reach inside. Just open it and then step away.'

'You don't have to worry, there are no guns on the ship,' said Dominik.

'I'm not worried, just do as you're told,' said Blue.

'OK, whatever you say,' said Dominik, kneeling down in front of the safe. There was a numeric pad next to the opening lever and he tapped in the six-digit combination. He twisted the lever and then stood up and moved away. 'It's done,' he said.

'Sit down, over there,' said Blue, nodding at the blue corner unit beneath the portholes at the far end of the cabin. He waited until the captain had done as he was told and then he opened the safe. There was a bulky envelope carrying the papers and passports of the crew and he tossed that on the desk. Underneath the envelope were half a dozen bundles of dollar bills. Blue grinned as he examined one of the bundles. All the notes were hundreds and it contained ten thousand dollars. Another of the bundles was also hundred-dollar bills and four were twenty-dollar bills in bundles of five thousand dollars. He stacked the bundles on the desk. In all there was forty thousand dollars.

'Is there more?' Blue asked, turning to look at the captain. 'More money?'

Dominik pointed to his desk. 'Top drawer on the right,' he said.

Blue pulled open the drawer and took out a bundle of notes. 'Bag?' he said.

Dominik pointed at a cupboard. Blue opened it and took out a grubby white holdall. He put the money in it then threw in the envelope and zipped it up. He tossed the bag at Dominik. 'Carry for me,' he said, and waved for the captain to go out into the corridor. On the other side of the corridor was a door with a sign saying 'Chief Engineer'. Blue opened it. The cabin was large with a bathroom and three windows looking out over the containers at the front of the ship. Only one of the windows could be opened but Blue could see that there was no way anyone could escape through it. There was a telephone on a desk and Blue ripped it out and threw it into the corridor, then told Dominik to go back to the bridge.

By the time they got there, Tomasz and Konrad were there, with Feliks and the Filipino second engineer. They looked over at the captain but he shook his head, warning them to keep quiet.

'Can I say something, Blue?' asked Dominik, placing the holdall on the chart desk.

'What?'

Dominik pointed at the controls. 'The engine's not working,' he said. 'You can't move the ship.'

'We can move it,' said Blue.

'The engine's stopped,' said Konrad. 'You need us to fix it. If the engine's not fixed we're not going anywhere.'

'The engine is OK,' said Blue. 'Working soon.'

Konrad laughed harshly. 'So now you're an engineer and a pirate?'

Blue took three quick steps towards Konrad, raised his AK-47 and brought the butt crashing down on to the engineer's nose. The cartilage splintered, blood spurted and Konrad collapsed on to the floor, sobbing. Blue glared at Dominik. 'You see? You see what happens?'

'OK, OK,' said Dominik. 'We'll do whatever you say, whatever you want.' He went to help Konrad but Blue blocked his way and pushed him back with the point of his gun. 'Stay away from him.'

'He's hurt,' said Dominik.

'He's hurt because he didn't do what he was told,' said Blue. He raised the butt of his Kalashnikov and jabbed it at Dominik's face. 'You want the same?'

Dominik put his hands up. 'None of us want to give you any problems,' he said, speaking slowly and calmly. 'Whatever you want us to do, just tell us.'

'I want you all to do as you're told!' screamed Blue. He turned and pointed his gun at the crew. 'If you do not do what we say, we will kill you all,' he shouted. He turned to five of his men who were standing with their guns trained on the Filipinos. 'Take them to the deck below,' he said in Somali. 'Deck G. Take them to the chief engineer's cabin and lock them up. And make sure there's nothing they can use. Check them for weapons, for knives, for everything.'

He pointed at Dominik. 'The captain stays on the bridge but everyone else stays in the cabin. Nobody leaves. And always have two men outside the door. Every hour, every minute, two men outside.' He nodded at Marlboro. 'You make sure, OK?'

The five pirates moved towards the crew and herded them off the bridge and down the stairs.

'I know you don't want to hear this, but this ship can't go anywhere,' said Dominik.

Blue looked up at the clock. 'Twenty more minutes and the engine will work,' he said. 'You have called your company already?'

Dominik nodded. 'Before you boarded us. It's policy.'

'Where is the sat-phone?'

Dominik pointed to the sat-phone receiver, near the door. Through the side window of the bridge he saw the two skiffs heading back the way they'd come.

Crazy Boy was using his shotgun to blow out the windows of a bar when his mobile rang. He paused the video game and took the call. It was Blue. 'Everything is good,' said his uncle. 'We are on the ship.'

'Excellent,' said Crazy Boy. He looked at his watch. 'And you are ready to move?'

'Yes,' said Blue. 'I am waiting for the company to call.'

'It won't be long, I'm sure.'

'I could call them first.'

'No, brother of my father. Let them do the chasing. Just make sure that the ship is moving, as we planned.' He ended the call and grabbed a handful of khat leaves from the crystal bowl by his side.

Two Knives walked in. 'OK, brother?' he asked.

'Perfect,' said Crazy Boy.

Shepherd felt the ship begin to vibrate and slowly move forward. He crawled out of the container and looked left and right down the passageway. He could just about see the waves off the port side; the ship was definitely moving. That didn't make any sense at all. He crawled back into the container. He wanted to phone Charlotte Button but he didn't want to risk it during the day in case one of the pirates decided to come out on to the deck.

He hadn't heard any gunshots after the pirates had boarded the ship and he'd taken that as a good sign, but he would not know any more about what was happening until he was able to call Button.

The man whom the shipping company had sent to handle the negotiations was a former London detective who now headed up their security section. His name was Chris Thatcher and he was wearing an expensive suit with a sombre tie and a perfectly starched white shirt and gold cufflinks, which Button thought was actually overdressed considering they didn't know how long they'd be stuck in the operations room. He was tall, in his early sixties with a close-cropped grey beard, and he looked at her over the top of his spectacles before offering a well-manicured hand. He had a gentle but firm grip when she shook it. With him was a portly black man in a tweed jacket and grey flannel trousers. 'This is Omar Yusuf,' said Thatcher by way of introduction. 'Omar was born in Puntland, he's a consultant with our company.'

Button shook hands with the Somali. 'Thank you for coming,' she said.

'I am more than happy to be of assistance,' he said, in accented English.

Thatcher looked around the room and nodded appreciatively. 'Well, this beats the hell out of our operations room,' he said, taking off his jacket and hanging it on the back of one of the chairs.

'We try to please,' said Button. She had arranged to use a briefing room in MI6's headquarters at Vauxhall Cross, on the Albert Embankment overlooking the Thames. It had been the high-profile headquarters of the Secret Intelligence Service, or MI6 as it was more commonly known, since 1995 and had become one of the most famous landmarks in the city, partly because the Real IRA had once fired a ground-to-air missile at it and blown a big chunk of masonry to dust, though doing little in the way of serious damage.

Thames House was notoriously cramped and MI6 had much better facilities, including instant access to the nation's surveillance satellites and direct links to GCHQ. There were desks against three of the walls, each with two telephones, and a bank of twelve LED screens on the main wall, most of which were blank. One showed a computer map of the Arabian Sea with small triangles showing the position of the vessels that could be identified by means of their AIS transmitters. Another was a rolling weather report interspersed with any instances of piracy that had been reported to the United Kingdom Maritime Trade Organisation and the Maritime Security Centre – Horn of Africa.

Button sat down next to Thatcher. There were two other men in the room sitting in front of terminals, wearing lightweight headsets, and a young woman was monitoring the screens on the wall. 'I'd like to handle the negotiations, if that's all right with you,' said Button. She waved for Yusuf to take one of the empty seats. He removed his jacket, revealing bright red braces, and hung it on the back of the chair before sitting down.

Thatcher grimaced. 'My bosses said that I should defer to you on all operational matters,' he said. 'Actually they said I was to defer to you on pretty much everything. But in this case it might be better if I do the talking.'

Button opened her mouth to argue but Thatcher held up his hand and smiled apologetically. 'The thing is that Somali men tend not to do much talking to their women. Men rule the roost, and I'm afraid they take the view that women should be seen and not heard. And there's a good chance that the pirates will be Muslim, in which case dealing with a woman could cause all sorts of additional problems. I'm sorry if that sounds sexist – believe me, I have a wife and three daughters so there isn't a sexist bone in my body. It's just the way it is.'

'I've been in situations before where it was considered an advantage for me to be a woman when dealing with Muslims,' said Button. 'It puts them on the back foot.'

Thatcher looked across at Yusuf for support. The Somali nodded in agreement. 'Mr Thatcher is correct,' he said. 'The men in Somalia are brought up to believe that a woman should be seen and not heard.' He raised his hands palms upward. 'I sometimes wish it was that way in my own home.' He smiled amiably. 'I am joking, of course. It would be best if it was a man talking to them. With a man, there would be no doubt in their minds that they were talking with an equal. We Somalis have a saying. Your woman should be in the house or in the grave. It is not one of our better proverbs but it does show the attitude of the men in Somalia.'

Thatcher nodded. 'It might well put them on the defensive if they're in an orange jumpsuit in Guantanamo Bay but in this situation they'll be feeling in control and would see a woman's involvement as being insulting.' He smiled. 'No offence,' he added.

'None taken,' she said. 'But I should tell you that I've already commenced negotiations with the pirates who have taken the yacht.'

'And how's that going?'

Button smiled thinly. It hadn't been going well, but she hadn't considered that her being a woman was the problem.

'Look, I'm more than happy for you to listen in, and equally happy to hear your advice,' said Thatcher. 'And as I already said, my bosses have made it clear that you're running the show. I just think that when it comes to negotiating, they'd be more comfortable talking to a man.'

'I get it,' said Button. 'And it's been explained to you that we want the ransom to include the release of the crew of the yacht that they are also holding?'

'Absolutely,' said Thatcher. 'I plan to open negotiations for the *Athena* and to get an opening figure from them, and then once we start haggling I'll bring up the yacht crew. Once the negotiation has some sort of momentum we can expand it to encompass the yacht and its crew.'

'Then we're definitely on the same page,' Button said. 'But what if they start opening the containers?' she asked. 'There are Chinese weapons in there and the last thing we want is for them to be bristling with RPGs and ground-to-air missiles.'

'They'd have to be smart enough to take a look at the

manifest, and in my experience they're not that smart,' said Thatcher. 'It'll be on the bridge somewhere but I doubt that they'll ask for it.'

'You've dealt with a lot of hijackings?'

'Actually this is only my second. Our company is pretty sensible about its anti-piracy precautions, especially on our smaller vessels. But I've sat in on several negotiations. The shipping companies tend to help each other out when things go wrong.'

'And tell me, do things generally work out?'

Thatcher nodded. 'Provided both sides stick to the script, it usually works out just fine,' he said. 'They want money, the owners want their ship and crew back. There's a lot of back and forth but eventually we should reach some middle ground that both sides can be happy with.'

'You make it sound like a game.'

'It is, partly. They know the value of these ships and their cargo and that they're asking for a tiny fraction of what they're worth. They also know that every day a ship isn't moving the company loses hundreds of thousands of dollars. We know we're going to pay, we just want to pay as little as possible. But let's not forget that we're talking about ill-educated fishermen with guns who are probably high on khat and for whom life is pretty cheap. If they do think that we're trying to cheat them they will start killing hostages. It's up to us to make sure that doesn't happen.'

'So what do we do now? Do we wait for them to call?'

'What we do first is get a pot of coffee going. I take mine strong but with lots of milk and two sugars.' He looked around the room. 'Can we get a machine or something in here? I drink a lot of coffee.'

'I'll get it arranged,' she said. 'Any particular brand of biscuit?'

He chuckled. 'I detect a note of sarcasm, but if there is even a hint of sincerity in that offer then I would absolutely love some Jaffa Cakes.'

'Actually, so would I,' she said. 'I'll get some in.' She looked across at Yusuf. 'Coffee, Mr Yusuf?'

'Tea, please.'

Button smiled. 'A man after my own heart.' She looked back at Thatcher. 'Going back to my question, how do they get in touch?'

'They don't,' said Thatcher. 'There's a sat-phone on the bridge and another in the administration cabin. We call them.'

Blue looked at the screen that showed the position of the *Athena*, with Somalia to the south and Yemen to the north. 'Keep on course three-five-zero,' said Blue. 'Full speed.'

Dominik was sitting in the right-hand chair, his left hand on the telegraph. 'You know we're heading north, don't you?'

'Just do as you are told,' said Blue.

'But Somalia is to the south.'

Blue jabbed the barrel of the AK-47 against the captain's neck and tightened his finger on the trigger. 'Shut up.'

'OK, no problem,' said Dominik.

'You think I don't know what I'm doing?'

'I'm sorry,' said Dominik.

'I know what I'm doing. You keep your mouth shut.'

Dominik nodded and said nothing.

Blue was about to say something else when the sat-phone rang behind them. Blue whirled around and stared at it.

'It's the sat-phone,' said Dominik.

'I know.'

'That'll be the company phoning,' said Dominik. 'You should answer it.'

Blue took two steps towards the captain and slammed the butt of his AK-47 against his shoulder. Dominik yelped. Blue lashed out again and this time he caught Dominik under the chin and a tooth broke. Blood trickled down Dominik's chin and he wiped it away with his hand. 'You don't tell me what to do!' screamed Blue. He glared at the captain and then went over to the sat-phone and picked up the receiver.

'My name is Chris, who am I talking to?' said a voice.

'Who are you? Do you work for the company?'

'I represent the company,' said the man. 'Can you tell me your name?'

'My name doesn't matter,' said Blue. 'I want ten million dollars.'

'I understand that, but I need to know who I am talking to so that when I call back I know who to ask for. So what is your name?'

'Blue. You can call me Blue.'

'That's good, Blue. Now, like I said, my name is Chris. No one else will be calling you, just me.'

'I want ten million dollars. Or I kill the crew.'

'I understand,' said the man. 'But first I need to talk with the captain, Blue. Can you put him on the phone for me, please?'

'You talk to me,' said Blue.

'Yes, I will, of course I will, but first I need to talk with the captain. I have to check with the captain that the crew are OK. Once he has confirmed that the crew are safe you and I can talk. So please put him on.'

Blue held out the phone to the captain. 'Talk to him,' he snapped.

The captain took the phone. 'This is Dominik Kaminski,' he said, dabbing at his mouth with a handkerchief.

'Dominik, this is Chris Thatcher. I'm acting for the company. Are the crew with you?'

'They're locked in the chief engineer's cabin.'

'And they're safe?'

'So far, yes.'

'And the pirates have guns?'

'Yes.'

'AK-47s?'

'Yes.'

'I need to know how many pirates there are on board, Dominik. More than five?'

'Yes.'

'More than ten?'

'No.'

'Nine?'

'Yes.'

'They have turned off the AIS?'

'Yes.'

Blue grabbed the phone and pulled it away. 'You spoke to him, now I want my money,' he said. 'No money, the crew dies.'

'Nobody wants anybody to get hurt, Blue,' said the man. 'But you have to know that nobody pays ten million dollars for a ship. Nobody.'

'Ten million dollars or they die!' shouted Blue, and he

switched off the phone. He slammed it down on the table. He walked over to the left-hand chair and sat in it, keeping the barrel of his Kalashnikov pointed at the captain.

Dominik said nothing as he stared out through the window, holding his handkerchief to his bleeding mouth.

Shepherd looked at the luminous dial of his Rolex Submariner. It was just after one o'clock in the morning. He slowly crawled out of the container and on to the metal walkway. He stood up and listened for a full minute before creeping towards the starboard side. He peered cautiously down the deck towards the superstructure. There was enough moonlight to satisfy himself that there was no one on the deck close by, but the rear of the deck was shrouded in darkness. He stood and listened carefully, but there was only the sound of the ship coursing through the waves. He was holding the sat-phone and he slipped it into his pocket, knowing that if he did stumble across a pirate he'd need both his hands. He looked towards the bow and frowned as he saw the North Star, directly in front of the vessel. He scanned the night sky, thinking that he'd made a mistake, but saw the Plough with its handle pointing towards the North Star and realised that he had been right the first time.

He headed along the deck to the bow and knelt down by one of the anchor chains before switching on the sat-phone. The phone searched for a satellite link and as soon as he had one he tapped in Charlotte Button's number.

'Thank goodness,' she said. 'Are you OK?'

'I'm fine,' he said. 'I figure that most of them will be asleep by now.'

'Where are you?'

'Hiding in a container close to the bow. There's no reason for them to be out here and even if they were they'd have to look hard to find me.'

'Just be careful, OK? We've started negotiations. The pirates want ten million, which is ridiculous, but that's just the opening shot. We'll get this sorted as quickly as we can.'

'And then what?'

'If we can tie the yacht crew with the *Athena* then we can arrange the money drop in Puntland. Martin and his people can go and get the crew.'

'And what about the *Athena*?'

'We'll send in the Increment. They're already out on one of the task force's British vessels.'

'But what if the pirates on board warn the guys in Somalia?'

'That won't happen. We'll be blocking all communications from the *Athena* once we've done a deal with the pirates in Puntland,' she said. 'Don't worry, Spider, we've got all the bases covered. Now listen, they've switched off the AIS so we don't know where you are. I need you to keep the sat-phone on for a while longer so that we can use the GPS to fix your position.'

'I can do that, but it's going to drain the battery,' he said.

'Understood,' she said. 'Leave it on until we've got a fix and then we'll end this call. Then tomorrow switch the phone on at this time. Even if you don't make a call we'll be able to see your position.'

'I think we're heading north, towards Yemen,' he said.

'That wouldn't make sense,' said Button.

'They might just be moving us out of the main shipping

lane, but you'd have thought that they would go to Somalia rather than Yemen.'

'Here we are,' she said. 'We've just got you. Yes, you've moved about thirty miles north of the last position we had on the AIS.'

'I'll switch on again this time tomorrow,' said Shepherd, and he turned off the phone.

Liam was sucking his pen and trying to work out whether to do his history homework first or whether he should try to memorise the twenty French words that he was going to be tested on the next day. His books were spread out on the coffee table and he had the television on but with the sound muted because Katra was in the kitchen and she wouldn't let him watch television while he was doing his homework. She had promised to cook fish fingers, chips and baked beans for him once she'd finished the ironing.

He decided to memorise the French vocabulary and picked up his exercise book, but even before he'd flicked through to the right page the doorbell rang. Liam jumped up off the sofa. 'I'll get it!' he shouted, and rushed down the hall to the front door. There was a woman on the doorstep, wearing a dark brown coat and holding a clipboard. She flashed him a beaming smile. 'Hello, is your daddy home?' she asked. She had red hair with a black clip in it and she reminded Liam of one of the ladies who worked in the canteen. She had a similar accent, too. Irish.

'No, sorry,' said Liam.

The woman looked at her clipboard and frowned. 'Mr Daniel Shepherd, is that right?'

Liam nodded. 'That's my dad.'

She handed him a glossy brochure filled with photographs of cars. 'I wanted to ask if he would take part in a survey we're doing about SUVs,' she said. 'Your father owns a BMW and a CRV.' She half turned and pointed at the two cars in the driveway. 'Which one does your father usually drive?'

'The X3,' said Liam.

'That's good because we wanted to ask him about his driving experiences and offer him a test drive of the new BMW X6.'

'Really?' said Liam. 'The X6 is a cool car. Really cool.'

The woman smiled. 'You're a fan, are you?'

'Of the X6? Sure.'

'So when will your father be back? As soon as we do the survey he can get the test drive. We'll deliver it and let you have it for a day or two.'

Liam sighed. 'I don't know when he'll be back, actually.'

The woman clicked a ballpoint pen. 'If you give me his mobile phone number I'll give him a call.'

'That won't work,' said Liam, looking at the brochure. 'He's not in England. And he always turns his mobile off when he's away.'

'Oh dear.' The woman sighed. 'That's not much fun, is it? What job does he do that keeps him away from home for so long?'

'He's a policeman, sort of.'

'Sort of?' The woman chuckled. 'How can he be sort of a policeman?'

'He's not really a policeman. But he used to be.' He shrugged. 'It's complicated.'

The woman put her pen away. 'Probably best if I come

back again in a week or so, then,' she said. 'You can keep the brochure. What's your name?'

'Liam,' he said. 'Thanks.'

'Is your mum home?'

Liam shook his head. 'She's dead.'

'Oh, honey, I'm sorry.'

Liam shrugged. 'It's OK. It was a long time ago.'

'So who looks after you?'

'Katra. She's an au pair.'

The woman smiled. 'That's good,' she said. 'You take care now.' She waved and walked down the path.

Liam closed the door and went back to the sitting room. 'Who was it?' called Katra from the kitchen.

'No one,' said Liam, dropping down on to the sofa and picking up his exercise book.

Chris Thatcher looked at the clock on the wall. It was just after ten o'clock in the morning. 'Right,' he said. 'Let's give it another go.'

Charlotte Button nodded and hit the button to dial the number of the sat-phone on the *Athena*. They were both wearing headsets but Button had removed the microphone from hers. She had a notepad and pen in front of her.

The phone rang out and was answered after half a dozen rings. Thatcher was holding the handle of his coffee mug in his right hand and a bright orange stress ball in his left. He squeezed the ball as he spoke. 'Blue? This is Chris. Is everything OK?'

'You have my money?'

'Blue, you know it isn't as easy as that. We have to talk to the insurance company, it's their money. And they say that ten million dollars is not possible. You know that nobody pays ten million dollars for a ship.'

'The *Athena* is a big ship with many containers.'

'Yes, but the insurance company says that it won't pay ten million dollars. I'm sorry, I'm as upset as you. I'm on your side, Blue. I want to get the crew back with their families and I will do whatever is necessary to do that.'

'So pay me ten million dollars.'

Thatcher smiled at Button. He seemed relaxed but his left hand was working the orange ball hard. 'They say they won't pay ten million dollars.'

'How much will they pay?' asked Blue.

Thatcher sighed theatrically. 'They say that the ship's insurance policy only allows them to pay two million dollars.'

'Liar!' shouted Blue.

'Blue, I'm telling you the truth,' said Thatcher, speaking slowly and clearly. 'They've told me that they can pay two million dollars. They have the money ready. You can have it right away.'

'Two million is not enough!' shouted Blue. 'I will kill the hostages! They will die and you are to blame.' He cut the connection.

Thatcher took off the headset. 'That went well,' he said.

'You're not worried that he'll carry out his threat?' asked Button.

Thatcher shook his head. 'They rarely kill the hostages,' he said. 'And it's early days yet. He's just playing his part, the same as we are.' He looked across at Yusuf. 'What do you think?'

The Somali nodded thoughtfully. 'He is tense,' he said. 'But I think that is the khat.' He smiled at Button. 'They tend to chew a lot of khat while they are on the skiffs. The boats are small and the seas are rough and the khat helps prevent seasickness. But khat is also a stimulant, and I think that's why he sounded so aggressive.'

'What happens now?' asked Button. 'Will he call back?'

'He's left the ball in my court,' said Thatcher. 'Now he'll wait for us to phone him. And we can't do that too quickly because then we'll appear too eager.'

Button nodded. 'It's a mind game,' she said.

Thatcher nodded. 'On both sides,' he said. 'But he's up against experts. We'll get him to do exactly what we want, don't worry.'

Shepherd finished eating an apple, took a swig from a bottle of water, then checked his watch for the hundredth time. It was one o'clock in the morning. He switched on the sat-phone but after several minutes it had failed to log on to a satellite. He figured that the container was blocking the signal so he eased himself out and down to the walkway, then crept across to the starboard deck. He took a quick look left and right, then went back along to the bow. By the time he'd crouched down by one of the two huge anchor chains the sat-phone had a signal. He phoned Charlotte Button but kept the call short, talking just long enough for her to log on to his position, which was now just twenty miles off the coast of Yemen. Button gave him a rundown on the negotiations and then ended the call. Shepherd phoned Martin O'Brien to check that he was ready to go and then switched off the sat-phone to conserve what power it had left. He knew that he should go back to his container but he couldn't face sitting in the metal box all night so he stayed where he was, staring out to sea and allowing the wind to blow across his face.

At some point he fell asleep but he was jerked awake by the sound of the massive anchor chains playing out. They had stopped and were dropping the anchors. It was still dark and according to his watch it was just after four o'clock. He'd only been sleeping for half an hour. He got to his feet, checked the starboard deck was clear and then hurried back to his hiding place.

The captain looked across at Blue. 'The anchors are down,' he said. The pirate was looking out across the sea, north towards Yemen. Dominik glanced at the GPS display. The nearest ship was forty miles away, sailing towards the Red Sea.

Blue was holding his portable GPS unit and staring at the display. He nodded. 'Good,' he said.

'You are going to wait here until they pay the ransom?'

Blue put the GPS down on the shelf in front of the window. He turned around slowly, pointing the barrel of his AK-47 at Dominik's stomach. 'Out,' he said.

Dominik frowned. 'Out?'

Blue waved the gun towards the door. 'Out of the bridge,' he said.

Dominik climbed out of the chair and Blue followed him out, jabbing him in the small of the back with the weapon. Blue marched him down to G-Deck and along to the chief engineer's cabin, where Marlboro was standing with a teenage pirate. They were both leaning against the wall smoking and laughing but straightened up when they saw Blue and the captain.

'Everything OK in there?' asked Blue in Somali.

Marlboro nodded. He squashed the butt of his cigarette against the wall and threw it on the floor. 'They want more toilet paper but I told them to lick themselves clean,' he said, and laughed.

'Give them toilet paper,' Blue said. 'We are not animals.'

The smile vanished from Marlboro's face and he nodded.

'What about food?' asked Blue. 'You feed them twice every day.'

Marlboro nodded again. 'Rice and meat and they have water.'

'No glasses or bottles or knives or forks, nothing they can use as a weapon,' said Blue. He prodded Dominik with the AK-47. 'Inside,' he said.

Dominik opened the door to the cabin. Cigarette smoke billowed out and there was a cheer from the men inside when they saw it was the captain. Dominik waved and walked in. The Filipinos were whooping and slapping him on the back and Hainrich gave him a thumbs-up. Blue closed the door.

'What about the money?' asked Marlboro.

'They will pay,' said Blue. 'We are just agreeing the figure.' He went back on to the bridge and placed his AK-47 on the map table, then went over to the sat-phone. He took out a small piece of paper from his back pocket and smoothed it out. It was the number of a mobile phone in London. He carefully tapped out the number and put the receiver to his ear.

The phone rang out for almost a minute and Blue was about to dial again when Crazy Boy answered. 'Yeah?' he said.

'We're in position,' said Blue.

'Excellent,' said Crazy Boy. 'And how are the negotiations?'

'They are offering two million,' said Blue.

'Which means they will pay five,' said Crazy Boy. 'But make no agreement until tomorrow, no matter what they offer.'

'This ship is one of the biggest I have ever seen, son of my brother. With thousands of containers. They will pay a lot more.'

Crazy Boy chuckled. 'Do not be greedy, brother of my father,' he said. 'This time it is not just about the money, remember that.'

Shepherd was sleeping on his side, his head resting on his left arm. It was stuffy in the container but the air was breathable. He woke to the sound of a helicopter flying overhead. He looked at his watch. It was five o'clock in the afternoon. He sat up and ran a hand through his hair. The helicopter sounded like it was big, or very close, and for a while it sounded as if there were two rotors, but that could have been an echo. He crawled over to the doors and gently pushed them open. The ship was rocking from side to side, buffeted by the waves. The engine had stopped again. He squinted upwards but there was only a thin strip of sky between the towering containers. He didn't want to risk going out in daylight so he pulled the doors closed and sat back on the wooden floor, wondering what was going on.

Chris Thatcher sipped his coffee as Charlotte Button put on her headset and sat down next to him. 'Ready?' he asked.

Button nodded and tapped out the number of the *Athena*'s sat-phone.

Thatcher squeezed his stress ball with his left hand and took a deep breath. The phone rang out and then it was answered. 'Blue? This is Chris.'

Yusuf put on a headset and listened intently.

'You have my money?' asked Blue.

'I have good news for you, Blue. The insurance company say that they are willing to pay three million dollars.'

'That's not enough!' interrupted Blue. 'I said ten. I want ten million dollars.'

'I know you do, Blue. But they just won't pay that much.' He paused for effect and winked over at Button. 'But there's a way we can maybe get them to pay more.'

'How?'

Thatcher paused again. 'You have heard about a yacht called the *Natalya*? Some of your people seized it several weeks ago.'

'How do you know about that?' snapped Blue.

'I'm just telling you what the insurance company is telling me,' said Thatcher. 'They want the crew of the yacht and are willing to pay for it. If we can include the yacht crew then I think we can get them to pay more.'

'How much more?'

'Four million dollars maybe. That sounds like a good idea, doesn't it, Blue? I know you've had problems getting a ransom for the yacht crew. This way you get more money and you get rid of the hostages. Can we go ahead and agree on that?'

'I need time,' said Blue.

'Take all the time that you need, Blue. But this is a very

good deal for you. Four million dollars is a good price and the company tells me that they can get that money to you right away. So can we agree on this, Blue? Can we move this forward?'

'Four million is not enough!' shouted Blue.

'OK, OK, then let me talk to the company again. But we want to release the ship and get the crew of the *Natalya* back. Can we do that?'

'I will think about it,' said Blue.

'That's great, Blue. Thank you. And what we were thinking was that we could pay the ransom wherever you have the crew of the yacht. We can deliver the money there and collect the hostages. Can you arrange that?'

The line went dead.

Thatcher sat back in his chair. 'He can't make the decision,' he said. 'He's got to ask someone else.'

Button nodded. 'That's right.'

'But I think we're getting there. This is the home stretch.'

'I hope you're right,' said Button.

The entryphone buzzed and Two Knives went over to look at the CCTV monitor while Crazy Boy sat on the sofa listening to his iPod, nodding his head back and forth in time with the 50 Cent song. Crazy Boy was a big fan of 50 Cent. Like Crazy Boy, the American rapper had come from nothing to be a rich and powerful man, a convicted drug dealer who was now one of the world's most successful rappers. In 2000 he was shot nine times and survived. That impressed Crazy Boy, as did the fact that 50 Cent had a fortune of more than four hundred million dollars. But despite all the money 50 Cent had never lost touch with his roots and his songs spoke from the heart. Crazy Boy's plan was to one day own his own record label and record his own songs.

Two Knives looked over at him. 'They're here,' he mouthed, and Crazy Boy grinned and gave him a thumbs-up. He'd ordered four hookers from one of the escort agencies that he used regularly. It was run by a group of Bosnians who brought in fresh young girls from Europe, and they made a point of notifying Crazy Boy whenever they had in a new batch. He'd been promised that the four that were being sent around were very young, very blonde and almost virgins.

Two Knives pressed the button to open the front gates and watched on the monitor as the minicab drove in.

Crazy Boy's mobile phone began to vibrate and Two Knives pointed at it. Crazy Boy switched off his iPod and took the call. It was his uncle, calling from the ship. 'They are offering four million dollars but I think they will pay more,' said Blue.

'I told you that,' said Crazy Boy. 'They will pay five million. Five million is covered by insurance so it costs them nothing.'

'There is something else. They want us to free the other hostages.'

'What hostages?'

'The yacht that Roobie seized. He has been trying to get a ransom for the five crew that he took. But no one will pay.'

Crazy Boy frowned. 'But why does the shipping company want to pay for them?'

'I don't know. But they say they want to pay four million and hand it over when they get the crew of the yacht.'

Crazy Boy pursed his lips as he considered his options. It was important always to have the upper hand in nego- tiations and never to give away points to the other side, but there were advantages in having the money paid ashore instead of being delivered to the ship.

'What do you think?' asked Blue.

'We want the ship to continue on its way as quickly as possible. Tell them you'll take the one ransom for the *Athena* and for the yacht. But don't roll over too easily. Play hard to get.'

'What about Roobie?'

'I'll speak to him. I'll do it now. We can do the exchange at the airfield. Well done, brother of my father.'

He ended the call. The doorbell rang and Two Knives went to open the front door and reappeared with the four girls. Two of them looked as if they might be sisters, short and busty with perfect skin and blue eyes. One was wearing black hot pants and a silver halter top under her coat and the other had on tight-fitting jeans and a low-cut T-shirt that showed several inches of cleavage. 'Put those two in my room,' he said, pointing at the two girls.

'Are you the boss?' asked the girl in the halter top. Her lipstick was blood red and matched her fingernails, and she had long eyelashes that looked as if they might be false.

'You're not here to talk, you're here to fuck,' said Crazy Boy, turning his back on her. He went through to his study and switched on his computer. He preferred to make calls on Skype whenever he could as it was more secure. He regularly changed his mobile phones but he knew that talking on any phone line was always taking a risk, but Skype conversations were hidden among the billions of gigabytes that whizzed around the world every minute of the day. Skype conversations were only vulnerable when one of the parties was on a mobile or a landline, but Crazy Boy made sure that all his people regularly changed their phones and Sim cards.

He launched his Skype program and dialled the number of Roobie's latest mobile phone. It rang out for almost half a minute, and when Roobie answered he sounded angry. 'Who is this?' he barked in Somali.

'It's me, cousin,' said Crazy Boy.

'Your number didn't show,' said Roobie. 'Where are you?'

'In London, cousin. The yacht you seized, you have not agreed a ransom yet?'

'They are saying they have no money,' said Roobie. 'I might have to kill one of the crew to show that I am serious.'

'No need,' said Crazy Boy. 'I have a proposal that will kill two birds with one stone. Your father has taken a ship, a big one, and they will pay big money. As part of that deal, they want the yacht too.'

'The yacht is mine, cousin.'

Crazy Boy felt a wave of anger wash over him but he held his tongue. What was happening on the *Athena* was far too important to be jeopardised by Roobie's stupidity. There would be time to deal with Roobie down the line; all that mattered now was that the ransom was paid and the ship sent on its way. 'Of course it is, cousin. But this is good news for both of us. This way we can get the ransom paid in Puntland, and you can get rid of the hostages.'

'How much will they pay?'

'They have offered four million dollars.'

'For the yacht?'

Crazy Boy bit down on his lower lip so hard that he tasted blood. He was not used to having his decisions questioned and Roobie would pay for his insolence at some point. But not today. 'For the ship and for the yacht,' he said.

'Four million is nothing,' said Roobie. 'They are making fools of us.'

'Four million dollars is a lot of money, cousin. We might be able to get them to pay five.'

'And who gets that money, cousin? How much goes in your pocket and how much comes my way?'

'We can talk about that once the ransom has been paid.'

'No, cousin, we can talk about it now. I'm asking for four million dollars for the yacht and the crew.'

'But as you say, they do not have the money to pay. The money I am talking about is ready to go. The shipping company will pay, guaranteed cash. It is a bird in the hand, much better than any number of birds in a bush.'

'The bird is no good to me if it flies to your hands, cousin,' said Roobie.

Crazy Boy took a deep breath. If he had been standing in the same room as Roobie he would have put a bullet in his brain there and then, but that wasn't possible. He had to stay calm, he had to negotiate, he had to persuade. But down the line, at some point in the future, he was going to take a great deal of pleasure in killing Roobie. 'I would like this deal to go ahead, cousin,' said Crazy Boy. 'I agree that the yacht is yours, and that the ship is mine. We should share the proceeds.'

'Fifty-fifty?' said Roobie. 'Half for me, half for you. Whatever they pay, we split down the middle.'

'That is only fair,' said Crazy Boy.

'And I want you to bring me to London,' said Roobie.

'I can do that,' said Crazy Boy. 'As soon as the ransom has been paid, I will arrange it.'

'Then I agree,' said Roobie.

Crazy Boy could almost hear the sneer on his face and he bunched his hands into tight fists. 'Thank you, cousin,' he said. 'I shall not forget this.' He ended the call and slammed his fists down on to the table, his face contorted with rage.

Charlotte Button took off her headset and looked across at Yusuf. 'Would you mind translating, Mr Yusuf? Somali isn't one of my languages, I'm afraid.' Yusuf translated both conversations while Button made notes on a pad. They were able to pick up all the conversations that Crazy Boy made from the computer and had patched in to the ship's sat-phone so they could eavesdrop on all conversations made to and from the *Athena*.

When he'd finished, Button looked across at Thatcher. 'Perfect,' she said. 'He fell for it.' She turned to Amir Singh, who was peering at a computer screen as he tapped away on his keyboard. 'Do we have a location for Roobie?' she asked.

'Working on it,' he said. 'Give me a few minutes.'

'What did he mean about wanting to get the ship on its way?' Thatcher asked Button.

'I assume he meant he wanted the money as quickly as possible,' she replied. She looked up at the clock on the wall. 'When should we call the ship?'

'Let's do it tomorrow,' said Thatcher. 'We don't want him to think we're desperate.'

'OK, I have the location of the mobile,' said Singh, looking up from his computer. 'Northern Puntland, so no surprises there.'

'Can you be more specific?'

'To within a few miles,' said Singh. 'We don't have his GPS identifier so all we can do is identify the transmitting tower.' He read out a longitude and latitude reference and Button scribbled it down.

There was a large-scale map of Africa up on one wall and she went over to it. 'It's about eighty miles inland from Eyl, where they took the yacht,' she said, tapping the map.

She went over to one of the MI5 technicians, a bookish man in his twenties in a corduroy jacket, and gave him the piece of paper. 'Can you get me a satellite picture of those coordinates, as current as possible?'

The technician nodded and began tapping away on his computer keyboard.

'So tell me, Charlotte,' said Thatcher, leaning back in his seat and stretching his arms up. 'I get what the plan is. You send in your people with the ransom and they rescue the hostages and keep the money. But what about the *Athena*? The pirates will still be on board. They're not going to leave until the ransom's paid.'

'Sorry, Chris, operational matters have to stay classified. But don't worry, we'll get your ship back. And the money.'

'Glad to hear it,' said Thatcher.

'OK, I have a sat feed,' said the technician. 'I'll patch it over to the main screen.'

A satellite photograph of African scrubland filled one of the flatscreen monitors.

Button smiled as she looked at the screen. Right in the middle was a small airfield with a single dirt runway and several buildings. 'Well, I think we know where the hostages are,' she said.

Blue looked at the GPS screen. There were two dozen ships heading east, coming from the direction of the Suez Canal on the way to the Arabian Sea. It was a convoy, and a convoy meant warships. Dominik was back in the right-hand seat, smoking and staring out of the window, straight ahead. 'Keep away from the ships,' said Blue.

The captain looked at the radar screen on the right that gave a view for twenty miles ahead of the *Athena*. 'We won't even see them,' he said. The rest of the crew were still in the chief engineer's cabin, under guard. Since the ship had started moving again, Dominik had been on the bridge twenty-four hours a day. When he was too exhausted to keep his eyes open he slept in the seat with his feet on the console.

Blue also spent most of the time on the bridge, but when he needed to sleep he went downstairs to the captain's cabin while two pirates with AK-47s kept watch over Dominik.

'Can I ask where we're going?' asked Dominik. They were heading on a course of 225, south-west, towards Somalia, at quarter-speed.

'No,' snapped Blue. 'It is not your business.'

Dominik shrugged. 'You're the boss,' he said.

'Yes,' said Blue. 'I am.'

The sat-phone rang and Blue hurried over to it. It was the man called Chris in London. 'Is everything all right there, Blue?'

'Five million dollars. You have it?'

'Good news on that front, Blue. Yes, the company will go to five million dollars if you release the ship and the crew of the yacht.'

Blue grinned. 'The ship is worth more,' he said. Crazy Boy had told him not to make it too easy for them.

'Five million is all the company will pay,' said Thatcher. 'But they have the money ready now and they can deliver it to you in Somalia.'

'If you try to trick us, the hostages will die,' said Blue. 'And we will take the cargo to Somalia. We will steal everything.'

'Blue, no one is going to trick you,' said Thatcher. Blue could hear the fear in the man's voice and he grinned. 'We won't do anything that would put our people at risk. We just want our people safe and our ship working again.'

'When can I have the money?'

'Where can we deliver it to you?' asked Thatcher. 'The company would be happier if we could fly in the money by plane rather than bringing it overland. Somalia is a dangerous place to have five million dollars.'

Blue laughed. The Englishman was right. Somalia was indeed a very dangerous place. 'Do not worry, Chris,' he said. 'I know a place where the money will be safe.'

Shepherd was hungry but he only had one apple left. He chewed it slowly, eating it core and all, and swallowed a few mouthfuls of water. If the hijacking went on much longer he would have to risk going back into the accommodation for supplies, and he wasn't looking forward to that. He looked at his watch, focusing on the luminous dots in the gloom. It was almost one o'clock in the morning. He eased himself out of the container and on to the walkway, then stood there listening until he was sure there was no one near by. The ship was moving again.

He crept along to the bow and sat as before next to one of the massive anchor chains. As he looked up at the night sky he realised that the *Athena* wasn't heading towards the North Star. He got up again and searched the sky, looking for the Plough. Eventually he found it, towards the stern, and saw the handle of the Plough pointing towards the North Star. It was behind them. They were sailing south.

The sat-phone keyboard glowed as soon as he pressed the first digit. He tapped out Charlotte Button's number.

'Spider, everything OK?'

'Just eaten the last of my food but I've got water for a few more days,' he said.

'Where are you now?'

'Me or the ship?'

Button chuckled. 'Both.'

'I'm still in the container,' he said. 'The pirates never leave the accommodation. Hardly ever, anyway. One might take a walk around the Upper Deck but they're looking out to sea mainly. They'd have to look bloody hard to find me. The ship is moving again. By the look of it we're going south now towards Somalia.'

'Are you OK?'

'I could do with a shower and a good meal, but other than that I'm doing fine. It's been quiet, no shots, no shouting, everything's calm.'

'And the crew and officers?'

'No idea, they'll be locked up somewhere. Was there a helicopter checking up on us this afternoon? About five?'

'What do you mean?'

'There was a big chopper flying over the ship. I don't know what they were up to.'

'It wasn't one of ours, we're keeping well away while the negotiations continue. We don't want to spook them.'

'How are the negotiations going?'

She didn't answer.

'Charlie? Can you hear me?'

There was still no answer. Shepherd took the phone away from his ear and looked at it. It was off. He cursed as he realised that the battery must have died. And the charger was in his cabin.

He stared at the sat-phone and considered his options. There was no point in being on the ship if he couldn't communicate with Button and O'Brien – all the intel in the world was no use if he couldn't pass it on to where it was needed. He had to go back to his cabin, no matter what the risks. It was late at night, so hopefully most of the pirates would be asleep and those that were awake would probably be up on the bridge.

He had two options. He could make his way along the Upper Deck to the superstructure or he could make use of the Below Deck Passageway. The Below Deck Passageway was probably the safer option but it led to the engine room, and with the ship moving there was a good chance that at least one of the pirates would be there. He shoved the sat-phone into his back pocket and started moving along the starboard deck.

He moved slowly, stopping every minute or so to listen

and to peer into the gloom, and it took him almost fifteen minutes to reach the base of the superstructure. He stood at the bottom of the outdoor stairway, looking up. There was no sound, other than the waves hitting the hull. He steadied his breathing as he planned his next move. The most likely area for the pirates to keep the crew would be A-Deck, where most of the storage rooms were, including those where the meat, fish, vegetable and provisions were kept, or in one of the mess rooms on B-Deck, or even one of the large cabins on G-Deck, directly below the bridge. There was no reason for any of the pirates to be on F-Deck, where his cabin was.

He took a deep breath and then started up the metal stairway, sticking to the shadows wherever he could. He stopped at each level, checking through the windows, but didn't see anyone as he moved up to F-Deck. He pulled open the door and stepped into the corridor, his heart pounding. He listened but heard nothing, so he closed the door behind him and tiptoed down to his cabin and slipped inside. The sat-phone charger was where he'd left it on his desk. He plugged in the sat-phone and the charging light glowed. He looked at his watch. Charging could take up to two hours.

He opened the fridge and took out a can of Coke and drank it as he sat on his bed and wondered what he should do. His stomach growled. There was no food in the cabin, but he was going to need protein soon. There was plenty of food in the galley on B-Deck, but he'd be taking a risk going there, even late at night. His stomach growled again. He finished his Coke and put the empty can in the waste-paper bin. He paced around the room. He wasn't sure how much longer he was going to have to remain in hiding, and while he could go without food for weeks if necessary he knew that hunger would reduce his efficiency. He opened the cabin door and listened but heard nothing. He tiptoed to the stairs and stood in the doorway for five minutes to satisfy himself that no one else was moving around, then he slowly went down the stairs.

When he reached B-Deck he stopped again. He tilted his head from side to side listening, but the only sound was the occasional creaking of the hull. His heart was racing and he took slow, deep breaths before moving silently down the corridor. The door to the galley was closed and he put his ear against it but heard nothing. He turned the handle and slowly pushed the door open. The galley was empty and the door from it to the crew mess was wide open and he could see that there was no one there. He looked to the right through the door that led to the officers' mess and that too was empty. Shepherd smiled to himself as he stepped into the galley and pushed the door closed behind him.

There were two sticks of French bread on a metal counter. They had gone stale and were as hard as rock but he could dampen them with water and they'd be edible. He needed protein, though. He opened one of the metal cabinets and found three unopened boxes of cereal, two of cornflakes and one of muesli. The cornflakes were mainly sugar but the muesli was a good source of nutrition, albeit with a high sugar content. On the floor was a cardboard box that had once contained cans of peas. Shepherd placed it on the counter and tossed in the box of muesli. He opened another cupboard and found three plastic bags of fruit, one of apples and two of bananas. He threw them into his box.

He grinned when he pulled open the third cupboard door. It was full of tins of the tuna that the chief officer ate with his salad every night. He took out a can and his grin widened when he saw that it opened with a ring pull. Shepherd was no great fan of canned tuna but it was full of protein and what was in the cupboard would keep him going for weeks. He added the cans and the bread to the cardboard box. There was a large metal fridge at the end of the galley and Shepherd pulled it open. It was filled with bottles of mineral water and white wine and cans of soft drink. He took as much water as he could carry and a couple of cans of Coke for good measure. At the bottom of the fridge, in a crisper section, there were a dozen iceberg lettuces, several long cucumbers and a carton of tomatoes, but he rejected them as they had next to no nutritional value.

The box was pretty much full so he picked it up, eased open the galley door and slid into the corridor. He listened but there was only the sound of the sea slapping against the hull. He moved on tiptoe towards the stairs, but froze when he heard the lift start to move. He stared at the floor indicator. It was on A-Deck, heading up. He moved into the stairwell. He doubted that anyone would bother taking the lift just one floor and he was right, it continued to move up to G-Deck before stopping. Someone was probably visiting the bridge, either that or someone from the bridge had called the lift so that they could go down. He waited but the lift stayed on G-Deck.

He moved up the stairs slowly, listening intently. He reached F-Deck, stepped into the corridor, then hurried back to his cabin. The red charging light was still on. He looked at his watch. It was just after two o'clock. He wanted to call Button back but didn't want to risk talking while inside.

He sat down on the bunk and opened one of the cans of tuna. There was a spoon by the kettle and he used it to eat the fish, chewing slowly and methodically to get the maximum nutrition from every mouthful. Bolted food was wasted food – one of the many survival skills that he'd learned during jungle training. When he'd finished he put the empty can in the box, along with the spoon. He used the toilet but didn't flush it. He would have loved to have used the shower but knew that was out of the question, so he dampened a towel, took off his shirt and wiped himself down. He threw his dirty shirt into the wardrobe and put on a clean one, then decided he might as well go the whole way and put on clean socks and underwear, too.

He checked the sat-phone again and the charging light had turned to green so he unplugged it and put the phone and the charger into the box. He popped his head around the door, listened to check that there were no sounds of anyone moving around, then carried the box along the corridor to the stairs.

The lift hadn't moved and it was still showing as on G-Deck. Shepherd stopped and listened again, then headed down the stairs. E-Deck was silent, and so was D-Deck, but when he got down to C-Deck he heard footsteps and laughter. Two men, heading down the corridor. Shepherd froze. If they carried on walking down the corridor then they wouldn't see him, but if they turned into the stairway there'd be no place to hide.

C-Deck was where most of the crew's quarters were, so they might have been going through the cabins looking for valuables. Or maybe they were sleeping there and were now heading back to the bridge. Either way they wouldn't be staying on C-Deck, which meant that they'd either use the stairs or the lift.

Shepherd turned and moved quickly up the stairs and hurried down the corridor of D-Deck, towards the gymnasium. The hatch to the deck was on his left and he put down the box so that he could twist the two chrome locking levers and push open the door. He smelled cigarette smoke and realised immediately that there was someone on the deck. It was too late to go back so he stepped through the hatch, his heart pounding. There was a man leaning against the rail, looking out over the sea, a Kalashnikov hanging over his back, barrel down. The man grunted as he turned and Shepherd saw the red dot of the burning cigarette. Shepherd's night vision hadn't kicked in so he couldn't make out the man's features but he saw the strip of white as his mouth opened in surprise and he lunged forward, knowing that he had to move quickly before the pirate could sound the alarm. His left hand found the man's chin and pushed hard, clamping the jaw shut. The man dropped the cigarette and it fell to the deck in a shower of sparks as Shepherd forced his head back and they staggered together against the railing. Shepherd punched the man in the throat with his right fist, the knuckle of the second finger protruding slightly, and he heard the satisfying crack of the trachea rupturing. He hit him again, hard, for good measure, and once more the cartilage splintered.

He released his grip on the man's jaw, knowing that there was now no way he could cry for help; his throat was already filling up with blood. He grabbed the back of the man's head with his left hand, the chin with his right hand, gave the head a slight turn to the left and twisted with all his strength to the right. The man's neck snapped like a dry twig and he slumped to the deck. Shepherd caught him under the arms and lowered him face down, then stood up and listened. It had taken him less than three seconds to kill the man, and unless there was anyone else out on deck he was sure that no one would have heard anything. His eyes were starting to get accustomed to the lack of light and he could see that the deck around him was clear and there was no one at the railings of Decks E, F and G above him. He leaned over the railing and looked down at the decks below but couldn't see anyone.

The pirate's left leg twitched but it was a muscular reaction, nothing more, and it soon went still. Shepherd knelt down and undid the fastening on the strap of the AK-47 and pulled the weapon away. He placed it on the deck then took the machete and scabbard off the man's belt and put them down next to the AK-47. He grabbed the pirate under the arms and heaved him over the railing. The body spun through the air and splashed into the sea far below.

Shepherd slung the Kalashnikov over his shoulder and fastened the machete to his belt. He retrieved his box of provisions, shut the hatch and took the outside stairs down to the Upper Deck. He stopped and listened for a full two minutes until he was certain that there was no one else around, then he headed down the port side of the deck towards the bow.

By the time he reached his hiding place his night vision had fully kicked in. He climbed up the metal ladder and shoved the box into the container after taking out a couple of bananas and the sat-phone. He went forward and sat down in the deck area between the two anchor chains, then he tapped out Button's number. 'Sorry about that,' he said. 'The battery died. And I had to kill a pirate.'

'Please tell me that's your idea of a sick joke,' said Button.

'Couldn't be helped,' said Shepherd. 'It was him or me.'

'Any repercussions?'

'No one saw what happened and his body's in the sea. The good news is that I've got his AK-47 and a very big knife.'

'Won't they start looking for him?'

'It's a big ship. They won't notice it right away and even if they did, they don't know that I'm on board. Worst possible scenario, they think they have a man overboard. So how are the negotiations going?'

'Blue has agreed to a joint deal, he'll release the yacht crew at the same time as he releases the ship. The money is to be delivered to an airstrip in Puntland.'

'That's a first, right? In the past Crazy Boy's had the cash delivered to the ships, right?'

'We persuaded him,' said Button. 'This way we get the yacht crew and the money in the same place. The cash gets flown in to Puntland, and the crew can fly out on the same plane that brings the money in. I've spoken to Martin, he'll be ready to go in tomorrow.'

'But what about the *Athena*? The pirates here aren't going to leave until they know the money has been handed over. If they hear that there's been a rescue then they might kill the hostages here.'

'They won't know. We can cut the ship's sat-phone connection. They have no other way of communicating so they'll be in the dark.'

'And then what? You send in the Increment?'

'They're ready to move in, as soon as you give the word.'

'The crew are being held at gunpoint, Charlie. They could get killed.'

'The Increment are expert at situations like this, Spider. You more than anyone know that.'

'But this is a difficult situation. The hostages are inside and the pirates are all armed. I don't see how they can be taken by surprise. And how are they going to get to the ship?'

'They want to go in by helicopter,' she said.

'Then they'll be seen for miles.'

'Not if they come at night.'

'Then they'll be heard.'

'Do you have a better idea?' asked Button.

'I think I do, yeah.'

John Muller was surprised at how little space five million dollars took up when it was in hundred-dollar bills. The sixty-year-old American stroked his chin as he studied the plastic-wrapped parcels on the table in front of him. He had brought two Samsonite cases with him, just small enough to be taken on board a plane as hand baggage, provided that he was flying first class. There was no way that he was going to check five million dollars into the hold on any airline, especially one in the Middle East. He was on the top floor of the bank's headquarters in Dubai, in a room with double-height windows offering breathtaking views of the Persian Gulf, centring on the Burj Al Arab, the luxurious hotel built in the shape of an Arab dhow on its own artificial island.

The banker organising the transaction was an Englishman wearing a dark blue pinstripe suit and a starched white shirt with gold cufflinks and spoke with an accent that reminded Muller of a PBS costume drama. He had a double-barrelled name that Muller couldn't be bothered to remember because he doubted that he'd ever be meeting the man again.

A bank official, a portly middle-aged Arab in his thirties, was feeding the bundles of notes through a counter and checking for forgeries. 'We don't have to do this,' said Muller. 'I trust you.'

'It's not about you trusting us,' said the banker disdainfully. 'It is to ensure that you receive the correct amount.' He handed Muller a letter in a crisp white envelope. 'Here is the letter to show on your departure if necessary.'

Muller took out the letter. It was on the bank's headed notepaper and detailed where the money had come from, the accounts that it had passed through, and that the cash was to be used for 'humanitarian disbursement in Africa'. Muller smiled. There was nothing humanitarian about the disbursement of the five million dollars sitting on the table. The subterfuge was necessary to ensure that no overzealous official wanted to stop the cash from leaving Dubai.

'They'll let the money out on the basis of this?' asked Muller. 'It seems very vague.'

'The officials at the airport are used to large amounts of cash leaving in hand luggage,' said the banker. 'Provided they have no reason to suspect that money-laundering is involved, they will not detain you. More often than not the money is allowed through without comment, but if they do stop you that letter will suffice. Most of the NGOs operating in Africa have to pay their people in cash so large amounts of money fly out every day.'

Muller put the envelope into his jacket pocket. The bank

official continued to feed notes into the counter. 'Any chance of a coffee while we wait?' he asked.

Katie looked up anxiously as the door was pushed open. It was Roobie, holding a bottle of whisky and a large machete. He was grinning and there was a manic look in his eyes. 'You're going home,' he said. 'The ransom is being paid.'

Katie looked across at Joy, who was sitting next to her, wondering if she had misheard. Joy's mouth was open wide in astonishment.

'Who paid?' asked Hoop. 'Where did the money come from?'

Roobie laughed and waved his machete at Hoop. 'Why do you care?' he asked. 'The money is coming. You will go home. And I will be rich.' He laughed again. 'Maybe one day you will see me in London. I will be English, same as you.' He did a soft-shoe shuffle across the dusty concrete floor.

'When can we go?' asked Hoop.

'When we have the money, you go home,' said Roobie. He laughed again and waved the machete above his head. 'I tell them I will cut off your heads and they beg me to spare you. "Please, do not cut off their heads," they said. But I was merciful and now I am rich.'

Eric looked at Hoop. 'Is it true?' he asked. 'Did somebody pay?'

Hoop shrugged. 'Somebody must have,' he said. 'Maybe the owner came through.' He looked up at Roobie. 'If we're going home, how about some food? You've won, right? The least you can do is to give us a decent meal before we go.' He pointed at the bottle of whisky. 'What about a drink for a start?'

Roobie looked at the bottle he was holding as if seeing it for the first time. 'You want whisky?' he said. He laughed again as he walked over to Hoop. 'You want whisky?' he repeated, then poured it over Hoop's head. Hoop turned away but Roobie kept pouring until the bottle was empty, then he threw it hard against the wall and it shattered into a hundred shards.

Roobie spun around in a drunken pirouette and then waved his machete at Katie. 'So, you will go home soon,' he said. He pointed the knife at Joy and leered at her. 'But first we will celebrate.' He held out his left hand. 'Where is my whisky?' he said. He frowned when he saw the bits of glass on the floor. 'I need whisky,' he said. He ambled out of the hut, muttering to himself.

'Is he serious?' asked Joy. 'Are we going home?'

'Don't get your hopes up,' said Hoop, shaking whisky from his hair. 'He might just be screwing with us.'

'He wouldn't joke about something like that,' said Andrew.

'He's a sick bastard,' said Katie.

The door crashed open and Roobie stood in the doorway holding a fresh bottle of whisky. He took a long drink and then walked into the hut and kicked the door shut behind him.

'So, who wants to suck me?' he said, waving his machete at Joy and Katie. 'Did you decide? Or will I have to decide for you?'

He tapped Katie on the head with the machete. 'Should I choose you?' he said. He placed the blade on Joy's head. She trembled and began to cry. 'Or you?' he said. Back to Katie's head went the knife. 'You?' He tapped Joy with the blade. 'Or you?' He threw back his head and laughed, then took a swig from the bottle before wiping his mouth with the back of his arm and belching. 'Which one of you wants to suck me? You can choose because I don't care.' He took another swig from the bottle. 'But hurry, yeah.'

The two girls cried and hugged each other.

'Why can't you just leave us alone, you bastard!' shouted Andrew.

Roobie swaggered across the floor to him. 'You want to suck me, is that it?' He roared with laughter and groped for his zip with his left hand.

Andrew got to his feet and shoved Roobie in the chest so hard that he staggered back and crashed against the wall. 'You bastard!' screamed Andrew. 'We're not animals. We're human beings!'

Roobie snarled and lashed out with the machete in a wide sweeping motion and it sliced through Andrew's throat. Blood spurted up towards the roof and Andrew fell back, clawing at his neck. Joy and Katie screamed in horror and Eric and Hoop scuttled away from the dying man as he fell to the floor in a pool of blood. Andrew slumped back; bloody froth welled up from between his lips and his feet began to drum on the floor. His whole body began to jerk as if he was being electrocuted and Joy began to shriek uncontrollably.

Roobie stood over the dying man and whooped with laughter. 'Happy now?' he screamed, swinging his bloody machete from side to side. 'You die like a dog and your wife is still going to suck me. Happy now?'

Andrew went still and the life faded from his eyes. Roobie spat in the dead man's face and then turned around to leer at Joy. 'Come here, bitch,' he said.

* * *

Blue used the sat-phone to call Crazy Boy's mobile. 'They have agreed to pay five million dollars,' he said. 'They say they can get the money to the airfield tomorrow.'

'Excellent,' said Crazy Boy.

'I've called Roobie already. He knows he has to check the money before he releases the hostages. And he will hold the money for us.'

'He'd better,' said Crazy Boy. 'So he will let you know when he has the money and then you and your men leave the *Athena*?'

'That is the plan,' said Blue. 'I will go straight back to the airfield and look after the money.'

'Well done, brother of my father,' said Crazy Boy. 'We will get our reward in heaven for this.'

Blue laughed. 'I'm satisfied with my reward in this life,' he said. He put down the phone. There were two pirates on the bridge, one at either side, using binoculars to check the sea around the *Athena*. 'Any of you seen Marlboro today?' asked Blue.

The two men shrugged and shook their heads.

'If you see him, tell him to come to the bridge.'

Martin O'Brien grinned when he saw John Muller walk through the sliding doors into the arrivals area. 'There he is,' he said. 'The one dressed like a jungle explorer.'

John Muller was tall, well over six feet, with grey swept-back hair and a neatly trimmed moustache. He was wearing a pale blue safari suit with short sleeves, towing a Samsonite suitcase.

Standing next to O'Brien was Jack Bradford, in his early

thirties with broad shoulders and unkempt brown hair that was too long to be fashionable. 'A Yank?'

'Yeah, but he's OK in spite of that,' said O'Brien. 'He was in Vietnam when he was a teenager. The Phoenix Program. Winning the hearts and minds of the VC, and when that didn't work throwing them out of helicopters. He's mellowed a bit since then.'

Just behind Muller was a second man in a dark suit pulling an identical Samsonite suitcase, and they were flanked by two other men without luggage in dark grey suits and wearing Oakley sunglasses, the brand favoured by mercenaries around the world.

Muller grinned as he saw O'Brien. He strode up to him, let go of the suitcase and gave him a tight bear hug, slapping him on the back. Then Muller did a double-take when he saw the man standing next to O'Brien. He was the twin of the man behind him, towing the second Samsonite suitcase.

'Jack Bradford,' said O'Brien, by way of introduction. 'Billy's twin.'

'Billy didn't say anything,' said Muller.

'He's a bit embarrassed because I'm the good-looking one,' said Jack, shaking hands with Muller.

'Any problems, John?' asked O'Brien.

'None, mate,' said Muller. 'I had these two guys to run interference if we needed it but we were waved right through.' He flashed a thumbs-up at the two men in dark glasses and they both threw him mock salutes and headed for the exit.

O'Brien grabbed the handle of Muller's case. 'We'll take it from here, John, thanks.'

'No you won't,' said Muller, taking the case off him.

'You're not just using me as a delivery boy. If there's action to be had, I want in.'

'With the greatest of respect, John, you're a bit long in the tooth for this.'

Muller took a step closer to O'Brien, his eyes hardening. 'You watch who you're calling long in the tooth,' he said. 'I'm not too old to give you a good hiding, even with all that Jewish aikido crap that you've studied.'

'It's Krav Maga, and it's Israeli, not Jewish.'

'Yeah, tomayto, tomato,' said Muller. 'I'm coming with you, you Irish bastard.'

O'Brien's face broke into a grin. 'Yes, John, I guess you are.'

Shepherd sat up as he heard shouting from somewhere on the deck. He looked at his wristwatch. It was just after seven o'clock in the morning. He went over to the container doors and nudged them open. There were two men shouting, one on either side of the ship, and it sounded as if they were moving closer. He pulled the doors closed and switched on the sat-phone. He sat with his back against the wall of the container as the sat-phone tried and failed to log on to a satellite, then switched it off.

He waited for thirty minutes and then carefully pushed open the doors again. The shouting had stopped. He was pretty sure it was the pirates looking for the man that Shepherd had thrown overboard. He pushed the doors open wider. He didn't like going out in the daytime but he didn't have a choice. If they started a full-scale search of the vessel and its containers they might well find his hiding place, and then it would all be over.

He switched on the sat-phone and tucked it into his back pocket, attached the machete to his belt, then slung the AK-47 over his shoulder and climbed down to the walkway He crept along to the starboard side, bending double to make himself a smaller target. He reached the side and carefully checked left and right, then headed for the bow, cradling the Kalashnikov across his chest, the safety off. He knelt down between the anchor chains and took the sat-phone from his pocket. It already had a signal and he called Charlie Button.

'They're starting to search the ship,' said Shepherd. 'I don't think hiding is an option for much longer.'

'We're ready with the ransom now,' said Button. 'We're in direct communication with the group that's holding the yacht crew and we have agreed the time and place of the handover.'

'So what's the plan?'

'Martin is going to deliver the money this afternoon at four. By plane.'

'Where is he now?'

'He's close to the Ethiopia–Somali border, ready to go. The money is already there.'

Shepherd heard a footfall to his left. He switched off the phone and shoved it into his back pocket, then got up in a crouch, his finger on the trigger of the AK-47. He hid behind the forward mast, keeping the AK-47 close to his chest. He heard another footfall, a sandal brushing against the deck. Then a man came into view, tall and gangly, his skin the colour of coal, wearing a red and white checked bandana and ragged multicoloured surfer shorts. He was bare chested and a Kalashnikov was hanging from a sling by his side, and there was a machete in a leather holster on his left hip. As Shepherd watched, the man stopped and cupped his hands around his mouth and then shouted something up at the containers. It sounded like 'Marlboro'. Shepherd remembered that the man he'd killed had been smoking, so maybe that was his nickname. The pirate shouted again and then began walking towards the bow. Shepherd stared at him grimly. If he turned around, the pirate would be looking right at him.

Shepherd could shoot the man easily, he was as proficient a shot with the Kalashnikov as he was with the SAS's standard-issue MP-5 and Glock, but if he did he'd be giving himself away. The pirate had to be dealt with silently.

He slid his finger off the trigger and upended the AK-47, then rushed forward, towards the pirate. At the last moment the pirate began to turn but it was too late, Shepherd was moving quickly, and he brought the butt of the assault weapon crashing down on the back of the man's neck and he dropped without making a sound.

Shepherd whirled around, bringing the AK-47 up into the firing position, but there was no one else on the deck. He moved over to the port side and peered around but the whole of the Upper Deck was clear. He went back to the unconscious pirate and heaved him over the side into the sea. He ejected the magazine from the AK-47, shoved it in his pocket, and tossed the weapon into the sea after him.

He took out his sat-phone and called Button again.

'What happened?' she asked.

'I've just had to deal with another pirate,' he said. 'No one heard anything but that's me blown. I might have been able to get away with one missing pirate but now they're sure to realise that something's up.'

'What do you want to do, Spider? It's your call.'

'Kill the ship's sat-phone now,' said Shepherd. 'That way they can't contact Crazy Boy or the pirates in Somalia no matter what happens on the *Athena*.'

'Do you want me to send in the cavalry?'

'No. The crew's under lock and key. If the pirates panic then they could start shooting the hostages. Let me see if I can handle it. How soon can the Increment be here?'

'They're thirty miles away, just over your horizon,' said Button. 'Fifteen minutes, tops. We've got two helicopters on stand-by.'

'Make sure they're ready to go,' said Shepherd. 'As soon as I give the word, get them on their way.'

'They'll be ready. You're sure about this?'

'It's the only way,' said Shepherd. 'I'll do what I can to contain the situation here. Or at least minimise the risks to the crew. But once the Increment are on board, I want one of the choppers to take me to Martin.'

'Not a problem,' said Button. 'But you be careful, OK?'

'Always,' said Shepherd.

He ended the call and shouldered his AK-47. He heard shouting from the port side. He took a quick look and saw two pirates walking along the Upper Deck, towards the bow. They were moving slowly, checking any hiding places, and were about a hundred and fifty yards away.

Shepherd stepped back and then hurried over to the hatchway that led from the bow down to the Below Deck Passageway. He turned the wheel to open it and climbed through, then closed it behind him and headed down the ladder to the passageway.

He went to the port side and jogged towards the stern, counting off his steps. Once he got to a hundred and fifty he took the next stairs up and opened the hatchway to get back on to the Upper Deck. The two pirates were ahead of him, still moving towards the bow. Shepherd looked over his shoulder; there was no one behind him but even so he couldn't risk using the AK-47 because it would be heard all over the ship.

He drew the machete from its scabbard and moved towards the two pirates, staying up on the balls of his feet, his left arm out for balance. The pirate closest to him was peering up a walkway between two lines of containers while the other one was shouting something in Somali, obviously looking for his friend.

As he got to within ten feet of the pirate, Shepherd raised his machete. He quickened his pace, grabbed the man around the mouth and, clamping his jaw shut, forced the tip of the machete into the man's back and angled it upwards. The machete was designed for slashing rather than stabbing but there wasn't enough room to swing the weapon properly and guarantee a kill with the first blow so Shepherd forced the blade up into the man's diaphragm and on into the lungs, keeping a tight grip on his mouth to stop him making any sound.

Blood spurted over Shepherd's hand and the pirate struggled but the catastrophic bleeding caused him to pass out within seconds. Shepherd pulled out the machete and then lowered the dying man carefully to the ground, keeping his eyes on the back of the remaining pirate, who had his gun over his shoulder and was still calling out in his own language.

Shepherd got up as the pirate at his feet took his last breath and died with a brief shudder. He began to move towards the remaining pirate, the machete at the ready, but he'd only taken two steps when the ship was hit by a bigger than usual wave and the deck lurched. Shepherd banged against the railing and the pirate whirled around.

His mouth opened in surprise when he saw Shepherd and he fumbled for his Kalashnikov. He was about twelve feet away from Shepherd and Shepherd realised that the pirate would be able to get off at least one shot before he reached him, so he drew back the machete and threw it as hard as he could. It spun through the air and the blade buried itself in the man's throat. He fell back and smashed into the deck, his hands clawing at his neck. Shepherd ran towards him and grabbed the handle of the machete, twisting it to increase the damage. Bloody froth erupted from the wound in the man's throat and his eyes stared glassily up at Shepherd, seconds away from death. Shepherd grabbed the man's belt, heaved him up against the railing and rolled him over. The body spun through the air, hit the side of the ship, and splashed into the water far below.

Shepherd went back to the first pirate, took the man's magazine from his AK-47 and then threw the body, and the gun, into the sea.

He stood where he was, his chest heaving from the exertion, listening to see if anyone was sounding the alarm, but all he could hear was the sea and the throb of the *Athena*'s massive engine.

There had been twelve pirates in the two skiffs, and nine had come on board. Shepherd had killed four, so that meant that there were five men still on the ship, assuming that no more had boarded without Shepherd knowing. The odds weren't great, but they were improving.

There were bloodstains on the deck but they didn't matter because one way or another it would soon be over.

He went back to the hatch and climbed down into the Below Deck Passageway, then jogged down the tunnel to the engine room. He stopped at the hatch that led to the engine room workshop. He turned the wheel to release the hatch and carefully eased it open. The room was deserted. He moved through the workshop and opened the door to the engine control room. It too was empty. The engine was throbbing and all the computer screens were on; Shepherd couldn't see any warning messages. Whatever the problem was that had stopped the ship, it had now been resolved.

Shepherd stood in front of the engine controls that Konrad had shown him a few days earlier. He pressed the button that Konrad had said switched control to the engine room, and then he pulled the telegraph back to the Full Stop position. The engine began to slow.

'What did you do?' shouted Blue. 'What did you do to the engine? Why are we stopping?' He swung his Kalashnikov around and pointed it at the captain.

Dominik put his hands in the air. 'I didn't touch anything,' he said. The telegraph was still in the Half Speed Ahead position but the ship was clearly slowing and the computer screen showed that they had already dropped to four knots.

Blue slipped his finger inside the trigger guard as he aimed his Kalashnikov at Dominik's chest. 'I want the engine on now. When we leave the ship I want to be closer to Somalia.'

'I didn't do anything,' said Dominik. 'Look for yourself. The telegraph hasn't moved.'

Blue looked at the lever. The captain was telling the truth.

'Is it something you did?' asked Dominik. 'You stopped the ship before.'

'This is not me,' said Blue angrily. 'This is something you did.'

'Why would I stop the ship?' said Dominik. 'How does that help me? I want you all off, why would I stop you from going where you want to go?'

'Then tell me what is wrong!' shouted Blue. 'Why have we stopped?'

Dominik looked at the instruments on the console. Everything was as it should be, but the ship was definitely coming to a stop. 'There must be a problem with the engine,' he said.

'Then fix it!' shouted Blue. 'Fix it or I'll kill you now!'

'I'm not an engineer,' said Dominik calmly. 'I'm the master. I run the ship, but the engineers take care of the engines.'

Blue growled and pulled the crew list from the back pocket of his shorts and thrust it at Dominik. 'Who?' he shouted. 'Who is engineer?'

Dominik got out of his chair and tapped Tomasz's picture. 'Him. Tomasz. He's the chief engineer. He's the one you want.' He tapped the second engineer's picture. 'Him, too. They'll know how to fix it.'

Blue called over one of his men and pointed out the two photographs. 'Go down and get them, and bring them here,' he said in Somali. 'And be quick.'

The man hurried off the bridge and down the stairs to G-Deck.

Blue shoved the barrel of the AK-47 under Dominik's chin and pushed it up, forcing the captain's head back. 'If this is a trick, I will kill you, I swear.'

Dominik nodded but said nothing.

Blue kept the barrel against Dominik's throat until the man returned with Tomasz and Konrad. 'Tell them what to do,' said Blue. Konrad had a large plaster across his nose and he had two black eyes. His lip was split and his hand went up to his mouth as he glared sullenly at Blue.

Dominik looked over at Tomasz. 'We've lost engine power,' he said. He switched to Polish. 'Engine room has taken control, there must be someone down there.'

Blue pulled back his gun and smacked Dominik in the stomach with the butt. The captain's breath exploded from his body and he bent double, coughing and wheezing. 'English!' screamed Blue. 'Only English. What did you say to him?'

Dominik tried to speak but all he could do was to gasp for breath.

'He said I should check the turbocharger, that's all,' said Tomasz calmly. 'Sometimes it's easier for us to talk in our own language.'

Blue turned the gun around and pointed it at the chief engineer. 'If you are lying, I will kill you.'

'Why would I lie?' said Tomasz. 'Do you want me to fix it or not?'

'Yes, you fix now!' said Blue. 'We have to move.'

Dominik leaned against his chair, his hands clutched to his stomach, still trying to catch his breath. 'Are you OK?' Tomasz asked him. Dominik nodded.

'Don't talk to him!' shouted Blue. 'You talk only to me. Now fix the engine!'

'I can't do it from here, can I?' said Tomasz. 'I have to

go to the engine room.' He pointed at Konrad. 'He'll have to come too.'

Blue shook his head. 'You go first and find out what is wrong.' He jabbed at Konrad with his gun. 'He stays here. If you do anything bad, I will kill him.'

'We just want to get the ship moving,' said Dominik, rubbing his injured stomach. 'Then we can get on with our lives.'

The ship's speed had dropped to three knots and, having lost momentum, it was beginning to be buffeted by the waves.

Blue waved over the pirate who'd brought the engineers on to the bridge. 'Take him down to the engine room,' he said in Somali. 'Watch him like a hawk. If he does anything wrong, anything at all, you shoot him. We have two more engineers, we can lose one.' Blue looked over at Tomasz. 'I told him to kill you if you try to do anything other than fix the engine.'

Tomasz held up his hands. 'You won't have any problem with me,' he said.

'I'd better not, because he will kill you,' said Blue.

The pirate took Tomasz down to G-Deck at gunpoint and pressed the button to open the lift. They rode down to the engine room in silence. When the door rattled open the pirate jabbed his gun in Tomasz's ribs and motioned for him to go first. Tomasz stepped into the engine room, pulled back his shoulders, and walked over to the console. The pirate followed him and then dropped like a stone as a heavy spanner smashed into the back of his skull.

Shepherd stood over the pirate but the man didn't move. 'Have we got anything we can use to tie him up?' Shepherd asked the chief engineer. He put the spanner down next to the body.

Tomasz found a roll of duct tape and tossed it to Shepherd, who used it to bind the pirate's wrists and ankles. Then he wound a length around the man's mouth as a makeshift gag.

'What are you doing?' asked Tomasz. 'They're going to pay the ransom, they'll be leaving soon.'

'I need to get off the ship now,' said Shepherd.

'You stopped the engine?'

'Yes, I did,' said Shepherd. 'How many pirates are there up there?'

'Why do you need to get off the ship?'

'Tomasz, I need you to focus. How many men are there upstairs?'

Tomasz shook his head, clearing his thoughts. 'There's two on the bridge. The leader, and another one with him.' He nodded at the unconscious pirate. 'Plus this one. And there's two on G-Deck, guarding the crew. And four more, I think.'

'Don't worry about the four,' said Shepherd. 'I've taken care of them. So there's only four left? Two guarding the crew and two on the bridge?'

'I think so. But I've been locked in my cabin since this happened.' He looked down at the unconscious pirate. 'What do you mean when you say we don't have to worry about the four others?'

'I took care of them,' said Shepherd. 'Look, I need you to think carefully, Tomasz. Could there be more than four?'

Tomasz shrugged his massive shoulders. 'For all I know there could be a dozen of them with RPGs sitting in the crew's mess right now.' He scratched his chin. 'You know this is totally against company policy. We're told not to use firearms, or to offer any sort of resistance once they're on the ship.'

'Screw company policy,' said Shepherd.

Tomasz's face broke into a toothy grin. 'Exactly,' he said. 'So what do we do now?'

The bridge phone rang and Dominik looked over at Blue. 'Can I answer that? It'll be Tomasz, down in the engine room.'

Blue nodded and Dominik picked up the phone. 'I need Konrad down here,' said Tomasz.

'Why?'

'Because it's a two-man job and I need an extra pair of hands. And the quicker he's down here the quicker I can get this done.'

'Is everything OK?'

'It will be when Konrad gets down here,' said Tomasz.

Dominik took the receiver away from his face. 'He needs the second engineer.'

'Why?'

'It needs two men. There's a lot of heavy equipment down there.'

Konrad was standing behind the captain's chair, looking at the radar screens.

Blue looked around the bridge. There was only one man with them; his name was Teardrop and he was a big man with a rope-like scar across his right forearm and a large black mole under his left eye. He was standing at the starboard side of the bridge, an AK-47 cradled in his arms. 'Where is everybody?' Blue asked him in Somali.

'They went to find Marlboro,' said Teardrop.

'Where exactly?'

'They were searching the decks. They only just went out.'

Blue pointed at the outside wing. 'Go out and call them,' he said.

Blue kept his gun trained on Dominik and Konrad while Teardrop went outside and shouted for the other pirates. After several minutes he came back in. 'They must be near the bow,' he said. 'With this wind, they can't hear us.'

Blue cursed. 'OK, you take him down to the engine room. If he tries anything, shoot him.'

Teardrop nodded and gestured for Konrad to leave the bridge.

As the two men went to call the lift, Blue aimed his AK-47 at the captain's chest. 'If your men try any tricks, I will kill you,' he said. 'I will kill you and all your men.'

'No one's going to try anything,' said Dominik.

The lift lurched upwards and Shepherd nodded at Tomasz. 'There it goes,' he said. He pointed at the far end of the engine control room, 'You stand over there by that equipment so that they see you as soon as the lift door opens. Then call them over.'

Tomasz walked over to the spot that Shepherd had indicated. Shepherd stood to the right of the lift, the spanner in his hand. They'd dragged the bound and gagged pirate, still unconscious, into the tool room. Shepherd watched the deck indicator as it clicked up to G-Deck and then began the slow journey down. He took slow, deep breaths as he tried to stay calm. He was sweating, and he transferred the spanner to his left hand as he wiped his right hand on his trousers.

There was a dull thud as the lift arrived and then the door rattled open. Shepherd pressed his back against the wall. Tomasz waved over at Konrad and shouted to him in Polish. Konrad stepped out of the lift and started walking towards him. Shepherd saw the tip of the pirate's AK-47 and then his shoulder and then the back of his head, and then he moved, bringing the spanner crashing down on the man's temple. There was a satisfying crunch and the pirate dropped like a stone, the Kalashnikov clattering on the floor.

Konrad whirled around and then grinned when he saw the unconscious pirate. He made a whooping noise and began kicking the pirate in the head, cursing him in Polish. 'Hey, leave him alone,' said Shepherd, pulling him away.

'Screw you!' said Konrad. He pointed at the bandage across his nose. 'Have you seen what they did to me? Hit me in the face with a gun. Broke my nose and smashed my teeth.' He pushed Shepherd away and kicked the pirate hard in the stomach.

Shepherd figured that Konrad had a point so he left the scond engineer to get on with it while he went over to Tomasz. 'So there's only the captain on the deck,' said Shepherd. 'If we ask him to come down here, do you think they'd let him?'

Tomasz shook his head. 'The leader's too suspicious,' he said. 'He'll know that something's wrong.'

'There are three pirates left,' said Shepherd. 'I'm going to need your help.'

Konrad stopped kicking the unconscious pirate. He knelt down and pulled a handgun from the pirate's belt and pointed it at the man's stomach.

'Hey!' shouted Shepherd. 'Don't!'

Konrad looked over at Shepherd. 'I want to kill this bastard,' said Konrad.

Shepherd went over and put his hand on Konrad's

shoulder. 'We need to take the ship back,' he said. 'If we start losing control they'll hurt the captain and the crew. Now's not the time to get angry, OK?'

Konrad frowned, but then nodded. 'OK.'

Shepherd took the gun off him. 'We need this,' he said. 'How many pirates were on the bridge when you left?'

'Just the leader.'

'And the others are on G-Deck? In the corridor?'

'There are some on the deck.'

'Don't worry about them,' said Shepherd.

Tomasz said something to Konrad and Konrad raised his eyebrows. 'You killed them?' he said.

Shepherd ignored the question. He examined the gun. It was a Beretta M9, the handgun of choice of the United States and French armed forces. Shepherd wasn't a fan of the weapon and had heard stories of the sliders breaking after extensive use, but it was serviceable enough and would do the job. He looked at Tomasz. 'I need two tubes, one a bit larger than the barrel, another about three inches in diameter. Wire wool. Duct tape.'

Tomasz jerked his thumb at the door to the tool room. 'In there,' he said.

Shepherd looked over at Konrad. 'Get some duct tape, bind him and gag him. Careful with the gag, we don't want him suffocating but we don't want him making any noise.' Konrad nodded and went through to the tool room. Shepherd and Tomasz followed him. The chief engineer found a length of aluminium pipe and showed it to Shepherd. Shepherd slid the barrel of the gun inside the pipe and nodded. 'We need to drill holes in it, each hole about five millimetres in diameter. Lots of them.'

'You are making a silencer?'

'It's called a suppressor, but yes, that's the basic idea. Now what about the larger tube? Something like a tin can will do.'

'Coke?'

'Perfect.'

Tomasz opened a cupboard and pulled out a six-pack of Coke. He ripped out one of the cans, popped the tab and drank it.

'So here's what we need to do,' said Shepherd. 'Cut a length of the thin pipe and drill holes in it. Cut holes in either end of the Coke can so that the tube can fit through it. Then pack the space between the tube and the can with wire wool. Can you do that?'

Tomasz grinned. 'Ten minutes,' he said. He put the tube in a vice and reached for a hacksaw. 'You can time me.'

Shepherd patted him on the back and went through to the engine control room, where Konrad was winding tape around the unconscious pirate's mouth. 'Why don't we just kill him?' asked Konrad.

'Use any more of that tape and you will do,' said Shepherd.

'They're scum,' said Konrad. 'They'd have killed us without a second thought.'

'We're not them,' said Shepherd. 'Don't forget that.'

A phone rang out. 'That'll be the bridge,' said Konrad. 'We'll have to answer it or they'll know something is wrong.'

'We need fifteen minutes,' said Shepherd. 'Just tell them that you're working on it and that we'll be moving soon.'

Konrad nodded and went over to the phone. He answered it in Polish but then switched to English.

Shepherd went back to the tool room and watched as Tomasz finished the suppressor.

Shepherd took it and inserted the barrel of the Beretta into the tube. There was a gap but it was a reasonable fit. He picked up a roll of grey duct tape and began winding it around the can and the barrel. He used the entire roll, and when he'd finished he nodded at Tomasz. 'OK, now I'm really going to need your help,' he said.

There were two Somalis standing guard outside the chief engineer's cabin. Silver Tooth was the taller of the two, tall and lanky and wearing his favourite Manchester United football shirt. He had a Kalashnikov hanging from a canvas sling and a machete in a nylon holster and he was working at his gums with a toothpick. Silver Tooth was always having trouble with his teeth, a situation that wasn't helped by the fact that there wasn't a decent dentist to be found in Somalia. He prodded at the flesh around the silver tooth at the back of his mouth that had been put in by a Russian dentist fifteen years earlier and then stared at the pick's bloody tip.

The other Somali was shorter and fatter, his black skin mottled and scarred from a childhood accident when he'd pulled a pan of boiling fat over himself while his mother lay on her bed drugged from too many khat leaves. His name was Abdu the Liar because given the choice between telling the truth or concocting a story, Abdu always chose the latter. He was armed with a pistol and had a large stainless-steel diving knife strapped to his left leg.

They were arguing over whether they had another hour or two before they were relieved when they heard the lift judder to a stop along the corridor. As the door rattled open, Silver Tooth took his gun off his shoulder and held it in front of him.

'Who is it?' asked Abdu the Liar.

'How would I know, fool?' said Silver Tooth, clicking off the safety.

Nobody stepped out of the lift so both men started walking towards it. Abdu the Liar pulled his pistol from its holster and pointed it down the corridor ahead of them.

A figure stepped out. It was one of the officers that had been taken upstairs to the bridge.

'What is happening?' asked Silver Tooth. He spoke Somali because he knew no English.

The man raised his hands and said something but Silver Tooth couldn't understand him. He waved his AK-47. 'Stay where you are!' he shouted. 'Do not move!'

The man carried on walking and said something else. A second white man stepped out of the lift. It was the other officer who had been taken up to see Blue, the one with the broken nose.

'What are they doing?' Silver Tooth asked Abdu the Liar.

Abdu the Liar shook his head. 'Where is Blue? Why are they here alone?'

The two men got down on to their knees as if they were praying.

'What do we do?' asked Silver Tooth.

Abdu the Liar opened his mouth to speak but then his face exploded in a shower of blood and bone fragments and he staggered forward. He fell to his knees and then slumped to the floor.

Silver Tooth shrieked and jumped back and then he felt as if he'd been slapped behind his right ear and he whirled around and saw a man standing by the doorway at the end of the corridor, a bulbous grey thing in his hands. Silver

Tooth tried to swing up his AK-47 but it suddenly felt as if it was made of lead and he couldn't lift it and then the bulbous grey thing jerked and everything went black.

Shepherd went out on to the metal stairs on the starboard side and switched on his sat-phone. He waited for it to log on to a satellite and then he phoned Charlotte Button. 'Tell the cavalry to come now,' he said.

'I'm on it,' said Button. 'Are you OK?'

'Fine and dandy,' said Shepherd. 'There's only one pirate left and no matter how it pans out your guys will have to come in now.'

'What about the crew?'

'The crew's safe. They're on G-Deck and I'll get them to stay there. The captain's on the bridge with one pirate and I'm on my way there now.'

'Be careful,' she said.

Shepherd laughed. 'You really must stop saying that,' he said. 'Being careful just doesn't fit with the job description.'

He ended the call and waved Tomasz over. 'Do you want to help me save Dominik?'

'Of course.'

'It means using you as bait again.'

Tomasz grinned. 'I trust you, Company Man,' he said.

Konrad was in the cabin, explaining to the crew what had happened. Shepherd and Tomasz dragged the two dead pirates into the captain's cabin and then closed the door.

The Filipinos were chattering and slapping each other on the back and Shepherd raised his hands and called for their attention. 'Guys, listen to me,' he said. 'This isn't over yet. I need you to all stay here, with the door shut. Help is on its way but we still have to get the captain out of harm's way.'

The crew fell silent.

'I suggest you all lie down and stay low. Don't make any noise, and when the door opens just stay where you are and follow any instructions you're given. Do you understand?'

He was faced with a wall of nodding heads but no one moved.

'Now!' said Shepherd. 'Down on the floor.' One by one the crew followed his instructions. Shepherd gestured at the second engineer. 'Konrad, I'll need you.'

Konrad followed Shepherd out of the cabin and closed the door behind him. 'Right,' said Shepherd, 'we're going to have to move quickly.'

The transceiver in front of Dominik crackled and he heard Konrad, speaking in Polish. 'Captain, are you there?'

Dominik looked over at Blue, who was standing by the door to the bridge, his Kalashnikov against his chest. 'OK if I talk to him?' asked Dominik.

'Tell him I want the ship fixed now,' Blue said. He walked over to the middle of the bridge, keeping his weapon aimed at Dominik's chest.

Dominik picked up the transceiver and clicked transmit. 'What's happening?' he asked.

Konrad continued to talk in Polish. 'When you see Tomasz at the window, get down and stay down,' said Konrad. 'Do you understand?'

'English!' shouted Blue. 'Tell him to speak English!'

Dominik nodded and pressed the transmit button again. 'He says you're to speak English. And yes, I understand.'

'What do you understand?' shouted Blue. 'What are you talking about?'

'He said that they're working on repairing the engine.'

'What's wrong with it?' asked Blue, taking a step towards the captain, his finger on the trigger of his weapon.

'They're not sure yet.'

'I want to speak to my men,' said Blue. He held out his hand. 'Give me the radio, I want to talk to my men.'

'It's OK, everything is under control,' said Dominik. 'We can fix it.'

'Give me the radio!' screamed Blue.

Tomasz appeared at the window close to the door leading to the starboard bow. He waved at Dominik, then rapped on the window with his knuckles. As Blue whirled around, Dominik dropped down by the side of his chair.

Blue screamed and aimed his Kalashnikov at Tomasz, but the chief engineer was already ducking out of the way. Then the window on the port side shattered and a hail of bullets ripped through Blue. The pirate's finger tightened instinctively as his body went into spasm and bullets sprayed around the cabin as he fell to the floor. The firing stopped as suddenly as it had begun and Blue lay still as blood pooled around him. Dominik's ears were buzzing from the loud explosions in the confined space and his eyes were watering from the cordite, but despite his discomfort he began to laugh.

Shepherd pushed open the door from the port wing of the outdoor bridge and kept his gun pointed at Blue's body as he walked over to it. 'Are you OK?' he called over to the captain. The pool of blood was continuing to spread around the body. Blue's left leg twitched once and then went still.

Dominik got to his feet, laughing nervously.

'Dominik, take slow breaths. You'll be fine.' Shepherd kicked Blue's Kalashnikov away, then went over to the starboard door and opened it. Tomasz had run down the stairs and was standing on the landing outside G-Deck. 'Tomasz, it's over!' shouted Shepherd. 'Come on back up here!'

Off to the right, two helicopters were flying towards the *Athena*, a few metres above the waves. They were Lynx Mark 8 anti-surface helicopters, both fitted with machine-gun pods. Shepherd took out his sat-phone and called Button. 'All done and dusted,' he said. 'Tell the cavalry that they can holster their weapons.'

'Are you OK?'

'I'm fine,' he said. 'No casualties among the crew.'

'Well done you.'

'You can save the congratulations until we've got the yacht crew back,' said Shepherd. He put the sat-phone in his back pocket and hurried back to the bridge.

'What's happening?' asked Dominik, lighting a cigarette with trembling hands.

'You're back in command of your ship,' said Shepherd, placing his Kalashnikov on the chart table. 'The crew's fine. No one got hurt.'

Tomasz joined them on the bridge. He said something to Dominik in Polish and the captain looked at Shepherd in astonishment. 'You killed them? The pirates?'

'Some of them,' he said. 'Look, in a few seconds there are going to be soldiers here. They'll secure the ship but pretty soon you'll be on your way.' He went back outside to the starboard wing and watched as the two helicopters moved apart. One hovered over the port wing and two ropes dropped down directly over the yellow P on the deck. Two SBS troopers dressed all in black abseiled down, followed in quick succession by another four. They took their MP5 machine guns off their slings and rushed through to the bridge, where Dominik and Tomasz instinctively raised their hands.

One of the troopers walked through the bridge and out to the starboard wing, where Shepherd was watching the second helicopter moving in. 'You Shepherd?' asked the trooper. He was wearing an armoured helmet over a Nomex flame-retardant balaclava, a black Nomex one-piece assault suit, knee and elbow pads and a bullet-proof armoured waistcoat with ceramic armour plates covering his front, back and groin.

'That'd be me,' said Shepherd. 'The crew are on the deck below us. There are two pirates bound and gagged in the engine room.'

The trooper grinned. 'Sounds like you didn't need us.' He headed back into the bridge.

The Lynx went into a hover about twenty metres above the bridge and more troopers began abseiling down. Shepherd stood back and they ran past him, cradling their MP5s. As the last trooper ran by him, a bright orange harness appeared at the hatchway. The downwash from the helicopter's rotor ripped at Shepherd's hair as he looked up. Dominik came out joined him and they both watched as the bright orange harness was winched down, whirling around in the wind as if it had a life if its own. Shepherd could see the winchman, looking out of the hatchway, peering down the cable.

'Who are they, the men in black?' asked Dominik.

'SAS and SBS,' said Shepherd. He grabbed at the harness and slipped it under his arms. 'Special forces.'

He looked up and made a circling motion with his right hand, letting the winchman know that he was ready to be winched up.

'Answer me one question, will you?' said Dominik.

'Sure,' said Shepherd. The helicopter's engine pitch increased and the rope tightened.

'You don't really work in human resources, do you?'

Shepherd laughed as his feet left the deck and he headed upwards. The helicopter banked towards Somalia as the winch pulled Shepherd away from the *Athena*.

Shepherd peered out of the open door of the Lynx as the helicopter circled around an airfield far below. The pilot was talking to someone on the ground as Shepherd caught glimpses of a dirt track running through arid scrubland, then a line of white SUVs and half a dozen tents.

The co-pilot twisted around in his seat and gave Shepherd a thumbs-up and Shepherd grinned back. The helicopter landed in a cloud of choking dust and Shepherd climbed out and jogged away, bent double and coughing.

As he straightened up he saw Martin O'Brien grinning at him. O'Brien was wearing khaki fatigues and had a floppy camouflage hat on his head. 'Welcome to Ethiopia,' he said, and clapped him on the back. 'Nice flight?'

'Not much in the way of in-flight entertainment and I prefer flat beds, but yeah, it was OK.' The Lynx's twin turboshaft engines roared and the helicopter lifted off and banked to the right before heading north.

There was a group of men standing behind O'Brien wearing similar fatigues and Shepherd grinned when he realised that one of the figures was a woman. 'Bloody hell, Carol Bosch,' he said. She had shoulder-length wavy black hair tied back in a ponytail and charcoal-grey eyes that sparkled with amusement. She had an Uzi hanging from a nylon sling.

'Bastard,' she said. 'You never called.' The last time Shepherd had seen Bosch they had been in Iraq four years earlier. 'And you forgot my birthday. I hit the big three zero last month.'

She hugged him, then screwed up her face. 'You're a bit ripe, Spider,' she said. 'Have you given up showering? And the facial fuzz really doesn't suit you.'

Shepherd ran a hand over his stubble. 'Long story, Carol,' he said, and kissed her on the cheek. 'And really, it's good to see you.'

'Couldn't let you do this on your own, could I?' said Bosch. 'When Martin said you'd got out of your depth again we had to offer to pull your nuts out of the fire – again.' She turned and gestured at three of the men behind her. 'You remember Joe, Ronnie and Pat?'

'Of course,' said Shepherd, and he shook hands with the three men and hugged them in turn. Like Bosch they were South African mercenaries, and the last time he'd seen them had been in Iraq. Joe Haschka had a shock of red hair and freckles across his nose and cheeks. He was a big man and was carrying a Kalashnikov. Ronnie Markus was tall and thin with a straggly moustache and had a pump-action shotgun hanging across his back. Pat Jordan was in his early fifties with a grey crew cut and a fading tattoo of a leaping panther across his left forearm. He had a handgun on either hip and a combat knife strapped to his right leg.

O'Brien introduced Shepherd to the rest of the team, most of whom were former SAS. With the introductions out of the way, O'Brien clapped Shepherd on the back. 'Carol's right about you being a bit ripe,' he said. 'You've got time for a shower and a feed if you want one, and I'll get you clean clothes. Then we'll have a briefing.' He looked at his watch. 'We're going to be moving out in about an hour.'

Roobie's mobile phone rang and he put down his bottle of Johnnie Walker Red Label and picked it up. It was Crazy Boy. 'Cousin, have you heard from your father?' he asked.

'Not since yesterday,' said Roobie. 'The money is coming today, you know that?'

Crazy Boy ignored the question. 'What did he say when he spoke to you?'

'He wanted to know that everything was OK with the hostages. And that I was to take good care of the money. Is there a problem, cousin?'

'He hasn't called me today and he said that he would.'

'He might be waiting until we have the money.'

Crazy Boy didn't say anything.

'Cousin, I said he might be waiting until we have the money.'

'He should have called me, and when I tried to call the ship's sat-phone I couldn't get through.'

'You think something is wrong, cousin?'

'The last time your father contacted the company about the ransom, everything was as it should be?'

'That was days ago,' said Roobie. 'But they said that they will deliver the five million dollars today. That is agreed.'

'And the hostages are OK?'

Roobie flinched and took a swig from his bottle of whisky. 'There was a problem.'

'What sort of problem?' asked Crazy Boy quickly.

Roobie closed his eyes. 'Cousin, he attacked me. I had to defend myself.'

'What happened? What did you do?'

'One of them attacked me and he died.'

'He what?' exploded Crazy Boy.

'He died. I had no choice.'

'You killed one of the hostages? How could you do that?'

'I had no choice, believe me. He went crazy, he tried to kill me and I had to stop him.'

Crazy Boy went quiet.

'Cousin, are you there?' asked Roobie.

'Do they know?' said Crazy Boy coldly. 'Does the company know?'

'I have only told you. I didn't tell my father.'

Crazy Boy cursed. 'What do you think is going to happen when they find out that you've killed a hostage?'

'It's the ship they want and they're getting that back, aren't they? Why would they care about one hostage more or less?'

'You don't understand these people,' said Crazy Boy. 'We did a deal, we said that they would get the ship, the crew and the hostages, and now you're telling me that you've killed a hostage.'

'They will still pay us the money,' said Roobie. 'And if they don't, we can take it from them.'

'That's not how it works,' said Crazy Boy.

'They are bringing the money here,' said Roobie. 'What can they do?'

'You don't understand what's happening,' said Crazy Boy. 'That ship has to be released. It has to be on its way, and soon.'

'It will be, cousin. We will take their money and we will give them back their ship. What is the problem?' He took another swig from his whisky bottle.

'Listen to me and listen to me carefully, Roobie. Nothing must go wrong today. Nothing. If anything does go wrong, it is on your head.'

Before Roobie could reply the line went dead. Roobie sneered and tossed the mobile phone on to the table. Nothing was going to go wrong. Roobie would get the five million dollars and he would keep it for himself. He would use the money to buy himself passage to London and then he would teach Crazy Boy a lesson that he would never forget. Roobie laughed and reached for a khat twig. Crazy Boy had no idea about the world of hurt that was heading his way.

Shepherd showered in a makeshift shower unit connected to a water tank, then shaved and changed into a clean polo shirt and jeans before heading to the briefing tent. There was a twin-engine Sherpa plane parked to the side of the dirt runway. The C-23 Sherpa reminded Shepherd of a shark, with a strip of windows above a pointed nose and the thirty-foot-long grey body tapering back to a twin tail. The wing was above the body with a Pratt & Whitney turboprop on either side.

Shepherd had seen several versions of the Sherpa during his years in the military. It could be converted to carry thirty passengers in airline-style seats, or outfitted as a troop carrier able to drop two dozen paratroopers, used to carry and drop freight on pallets, or be set up as an air ambulance with eighteen stretchers. It had a top speed of more than 200 mph flying at 10,000 feet and a range of almost a thousand miles, and was the perfect all-purpose workhorse.

Shepherd was the last to arrive in the briefing tent. There were fifteen men in camouflage fatigues sitting on camp stools. Between them they were carrying a variety of weapons, including Kalashnikovs, pump-action shotguns and Uzis, and with various handguns in holsters attached to pretty much every part of their body. Bosch was standing at the entrance to the tent and she nodded her approval at his improved appearance. 'You look OK when you're scrubbed up,' she said.

'Thank you, ma'am.'

'You got yourself a girlfriend yet?'

Shepherd laughed and walked over to O'Brien. O'Brien had changed into a denim shirt and chinos, and for the first time Shepherd saw John Muller and Billy Bradford, who were also dressed casually. Shepherd hugged Muller, whom he had last seen in Dubai, then shook hands with Bradford. 'Where's Jack?' asked Shepherd.

'Taking care of the plane,' said Bradford. 'He's fitting extra fuel tanks, just to be on the safe side.'

'OK, let's get started,' said O'Brien. He was standing by a large sheet of plywood on which had been pinned several maps and satellite photographs. Next to it was a whiteboard on which he'd drawn a rough diagram of the airfield where the hostages were being held.

He tapped the two watchtowers that overlooked the airfield. 'Generally there are two men in each of these towers. Now more often than not the guards are stoned or asleep or both, so they're not a major problem, but we already have two sniper teams in place. As soon as it kicks off the snipers will take out the four guards and then pretty much take care of any hostiles they see.'

He tapped the huts behind the main control tower building. 'There are three huts here and the hostages are being held together in the middle one. There is a single door and the windows are barred. The door is usually closed and there are two guards stationed outside. We're not going to wait until the pirates bring them out because with bullets flying they'll be safer in the hut. The walls are made from concrete blocks so the rounds won't penetrate.'

He drew a plane on the diagram's runway and there were a few sniggers from the men. 'I never claimed to be Van Gogh,' said O'Brien. He drew an arrow from the plane to the control tower building. 'We figure this will be the place where they'll count and check the money.'

'The money's real, right?' asked Haschka.

O'Brien pointed a warning finger at him. 'Don't get any ideas, Joe. We've got the number of every note.'

'I'm asking because I was wondering why we're going in with genuine cash if we're going to be taking it back anyway.'

'Fair point,' said O'Brien. 'If we used counterfeit then the game's up as soon as they spot the fakes. Using real money gives us extra time.' He tapped the drawing of the plane. 'We land and we taxi to this end of the runway. Before we stop we'll position the plane so that we're ready for take-off and Jack will keep the engines running. Four of us will get off with the money. Everyone else stays on the plane and stays hidden. They won't expect us to be alone but if they see you lot they'll know that something's up.'

Bosch raised her hand. 'I know what you're going to say,

Carol, and I know you want to be in the thick of it, but the sight of a woman will probably set them off.'

'Even one as ugly as you,' said Jordan, laughing.

Bosch smiled thinly then grabbed Jordan's testicles with her right hand and squeezed. 'Be nice, Pat,' she said.

'Sorry, honey,' said Jordan, and she let go of him.

'I'm serious, Carol. Head down, OK?'

'I hear you,' said Bosch.

'So, I'll be walking off the plane with the money, along with Spider, Billy and John,' O'Brien continued. 'As you can see, we're in casual clothing. Please try to remember that when the shooting starts.'

There were several laughs and catcalls and O'Brien held up his hand. 'I'm serious, guys, we don't want any collateral damage. We're a long way from home and we've no medivac on tap. Now, John looks the part so he'll be playing the company man and Spider, Billy and I will be his security. The money is in two suitcases. John will have one, so will Billy. We take the money to this building here.' He tapped the drawing of the control tower building. 'As I said, this is where we figure they'll count and check the money. They always do on piracy operations. They'll have electronic counters and gizmos to check for forgeries. We'll be armed and we're going to be insisting that we keep our guns with us. If there's a problem with that, I'll take out this hand-kerchief and wipe my head.' He pulled a red handkerchief from his pocket and waved it around. 'If you see this, it means you come out shooting. It'll also be the signal for the snipers to start taking out the guards in the watchtowers.'

He put the handkerchief away and tapped the control tower building again. 'If everything goes to plan the four of us will go inside with the money. We'll choose our moment when we're inside and hopefully we can take the leader hostage and get him to release the crew without any shooting. But if it goes tits up and you hear shooting, then you pile out and we're at war. Once the four of us are away from the plane, Jack will lower the rear ramp so that you can all make a quick exit when necessary. And he'll keep the ramp down until we're all back on the plane.'

He looked at his watch. 'OK, ten minutes and then we're off. Any questions?'

Several of the men made loud grunting noises.

'That's it, then,' said O'Brien. 'Let's rock and roll.' The men filed out of the tent.

'Who are the snipers?' Shepherd asked O'Brien.

'No one you know,' said O'Brien. 'Two of them are SAS that Jack and Billy met in Iraq, and two are former Irish Rangers. Before my time but they come highly recommended and they're Irish so they've got to be good. They went overland last night and they're already dug in with clear views of the buildings.'

'Let's try to do this without hurting anyone,' said Shepherd.

'We'll give it a go,' said O'Brien.

Jack Bradford kept the plane below eight thousand feet during the flight through Ethiopian airspace then dropped down to below a thousand feet for the flight across Somalia to the pirates' airfield. They kept away from any populated areas and all they saw below them was scrubland, red-brown earth, rocks, and whatever vegetation could suck enough moisture from the ground to survive.

Ten minutes before landing, O'Brien unbuckled himself from the co-pilot's seat and went back to the main cargo area. There were no seats on the plane so everyone was sitting on the floor, their equipment between their legs. 'Sorry about the lack of creature comforts,' he shouted above the noise of the engines. 'The plane's normally used for flying goats out to starving farmers.'

Jordan bleated like a goat and everyone laughed, more from the tension than the humour.

'The runway isn't exactly Heathrow but this plane is designed for short take-offs and landings so it might be bumpy but we'll be just fine.' He grinned at Shepherd, who was sitting next to Bosch. 'If you can find anything soft to grab on to, go for it,' he said.

Bosch looked at Shepherd. 'Don't even think about it,' she said.

O'Brien made his way back to the co-pilot's seat as Bradford began his descent. He made a slow pass over the airfield, which was little more than a dirt track in the brush, then flew away from it before making a sweeping left turn and then a sharper one, and then he throttled back the engines and brought the plane into land. It hit the ground smoothly enough but bumped and shook and rattled as it rolled over the uneven clay surface.

It came to a stop fifty feet or so before the end of the runway and he made a tight 180-degree turn before taxiing back to where it had landed, then he made another tight turn before throttling the engines back to idle.

O'Brien got out of his seat and patted Shepherd on the shoulder. 'Right, let's do it,' he said. 'Remember, John's the boss so let him do the talking.'

O'Brien threaded his way to the side door at the rear of the plane and unfolded the metal stairway. He stepped out on to the runway. Shepherd followed him.

Half a dozen pirates were standing around three open-topped Land Rovers just off the runway with their backs to the control tower building. They were all holding Kalashnikovs. O'Brien and Shepherd moved away from the plane while Muller climbed down. The American flexed his shoulder muscles and stood with his hands on his hips. He was wearing a beige safari suit and brown loafers. He waved a hand at Shepherd. 'Help Billy with the cases,' he said, and strode towards the group of pirates, his chin thrust up arrogantly.

'He loves this, doesn't he,' Shepherd whispered to O'Brien, before hurrying over to the plane to help Billy bring out the two Samsonite suitcases.

'Who's in charge?' shouted Muller. 'Where's the big boss?'

A pirate striding over from the control tower building let loose a burst of gunfire and everyone ducked. He was in his thirties, tall with jet-black skin, bare-chested and wearing red and blue surfer pants and flip-flops. He had greasy ringlets and around his neck was a large shark's tooth on a leather necklace. There was a manic look in his eyes and in his left hand he had a bottle of Johnnie Walker Red Label whisky. 'I am Roobie,' he shouted. 'These are my men.'

'We need to see the hostages,' said Muller.

'Money first,' said Roobie, striding towards him.

Muller folded his arms across his barrel-like chest. 'Hostages first,' he said. 'We need proof of life.'

Roobie brought his gun to bear on the American's chest. 'Fuck proof of life. Money first, then you see the hostages.'

Muller sighed and then nodded slowly. He reached behind

his back and pulled out a Glock, which he pointed at Roobie's face. 'Then we'll just get back on the plane and take our money with us,' he said.

The group of pirates all jerked into life, pointing their AK-47s at the four men and shouting. Shepherd looked up at the watchtower nearest them. There were two men standing looking down, sighting along their Kalashnikovs.

'John . . .' said O'Brien. 'Don't antagonise them.'

Muller ignored O'Brien and walked towards Roobie, holding his gun out in front of him. He stopped a few paces in front of Roobie and stared at him coldly. 'I'm a professional, and I would hope that you are as well,' he said. 'In this business we always check on the health of the hostages before we hand over any ransom. That is what professionals do.'

Shepherd saw O'Brien's hand move towards the red handkerchief in his back pocket.

Roobie stared at the American with undisguised contempt, and then he smirked. He nodded slowly. 'Professional,' he said. 'Yes. We are professional. One of your men can go check.' He waved his Kalashnikov at the control tower building. 'Over there,' he said. 'One of the huts.'

O'Brien nodded at Shepherd. Shepherd walked across the runway and past the group of pirates. There were a dozen more pirates standing around the building, all of them armed.

Shepherd walked by a tent in which there were another dozen or so pirates lounging on camp beds. There were empty whisky bottles everywhere and plastic bags filled with khat leaves and a stack of assault rifles and an RPG on a table. Several of the men were snoring loudly.

There were two guards in front of one of the huts, barely more than teenagers. One had a bolt-action Mosin-Nagant

Russian military rifle and his companion had a machete and what appeared to be a Russian copy of a Smith & Wesson revolver.

The pirate with the machete pushed the door open and waved for Shepherd to go inside. Even before he stepped across the threshold his stomach lurched from the foul smell within – sweat, urine and faeces. There were four people in the small hut, two men and two women. He recognised Katie Cranham, though she looked a good ten years older than in the picture he'd seen. There were dark patches under her eyes, her skin was covered in spots and sores and her hair was matted.

Four pairs of eyes stared at him in disbelief. 'I'm here to get you out,' he said.

'Oh my God, you're English!' gasped Katie.

'Yes, I am,' said Shepherd. 'I just need you all to stay here a little longer.'

Katie hugged the woman next to her. She was in an equally bad state. Joy Ashmore. 'We're going home, Joy,' said Katie. 'We're going home.'

Shepherd looked at the two men. One of them was getting unsteadily to his feet. He was filthy and unshaven and there was a dead look in his eyes that Shepherd had seen in battle-scarred soldiers. Graham Hooper, the Australian captain. Hooper held out his hand unsteadily and Shepherd shook it, even though the fingers were crusted with black mud and dried blood. 'Please, sit down, best you all keep down for a while.'

He looked across at the other man, who was sitting with his legs drawn up to his chest, a dazed look in his eyes. Eric Clavier, the Frenchman.

Hoop sat down heavily and stretched out his legs. 'We're really going home?'

'Soon,' said Shepherd.

'Someone's paid the ransom?'

'Sort of,' said Shepherd. 'Where's Andrew? Andrew Ashmore?'

Joy Ashmore started crying and Katie hugged her.

'He's dead,' said Clavier. 'They killed him.'

'What happened?'

'The leader, the one called Roobie, hacked him to death. They hauled away the body and washed away the blood.'

Hooper buried his face in his hands.

'Can we go?' asked Clavier.

'Soon,' said Shepherd. 'There's a few things to be done yet.'

'But the ransom's being paid?' asked Katie.

'There are men outside handling that,' said Shepherd. 'But I need you to stay here and keep down, no matter what happens outside. And when we come to get you, do exactly as we say with no talking. We have a plane outside and we'll get you there. Do you all understand?'

They all nodded.

Shepherd reached for the door. 'Don't go!' begged Joy. 'Please don't leave us.'

Shepherd went over and knelt down beside her. She was battered and bruised and she had the eyes of a frightened animal. 'I'm going to get you out of here, Joy,' he said. 'I swear.' He stroked her matted hair and she tried to smile but started crying again. Shepherd stood up and went out.

The two guards laughed when Shepherd came out of the hut and the one with the rifle said something in Somali.

The other one laughed and wiped his nose with the back of his hand.

'Does you speak English?' Shepherd asked.

The two men looked at him blankly.

'Does either of you two scumbags speak English?'

The man with the machete said something to Shepherd in Somali and the other one laughed.

Shepherd smiled. 'That's a pity,' he said. 'Because I want you to know that I'm going to shoot the both of you.' He made a gun with his hand and pointed it at the chest of the pirate with the rifle. 'Bang, bang,' he said quietly.

The two pirates roared with laughter as Shepherd walked away.

Muller and Roobie were still facing off, but they had lowered their weapons. Shepherd nodded at O'Brien. 'There are four hostages and they're not in great condition but they're alive,' he said in a low whisper. 'Andrew Ashmore is dead, though.' He jerked a thumb at Roobie. 'Apparently he did it.'

'Shit,' said O'Brien.

'Yeah,' said Shepherd.

'Now we count the money!' shouted Roobie. He pulled the trigger of his Kalashnikov and fired a short burst into the air.

'There are a dozen soldiers in a tent over there, drunk and drugged,' whispered Shepherd. 'I've got a bad feeling about going into that building.'

'Yeah, you and me both,' said O'Brien. 'Best we do this out in the open. The Land Rovers will provide cover.'

'Agreed,' said Shepherd. 'John, let's roll.'

Muller shoved his gun back into his holster and pointed at the control tower building. 'Let's go,' he said.

Roobie grinned and took a drink from his bottle.

'I'm going back to the hostages,' said Shepherd.

'Roger that,' said Muller. He grabbed the handle of one of the Samsonite cases and Bradford took the other. They started walking after Roobie, who was swaggering towards the control tower building.

Shepherd looked up at the two watchtowers. The men in both had relaxed and were no longer sighting down their weapons.

The gang of pirates turned and followed Roobie. They all had their backs to the plane.

Shepherd began walking confidently towards the huts. He had a Glock in a nylon holster in the small of his back but he knew that the semi-automatic only had fifteen rounds and that wouldn't be enough for what he needed to do.

He looked over his shoulder. Muller and Bradford were about ten feet behind Roobie and his gang.

O'Brien was hanging back, his right hand reaching towards his pocket.

Shepherd began walking faster. He reached for his Glock as he broke into a run.

The two guards outside the hut looked up, their mouths open in surprise. As Shepherd pulled out his gun he heard the double crack of sniper rifles and he knew that it had started. He shot the nearest pirate in the chest, just above the heart, then shot the other in the face. Both men went down without a sound.

As Shepherd turned away from the hut he heard more sniper fire and saw Carol Bosch leading the charge from the rear ramp of the Sherpa.

Muller and Bradford had both hit the ground and were firing their handguns at the pirates grouped around Roobie.

Shepherd reached the tent where the pirates were sleeping off their drugs and drink. One or two were sitting up, but most still hadn't reacted. Shepherd figured that gunfire was probably a regular occurrence at the camp.

One of the pirates stumbled over to the table, groping for a weapon, but Shepherd put two rounds in his chest and he fell back on to a sleeping pirate.

More men started getting to their feet, shaking their heads in confusion, and Shepherd shot three of them, each with a single round.

He'd been mentally counting the rounds. Seven gone. Eight left.

The men in the tent began screaming and several crawled under the canvas and ran away. Two made a run for the table and Shepherd shot them both in the chest. Six left.

Behind him he could hear the rat-tat-tat of automatic-weapons fire.

Shepherd stood at the tent entrance, covering the men inside. Most of the pirates left were lying on their camp beds, transfixed with horror. One of the men that Shepherd had shot was curled up in a ball, screaming.

If the pirates stayed in the tent Shepherd knew that he'd have to shoot them all. He couldn't leave them, not when all their guns were lying on the table. He fired the rest of his rounds as he ran towards the guns, then grabbed a Kalashnikov, checked that the safety was off, and swung it around. 'Get out now!' he screamed. He waved the gun towards the rear of the tent, then fired a burst into the ground.

The remaining pirates bolted to the back of the tent and scrambled under the canvas. Shepherd fired another burst, then turned around.

O'Brien's men had formed a semicircle and had taken up positions behind the three Land Rovers. There was gunfire coming from the control tower building. Shepherd couldn't see Roobie's body among the dead scattered in front of the building and figured that he'd made it inside.

He tossed the Kalashnikov on to the table and picked up the RPG. It was a Russian-made reloadable RPG-7, the middle of the steel tube wrapped with wood and the end flared to shield the user from the blast. The bulbous grenade was a PG-7VL standard high-explosive anti-tank round and the weapon was armed and ready to fire.

Shepherd turned and hurried away from the tent, then went down on one knee and sighted on the door to the control tower building. He had been trained in the use of RPGs during his time with the SAS and was confident that he'd hit the target. He pulled the trigger and the gunpowder booster charge started the grenade on its deadly trajectory. After ten metres the grenade's rocket motor kicked into life and two sets of guidance fins clicked into place to keep it on target. It left a plume of white smoke behind it as it streaked towards the building, then the door erupted in a ball of flame and the ground juddered from the force of the explosion.

O'Brien's team held their fire. There was no more shooting from the burning building, just the occasional crack of sniper fire in the distance.

Shepherd dropped the RPG tube and went back for a Kalashnikov before running over to the hut. He pushed open the door. The four hostages were huddled together at the rear of the building.

'It's OK,' said Shepherd. 'Come with me.'

Hooper and Clavier helped the two girls to their feet and they followed Shepherd out of the hut.

O'Brien was running towards them. Behind him Muller and Bradford were pulling the suitcases back to the plane.

Haschka, Jordan and Markus were following Bosch as they ran over to the control tower building, bent low but not under fire.

'The area's secure,' said O'Brien. 'There's a dozen or so hostiles still armed but they're too far away to do us any damage.' He helped Hooper with Katie and they headed to the plane.

Shepherd ran alongside the Frenchman and Joy with his AK-47 at the ready but O'Brien was right, the shooting had all but stopped.

They went up the rear ramp into the cargo area, where Muller and Bradford were already sitting next to the cases. 'Goddam it, that was a blast!' said Muller, pumping the air with his fist.

O'Brien's men began filing into the plane and taking their places, and the pitch of the engines increased as Jack Bradford prepared for take-off.

Bosch was the last to get on board and she winked as she sat down next to Shepherd. She was bleeding from her right forearm and Jordan pulled out a field dressing and slapped it on to the wound. She grinned when she saw the look of dismay on Shepherd's face. 'Flesh wound,' she said. 'But you're welcome to suck the poison out if you want.'

'Let's go, Jack!' shouted O'Brien as he headed towards the co-pilot's seat.

The rear ramp rose and clicked into place and the plane started to roll, picking up speed quickly. Less than twelve minutes after they'd touched down on the runway they were back in the air and heading for Ethiopia.

Crazy Boy slipped into the Hilton Hotel through its revolving door and headed straight for the lifts. He was wearing a black baseball cap and he kept his head down. He rode up to the top floor and walked along to al-Zahrani's suite. There were two bodyguards standing outside the suite's double doors and they patted Crazy Boy down before allowing him inside.

Al-Zahrani looked as immaculate as he had done when he'd visited Crazy Boy's house in Ealing. He got up off the sofa when Crazy Boy walked in and held out his arms. His suit was Armani, his shoes Bally and there was a diamond-encrusted Rolex on his left wrist. 'My brother,' said al-Zahrani. 'Welcome to my temporary home.' He hugged Crazy Boy and kissed him on both cheeks. Crazy Boy smelled a sweet and clearly expensive aftershave. Another bodyguard, the one who had accompanied al-Zahrani to Crazy Boy's house, was sitting by the window wearing his trademark impenetrable sunglasses.

Al-Zahrani released Crazy Boy and waved for him to sit on an overstuffed easy chair. 'Can I get you a refreshment?' he asked.

Crazy Boy shook his head. 'You said you are leaving tomorrow?'

'My work is done here and I have things to do in the Gulf,' al-Zahrani replied.

Crazy Boy took off his baseball cap. 'It all went wrong,' he said. He put his head in his hands. 'I've lost everything. My uncle is dead, most of my men are dead or injured. The

Somali government has moved into my base and is hunting down the rest of my gang. My bank accounts have been frozen. They've been around to my businesses. The cops here are on to me. I was being followed but I shook them off.'

'I am sorry, brother,' said al-Zahrani.

'My life here is over,' said Crazy Boy. 'I have lost everything.'

'You have your life, brother. And you have your faith. Remember what the Koran says. "Those who readily fight in the cause of God are those who forsake this world in favour of the Hereafter. Whoever fights in the cause of God, then gets killed, or attains victory, we will surely grant him a great recompense." You will get your reward in the Hereafter, brother.'

'But there has been no victory,' said Crazy Boy. 'They killed my men, they killed my family, they took the money back. Where is the victory?'

Al-Zahrani smiled. 'Why, the ship, of course. Even as we speak it is sailing to its destination. You are helping to change the world for ever, brother. Your victory is on the horizon.'

Crazy Boy's eyes widened. 'It will still happen?'

'Of course. Inshallah. God willing.'

Crazy Boy leaned forward. 'I want to help,' he said.

'You have already helped. This has only been possible because of you.'

'I want to do more,' said Crazy Boy.

'You are sure about this?' asked al-Zahrani.

Crazy Boy nodded enthusiastically. 'They sent their soldiers to kill my uncle and my men. I want to make them pay.'

Al-Zahrani nodded sympathetically. 'Then make them pay you shall, brother,' he said.

* * *

Charlotte Button raised her glass to Shepherd. 'Job well done, Spider.' They were in a wine bar overlooking the Thames, a stone's throw from MI5's headquarters, sharing a bottle of Bollinger. Shepherd had taken a taxi from Heathrow Airport, straight off a ten-hour Ethiopian Airways flight from Addis Ababa.

Shepherd clinked his glass against hers. 'To dry land,' he said.

'*Terra firma,*' she said. They both drank. 'The PM's very pleased, obviously,' she went on. 'I've been asked to pass on his personal thanks.'

'Even though it never happened.'

'Oh, it happened, it's just that the British government wasn't involved. It couldn't have gone better, Spider. Kudos.' Her face tightened a little. 'That was a stupid thing to say, of course. What with one of the hostages being killed.'

'At least it wasn't our guys that did the killing,' said Shepherd. 'He was long dead by the time we got there.'

'Horrible business,' said Button. 'But at least we got the rest of the hostages back, freed the ship and recovered the ransom.'

'And got rid of a few pirates to boot,' he said. 'That's what the so-called task force should be doing, of course, instead of shepherding ships in convoys. Send in the SAS and blow them apart.' He raised his glass. 'It's never going to happen, of course.'

She raised her own glass in salute. 'Seriously, you and Martin and the boys deserve a medal for what you did.'

'Do you think I'll get one?' He smiled at the flustered look on Button's face. 'I'm joking,' he said. 'Just so long as all the bills are paid. Martin spent a hell of a lot setting it up.'

'It'll all be covered,' she said. 'After he got his god-daughter back in one piece, the PM's not going to be quibbling about any budgets, not for a while at least.'

'And what's the press going to be saying?'

'The Somali government is taking the credit for the raid in Somalia. Makes them look good, suggests that they're serious about dealing with the pirate problem. The hostages were in a state of shock so they're not sure what happened.'

'And the ship?'

'British special forces saved the day. More power to the men in black overalls.'

Shepherd sipped his champagne. 'And Crazy Boy? Is he in custody?'

Button grimaced. 'That's the one fly in the ointment,' she said. 'He's vanished. His house in Ealing is empty and his close associates have all disappeared too.'

Shepherd's forehead creased into a frown. 'What? How the hell did that happen?'

'He was in his car, we had two vehicles tailing them and he gave them the slip. And he hasn't been seen since.'

'And when did this happen?'

'Forty-eight hours ago. When the hostages were rescued.'

'Do you think he knows we're on to him?'

'We're not sure,' said Button. 'It depends if he's on the run or if we've just misplaced him.'

'I know what happened. Somebody screwed up.'

'Spider, sometimes targets give their surveillance the slip. It happens. Tailing isn't an exact science. We'll pick him up again eventually. In the meantime we're shutting him down, going after his assets. We'll take everything and at the end of the day we'll put him away on conspiracy and piracy charges.'

Shepherd ran a hand through his hair. 'There's something not right about this whole scenario,' he said.

'What, exactly?'

'It just feels, I don't know, like something's not right.'

'Specifically?'

Shepherd sighed and swirled champagne around his glass. 'The ship was far bigger than any other vessels his men had taken,' he said thoughtfully. 'I told you that before I went out to Malaysia. Big ships are really difficult to board.'

'But they managed, didn't they?'

'Yes, but that's what doesn't feel right,' he said. 'The way the ship was taken wasn't the way he usually operates. Something went wrong with the ship. Some sort of computer malfunction that brought us to a stop. And that was when his men turned up. We were dead in the water so it was easy for them to get aboard.'

'So they were lucky?'

Shepherd shook his head. 'No one is that lucky, Charlie. We were in the middle of nowhere when it happened. There was no sign of any other vessel, no mother ship or anything. That means the skiffs had to have been waiting for us.'

'Sure, because they were after the *Athena*. They were tracking you.'

Shepherd sighed in exasperation. 'But how did they know that the *Athena* would break down at that particular point? If the ship hadn't stopped they wouldn't have been able to board.'

'You don't know that for sure.'

'Trust me, Charlie, a group of guys in a small boat have next to no chance of getting close to a ship the size of the *Athena*, never mind boarding her. If there hadn't been a computer problem the ship would have gone right by them.

Even if they'd given chase they'd soon have run out of fuel. And like I said, there was no mother ship close by.'

'So what are you suggesting? That the breakdown was prearranged?'

Shepherd nodded. 'Exactly.'

'How?'

Shepherd shrugged. 'I don't know for sure. We were heading along just fine and then the alarms started to go off. The alarms were saying that the engine was overheating, but according to the engineer everything was just fine. They had to stop the engine to check and that was when we were boarded. But half an hour after the pirates took over the ship we were moving again. The engine was fine and the alarms were off.'

'So someone sabotaged the ship?'

'The computer, maybe. We should get some experts on to find out what happened. Because if the computer wasn't nobbled, maybe one of the engineers was working for Crazy Boy.'

'An inside job?'

'That would explain why the ship stopped exactly where his men were waiting. But there's more, Charlie. So much of what happened didn't fit Crazy Boy's method of operating. Before the *Athena* they always seized their ships in the Arabian Sea, as they were joining or leaving the secure corridor. But they took the *Athena* well into the Gulf of Aden, almost at the Red Sea.'

'Maybe it was easier to do it that way.'

'But it wasn't, was it? If they had organised the breakdown then they could have done it off the east coast of Somalia, before they were anywhere near the secure corridor. They could have done it in their old stamping ground. Why choose a new place?'

Button threw up her hands. 'I don't know. But I don't see that it matters. How do we know what was going through their minds? They're pirates, not master criminals.'

'But Crazy Boy is smarter than the average pirate, remember? And this was all pre-planned. He chose to take the *Athena* where he did, we just don't know why he made that choice. And there's something else. Once his people had taken the ship, they headed north, to Yemen. Why didn't they go south, to Somali waters?'

'Maybe they didn't care where they went, so long as they avoided the task force.'

'But they could have gone south, couldn't they? It was another choice, to go north. To Yemen.'

'But they weren't looking to dock. They just wanted the ship out of the way while they negotiated the ransom. I think you're making a mountain out of a molehill here.'

'But then they went back to Somali waters,' Shepherd continued. 'That made no sense at all. And there's another thing. Crazy Boy went to Somalia before the ship was taken. Why? Has he done that before?'

'Not so far as we know, but he's been taking ships for years and we've only been looking at him for six months.'

'What was so important that he had to go in person?' said Shepherd. 'He went to see his uncle, right?'

'We assume so. He flew to Nairobi and then chartered a small plane to the airfield.'

'So why didn't he phone? Or use Skype like he usually did? Charlie, there's something not right about this. And the key is finding out how he stopped that ship the way he did.'

Button sipped her champagne. 'OK, I'll get that looked at. But in the grand scheme of things I really believe it's a small point, just a loose end that needs tidying up. We got the ship back, we got the pirates and we rescued the crew of the yacht with only one hostage killed, and he didn't die in the rescue.' She raised her glass to him. 'Go home, spend time with your boy. You deserve a rest.'

'And a pay rise?'

Button's smile tightened a fraction.

'I was joking, Charlie,' he said, and raised his glass to her. 'You know I don't do it for the money.'

Lisa O'Hara's heart began to race when she saw the minicab pull up outside Shepherd's house. She was parked far enough away that he wouldn't see her but she still slid down in her seat as she watched him walk towards the front door carrying a black holdall. He let himself into the house and closed the front door behind him.

It was definitely him, she didn't even have to check the photograph in her handbag. Daniel Shepherd was Matt Tanner and before long he would be dead.

She smiled to herself as she started her car and drove away. She had a call to make but she never used mobile phones so she drove to a British Telecom payphone in the centre of Hereford. The man she called was one of the Real IRA's top bombmakers. He lived in Cork, where he ran a computer repair business, and he promised to be over within twenty-four hours. O'Hara had already obtained the explosives that he would need for the construction of the device. The Semtex had arrived in Ireland in 1985, a gift from Libya in the days when Gaddafi had been an enemy of the free world, long before Tony Blair had visited the country and British companies had started making fortunes from Libyan oilfields. The Real IRA had received more than a ton of legacy weapons from the Provisionals during the time when the government was demanding that the weapons be handed in and the IRA were arguing that decommissioning was enough. The Semtex had been taken, as had Kalashnikov assault rifles, half a dozen RPGs and thousands of rounds of ammunition. The government had never called the Provisional IRA to account for the missing ordnance; all they had been concerned about was the public relations value of being able to say that the IRA had laid down its arms.

The Republicans had put the explosive to good use. It had been the main component of the 1983 bombing of the Harrods department store in London, and the Enniskillen Remembrance Day massacre that left eleven people dead, and later it was used by the Real IRA when they killed twenty-nine men, women and children in Omagh in 1998. There wasn't much left of the Semtex that Gaddafi had sent, but there was more than enough to blow Daniel Shepherd to kingdom come.

Liam was sitting at the kitchen table with his homework spread out in front of him and Katra was busy at the sink when Shepherd walked in. 'Dad!' shouted Liam, and he got up and hugged his father.

'You should have said you were coming,' said Katra. 'I'd have picked you up.'

'I didn't want to bother you,' he said.

'Everything OK?' asked Liam.

'Sure.'

'Where's your bag?' asked Katra.

'I had to leave it behind,' said Shepherd.

'On the ship?'

Shepherd nodded. 'Yeah, it was all a rush.'

'But you're home for a while?'

Shepherd sat down at the kitchen table and Katra went over to switch on the kettle. 'Yes, I hope so.'

'You work too hard,' said Katra, taking a coffee mug from the draining board.

'Yes, I do,' agreed Shepherd. 'But now I'm going to take it easy for a while.'

O'Hara brought the rental car to a halt. 'That's the house,' she said. 'See the two vehicles, the CRV and the X3?' Eleven days had passed since O'Hara had watched Shepherd return home and it had been time well spent.

The man in the passenger seat nodded. His name was Eamonn Foley and there wasn't a man in Ireland who knew more about blowing up cars. Foley's forte was small controlled explosions that would kill the driver without causing much in the way of collateral damage. One of his devices had blown the legs off a High Court judge at the height of the Troubles but left his wife and two young children unharmed by the blast. It was all a matter of using the right amount of explosive and placing the device in the correct position. There were a multitude of factors to be taken into account, including the make and model of the vehicle and the weight and size of the target.

Foley had spent days studying technical diagrams of the BMW X3 and had researched everything from the thickness of the steel used in the body shell to the weight of the chassis, and he had visited several BMW showrooms to get a feel for the real thing. The bomb that he had in the holdall at his feet was a one-off, designed and built specifically for the vehicle that Shepherd drove.

The house was in darkness. The sky was overcast and the cars were far enough away from the street lights that even if someone walked by they wouldn't be able to see anything.

'How long, do you think?' asked O'Hara.

'Ten minutes, max,' said Foley. 'I just need to link it to the ignition circuit.'

'It's always the best way,' said O'Hara. 'Fewer mistakes.'

Foley winked. 'No argument there,' he said. He reached for the door handle. 'Keep an eye on the lights,' he said. 'If you see anything, two beeps on the horn.'

Shepherd woke at just after nine o'clock. He didn't bother showering or shaving, he just rolled out of bed and pulled on his running gear and went downstairs to get his rucksack from the cupboard under the stairs.

'Dan, do you want breakfast?' called Katra from the kitchen.

'Later,' said Shepherd, sitting down and pulling on his boots. They were more than ten years old and had moulded to his feet. They were comfortable but heavy. Running in high-tech Nikes or Reeboks was all well and good, but in his experience when you really needed to run to save your life you didn't have time to change into fancy footwear.

He carried his rucksack through into the kitchen. 'I'll have a coffee, though, I could do with the caffeine kick-start,' he said.

Liam was sitting at the table, tucking into cheesy scrambled eggs and toast. 'You know what I don't get, Dad?' he asked.

'Basic algebra?' said Shepherd, dropping the rucksack on the floor and sitting down.

'Ha ha,' said Liam. He jabbed his fork at Shepherd's rucksack. 'The bricks. I don't understand why you don't use proper weights.'

'Bricks are weights,' said Shepherd. Katra made him a cup of coffee with a splash of milk and he smiled his thanks. 'Doesn't matter what the weight is, so long as it's heavy.'

Katra picked up the rucksack and grunted. 'Wow, that's heavy.' She let it fall back on to the floor. 'Doesn't it hurt?'

Shepherd shrugged. 'You get used to it,' he said.

'And it makes you run better?'

'Not better,' said Shepherd. 'But it makes you fitter.'

'You've heard about gyms, right, Dad?' Liam put a forkful of egg into his mouth and chewed noisily.

'Yes, and have you heard about eating with your mouth closed?' He sipped his coffee. 'Gyms are OK but they're boring. I want to run outside, on the street or across fields. And it's better training. Who wants to run while they watch a video or listen to their iPod?'

'Who wants to run anyway?' said Liam. 'That's why they invented cars, right?'

'You know, the more conversations I have like this, the more I'm looking forward to you being in boarding school,' said Shepherd. He put down his mug and swung his rucksack on to his back. 'OK, I'm off. What are you doing?'

'Facebook,' said Liam. 'And Farmville.'

'You should try the real world some time,' said Shepherd. 'We'll have a kickabout when I get back.'

He headed out of the front door and ran along the pavement for a mile before leaping over a five-bar gate and skirting a ploughed field. After ten minutes at half-speed he was starting to sweat and he upped the pace and ran at full pelt for a mile, then started jogging, settling into an easy pace as his breathing gradually slowed. He cut through a copse of trees, ducking under low overhanging branches, then ran at full speed again until he reached another gate that he vaulted without breaking stride. He slowed again as he headed down a road that led to a line of shops. A bookmaker's, a newsagent's and an off-licence. He stopped off at the newsagent's and bought himself a chilled bottle of Evian water, the *Mail on Sunday* and the *Sunday Times*. He drank the water and jogged the rest of the way home holding the newspapers.

Katra was loading the washing machine when Shepherd got back. He dropped his newspapers on to the kitchen table. 'I'll have that breakfast now, Katra,' he said. 'A couple of bacon sandwiches will hit the spot. I'll shower first.'

Shepherd went upstairs, showered and shaved, and changed into black jeans and a yellow polo shirt. By the time he returned to the kitchen Katra had put two bacon sandwiches and a mug of coffee on the table. He thanked her and sat down.

He pulled the *Sunday Times* towards him and flicked through the sections, discarding those that he didn't plan to read. He opened the main news section as he bit into one of the sandwiches and read through any articles that piqued his interest. The economy was limping along, the only growth industry seemed to be crime, the government was promising yet another crackdown on benefit fraud and councils were complaining that they were being swamped by immigrants. The only good news was that an unemployed single mother with three kids by three different fathers had won more than two million pounds on the National Lottery.

He turned the page and raised his eyebrows when he saw a huge photograph of the *Athena*, docking at Southampton harbour. There was also a map of the area where the ship had been seized, and photographs of Somali pirates in an inflatable. Shepherd scanned the faces but none of them were the men that he'd come across. It was probably a file picture.

On the left-hand page was a separate story on Katie Cranham under a large photograph of the girl standing with her parents in front of a rambling farmhouse in the Yorkshire dales. Katie looked much better than when Shepherd had last seen her, on the plane flying away from the Puntland airfield, but even though she was smiling at the camera Shepherd could see the sadness in her eyes. Katie's father had his hand protectively around her shoulder and her mother was holding her hand as if they both feared that she would be taken away from them again.

The feature was probably part of the pay-off for the Fleet Street editors who had held back on the story while the kidnap was in progress. Now that she was safe at home they had obviously demanded, and got, their pound of flesh. Shepherd scanned the article. Katie praised her rescuers and thanked the Somali government. There were no details of what had happened to her while she'd been held hostage other than her saying that it 'had been a horrible experience that she wanted to forget'. The prime minister had already been down to see her, and there was a quote from the man himself saying how happy he was that the situation had been resolved. Katie was planning to go to university and wanted to put the kidnap behind her. Shepherd wished her well with that, but he knew from experience that trauma wasn't so easily dismissed.

He looked back at the article on the rescue of the *Athena*.

A reporter had interviewed the captain and several crew members, and had obtained figures from the shipping industry showing the effects the ship seizures were having on freight charges through the Gulf of Aden.

It was a cuttings job, mainly, with most of the information taken from stories that had appeared previously, and the captain and crew hadn't said much other than that they were glad to be working again. When the captain was asked how he felt sailing back through the Gulf of Aden he'd told the reporter that he didn't think that lightning would strike twice.

Shepherd finished the first sandwich and took a sip of coffee. As he put his mug down his eyes settled on the photograph of the *Athena*. He frowned and then his face slowly hardened and he cursed under his breath.

'Is something wrong, Dan?' asked Katra, but he ignored her, ripped the picture out of the paper and dashed upstairs. He picked up his mobile and tapped out Charlotte Button's number. 'Where are you?' he asked the moment she answered.

'Home,' she said. 'What's wrong?'

'I need to see you in London,' he said. 'Now.'

'I'm with my daughter,' she said. 'Is it important?'

'Charlie, this is as important as it gets.'

'OK, I'll leave for the office now,' she said. 'Can you give me a clue as to what this is about?'

'Not on the phone,' he said. 'But there's a major problem with the *Athena*. I need to see the satellite photos of it when it was taken by the pirates.'

'I'll arrange it,' she said. 'You're in Hereford, right?'

'Yeah. I'll need you to arrange some transport,' he said. 'We've got to move fast.'

He ended the call and went along to Liam's bedroom.

'Sorry, I've got to go to London,' he said. 'Hopefully not for long.'

'You said we were going to play football today.'

'I know, I'm sorry, but this is important.'

'It's always important, Dad.' Liam looked away and concentrated on his iPad.

'Liam, don't be like that.'

'It's OK, Dad,' said Liam quietly. 'No big deal.'

Shepherd looked at his watch. He didn't have time to argue. He hurried back downstairs and picked up the keys for the X3. 'I don't know how long I'll be, Katra,' he said.

'Dan, you'd better take the CRV,' said Katra. 'The BMW is booked in for a service tomorrow.'

'No problem,' said Shepherd, taking the CRV keys instead. He picked up his mobile and started dialling as he hurried out to the car.

Shepherd drove the CRV to the SAS barracks and showed his MI5 identification card to a uniformed guard, who waved him through immediately, pointing towards a field where a helicopter was already warming up.

Shepherd parked his car and ran over to the helicopter. It was a Eurocopter Dauphin painted in civilian colours and with a civilian registration, but the two pilots were from 8 Flight Army Air Corps. The non-military configuration allowed the SAS to move around the country without attracting attention, and was also used to fly troops in and out of Northern Ireland during counter-terrorism operations.

'Spider!' Shepherd turned to see the Major jogging towards him in a black Adidas tracksuit.

'Thanks for arranging this, boss,' shouted Shepherd over the roar of the twin engines.

'No sweat. It'll have to be a one-way trip because we need it for an exercise tomorrow.' He clapped Shepherd on the back. 'Pity you won't tell me what's up. Never thought you'd go secret squirrel on me.'

'I'll tell you when I get back,' said Shepherd, and he climbed into the helicopter. The pilot in the left-hand seat turned around and flashed Shepherd a thumbs-up. Shepherd grinned as he recognised the man; they had flown together almost ten years earlier on a training exercise in the Brecon Beacons.

Shepherd slammed the door shut and was strapping himself in when the engine roared and the helicopter lifted off.

The flight to London took just over half an hour, the last five minutes curving along the River Thames until they reached the London Heliport, between Battersea and Wandsworth bridges.

The moment the helicopter landed Shepherd had the door open and was out on to the tarmac, bent low as the rotor wash tugged at his hair and clothes.

A blue-grey Nissan Primera was waiting for him, a black-suited driver ready with the rear passenger door open. There were two Metropolitan Police motorcycle cops in full-face helmets and fluorescent jackets, one at the front of the car and one at the back. Shepherd hurried over and showed his ID to the driver.

'We're going to Thames House, right?' asked Shepherd.

'Mrs Button wants you at Vauxhall Cross,' said the driver.

'She knows best,' said Shepherd. 'But I don't have time to sit in traffic.' He asked the cop at the rear of the car to hand over his full-face helmet, which he did reluctantly.

Shepherd jammed the helmet on his head and climbed on the pillion of the first bike. 'Let's go,' he said. The cop revved the engine and they roared off.

It took them just six minutes to get to Vauxhall House, zipping through any red lights with the siren on and the bike's lights flashing. The bike pulled up outside with its siren still going. Shepherd took off his helmet, gave it to the motorcycle cop, and ran to the main entrance. Charlotte Button was there waiting for him, dressed in a dark blue suit and a pale blue shirt. 'You made good time,' she said. 'Now do you want to tell me what's wrong?'

'Let's have a look at the satellite photographs,' said Shepherd. 'There's a chance that I'm wrong.'

'Wrong about what?'

'The clock's ticking, Charlie,' said Shepherd impatiently.

They both showed their MI5 ID cards to a blue-blazered security guard and walked through a metal detector arch manned by two more men in blazers. 'I've got us an operations room on the fourth floor,' said Button. 'And I've got a few other people there just in case we have to move quickly.'

'If I'm right, we will,' said Shepherd.

Button swiped her ID card through the sensor in the lift and it took them smoothly up to the fourth floor. As soon as the doors opened Button led Shepherd down the corridor to a room with two double doors that had been left open. Shepherd could see six men sitting down facing half a dozen large LED screens on the far wall. All the heads swivelled as Button and Shepherd walked in. Only one of the men was wearing a suit, the rest were in casual clothing, and one man in his thirties looked as if he had come straight from his garden, in a baggy green sweater with brown suede patches on the elbows, and threadbare corduroy trousers with damp stains on the knees.

'Gentlemen, apologies again for getting you all here on a Sunday but we have something of a situation. What that situation is I'm going to leave it up to Dan Shepherd to explain. Dan, over to you.'

Button stood with her back to the wall and folded her arms as Shepherd walked over to one of the female technicians and pointed at the photograph of the *Athena*, docked at Southampton. He pulled out the photograph that he'd ripped from the *Sunday Times* and gave it to the technician. 'Can you blow this up and put it on one of the big screens, and then give me one of the satellite photographs on the screen next to it?'

The technician nodded, scanned the photograph, and tapped on her keyboard. The *Sunday Times* picture filled the left-hand screen. A few seconds later there was a second picture of the *Athena*, taken from overhead, on the screen on the right.

'OK, so on the left is the *Athena* docking at Southampton,' said Shepherd. 'On the right is the ship at sea, just after it was taken by the pirates.'

Button looked at both screens and shrugged. 'I don't see it,' she said.

The men in the room were all frowning as they studied the two images. Then one of them, a grey-haired man in his fifties wearing a suit with a red and yellow MCC tie, put his hand up to his face. 'Good Lord,' he said. 'Why didn't we spot it before?'

'Will somebody put me out of my misery?' said Button. 'What am I not seeing?'

Shepherd walked over to the screens and pointed at the rear of the ship coming into dock. He ran his finger along the first line of containers on the top level. He pointed at them one by one. 'Green, red, white, white, blue, green, red, white, red, green,' he said. 'Ten.'

He walked over to the second screen, to the satellite picture of the *Athena* at sea. He pointed at the containers in the front row, one at time. 'Green, red, white, white, blue, green, red, white, red,' he said. 'Nine.'

'There's an extra container,' said Button. 'When the ship docked at Southampton, there was an extra container on board.'

'This green one, here,' said Shepherd, going back to the first screen and pointing at a container on the starboard side. 'I heard a helicopter one night after the pirates boarded. Twin rotors. Probably a Chinook.'

'The helicopter took a container to the ship? From Yemen?' Button frowned. 'Is that possible?'

Shepherd tapped the green container on the screen. 'This wasn't here before we were boarded,' he said.

'The *Athena* stopped at Jeddah, remember? On the way to the Mediterranean.'

'Only to drop cargo off,' said Shepherd. 'They weren't due to take on cargo there. I saw the manifest on the bridge. They unloaded thirty-two containers at Jeddah. They weren't due to take on any. And Jeddah was the only port it stopped at between being released and arriving at Southampton. That container could only have been put on board while we were at sea.'

'That would explain why they took the ship closer to land,' said the man in the MCC tie.

'So what are we thinking here?' said a young man with pointed sideburns and rectangular designer glasses. 'Drugs? Weapons?'

Button shook her head. 'No one's going to go to all that trouble over contraband,' she said.

'A container full of heroin would be worth hundreds of millions on the street,' said the man.

'Crazy Boy isn't geared up for a drugs deal of that size,' said Button. 'But he is chummy with al-Qaeda.'

The man's jaw dropped. 'You're thinking . . .' He ran his hand through his hair. 'You're thinking a bomb?'

'That's exactly what I'm thinking,' said Button. 'But let's not get ahead of ourselves. I trust Spider's trick memory, of course, but let's get some details of that container and check that it wasn't moved during the unloading at Jeddah. We need to contact the ship for a look at their manifest, and see if the people at Southampton can get us some sort of ID on that container.'

Crazy Boy switched on the left indicator and moved over to the inside lane, preparing to leave the motorway. 'Why aren't we going straight to London?' asked Two Knives. He had a bag of khat on his lap and he spoke through a mouthful of leaves.

'The Arab said it has to be checked first. There's no point if it doesn't go off. Everything will have been wasted.' He reached over and helped himself to a handful of khat. 'Don't worry, we won't be staying long.'

The two men had port IDs clipped to their overalls. The

IDs and the truck had been supplied by al-Zahrani, along with the necessary paperwork to collect the container from the *Athena*. The container had been one of the first to be unloaded and Crazy Boy was sure that hadn't been a coincidence. Al-Zahrani seemed to have planned everything to perfection.

A surveillance video flashed up on to one of the monitors. Button walked over to it and pointed at a truck driving out of Southampton Container Terminal. On the back of the truck was a dark green container. 'There it is,' she said.

The operator looped the video so that it replayed several times.

'Right,' said Button, standing up. 'We have now received confirmation that the green container at the stern was not on the ship when it left Port Klang in Malaysia. It was also not loaded at Karachi or Jeddah, but was on board when the *Athena* arrived at Southampton. We can only assume that it was taken to the ship by helicopter while the *Athena* was under the control of the pirates. The question is, where is it now?'

'GPS?' said one of the technicians. 'A lot of containers have GPS so they can be tracked by their owners.'

Button shook her head. 'The registration number of the container doesn't match any on record so we can't trace its owner. It doesn't exist officially.'

She nodded at the technician and a close-up still shot of the truck's number plate appeared on another screen. 'We have the registration number of the truck and again it's a ringer. The vehicle belonging to that plate is on the Continent as we speak. But at least we have something to go on. We're currently running the number through every

CCTV database we've got and every police force in the country is on the lookout for it.'

There was a knock on the door and a man in his sixties with slicked-back grey hair and wearing a tweed suit appeared. 'Dr Wilson,' he said. Button nodded at him. 'Dr Wilson sits on the London Fire and Emergency Planning Authority and is something of an expert on nuclear- and radiation-based incidents,' she said by way of introduction. 'I thought we might all benefit from a quick rundown on what we might be facing here.'

She thanked Dr Wilson for coming at such short notice and waved for him to take a seat. He sat down, took out a pair of steel-framed spectacles, and began polishing them with a large white handkerchief. He nodded and smiled at everyone in the room, as if making sure that he had their undivided attention. 'So, I gather that we might have an issue with a dirty bomb somewhere in the country,' he said. He had a faint West Country accent. 'The first thing to bear in mind is that in terms of immediate loss of life, a dirty bomb is not especially dangerous. We tend to refer to them as weapons of mass disruption.' He chuckled at his own joke but stopped when he realised that no one was smiling. He put his glasses on and linked his fingers on the table. 'What we're talking about is a radioactive source that is dispersed into the environment, probably by means of a small explosion. The purpose of the explosion isn't to kill but to spread the radioactivity across as wide an area as possible. It is a completely different animal to an atomic bomb.' He looked over the top of his glasses at Button. 'You are certain that we are not talking about a nuclear device?'

'There are no nuclear devices unaccounted for that we

know about, and if there were we'd have picked up intelligence chatter,' said Button. 'But we have heard whispers about several groups who are interested in putting together low-tech dirty bombs.'

'That's exactly what they are, low-tech,' said Dr Wilson. 'Basically all you need is an explosive, which could be as basic as dynamite. And a source of radioactivity, which could be something as simple as hospital waste or components from smoke detectors. If such a device were to be detonated in, say, Trafalgar Square, the initial explosion would cause very little damage and perhaps no loss of life.' He paused for effect. 'But the damage it would cause to the economy would run into billions. Literally billions.'

'And loss of life?' asked one of the technicians.

'Short-term there would be no immediate deaths caused by the radioactivity,' he said. 'There wouldn't be enough exposure to cause radiation sickness. I doubt that anyone would show any symptoms of any kind. We're not talking Chernobyl. What we would see over the decades following the explosion is a slight increase in cancer deaths. More leukaemia among children, more lung cancer and bowel cancer deaths among adults. The increase might only be of the order of a few per cent but considering the millions of people who live in London and who would be exposed to the radioactivity, it would mean hundreds, possibly thousands, of premature deaths.'

He sat back to let his words sink in. 'But it's not the deaths that would do the damage to the country. It's the terror that such an incident would cause. Who would choose to visit London? Or do business there? Can you imagine what would happen to property values?'

'But the radioactivity can be dealt with?' asked Button.

'Of course,' said Dr Wilson. 'In fact the first time there was a heavy rain shower most of it would be washed away. If there were no rain, a comprehensive washing of roads and buildings would deal with most of the radioactivity. Citizens would be advised to avoid any food or liquids that might have been exposed to radioactive dust but other than that there'd be no other precautions needed. But it isn't the true risk that matters, it's the perception that counts. Most of the indigenous population would have no choice other than to stay, but who would visit the site of a dirty bomb by choice? We've run numbers on this and we calculate that a dirty bomb in any average-sized city in the country would result in a £20 billion loss in GDP over five years. Quadruple that if it went off in central London. So for any terror group it's a pretty good return for an investment of a few thousand pounds.'

One of the technicians went over to Button and whispered in her ear. She stood up. 'If I can just interrupt you, Dr Wilson, there's something we need to see. We've managed to work on an image of the truck leaving the port.' She nodded at the technician. 'On the main screen, please.'

The picture of the *Athena* disappeared from the monitor and was replaced by a computer-enhanced image taken from the CCTV camera at the exit to Southampton Container Terminal. It showed the cab of a truck and the two figures in the driving seat and passenger seat were clearly visible. Young black men wearing baseball caps.

'That's Crazy Boy and his sidekick,' said Shepherd.

'Isn't it just,' said Button.

Crazy Boy reached into the bag of khat leaves, took out a handful and popped them one at a time into his mouth.

He held out the bag to Two Knives, and he helped himself. They were sitting on folding chairs at a wooden table in an industrial unit outside Basingstoke, thirty miles to the west of central London. There were two Smith & Wesson revolvers on the table in front of them. The doors of the container were open and two Pakistani men were inside wearing radiation suits and helmets. They were connecting detonators to the tops of aluminium barrels. Two Knives pointed at the container. 'If they're wearing suits, why aren't we?'

'It's only dangerous close up,' said Crazy Boy.

'That's what the Arab said, right?'

'We're only driving the truck for a few hours and the radiation is sealed in the metal barrels.'

'But you can't believe anything Arabs say,' said Two Knives.

'We'll be done soon,' said Crazy Boy. 'Once they've finished we drive it to the Olympic site and our work is done.'

'Who'll be detonating it?' said Two Knives.

'Someone else, it doesn't matter who,' said Crazy Boy.

'And after we're done, what are you going to do?'

Crazy Boy shrugged. 'Go back to Somalia,' he said. 'I have no choice. They'll take everything from me here.'

'They can't force you to leave,' said Two Knives. 'You're British.'

'But they can put me in prison,' said Crazy Boy. 'They can take away everything I have.' He slotted more leaves into his mouth and chewed as he watched the two men in the container. 'Whatever you do, you shouldn't stay in London,' he said. 'Go north, at least fifty miles.'

'You said there wouldn't be an explosion.'

'There will be a small explosion, but the wind will carry the radiation for many miles.'

'I will come with you, brother,' said Two Knives.

Crazy Boy grinned and pulled two airline tickets from his back pocket. 'I had assumed that you would.' He patted Two Knives on the back. 'It will be like the old days,' he said. 'Taking ships and making the infidels pay. And out in Somalia no one can touch us. We will be kings again.'

Two Knives nodded and helped himself to more khat.

'It'll be good to get back,' said Crazy Boy. 'England was making me soft. I know that now. I'll never be soft again.'

Shepherd put down a cup of tea in front of Button and she smiled her thanks. He sat down opposite her and sipped his coffee. CCTV images from around the country were flashing across the monitors as technicians worked away on their computers.

'I didn't realise that you could do this,' said Shepherd, gesturing at the screens. 'Use automatic number plate recognition on CCTV feeds from anywhere in the U.K.'

'Since 2006,' said Button. 'We have feeds from the motorways, main roads, all the council systems, the ring of steel around the City, down to petrol station forecourts. And we've got feeds from mobile police CCTV units. All the feeds are run through the National ANPR Data Centre at Hendon.'

Shepherd nodded. Hendon in north London was the site of the Police National Computer. 'That must be thousands of cameras,' he said.

'And every single one can be scanned for a specific plate,' said Button. 'The computer stores fifty million records a year. And we have total access.' She smiled. 'It really is Big Brother, actually. The government can cross-reference registration numbers with MoT test certificates and insurance companies and flag any vehicle that shouldn't be on the road. Not that MI5 does that, of course.'

'Not yet, anyway,' said Shepherd.

'The point is, Spider, police forces around the country and our good selves have instant real-time access to every single camera with the ability to pick out a single specific vehicle.'

Shepherd gestured at the technicians. 'So why aren't they pulling out any needles from the haystacks?'

'It takes time,' said Button.

'How long is this information stored for?'

'Five years,' said Button.

'Do you mean that you can track everywhere a vehicle has been over the past five years?'

'Not exactly everywhere because there are still places in the United Kingdom that don't have CCTV coverage,' she said. 'But certainly we can see what major roads they have been on.'

Shepherd sipped his coffee. 'You know where this is going, don't you?'

Button shook her head. 'Tell me.'

'They'll be tying this data to facial recognition systems and then you'll be able to follow every single person, no matter where they are.'

Button nodded slowly. 'You're probably right,' she said.

Shepherd opened his mouth to speak but he was interrupted by a female technician. 'I've got a hit!' she said excitedly. 'On the M3 outside Southampton.'

'On the screen, please, Daisy,' said Button.

The technician's fingers played across her keyboard and a view from a motorway CCTV camera filled the screen.

Among the traffic was the truck and its container. 'Freeze and zoom, please.'

The image zoomed in on the truck and they could clearly see the two black men in the cab.

At the bottom of the screen was a time code. It was three hours after the *Athena* had docked.

'Right, that's a start,' said Button. 'Let's concentrate on the M3. Where is that exactly?'

'Five miles from the city, heading north,' said the technician.

'Right, let's focus our search on the M3, and of course I don't have to point out that the M3 heads straight to the M25, which circles London.'

It was a relatively simple circuit but the two men wanted to be absolutely certain that it would work so they checked and rechecked it before activating it. The bomb had been well constructed by experts – Russian technicians who had been well paid for their work. They had put the bomb together in a disused factory on the outskirts of the seaport city of Aden using radioactive waste that had been obtained from a group of Chechen rebels. The Russians had designed and built the detonating circuit but had kept the individual components separate to be assembled when the container was close to its target.

The radioactive material was sealed in aluminium barrels and they had used a Geiger counter to check that the radiation levels in the container were not dangerous, so long as they wore their government-approved radiation suits and helmets.

Both men had been born in Scotland and attended university there, but when they spoke they spoke in Urdu because they did not want the two Somalis to understand them. 'It's done,' said the elder of the two. His name was Gadi Hussain and he had a degree in chemical engineering from Edinburgh's Heriot-Watt University. That was where he had met the second man, Chishti Akram, who was studying electrical engineering. They had joined the university's Muslim Society and after graduating had spent three months together in an al-Qaeda training camp in northern Pakistan.

Akram looked over his shoulder at the two Somalis who were sitting at a wooden table, eating leaves from a polythene bag.

'What is it with the leaves they chew?' he asked.

'That's khat. It's a stimulant.'

'And it's allowed? They are Muslims, right?'

Hussain chuckled. 'They are Muslims but they are Africans. They don't know any better.'

'But they are shahids. They must go to meet God in a state of purity and cleanliness, surely.'

Hussain lowered his voice, even though he knew that the two Somalis could not understand Urdu. 'They do not know, brother. They think that the bomb is going to be detonated by a mobile phone. They do not know that it is on a timer.'

'And they will die without knowing?'

'Inshallah,' said Hussain.

'Because they cannot be trusted?'

'They are Africans, brother. Who can trust an African? You have to count your fingers every time you shake hands with them.'

He turned and flashed Crazy Boy a beaming smile. 'We are ready,' he said. 'Everything is done. Help us close the doors.'

* * *

Charlotte Button paced up and down behind the technicians. On the screens on the wall behind her were six CCTV feeds showing the progress of the truck along the M3. One of the screens showed the truck leaving the M3 at the Basingstoke turn-off and since then there had been no sightings.

'Come on, everyone, let's find it,' she said, even though she knew they were working flat out and that the lack of success wasn't for want of trying. She rubbed her hands together and looked across at Shepherd. 'At least Basingstoke probably isn't the target.'

'You don't know that,' said Shepherd. 'You heard what Dr Wilson said, a dirty bomb anywhere in the country brings the economy grinding to a halt. And London is always going to be a harder target because . . .'

He was interrupted by one of the male technicians, who raised his hand. 'I have a hit,' he said. 'Camberley, thirty minutes ago.'

'Heading north?'

The technician nodded and put the recording on to one of the large monitors. The truck was in the inside lane, hemmed in by heavy traffic.

'They must have stopped off in Basingstoke and started their journey again,' said Button. She went over to a large-scale map of the country, tapped the M3 and ran her finger along it to the M25. 'They're probably on the M25 already,' she said. 'I need a live feed and I need it now, please.'

Liam was lying on the sofa watching an episode of *Two and a Half Men* on the television when Katra popped her head around the door. 'Are you OK?' she asked.

'Fine.'

'Homework all done?'

'Sure,' he replied, his eyes never leaving the screen.

'Do you want to go and play football?'

'With you?'

Katra grinned. 'What, scared to play a girl?'

'It's not that,' said Liam.

'You need some exercise,' said Katra. 'It's not good to lie around all day.'

Liam pulled a face.

'OK, what about going shopping? We can go to the Maylord Centre.'

'I don't need to buy anything.'

'We could get a game for your PlayStation.'

'Nah, there's nothing I want.'

'What about a movie?'

Liam sat up. 'Yeah, OK. What's on?'

'I don't know. We'll take pot luck. We'll go to the cinema and see what they've got. It's been ages since we've been.'

'Cool,' said Liam, using the remote to switch off the television.

Katra picked up the keys to the X3 and waited for Liam to get his jacket. They walked together to the BMW. 'Why did Dad take the CRV?' asked Liam.

'The BMW needs a service,' said Katra. She pressed the fob to unlock the doors.

'What do you think of the X6?' he asked.

'X6? What is that?'

Liam looked at her in disbelief. 'You don't know about the BMW X6? It's the coolest car.' He opened the passenger door and climbed in.

'I think this car is pretty cool,' said Katra, getting into

the driving seat. She put the key in the ignition. 'Fasten your seat belt,' she said.

One of the technicians jumped to her feet. 'I have a live feed!' she shouted. 'I've found it!' Everyone in the room turned to look at her. She was a Chinese girl in jeans and a baggy sweater that seemed several sizes too big for her. Her cheeks were flushed with excitement and her head was bobbing back and forth as she stared at her monitor.

'Where?' said Button, hurrying over to her.

'M25 heading east, between Junctions Eleven and Ten.'

'Patch it on to the main screen.'

The technician sat down, tapped on her keyboard and the CCTV image filled one of the monitors on the wall. The truck was moving slowly, hemmed in by traffic.

'Thank goodness for weekend roadworks,' said Button. 'OK, we have to take care of this before they reach London.'

'What do you have in mind?' asked Shepherd.

'The Increment,' said Button. 'We can't afford to take any chances with whatever they've got in that container.'

'You don't know how they're going to trigger it, Charlie,' said Shepherd. 'If the Increment goes in they might panic and detonate.'

'You think it might be a suicide bomb?' asked Button.

'If Crazy Boy is on the run he might think he's got nothing to lose,' said Shepherd. 'But suicide bomb or not, I'm not sure that the Increment is the way to go. Too many cooks.'

'How do you think we should handle it?'

Shepherd grinned. 'I thought you'd never ask.'

⋆　⋆　⋆

Two Knives swung his feet up on to the dashboard and stared at the slow-moving traffic ahead of them. 'It's Sunday, where are all these people going?' he asked.

'It's a sunny day so people want to go out,' said Crazy Boy.

'But go where? To sit in traffic with thousands of other people? The British are crazy. Maybe we should leave the motorway. We can drive up to London on the smaller roads.'

'We're safer here,' said Crazy Boy. 'Less chance of an accident, less chance of anything happening.' He pointed up ahead. 'And look, the traffic's starting to move.'

He reached over and took another handful of khat leaves. As he chewed a CCTV camera stared impassively down at them.

There were three police motorcyclists parked in front of MI6's headquarters, their engines running. Button handed Shepherd his motorcycle helmet. He had changed into a regular Metropolitan Police uniform and a yellow fluorescent jacket and had a Glock in a nylon underarm holster. 'Good luck,' she said.

Shepherd grinned. 'At least you're not telling me to be careful,' he said. He had a radio transceiver fixed to his belt and he fitted the earpiece before he put on the helmet. 'Just make sure that the cops are close to the truck, but not too close to be seen. And tell the Increment to hang well back.' He clipped the microphone to the collar of his fluorescent jacket.

'Will do,' she said. 'We'll keep tabs on the truck here. If they leave the M25 we'll tell you but otherwise we'll assume that you'll intercept them around about Junction Five, providing that they stay on and head north. But if they leave at the M26 you'll still be able to get them.'

'Got it,' said Shepherd.

'If they leave the M25 earlier and cut north into central London we'll let you know and you can do what you have to do.'

'Charlie, it'll be fine,' said Shepherd. Button nodded and Shepherd climbed on to the pillion of the second bike. He tapped the driver on the shoulder. 'Let's go,' he said.

The three bikes sped away, heading south. The three riders were experienced and they cut through the traffic like sharks through a shoal of fish. They had a well-practised technique for getting through red lights. The lead bike would hold up the traffic that had the right of way while the bike with Shepherd sped through, then the third bike would move to the front ready to deal with the next set of lights. The riders were so efficient that at no point did Shepherd's bike drop below thirty miles an hour, and for most of the time they were travelling well above the legal speed limits, sirens wailing and lights flashing.

They were soon driving through Bromley, and the traffic was lighter so they picked up speed.

'Spider, they've just passed Junction Seven,' said Button. 'We're looking at you on the map and I don't see that Junction Six is going to work so we'll stick with the original plan and get you on at Junction Five.'

'Roger that,' said Shepherd.

'We have two traffic cars behind the truck, one has eyeball on the vehicle and they're expecting you,' said Button.

The three bikes sped south along the A21 and then turned on to the A224. As they approached Junction 5 Shepherd called up Button. 'Just about to join the M25,' he said. 'Where are they?'

'Five minutes away,' she said. 'The traffic is thinner now and they're moving at about thirty miles per hour. Best you hang back and we'll see what they do.'

The riders were all tuned in to Button's frequency and they pulled in to the side of the road. Five minutes later she came back to say that the truck had passed Junction 5 and was still on the M25.

Shepherd's rider nodded at his two companions. From now on they would be travelling alone and without sirens and lights. The single bike sped off down the approach ramp and joined the motorway traffic. They kept on the hard shoulder until Shepherd saw the traffic car ahead of them. The rider had also seen the police car and he accelerated to bring them alongside. There were two officers in the vehicle. The passenger looked across at them and Shepherd motioned for them to pull in on the hard shoulder.

As soon as the car had stopped Shepherd handed his helmet to the rider and climbed off. He flashed the rider a thumbs-up and got into the back of the patrol car. 'Hi, guys,' he said. He pointed ahead. 'Follow that truck.'

The car edged into the traffic again, and then moved smoothly into the middle lane. Shepherd took out the Glock and checked the action. 'I'm Dan,' he said.

'Alistair,' said the driver. He was grey-haired and in his early fifties, probably close to retirement. 'Pleasure to have you on board.' He seemed totally unfazed by what was going on.

'Brian,' said the officer in the front passenger seat. 'What's going on?' He twisted around in his seat and his eyes widened when he saw the gun. He was in his early twenties with a rash of old acne scars across both cheeks.

'Nobody told you?' said Shepherd, putting the gun back in his holster.

'We were just told to keep an eye on that truck ahead, the one with the green container, and that somebody would be joining us,' said Alistair. He looked at Shepherd in the rear-view mirror. 'Someone from the Home Office, they said, which covers a multitude of sins.'

'We need to stop the truck and get the two men out with as little fuss as possible,' said Shepherd.

'That explains the Glock, then,' said the driver, with only the slightest trace of irony in his voice.

'We're going to make it seem like a regular traffic stop,' said Shepherd. 'Softly, softly, and I'll approach them on my own.'

'What do you need us to do?' asked the younger cop.

'Absolutely nothing,' said Shepherd.

Crazy Boy put his foot down on the accelerator and the speedometer needle pushed above fifty miles an hour. Two Knives held out the bag of khat and Crazy Boy took a handful of leaves. He was just about to put them in his mouth when a blue light flashed behind the truck and he heard the blip of a siren. Both men looked in their side mirrors.

'Cops,' said Two Knives.

The siren blipped again. The police car was directly behind them so there was no doubt that it was the truck that they were signalling to stop.

'I'm going to have to pull over,' said Crazy Boy.

'What do they want?'

'How the hell do I know what they want?' said Crazy Boy. 'We weren't speeding. Maybe it's a random stop.'

'Do they do that?'

'Who the hell knows?' said Crazy Boy. 'Maybe there's something loose at the back. Just stay cool, we'll be fine.'

Two Knives peered at the car in the mirror. 'It's a regular traffic car,' he said.

'Hide the khat,' said Crazy Boy as he slowed the truck and indicated that he was pulling in.

'Khat's legal in England,' said Two Knives.

'Just do it,' said Crazy Boy. 'Let's not give them any excuse.'

He pulled on to the hard shoulder as Two Knives shoved the bag under his seat. Crazy Boy watched in his side mirror as the rear door of the police car opened and a cop in a fluorescent jacket climbed out. The cop carefully put on his peaked hat and then walked towards the truck holding a clipboard.

'Get the guns ready, just in case,' said Crazy Boy.

'You think we've got trouble?'

'Let's see what he wants. But give me my gun.'

Two Knives opened the glove compartment and took out two Smith & Wesson revolvers. He gave one to Crazy Boy and held the other one down at his side in his left hand.

The cop walked up to Crazy Boy's window and motioned for him to wind it down. Crazy Boy did as he was told. 'Yes, officer, is there a problem?' He kept his gun down at the side of the door, his finger on the trigger.

Everyone in the room was looking up at the main screen, which was showing a live feed from a CCTV camera on the M25. They were looking at the truck from the rear, and even on full zoom they couldn't make out much detail. They could see the truck and the police car behind it, its lights still flashing. And they could see a figure in a fluorescent jacket standing next to the cab of the truck, holding a clipboard.

Button was fingering the thin gold chain around her neck. 'Please be careful, Spider,' she whispered.

Shepherd looked up at Crazy Boy. 'I need you to both step out of the vehicle, please, sir,' he said, keeping his voice flat and emotionless as if he was just a bored traffic cop doing his job.

'What's wrong?' asked Crazy Boy.

'I just need you at the rear of the vehicle. And your passenger. And bring with you any paperwork you have plus your driving licence and insurance.'

'We weren't speeding,' said Crazy Boy.

'Please, sir, if you would just get out of the cab we'll get this sorted and get you and your load on your way.'

'Get what sorted?' asked Crazy Boy.

Shepherd kept his face impassive and his tone neutral, concealing the growing tension that he was feeling. 'We just have to check your tyre pressures, sir, they appear to be a little deflated.'

'The tyres?' he said. 'This is about the tyres?' He spoke in Somali to Two Knives and both men laughed.

Shepherd stood to the side and Crazy Boy opened the cab door and climbed out. Shepherd couldn't see any sign of a weapon. 'And the passenger too,' he said.

He walked with Crazy Boy to the rear of the truck. Drivers were braking to see what was going on. Shepherd walked Crazy Boy around the back of the truck and on to the grass verge so that the vehicle was blocking the view of the passing traffic.

'Please stay where you are, sir,' said Shepherd, and he walked up to the passenger side. 'Can you get out, please. I need to see you at the rear of the vehicle.'

Shepherd reached for the door handle and pulled open the door. He caught a glimpse of a revolver and stepped back, dropping his clipboard and reaching inside his fluorescent jacket. He heard Crazy Boy shout something but all Shepherd's attention was focused on the man in the cab and the gun in his hand. He grabbed the butt of the Glock and pulled it out and fired twice just as Two Knives was swinging his weapon up. Both rounds caught Two Knives in the neck, just under the chin, and he fell back as blood sprayed across the dashboard.

Shepherd turned just in time to see Crazy Boy reaching inside his overalls. 'Stay where you are!' screamed Shepherd. 'Let me see your hands!'

Crazy Boy stared at Shepherd with undisguised hatred, froze for a fraction of a second, and then started to pull out a gun. Shepherd shot him twice in the chest and Crazy Boy fell back on to the grass, shuddered once and lay still.

Shepherd took a deep breath, then holstered his gun. He walked back to the police car. Traffic was continuing to drive by; the truck had shielded the killings from view and he doubted that anyone had seen what had happened.

As he reached the car his mobile phone rang. It was Major Gannon. 'Can you talk?'

Shepherd walked away from the car. 'Sure.'

'You done there with your secret squirrel stuff?'

'All taken care of,' said Shepherd. 'I'll fill you in when I get back.'

'I'd rather that was sooner than later,' said the Major.

'Is something wrong?'

'I need to see you in Hereford, now.'

'What's happened?'

'It needs a face-to-face, Spider. I'm sending a chopper.'

'I'm miles away from Battersea,' said Shepherd. 'On the M25.'

'I know exactly where you are,' said the Major. 'I took the liberty of using your GPS. The chopper's on its way to you.'

Shepherd heard the whop-whop-whop of a helicopter in the distance. He squinted up at the sky. It was a Eurocopter Dauphin. 'It's here,' said Shepherd.

'See you soon, then.' The line went dead.

'Spider, are you OK?' asked Button in his ear. Shepherd removed the earpiece and the radio and gave them to the driver of the traffic car, along with his fluorescent jacket, then he walked over to the field adjacent to the hard shoulder to wait for the helicopter.

The Dauphin did a slow circle around the Stirling Lines camp and then came in to land a short distance from a bright orange windsock that was hanging limply from a pole. Shepherd jogged away from the helicopter, bending low as the rotor continued to turn above his head.

The Major walked over from the main administration building. He was wearing a dark green T-shirt and camou-flage pants, his face set like stone. He was holding a manila envelope. 'What's happened, boss?' asked Shepherd.

'She put a bomb under your car, Spider. Lisa O'Hara. Tried to blow you to bits.'

'Liam – is he OK? Katra?'

'They're OK, Spider. I wasn't about to let anything happen to them.' He jerked a thumb towards the assault course. 'I've brought them here until we work out what you want to do.'

Shepherd felt relief wash over him. 'A bomb?'

'Nice little number, Semtex, with a detonator wired into the ignition system.' The Major gave the envelope to Shepherd. Inside were several surveillance photographs showing a man in his forties approaching Shepherd's car, lying under it, and then returning to a parked car, where a woman was in the driving seat. 'The bombmaker's name is Eamonn Foley, he's back in Cork now. The woman's the one I told you about. Lisa O'Hara. The bomb under your car is the twin of the one they put under my Jag.'

'When was this, boss?'

'Late last night. Two o'clock in the morning, to be precise.'

'Then why the hell didn't you tell me when you saw me this morning?'

'I didn't know. I'd put four of our counter-terrorism guys watching your house. Two of them followed the car and the other two removed the device. I wasn't informed until after you'd flown to London.'

'You've had people watching my house?'

'It had to be done, once I knew that O'Hara was interested in you.'

'I never saw them.'

The Major grinned. 'They're professionals, Spider. There would have been something very wrong if they had stood out.'

Shepherd nodded. 'Now what?'

'Now I know who the bombmaker is, I'll take care of it.'

'And the woman?'

'That's what I wanted to talk to you about.' He put his arm around Shepherd's shoulder. 'Come and say hi to Liam. He's a demon on the overhead bars.'

Shepherd heard the click of a key being inserted into a lock and then the front door opened. He stayed where he was, sitting in the chair behind the door. There was no way that she would be able to see him until she was in the room and by then it would be too late for her to do anything. He doubted that she would be carrying a gun, and even if she was there would be no time for her to pull it out. He looked down at the Glock in his hand. The Major had given him the gun. It had come direct from the manufacturers and had only been fired on one occasion, during testing at the indoor range, and once Shepherd had done what he had to do it would be disassembled and destroyed.

He was wearing dark clothes and black leather gloves and was sitting in the dark. He had been in the room for six hours without moving.

He heard footsteps walking down the hallway to the kitchen and then the sound of bags of shopping being placed on the counter followed by the click of an electric kettle being switched on. More footsteps back into the hall and then the rustle of a coat being removed. Then the door was pushed open and she walked into the room. She was wearing a knee-length black skirt, a pale blue shirt and a dark blue jacket, and looked more like a bank cashier than a Republican enforcer with

blood on her hands. 'Shit,' she said. She was about to take a
step back to the door when she saw the gun in his hand.

Shepherd waved the Glock at the sofa by the fireplace.
'Sit down,' he said.

She did as she was told. He could see her looking around
for something to use as a weapon, which told him that she
wasn't carrying a gun. It didn't matter either way; now that
she was sitting she wouldn't have time to do anything.

'Cross your legs at the ankles,' he said.

She obeyed him.

'It wasn't personal,' she said.

'I'm not sure that's true.'

'You attacked us. You killed two of our people. I'm sure
you'd say that wasn't personal either.' Her voice was calm
and measured with hardly any trace of the stress that she
was under. Shepherd knew that her adrenal glands would
have gone into overdrive and that she'd be geared up for
flight or fight, but that wasn't going to happen. And with
her legs crossed she wouldn't be able to spring at him.

'OK if I smoke?'

'Where are your cigarettes?'

'Right-hand jacket pocket.'

'Knock yourself out,' said Shepherd. 'But move very
slowly and if you pull out anything that looks remotely like
a weapon you're dead.'

She nodded and slowly took out a packet of Rothmans.
'I've a lighter in my pocket, too. Gold.'

'Gold?'

'Gold plated. It was a gift from my father.'

'Take it out nice and slowly,' said Shepherd. 'No sudden
movements.'

O'Hara took the lighter out, flashed him a tight smile, and then lit a cigarette. She put the lighter back in her pocket and blew smoke at the ceiling, her green eyes fixed on Shepherd.

'You attacked my family,' said Shepherd. 'That's as personal as it gets.'

'I'm a soldier in the Real IRA,' she said flatly. 'We're at war with the occupying forces, of which you form a part.'

'You attacked my son and my au pair. You put a bomb in my car knowing that they would use it.'

'Thousands of Irish citizens have been killed in the fight for independence,' she said. She took another pull on her cigarette and held the smoke deep in her lungs.

'My son has nothing to do with any of this, but you made him a target,' said Shepherd. There was no anger in his voice, he was simply stating a fact.

'You drove the X3. It was your car. The au pair used the Honda and we left that alone. We put the bomb in the X3 and didn't go near the Honda.'

'And I'm supposed to be grateful for that?'

'I'm just telling you the facts. You're making it sound as if I was deliberately trying to kill your son, and that's not what happened. I can understand why you want to believe that.'

'Why's that?'

'Because it makes it easier for you to do what you've come here to do. It gives you the moral high ground.'

'And you think I need that?'

'I do what I do because I believe in what I'm doing. I believe in a united Ireland. I believe that Britain is an occupying power that has no right to be in my country and I will do whatever is necessary to drive them out. I have a cause, and I believe in that cause. But you, Shepherd, why do you do what you do? Why did you kill those two men in Belfast? For four thousand pounds a month plus expenses.'

'A bit more, actually.'

'But you're a hired gun. You killed for money. Same as all the bastard soldiers and cops who work for the British. So which of us really has the moral high ground?' She blew smoke, then leaned over to an ashtray and stubbed out what was left of her cigarette. 'There's no point in continuing this conversation,' she said. 'Just arrest me and have done with it.'

'MI5 don't have powers of arrest,' said Shepherd. 'I thought you'd have known that.'

'Fine,' she said. 'What's the worst you can do to me? I'll spend a few years as a political prisoner and then the negotiations will start and eventually I'll be released. I might even be an MP one day. Join Martin and Gerry on the House of Commons gravy train. Now wouldn't that be a fine thing?'

Shepherd said nothing but continued to stare at her, his eyes as hard as granite.

'And the black looks don't scare me, Shepherd. Just call the cops and have done with it.'

'It's not as simple as that,' said Shepherd. He reached into his jacket pocket and took out a black cylindrical suppressor, a professional job that bore little resemblance to the one that Tomasz had built in the *Athena*'s workshop but which was several times more efficient. Any shot, even in the confined space, would sound no louder than a muffled thud. He screwed it into the barrel of the Glock, then pulled the trigger and shot her in the chest, just below the heart. She gasped, put a hand up to the wound, which was pulsing with blood, then raised it to her face and stared in disbelief at the bloody palm. Then she sighed and fell sideways.

Shepherd stood up and went over to her. Bloody froth appeared at her lips and her eyes widened in panic. Her mouth began to move but no sound came out, just froth, redder and more liquid with each movement of her lips.

She was seconds away from dying, she knew it and Shepherd knew it. But it wasn't about time, it was about certainty, about making sure, so Shepherd shot her again, once in the heart and finally between her disbelieving green eyes.

The Major was waiting for him outside.

'It's done,' said Shepherd, climbing into the car.

'It needed to be done,' said the Major.

Shepherd nodded. 'Thank you. Thanks for everything, yeah? For saving Liam and Katra, and for . . .' He left the sentence unfinished.

'No need for thanks, Spider. We're beyond that.'

Shepherd took a deep breath and exhaled slowly. He felt different, but he wasn't sure in what way he'd changed. He'd crossed a line, he knew that, but it was a line that needed to be crossed. 'She deserved it,' he said.

'Bloody right she did,' said the Major. 'Don't give her another thought.' He put the car in gear and drove away from the kerb. 'She was fair game.'

Shepherd nodded, but he knew it wouldn't be that easy. He'd shot a woman in the heart and the head, a woman who had been no immediate threat to him. He wasn't particularly worried about what he'd done, or what the repercussions might be. What worried him most was that he didn't feel in the least bit guilty about killing her and he knew that his life would never be the same.

If you enjoyed *Fair Game* then we think you'll like the latest thriller from Matt Hilton, *Dead Men's Harvest*.

An ex-Black-Ops soldier, Joe Hunter is an all action hero with a strong moral code. He will use his weapons and his fists – but only to save the victims from the bad guys.

When Rink is ambushed by a team of highly skilled killers, Joe is pretty sure his friend is being used as bait. And the intended prey is Hunter himself.

Forced to operate without official sanction, Joe penetrates the kidnappers' lair and finds his ultimate quarry is back from beyond the grave – and with a bone to pick . . .

'SOME MAY CALL ME A VIGILANTE. I THINK I'VE JUST GOT PROBLEMS TO FIX.'

Dead Men's Harvest is Joe Hunter's sixth ferocious adventure and sees the return of one of his most lethal foes.

Read on for a tantalising extract . . .

Out now

HODDER &
STOUGHTON

Conchar is an ancient Gaelic term for those who admire the king of all hunters: the wolf.

To some, the wolf is a magnificent beast, the pinnacle of predatory evolution. To others, the wolf is a thing of nightmare.

Castle of the wolf: it was a good name for an Army Confinement Facility. Imprisoned within its walls were men and women who were ultimate predators and also, often, things of nightmare.

Criminals housed at Fort Conchar generally fell into four categories: prisoners of war, enemy combatants, persons whose freedom was deemed a risk to national security and, lastly, military personnel found guilty of a serious crime.

Occasionally it housed criminals who did not meet any of these criteria, but that was an extreme circumstance. Only once had it opened its arms to a man who checked all four boxes and then some. Designated Top Secret, his name was withheld even from those who guarded him night and day. Known only by a number – Prisoner 1854 – he was a cipher in more ways than one.

Mostly he refused to speak to his jailers. Some even thought him incapable of speech. But his mystery went much deeper than that.

He was a living dead man. According to official records he had died, not once, but twice. And yet he still breathed.

If all went to plan, the dead man would, like Lazarus, rise again. And people would know him. And they would scream his name in fear.

I

A breeze stirred and the susurration of foliage was like the whispering of lost souls. Frogs croaked. Water lapped. All sounds indigenous to the Everglades pine lands. Jared 'Rink' Rington ignored the natural rhythms of the Florida night, listening instead for the soft footfalls of the men hunting him.

There were at least four of them: men with guns.

From the cover of a stream bed, Rink spied back to where he'd left his car. The Porsche was a mess. Bullet holes pocked it from front to back and had taken out the front windshield. He'd wrecked the sump when he'd crashed over the median and into the coontie trees. A wide swath of oil was glistening in the moonlight, as though the Boxster had been mortally wounded and crawled into the bushes to die. Rink cursed under his breath, more for the death of his wheels than for his own predicament, but it wasn't the first time he'd had to consign a car to the grave.

Neither was it the first time he'd been hunted by armed men.

It kinda came with the territory.

The stream was shallow, almost stagnant. He used its steep bank as cover as he headed left. Above him someone stepped on a twig and it was like the crack of a gunshot. The insects grew still. There was a hush on the forest now. Rink crouched low, pressing himself against baked mud.

A few yards further on, another twig creaked beneath a boot. Rink wormed himself out of the stream bed. A man moved along the embankment above him, periodically glancing down towards the water, but more often towards the road.

Through the bushes Rink saw another man was moving along the blacktop. This one held a Glock machine pistol, the elongated barrel telling him that it was fitted with a sound suppressor.

Frog-giggers want to do me in silence, he thought. Well, all right. Two of us can play at that game.

From his boot he pulled a military-issue Ka-bar knife, a black epoxy-coated blade that didn't reflect the light.

His options were few. He had to take out the men hunting him or die. Put that way he'd no qualms about sticking the man in front of him.

His rush was silent. His free hand went over the man's mouth even as he jammed the Ka-bar down between the juncture of his throat and clavicle. The blade was long enough to pierce the left aorta of the man's heart, killing him instantly. Rink dragged the corpse down to the ground.

The man on the road was unaware that his companion was gone.

From the dead man's fingers, Rink plucked free the Heckler and Koch Combat .45 and shoved it into the waistband of his jeans. There was no suppressor on this gun, so the knife would remain his weapon of choice for now, because the man with the Glock had to be done as silently as the first. Two other assassins were out there – possibly more – and he wanted to even the odds in his favour before exchanging rounds.

Rink was tall and muscular, built like a pro-wrestler. The man at his feet wasn't. But by exchanging jackets and with the man's baseball cap jammed over his black hair, he'd fool the other hunter for a second or so. Everything weighed and bagged, that would be all he'd need.

In the corpse's clothing, Rink moved through the bushes.

For effect he pulled out the .45 so the disguise was complete. He held it in a two-handed grip, or that would be how it looked in silhouette.

The man to his right gestured; soldier-speak that Rink recognised. These men weren't your run-of-the-mill killers; they too must have had military training. Rink hand-talked, urging the man in the direction of a stand of trees. As he moved off, Rink angled towards him. Ten paces were all that separated them. The moon was bright on the road, but its light helped make the shadows beneath the trees denser. If Rink moved closer he could forget the charade.

The man halted. Something stirred in the foliage ahead. He dropped into a shooter's crouch, his Glock sweeping the area. Then a bird, disturbed from its roost, broke through the trees in a clatter of plumage on leaves. The man sighed, turned to grin sheepishly at his compadre.

Rink grinned back at him and he saw the man's face elongate in recognition. Charade over, he whipped his Ka-bar out from alongside the .45 and overhanded it at the man. Like a sliver of night, the blade swished through the air and plunged through tissue and cartilage.

The man staggered at the impact, one hand going to the hilt jutting from beneath his jaw, the other bringing round the Glock and tugging on the trigger. Rink dropped below the line of fire, the bullets searing the air around him, making tatters of the bushes and coontie trees. It was a subdued drum roll of silenced rounds, but no less deadly than if the gun had roared the sound of thunder. The man was mortally wounded, though not yet dead, but the Glock was empty and no threat. Gun in hand, Rink moved towards him.

Weakened by the shock of steel through his throat, drowning in his own blood, he couldn't halt Rink's charge. He was knocked off his feet and went down under the bigger man.

Then Rink had a hand on the hilt of the Ka-bar. A sudden jerk sideways opened one half of the man's neck and that was that.

Dragging the corpse off the road, Rink concealed it amongst a stand of palmetto.

Two down, two to go.

Rink was beginning to fancy his chances.

Armed now with two reliable guns and his Ka-bar, he decided it was time to show these frog-giggin' sons of bitches who they were dealing with.

'My turn, boys,' he whispered.

A faint click.

'No, Rington,' said a voice from behind him. 'Now it's *my* turn.'

Rink swung round, his knife coming up in reflex, but it was too late.

Something was rammed against his chest and he became a juddering, spittle-frothing wreck as fifty thousand volts were blasted through his entire being.

2

The headstone was the only feature that held any colour. Everything else was the grey of a Maine winter, with sleet falling like shards of smoked glass across the monochrome background. Even the trees that ringed the small cemetery were dull, lifeless things, their bare branches smudged by the shifting sky. The sleet was building on the ground, not the pure white of virgin snow, but slushy, invasive muck that filled my boots with a creeping chill that bit bone deep.

I hunkered over the grave and wiped the accumulation of icy slush off the headstone. The granite marker stood four feet tall, pinkish-grey, with a spray of flowers carved down one side and painted in vivid splashes of red and green. The name had been inlaid with gold leaf, as had the date of her premature death: almost a year ago.

I'm not a religious man, not in the accepted sense, but I still mumbled a prayer for her. Religion, or more correctly the effects of others twisting it, had been a factor of my professional life. I'd seen people murder one another for having a different faith, I'd seen people tortured and mutilated. I couldn't believe that if there was a God, then such a benevolent, loving figure would allow such outrages in His name – whatever that might turn out to be. For fourteen years I'd fought men whose minds had been poisoned by fanatical teachings; they all swore that they were doing His bidding. Made me wonder who was guiding me when I put the bastards down. I hoped that Kate Piers was in more caring hands than those of the god of war that must have propelled me.

I rose to my feet and folded my hands across my middle, looking down at the grave. The sleet stung my face, but it was small penance for failing to save the woman I'd fallen in love with.

'Are you ready, Joe?'

Lost in the past, I'd momentarily forgotten that Kate's sister was standing beside me. I looked at her, and her eyes shone with tears. Her sister had died protecting her life, and Imogen had never got over it. She felt guilty that it was her little sister lying cold in the grave and not her. But, more than that, I knew her tears were because she feared the man she loved was thinking the same.

I took one of her gloved hands in mine, pulled her in close so that I shielded her under my arm and placed a kiss on her cheek. 'Ready,' I told her. 'Come on. Let's get out of this cold.'

Imogen leaned down and placed a single rose against the headstone, then together we walked across the cemetery towards the gates. The cemetery wasn't large, just a half-acre ringed by a stone wall, and now almost overgrown by trees. The Piers family plot held five generations, including the body of my old army friend, Jake. This was where Imogen would come when her time on earth was over. Made me wonder where I'd end up. Nowhere as sanctified as this, I supposed; more likely an unmarked hole in the ground. Perhaps that would be fitting, because I'd sent plenty of others to such an ignominious resting place.

Imogen's house was perched on a rocky bluff overlooking Little Kennebec Bay, a short drive from Machiasport. The cemetery was situated on the Piers land, but even the five-minute walk was unpleasant in this weather. We clambered into the warmth of my Audi A6. I'd had the foresight to leave the engine running and the car was snug. I felt the blood rushing to my cheeks. Imogen struggled out of her gloves while I headed the car up the incline towards the house. In this half-light Imogen's home looked like something out of a Poe story, its pitched roof and steepled corners rearing against the slate sky. We didn't speak in the car, nothing beyond complaints about the weather anyway, and the transition from vehicle to house was done in a hurry.

There was a fire burning in the hearth and I stoked it, piling on logs, while Imogen prepared hot, dark coffee for me, cocoa laced with something stronger for her. I never did get to drink the coffee. In the next few seconds we were in each other's arms as we navigated the stairs to her bedroom. Survivors' guilt syndrome is a powerful thing, but I couldn't blame that for the surge of passion that rose up in the two of us. She just looked so damn ravishing, her cheeks pink with a flush of warmth, her hair slightly in disarray from having pulled off her hat. She looked fragile and vulnerable and in need of reassurance. I hoped that actions were more profound than words. All I did was put down my coffee, take her cocoa from her hand and place it next to mine. Then I pulled her into a kiss, one that I meant dearly. That was all it took for us to wrestle our way through the house, undressing each other as we went.

Imogen's original bedroom had been violated when she'd been attacked by a misogynistic killer named Luke Rickard. Rickard had wanted to kill me and had targeted me through Imogen. She steered me past that room and into the one she had now commandeered. It was a big house for a single person, and the master bedroom only accentuated that. The bed would be best described as super king-sized, but we made use of every square inch.

Afterwards we lay side by side, our bodies glistening with perspiration, Imogen's hair in even more disarray. She lay with one hand on my stomach, tracing lazy circles with her finger-tips, enjoying for the moment the companionable silence. Perhaps there was more than that to the silence; there were things yet unspoken, but now was not the time or place. Beyond the windows night had fallen, and the sleet had turned to snow. It was like a shroud that blocked out the rest of the world. We were cocooned in our own little bubble and I wished that things could stay that way forever. But I knew they couldn't.

Some sixth sense in me had been anticipating the thrum of an engine and the squeak of tyres on the new snow. I sat up and looked through the window. The vantage didn't allow a view down to the parking area outside. Naked, I stood, and then stooped for my abandoned clothes. First thing first, I lifted my SIG Sauer P226 and racked the slide. After that I dragged on my jeans and then padded back to the window.

'Who is it?'

Without turning, I said, 'Don't know yet. You'd best get dressed.'

We weren't expecting visitors. On a night like this, with the blizzard driving in off the Atlantic, only someone very deter-mined would be out and about. In my world that meant law enforcement officers or enemies. Experience told me neither would be good news.

A vehicle crept into view. It was a dark-coloured SUV, the windows tinted so I couldn't make out who was inside, or how many. The snow didn't help because it was swirling on the breeze, dancing a dervish jig between me and the vehicle. I watched until it pulled up alongside my Audi. No one got out. Maybe they were running the tags on my car.

I quickly pulled on my T-shirt and a hooded sweatshirt. I shrugged into my leather jacket, still damp from earlier, even as I stepped into my boots. The clothes went on almost as frenetically as they had so recently come off. Behind me,

Imogen had pulled on a robe and cinched it round the waist. She joined me as I took another peek out the window.

'Joe,' she said in a whisper. 'Who could they be?'

'I don't know, but I don't like it. I want you to stay up here until I find out. OK?'

This was Imogen's home. She shouldn't have to live in fear within its walls, but she did. Once already it had been invaded by a killer, and a cop had died on the threshold, trying to help her. Luke Rickard wasn't the one she feared now. I'd killed that piece of shit. But there were others who might still want to harm her. I met Kate after Imogen had gone missing, running for her life to avoid the wrath of a Texan mobster and his sadistic enforcers, the Bolan twins. I had found Imogen and then took the war back to its source, but that was when Kate had died. Imogen didn't have to worry about Robert Huffman or the twins: I'd killed them too. But the mob was far-ranging and had a long memory and she waited for the day they'd seek retribution. She didn't argue with my request for her to stay hidden.

I went down the stairs and threw on the spotlights I'd fitted round the eaves. The light would momentarily blind those in the SUV. While they were blinking, I stepped out of the front door, the SIG hidden alongside my thigh. Enemies would do one of two things: reverse the car out of there, or come out with their guns blazing. I readied myself for either eventuality. Instead, the passenger door opened and a single figure emerged. He held his hands over his head, showing me that they were empty.

'Move away from the car.' I allowed the SIG to be seen, so he knew I wasn't taking no for an answer.

He nodded and took two exaggerated steps to the side. I left him standing there in the snow, his hands reaching for the heavens, while I angled for a look into the SUV. There was a driver, but no one I could see in the back. 'You as well, pal. Out of the car and show me your hands.'

These weren't men lost on the road and seeking directions, neither were they enemies. Their approach told me that quite eloquently. They showed they meant no harm by lifting their hands, without raising a fuss about their treatment. I waved the driver round the front of the car, ushering them both together. It was easier to keep an eye on them like that.

Both were alike the way men of military bearing are: strong and lithe, with short haircuts and hard eyes. They were dressed similarly in thick windcheaters, dark jeans and rubber-soled boots. Bulges under their left armpits told me they were packing, both of them right-hand draws. The only thing that differentiated them was that one was missing a chunk of eyebrow, and the other, slightly heavier, had ten years on his friend.

'You're not cops,' I said. 'So I'm guessing you're with the government.'

The older man was the designated driver, which made me conclude that the first man to get out the car was the one who'd come to speak. I wasn't wrong.

'We should get out of the storm.' He nodded towards the house. 'Better if we talk inside, Mr Hunter.'

He used my name as a tool, couching his words so that they were more than a suggestion. He wanted me to know who was really in charge. It didn't work that way with me. 'My girlfriend is inside.' I left things at that. Let them think what they wanted.

'She knows all about you?' The man was wily, and he left the hint about my past unsaid.

'She knows that I'm not the type to let strangers inside without checking them out first. So . . . who are you, and what brings you here?'

The men lowered their hands. The younger of the two reached towards his armpit. Left hand, so I didn't flinch. He pulled out a leather wallet and flicked it open. He showed me an FBI ID badge. I smiled cynically at him. 'I've got one just like that. I bought it off eBay for five bucks. Who supplied yours, Charles W. Brigham? The CIA, I bet.'

Brigham chuckled. His mouth twisted, and the skin on his face puckered all the way up to his damaged eyebrow. Once he'd been very lucky that a knife blade hadn't taken off his entire face. 'As you know, CIA agents aren't in the habit of carrying badges. It's too much of a giveaway. But that's my real name. You have the ability to check it out.'

I did, but I wasn't going to bother. There was no reason for Brigham to lie. 'And who are you?' I directed at the older man. 'Your name will do, forget the Mickey Mouse badge.'

'Ray Hartlaub.'

'Brigham and Hartlaub? It sounds like an accountancy firm to me.' I smiled to show I was only fooling, but also that they held no fear for me.

'That would be Hartlaub and Brigham,' the older agent said. 'Seeing as I'm in charge.'

I'd thought as much. The one in charge never gets out of the car first. Not when there's an armed man waiting for him. 'So why are you here?'

'We were asked to come fetch you.'

I shook my head, more an act of derision than to dislodge the snow off my hair. There was only one person who could be behind this round-up. My old CIA contact from when I was hunting terrorists. 'Walter Hayes Conrad. What has that old goat got up his sleeve this time?'

'Nothing,' Hartlaub said. 'In fact, you can forget about SDC Conrad upsetting your life ever again.'

'So old Walt's finally retired then?'

'No, Hunter, Walter Conrad is dead. He was murdered a few hours ago.'